The Seventh Chakra

by Kevin Frane

THE SEVENTH CHAKRA

Copyright 2010 by Kevin Frane

Published by Sofawolf Press
St. Paul, Minnesota
http://www.sofawolf.com

ISBN 978-0-9819883-5-1
Printed in the United States of America
First trade paperback edition
First printing, January 2010 • POD printing: May 2023

Cover art by Kamui

Dedicated to the guys in my local writing group—
Ryan and David and Watts and Paulie and Andy and Tim (again)

This book would never have been finished without your help.

Contents

*"**Fiat iustitia ruat caelum.**"*
—Let justice be done, though
the heavens fall.

1. In Shambhala

Arkady Ryswife looked up from the card table when a tall flute of fancy sparkling wine was set down in front of him. The ferret hadn't asked for it, but he knew full well where it had come from. The attendant held his now-empty tray at his side and bowed his head. He was a mouse, no older than his mid-twenties, wearing the same feminizing outfit that all the other male employees at Shambhala's casinos wore. Here in Tomosabaki, along with most other countries on the Continent, it was common for men in high-profile service positions to be made more girlish, so as to make them seem less threatening. Arkady found the custom outdated, even distasteful, though he'd long since grown used to it on his many trips to this part of the world.

This mouse certainly seemed the meek sort, if no less professional for it. "Sir," he said to Arkady. "Mr. Cibola would like to invite you to join him at his private table upstairs."

Arkady picked up the flute of wine and took a sip. This was the good stuff; his host-to-be was making quite the gesture. "I would be delighted," he replied. When he turned back to face his fellow gamblers at his current table, more than a few them were looking back at him with wide eyes, clearly recognizing the name that the mouse had just dropped. "Pardon me, friends," the ferret said to them as he reached out to rake in his remaining chips.

As he did so, the mouse attendant reached out with one paw and placed it gently atop the ferret's. "Please, sir, there's no need," he said. "Someone will be by to take care of that for you." Withdrawing his paw, the mouse then looked anxiously at his own fingers for a moment before regaining his professional composure. "If you would be so kind as to follow me?"

Leaving his chips without further protest, Arkady rose to his feet and offered a final farewell bow to the other players, toasting them wordlessly with the wineglass before downing the rest of the contents in one long gulp. He set the empty glass down, reached down to pick up the slender attaché case from underneath his chair, then motioned with a paw for the mouse to lead on before falling into step behind him.

The mouse attendant cut a path through the casino floor, moving like he was on rails. Arkady couldn't help but smile to himself as he followed, noticing that they were headed for one of the stairwells in the back as opposed to main elevator lobby out front. More than a couple gamblers glanced up from their slot machines and game tables to watch the ferret as he passed, as if he were exuding some kind of aura of importance that compelled them to look.

A female rabbit, wearing an attendant's outfit that wasn't appreciably different from the mouse's, made eye contact with Arkady as he reached the stairwell. She flashed him a knowing smile before disappearing back down one of the rows of slot machines with her full drink tray.

Before opening the door to the stairwell, the mouse presented his left wrist (more likely, he was actually presenting his wrist bangle) to the small panel on the wall. A tiny light on the panel flickered as a quiet beep sounded, and then the mouse pulled the door open. Inside was a carpeted staircase, its walls lined with high-end electric sconces that glowed more brightly when the mouse and Arkady walked by them. The stairs only went up a single story, ending at a small landing with another door, locked with the same type of mechanism as the first.

The door opened into a scene of pure opulence. Lavish though the previous casino floor already was, it didn't hold a candle to the splendor of this private area. The soft carpeting underfoot had a natural plushness and softness that no synthetic fabric could match. Along some walls, fine silks hung, draped between marble columns with ornate capitals; other sections of wall were left exposed to show off the intricate bas-relief carvings that depicted further scenes of luxury and excess.

Despite the old-fashioned, almost palatial motif, the full effects of modern engineering were also apparent. For one, regardless of a boisterous main casino area being just one level below, no sound made its way up through the floor. Likewise, the lighting was incorporated into the ceiling in such a way as to make it appear as though the stonework itself was glowing and giving the room its bright ambient light.

A small fortune had to have gone into creating just this room, and Arkady knew full well—as did anyone else here—that countless fortunes had gone into the making of Shambhala. The casino floor downstairs was just one of over half a dozen scattered throughout the massive skyscraper complex. Other sections of the building were home to entire shopping malls, high-end restaurants, even full amusement parks; still others housed offices of major corporations from all over Tomosabaki, the rest of the Continent, and overseas.

The mouse led Arkady to the semicircular table in the center of the large room. The dealer, some type of spotted feline of obviously mixed heritage, had her back to the stairway entrance. Facing Arkady were the players themselves, five in all. The one in the center, a raccoon who looked to be in his mid-thirties, seemed to light up when the mouse brought the ferret forward.

"Mr. Cibola," the mouse said, bowing to the raccoon. "Your guest."

Cibola stood and reached across the table, offering Arkady a paw. The odor of expensive cologne clung to him, drowning out his natural musk. "Delighted you could make it," he said.

Arkady took Cibola's paw and allowed the raccoon to squeeze firmly as they shook. "Mr. Cibola," he said. "I'm Christopher Hamilton. It's a pleasure."

"Mr. Hamilton, yes, of course," Cibola said as he sat back down. "Please, have a seat and join us."

The ferret took the open seat to the dealer's left, roughly across from Cibola himself, and set his attaché case down on the floor next to his chair. To Cibola's own immediate right was an elegant-looking black panther who Arkady recognized as Princess Ines of Afortunada; Arkady had known that she'd been here at Shambhala for the last few days, but hadn't figured her to be in attendance at a private card table like this. Next to her sat a short, stocky badger who reeked of cigar smoke, and next to him sat an equally stocky wolverine who nevertheless looked far more genial. Neither of them were anyone Arkady recognized.

To Cibola's left sat Kentian McEvoy, a young and somewhat muscular wolf who was, unbeknownst to Cibola, Arkady's partner on his mission.

"Would you care for a drink?" Cibola asked the ferret. When he did, the mouse attendant circled around the table and took up position near the raccoon.

"Please," Arkady said. Cibola simply held up two fingers to the mouse, who clearly understood the gesture; he bowed his head much as before, and began to walk off.

Before the mouse got more than a step, Kentian reached out with one paw and tweaked him on his skimpily-covered backside. "Hey, sugar," he growled, smirking at the mouse. "One for me, too."

Arkady nearly choked on his own tongue at that display. He'd known Kentian for close to five years, and knew full well that the wolf didn't swing that way. Clearly, Kentian had gone to quite the lengths, over the last several weeks, in assuming his cover identity for working his way into Cibola's good graces (the phony drawl he'd adopted was pretty convincing, too). Even so, if it weren't for the seriousness of the task at hand, Arkady would have sworn that the wolf had pulled that stunt just now merely to shock him.

The mouse, though, merely dipped his head toward the wolf, not appearing the least bit fazed. "Of course, sir," he said, before scurrying away without further interruption.

Given the smirk that tugged at the corner of Kentian's muzzle, Arkady wasn't entirely sure that the wolf *hadn't* done it just for the shock value. Then again, it wasn't as though either of them got to pretend to be high-rolling hedonists every day.

Cibola let out a good-natured chuckle of his own, then turned to Arkady. "My friend Mr. O'Donnell here says that you're quite the gambler," he said, gesturing with a paw to Kentian. "When I heard that you'd been wasting the last few days downstairs," he said, accenting that last word with some derision, "I knew that I had to make it up to you, on behalf of Shambhala itself."

"I can assure you that even downstairs is quite the establishment, considering some of the places I've been," the ferret replied. The badger sitting next to Princess Ines let out a snort that everyone else was polite enough not to acknowledge.

"Then I hope you enjoy yourself this evening all the more," Cibola said. The raccoon's eyes looked to be further back in his head than they should, and the mask of dark fur around them heightened the illusion further still, giving him an intense and unsettling gaze that doubtlessly served him well in his business dealings.

Arkady ran his tongue in between his teeth and upper lip. "I think the cards might be the ones to see to that," he said. "But then, let's not allow the mingling of business and pleasure to create any hard feelings."

"Indeed," Cibola replied, sharing a look and a smirk with Kentian.

By now, the mouse had reemerged from somewhere, bearing his tray. He first set down a drink in front of Kentian, earning himself a wink and a click of the tongue from the wolf. From the color of the liquid and the shape of the glass, Arkady surmised it was some kind of whiskey— another thing that he knew Kentian didn't normally indulge in. In front of Cibola, the mouse set down a tall, slender bottle and two minuscule glasses. The attendant then ducked back and left (and to Arkady's relief, his partner kept his paws to himself this time).

"Rasatsu vodka," Cibola explained as he poured into both glasses. "Finest in Tomosabaki." He picked up one of the glasses with two fingers and held it out for Arkady to take, and waited for the ferret to join him before taking a sip. It was smooth, ice-cold—*too* easy to drink, really, if one weren't careful. Careful was something Arkady could scarce afford not to be.

The dealer slid over a measured stack of chips in front of Arkady. A quick glance at the other players' respective stacks showed that they'd been playing for some time now. Another glance down at the actual denominations of those chips made Arkady's eyes widen, and when he opened his mouth to speak, Kentian held up a paw and, as if reading the ferret's mind, simply said, "It's taken care of."

And so the feline next to Arkady began the deal, her slender, spotted paws moving with the effortless precision of a machine. Cibola took another sip of vodka, then said, "The game is queen's cup, Continental rules."

"Continental rules," Arkady repeated, arching his brow. "Interesting choice."

Cibola waited until he had been dealt all his cards before taking a look. "We are, after all, on the Continent," he replied simply.

"Even downstairs they're all playing Archipelago rules," Arkady pointed out as he checked his own cards.

"Mr. Cibola doesn't much care for the way they do things on the Archipelago," the wolverine at the far end of the table said. He then looked up, but only to signal the mouse attendant over to himself.

"Sometimes I just prefer to do things the old-fashioned way," Cibola replied. "I trust that it's not an issue?"

Arkady grinned. "It's been a while," he confessed. "But I'm sure I'll recall the differences soon enough."

Continental rules for queen's cup hadn't been in wide favor (not even in Tomosabaki) since close to twenty years ago. Twenty years ago, back when Arkady had *actually* been the young twentysomething that he currently appeared to be. Hopefully, his deceptively youthful appearance would cause Cibola to underestimate him, if only a little.

Only a little, though. Arkady wasn't here to clean Cibola out: he just needed to play as well as he could to reinforce the illusion that he was the kind if high roller he was pretending to be, while still allowing the raccoon to come out on top by a narrow margin in the end. Of course, given the caliber of card players that the ferret was to be up against, his *real* problem was going to be not losing all his money inside of an hour.

"The first bet is to you, then," Cibola announced.

Arkady checked his cards a second time. He wished that Il-Hyeong could have been in his place. The fox had a much better head for numbers and patterns and probability analysis than either Arkady or Kentian did. More key was that he lacked the ability to come across as affable and rakish like Kentian in the role of Kay O'Donnell, or to play the part of a hobnobbing, attention-getting upstart like Arkady's role as Christopher Hamilton.

No, Il-Hyeong had different talents and proficiencies, and they were needed elsewhere right now. In the meantime, Arkady was just going to have to do the best he could, and have faith that he'd be good enough—that he *was* good enough.

"One thousand," the ferret announced as he tossed a single chip out in front of him. Kentian looked back at him, grinned, and began to consider his own cards in more detail.

Two hours later, the chip stacks had fluctuated more than a fair bit. Small fortunes had made their way all the way around the table and back again (and Princess Ines, it turned out, was quite the card player).

Arkady was doing as well as he'd hoped to be able: putting in a decent show while still losing out in the long term. When larger pots were at stake, he tried to lose to Kentian wherever possible, though not so frequently as to make it obvious (and thankfully, the princess was there to take him for a ride on a few occasions when he wasn't even trying to take a hit to his stack). The ferret had made some big wins, and most of those were when he was down a fair bit and trying to claw his way back up to even.

He was down only a modest amount from his starting bankroll; Kentian was up, and more importantly, so was Cibola. *That's it*, Arkady thought to himself. *Make him happy. Make him trusting. Make him drop his guard.*

The badger—Arkady had caught only his first name as Manfred— was down to about half of what he'd started with, a bulk of his money having gone to Kentian. As the dealer shuffled the deck between hands, the badger stood up. "I think I've had enough for one night," he announced. "If you'll excuse me."

Arkady noticed Princess Ines' attempt to hide a smirk. Cibola remained seated, but reached out to shake Manfred's paw. "Another night, perhaps," the raccoon offered, and the badger just grunted and nodded before heading for the back stair.

"Actually," Kentian then interrupted, "I guess this is as good a time as any for me to stop, as well. May as well quit while I'm ahead, right?"

Cibola turned to the dealer. "I think we're finished here for the evening, then," he told her. "In the meantime, I believe I have other business with you, Mr. O'Donnell, yes?"

"Only if it's not too late, of course," Kentian said. "I know that you have other guests and other matters to attend to, as well."

The raccoon got to his feet, then helped the princess get to hers by taking her paw. "Your Highness," he said to the panther, dipping his head to kiss that paw. "Shall I call upon you later this evening? I don't imagine that Mr. O'Donnell and I will take long."

"In the morning might be preferable, I should think," the princess replied. Even after the card game, her tone was still regal and reserved, making it hard even for Arkady to gauge her real attitude (no doubt, that same effect had served her play style well).

Cibola bowed once more. "Certainly, Your Highness," he said. "If you'll excuse me." Then he turned to face Kentian. "Shall we adjourn, then?" he asked.

While the princess busied herself in gathering up her personal effects, Cibola started to walk off, prompting Kentian and then Arkady to follow. The ferret held the attaché case casually at his side. The moment of truth was very nearly at hand, now.

The raccoon led them to a different stairwell than the one Arkady had come in through. This one was similarly furnished, but it led one floor up. Inside, the scent of Cibola's cologne became noticeable again. "So, Chris," Kentian said, breaking the silence now that they were out of earshot of the other players, "how's your visit to Shambhala coming along?"

"Oh, I'm having a fine time, so far," Arkady replied as he followed up the stairs. With one paw, he reached up and brushed his right ear, one of his claws turning on the transceiver tucked snugly within. "My time at the tables has gone pretty well for itself."

"Except for tonight, perhaps," Kentian said, and as they reached the top of the stairs together, Cibola smirked at him. "Still, glad to see it's not affecting your mood."

Within the shell of Arkady's ear, the transceiver let out a dull, electronic whine, followed by what sounded like a quick, sharp breath.

Arkady leaned against the wall as Cibola went about unlocking the next door in their way. "I've got no reason to be in a bad mood," the ferret said with a smile. "You know, I saw our old friend Ming-Jun downstairs in the casino, earlier. After we're done with this, I'm sure she'd love to see you."

"Arkady!" snapped the female voice in the ferret's ear. *"Arkady, what are—"*

"Once we're finished up here, I'd be happy to," Kentian replied. "Like Mr. Cibola said, I'm sure this won't take long at all."

"I shouldn't imagine so," Cibola said as he led them on through into a private elevator lobby. The walls and floors were lined with marble, smooth and polished, unadorned unlike the room downstairs. "Speaking of which," the raccoon continued, "are you okay with doing this in one of my private offices?"

"Damn it, get off this channel!" Arkady cleared his throat on reflex in order to mask the sound, even though he was sure that Cibola couldn't hear it from where he was standing. *"I'm turning this thing off before you blow my cover."* With that, the transceiver went dead with an electrostatic whine that made the ferret wince.

"One of your private offices would be fine," Kentian said, both he and Cibola seemingly unaware of the brief outburst that had sounded in Arkady's ear. "We'd insist on having building security present, however."

Cibola nodded. "Of course," he said. He rolled back his sleeve and brought his wristcomm up to his muzzle, pressing a button with his other paw. "This is Cibola," he said into the device. "Could I please have an observation detail sent up to fifty-one?"

Arkady gripped the handle of the attaché case a little harder. How could he let Kentian know what had just happened with Ming-Jun? What *had* even happened? What kind of trouble could she be in to cut her transceiver in the middle of the mission?

"Is this liable to take a while?" Arkady asked Cibola. "Because if it is, perhaps Mr. O'Donnell and I could wait downstairs?"

Kentian gave Arkady a wary look, but before the wolf could say anything, Cibola beat him to the punch. "Oh, no, not at all," the raccoon said. "Allow me to just get the merchandise and by then, security should be here to help us out."

"In that case," the ferret said, reaching up to rub his ear in an attempt to look sheepish—while sending an unmistakable message to Kentian, "I'm sure there's no problem."

"Excellent," Cibola said. "Then I will be right back." With that, the raccoon waddled down one of the hallways that branched off from the elevator lobby.

Once Cibola was out of sight, Kentian spun around and looked Arkady in the eye. "I hope nothing's the matter," the wolf said, still speaking as if someone might be listening in. The look on his face showed the irritation that his voice didn't.

"I'm just anxious, that's all," Arkady replied, again reaching up to scratch at his right ear. "I want to make sure that this deal goes off well."

"Is there some reason it shouldn't?" Kentian asked.

Cibola would be back at any second. If something had happened to Ming-Jun, if she'd somehow been compromised, then there was nothing Arkady or Kentian could do to help without blowing their own cover— and consequently, blowing the deal with Cibola. Still, if Ming-Jun had been taken out of the picture, somehow or another, then that likely meant that Il-Hyeong hadn't gotten Cibola's call for a security detail, and that might throw an even larger wrench into the rest of the operation all on its own.

It wouldn't blow it completely, though; it would just require some improvisation and some more bloodshed, most likely. The job itself would still be salvageable. Arkady and his team could still get what they'd come here for.

Arkady was the leader. It was up to him to call the shots, here. Did he pull the plug now, abort the mission and try to go after Ming-Jun, or did he press on and trust that he and Kentian could pull off the plan by themselves if it came down to it?

"No," Arkady told Kentian. "No, it should be fine. Like I said, I'm just anxious."

The wolf nodded. "All right, then," he said. "Like Cibola said, this shouldn't take long."

Arkady was able to keep from fidgeting as he awaited the raccoon's return. The silent earpiece was still cause for some worry, but if this mission went south now, there would never be a second chance. *Have faith,* the ferret told himself. *Everyone's played their part up through now. See it through.*

When Cibola finally returned, he was carrying a large, clunky case, the sort used for lugging around stereo or audiovisual equipment. It was far from what Arkady had imagined the raccoon might be bringing, and he knew as soon as he set eyes on it that he'd failed at keeping his eyes from widening.

The case was obviously heavy, but Cibola didn't appear to be struggling too much to carry it around. "Now, then," he said, opting to hold the case at his side instead of setting it down on the floor, "let's just wait for security to—aha!"

With that, the elevator chimed, and out stepped a lone, dusty-blond swift fox, dressed in one of Shambhala's black-and-gray security uniforms. At his belt, he openly wore both a shock baton and a state-of-the-art Duhamel Kurosaki-Reinhardt pistol.

Arkady knew that Il-Hyeong still preferred the older DKR-7 to the much newer DKR-8, despite it being a less optimally balanced weapon. Still, everything here at Shambhala was cutting edge, and that meant that, to sell the illusion, the fox needed to wear the DKR-8 instead. If everything went according to plan, he wouldn't need to fire it, anyway.

The fox turned to Cibola and dipped his head. "You requested security, sir?"

"Follow me, please," the raccoon said to the whole lot of them. He started to walk down a different branch of the hallway than before, his arm finally showing more strain at hauling the large case around. The office he stopped at, though, was only a few doors down from the elevator lobby.

Again, he refused to set the case down as he unlocked the door and then pushed it open. "Please," he said to Kentian and Arkady, "step in and take a seat at the far side of the table."

The office itself was like a small boardroom, with only minimal decorations, though the window offered a stunning view of the city far below. The real wood table in the center of the room served as yet another, if more subtle, reminder of the opulence here in Shambhala. Cleaning staff had been through with scent-scrubbers, too—probably sometime within the last few hours, given the clean, crisp lack of any single species' scent that might tip business negotiations to one side or another.

Asking Kentian and Arkady to sit at the far side of the table was a wise tactical move: the table itself acted as an effective makeshift barrier, and it put Cibola in prime position between the people he was dealing with and the only exit. If this were all an elaborate setup to pull a fast one, it limited the options any double-dealers would have in making a snatch and an easy getaway.

Luckily for Arkady's team, they weren't planning on running. This deal, this face-to-face meeting with Cibola behind closed doors, was exactly what they'd been aiming for, and now, at last, they had it.

As Arkady took his seat at the table, next to Kentian and across from Cibola, the only thing nagging at the ferret's mind was Ming-Jun. Where an actual Shambhala security agent should have shown up, Il-Hyeong had shown up instead, which meant that Ming-Jun had intercepted the message and passed it along to the fox as planned, but Cibola had made the call after Ming-Jun had cut contact with Arkady, when (presumably) something had gone wrong. What had made her panic, then?

Another element entered the picture to take Arkady's mind off of that distracted wondering: there was a telltale bulge of a pistol hidden under Cibola's jacket where there hadn't been one before. He must have armed himself while he'd gone to get the case. He'd done a very poor job of hiding it, too; whether that was due to clumsiness or deliberate intent would be seen soon enough, the ferret figured. Kentian whapped his tail against Arkady's leg to show that he'd seen it, too.

Still playing the part of the impartial observer, Il-Hyeong gave no outward signal as he closed the office door and stood silently beside it, but Arkady had no doubt that the fox had noticed the weapon, too. So long as Cibola didn't do anything stupid, this could all still go off okay.

Cibola shifted in his seat and looked at his two 'guests' with those sunken-back eyes of his. "All right, then, Mr. O'Donnell, Mr. Hamilton," he said. "Let's get down to business. You brought the payment, I take it?"

Arkady picked up his attaché case and set it atop the boardroom table, so that it was within Cibola's reach, the clasps facing out towards him. "This should cover what we agreed on," the ferret said.

The raccoon looked unconcerned with both Arkady and Kentian for a moment, but failed to fully mask a greedy smile, and he waggled his fingers before he went for the clasps on the case, unlocking and opening it while leaving it atop the table.

From within the briefcase, the raccoon pulled out a purple gemstone pendant. His dark little eyes seemed to pop further forward in his skull, and Arkady allowed himself a smug smile, speaking before the raccoon could vocalize his surprise.

"Is there a problem, sir?" the ferret asked.

Cibola let the pendant dangle from his paw, staring at both it and Arkady. "What is this?" he demanded, his voice quiet and cold.

"Not up on your gemology, are you?" Kentian chimed in. "That's iolite."

The raccoon's beady eyes seemed to bulge further out. "Iolite?" he choked out. "The Iolite League?" The pendant's chain slipped further through his stubby fingers.

"The same Iolite League to whom you promised to turn over those artifacts," Arkady said, nodding toward the case Cibola had brought with him. He then looked up at Il-Hyeong, clicked his tongue, and held up a paw. Without any hesitation, the fox lobbed his pistol over the table, and the ferret snatched it out of the air and pointed it at Cibola. "The same Iolite League that does not take kindly to being double-crossed."

Cibola quickly spun and looked back at Il-Hyeong, his muzzle gaping wide. With a snarl, he turned back to Arkady and clutched his paws at the table, his blunt claws digging into the polished wood. *That's it,* Arkady thought. *Keep them where I can see them.*

"You can see, I'm sure, why we'd be upset that you'd then try to go behind our backs and sell them to someone else before we had a chance to take them into custody," Kentian said. He'd dropped his phony accent and had reverted to his natural, lilting one.

The raccoon's cologne didn't do a good enough job of masking the tinge of fear that he now exuded. "Since... since when does the Iolite League resort to violence and thievery in their business?"

Next to Arkady, Kentian barked a clipped, amused laugh, and that made the ferret smile, too, in turn. "Thievery? Is that what you think this is?" Arkady said, running one finger along the trigger guard of the pistol. "You ought to give the Iolite League more credit, Mr. Cibola." His grin turned into a smirk. "Which, well, if you'd done that, you and I wouldn't be here right now, would we?"

"Look," the raccoon stammered, dropping the pendant on the boardroom table, freeing his paws. "I... I can explain"

"Explain what?" Arkady asked. "Explain how we weren't supposed to find out about your little deal with the Octavians?"

Kentian leaned in over the table, planting both paws down atop it. "You don't need to worry about them anymore, by the way; we've made sure that they won't be doing business with you again."

Cibola hesitated. He looked back and forth between the wolf and the ferret, his lips quivering as he searched for words and found none. He was trapped, and he knew it. "Take this back to your people as a message," Arkady said as he picked up the pendant and dropped it back into the attaché case, "that the Iolite League expects better from you in future dealings."

The raccoon's paws, still gripping the edge of the table, began to tense and shake. In the next moment, Arkady saw the look in the raccoon's shift from uncertainty to panic.

He was going to go for the gun. Stupid bastard had a weapon already trained on him, and he was still going to grab for his gun. His paw hadn't left the edge of the table yet, but already, the ferret could see the fingers starting to slip away.

There was no time to see how far Cibola would or wouldn't take this. There was no time to lunge over the table. There was no time to call out to Il-Hyeong.

Arkady fired twice before those fingers were even a hair's breadth away from the table. The first shot made Cibola's body snap backwards, and the second sent the raccoon and his chair right onto the floor. Il-Hyeong had his shock baton out before Arkady had even scrambled to his feet. "We're getting out, now!" the ferret snapped, grabbing Cibola's case from the table before vaulting over the boardroom table.

Kentian's eyes were wide in shock, his ears pinned back in response to the gunshots. "God in Heaven, Arkady, why the hell did you kill him?" the wolf asked, muzzle agape.

Arkady continued on toward the hallway, ignoring the question. "We've got about five seconds before—" The ferret's words were cut off by the shrill whooping of an emergency klaxon, accompanied by the flashing of red lights. "—before they start trying to lock down the floor," he finished, dropping the case in the door frame between the office suite and the corridor. The case was as heavy as it had looked, and so Arkady guessed that it was also sturdy enough to withstand the door closing on it, if the emergency lockdown system tried to shut them in.

"Il-Hyeong, can you get the elevator doors open?" Arkady said as the swift fox joined him at his side, baton still at the ready.

"They're probably going to lock them all down on the ground floor," Il-Hyeong replied, trotting off toward the elevators all the same. "Security will be coming in through the stairwells." Local law in Tomosabaki allowed private security to shoot on sight—and a world-class establishment like Shambhala hired world-class security to match.

"We'll slide down the cables, if we have to," Arkady said. "It's not like we have much choice." The ferret then reached up to his ear again. *Please, please answer,* he thought as he clicked his transceiver on again. "Ming-Jun, come in! Ming-Jun, where are you?"

"We spent weeks infiltrating this place so that we could send a message, not just kill him," Kentian snapped, beginning to get his thick arms out of his tight, heavy formal jacket. "And why the hell did you shoot when you knew it would set off the security systems?"

"If Arkady hadn't shot first, Cibola would have," Il-Hyeong called back, already busy at work popping the casing off of the elevator call button panel. Arkady was glad (though not surprised) that the fox had caught it, too. "And I—rrf!—might just be able to get us a ride on an elevator after all, so just sit tight."

Arkady turned to face the hallway that led to the nearest fire stairwell; if security was going to barge into the floor, they'd come through there, as opposed to the private back stair Cibola had led them in through. He held his gun at the ready in both paws, waiting and watching.

"Arkady, where *is* Ming-Jun?" Kentian asked. "Earlier, you—"

"I don't know, okay?" Arkady snapped back. "She went silent on me before we came upstairs." God, this had been a stupid idea, moving ahead with the mission when one of his teammates was out of commission.

Kentian shook his head, then looked down at the case at Arkady's feet. "Whatever's in that case had better be worth this."

It is, Arkady was about to reply, when another gunshot resounded in his already-ringing ears. The ferret heard Il-Hyeong spit out a curse that was then muffled by yet another gunshot. Snapping his head around, he saw Cibola, sprawled on his back where he'd been left for dead, one arm extended, pistol in his paw. The raccoon's grip on the weapon wavered as he tried to aim at Arkady upside-down.

Before the raccoon could get off a third shot, Arkady fired again, this time managing to hit Cibola cleanly in the head. With barely half a jerk, the raccoon went limp, eyes remaining open, his gun dropping from his paw.

The ferret swore under his breath and did his best to muster his composure before stepping back into the room to grab the discarded weapon, switching the DKR-8 security pistol to his other paw as he stuck the smaller gun into the waistband of his pants. As he knelt beside Cibola's corpse, he noticed that no red had welled up through the clothing where the raccoon had been shot twice in the chest. "Damn it!" Arkady snapped, spinning back around. "Bastard was wearing—"

Arkady's words trailed off when he saw the wide-eyed, unblinking stare on Kentian's face, the wolf having slowly started to slide back down against the wall of the office suite, leaving behind a shiny wet streak of red as he slipped towards the floor. Through the wailing of the alarm klaxon, the ferret heard the *ding* of the elevator bell as Il-Hyeong got the door open, and in the next moment, the swift fox turned around, the triumphant smile on his face fading away as he, too, caught sight of his companion.

"Kentian!" Il-Hyeong cried out, practically leaping down the hallway as he sprinted toward the wolf.

"Il-Hyeong, the elevator!" Arkady yelled, bolting past the fox in an attempt to grab the abandoned elevator door before it closed. He slipped on the hallway floor, sliding across the smooth marble tile, his outstretched paw managing to wedge its way in between the doors as they closed. They pinched and crushed in hard, but the car remained in place with the doors unable to shut completely.

Il-Hyeong was kneeling beside Kentian, holding his shoulders, attempting to rouse him back to his feet. "Come on, big guy," the fox said, his voice wavering. "Come on, you need to try to stand."

Arkady winced as the doors continued to put pressure on his paw, and he tried wriggling it to force them further apart. "Il-Hyeong!" he yelled again. "He's already dead! Just grab the case and let's go!"

"We're not leaving him!" Il-Hyeong yelled back. "Come on, Kentian, get up."

Watching the fox trying to help his fallen teammate in the moment's crisis made Arkady strain even harder to keep his paw from slipping free or getting crushed. "Il-Hyeong, we don't have time for that. Security's going to be on our tails any second now. Please, you need to get this door open."

Hefting the much larger, heavier wolf up with one arm nearly made Il-Hyeong buckle, and the fox then almost slipped as his foot slid through the pool of blood that had since formed. Kentian's eyes had already lost their spark, and his tail and ears were as limp as his limbs as the fox dragged him down the hallway, step by struggled step.

"Il-Hyeong, he's dead," Arkady said again, trying to fit his other paw into the tiny gap between the elevator doors. "We need to get the case and get out of here now, or we're all dead, too."

The dusty-furred fox's pelt was getting more and more matted in red by the moment. He bit his lip, whimpering as he shook his head. "No," he growled. "Not without Kentian. He might still be alive."

With a growl of his own, Arkady clenched his jaws. He considered trying to pull rank on the fox, but he knew that wouldn't fly, here. Instead, he closed his eyes tight, held his breath, and twisted his paw hard to one side. He squealed in pain as he felt one of his fingers break with a clean snap, but he was finally able to ball his paw up into a fist, forcing the doors open wide enough that the automatic sensors made them open up again.

The ferret scrabbled to his feet and stood between the open doors. He had no doubt, now, as he watched Il-Hyeong carrying Kentian's limp body along, that the wolf was dead. And if he wasn't, he'd be dead of blood loss long before they'd be able to even escape Shambhala, let alone get him to proper medical attention. Leaving his foot in place, Arkady leaned out and grabbed Il-Hyeong's other arm, pulling the fox and wolf both into the elevator.

"Hold the door," the ferret then gasped out, wincing again, having forgotten his broken finger when he'd grabbed for Il-Hyeong. "And take this." He slapped the DKR-8 security pistol into the fox's paw, then dashed to where he'd left the case in the office doorway. He grunted as he lifted it with both paws in order to ease the strain on his broken finger, and hauled it as fast as he could back into the elevator.

The blaring of the alarms went away as the elevator doors closed, leaving Arkady and Il-Hyeong trapped in a safe little box.

The stench of blood was nauseating. Now that he had a few moments, Arkady looked over Kentian in more detail, seeing that both of Cibola's shots had gotten the wolf in the chest. The ferret closed his eyes and growled, playing back in his mind the moment where he'd put two bullets in the raccoon's own chest.

"Body armor," Arkady murmured.

Il-Hyeong looked up. He'd been trying to use his claws to tear strips of fabric from the wolf's shirt for use as bandages. The fox's face had a large smear of blood down one side. "Body armor?" he asked.

"Cibola had body armor," the ferret replied. He cursed under his breath, wondering again just why the hell Ming-Jun had needed to cut her transceiver off. "Which means that he came here—or he was sent here—with the thought that this might turn out to be a trap."

The fox shook his head and went back to inspecting Kentian's wounds. "We'll look into it later," he said. "None of that is going to matter if we don't get out of here."

Kentian was a professional, Arkady reminded himself. He was a professional who knew the risks inherent in his job, and he went along with it. He'd stated on more than one occasion that he fought for a cause that he believed in. Arkady had no choice, then, but to tell himself that Kentian had been willing to die for the Iolite League, for Sahasrara and Project Scheherazade.

After a few seconds of just watching silently, Arkady couldn't stand to see Il-Hyeong continue his vain attempts to help Kentian. The ferret reached out and gently grabbed hold of the fox's wrist. The fox quickly shrugged it off. "Stop it," he muttered.

Arkady grabbed the fox's paw again. "Il-Hyeong, please," he said softly. "He's gone. There's nothing you can do."

Il-Hyeong looked up again. There weren't any signs of tears in the fox's eyes, but there was pain. He looked back at Arkady, as if searching the ferret's own eyes, and then he sighed, nodding, and let his paws fall away from Kentian's body. "I'm sorry," he said. Then, with more resolve: "God, how the hell did this happen?"

"Like you said," Arkady replied. "We'll figure that out once we get out of here." He glanced up at the numbers above the elevator doors, ticking down, one by one, bringing them ever closer to ground level. "They'll have security waiting for us outside the elevator, I'm sure."

"Probably," Il-Hyeong agreed. "They won't shoot us, though—not on the ground level in front of all their guests. Not unless they absolutely have to."

Arkady looked at himself, at Il-Hyeong in his stolen security uniform, and at the elevator. It was a gory, grisly scene, to be sure, and not something he imagined would buy them a lot of sympathy points. "They'll take the case," the ferret said. "And Ming-Jun's not going to be able to help us if Shambhala's entire security detail is waiting for us when we get off the elevator." He pressed the button marked '3.'

Looking much more composed than just a few moments ago, Il-Hyeong checked his gun again. He stood back up, leaned against the back wall of the elevator, and faced the doors, pistol at the ready as they continued their descent. With luck, Arkady thought, security would assume that whoever had perpetrated the shooting upstairs wouldn't know anything about Shambhala's floor plans or emergency protocols.

The elevator stopped on the third floor, and the doors opened to show nothing but an empty hallway. The third floor was another one of the casino levels, but because of the expert soundproofing, none of the noise reached the central elevator lobby. Both the fox and the ferret had guns drawn as Arkady hopped out and started to cross to the opposite-facing hallway.

Turning around, Arkady saw that Il-Hyeong was still in the elevator. The fox slowly dropped to one knee, next to Kentian, and Arkady hurried back. "Il-Hyeong," he said. "You know we can't take him with us."

"I know," the fox said, giving a solemn nod. "Just... give me a second." He reached out with one paw, touching the wolf on the bridge of the snout, and then he closed his eyes as he muttered something too quiet for Arkady to hear clearly. The ferret caught the reverent tone of voice, though, along with what he was pretty sure was the word 'Heaven.' Soon enough, the fox was done, and he stood back up and nodded to Arkady.

The two of them crossed the hallway, each of them taking point for the other as they rounded corners and headed for the east wing staircase.

If Ming-Jun was still patched into Shambhala's security channel, then she'd know that the big commotion was going on around the central elevator, and she'd therefore hopefully assume that they'd be taking the way down that would give them the easiest access to a street exit. Of course, Arkady wished fervently that he could just *tell* her where they were headed, but she was a smart girl. That just made it a matter of whether or not she was actually still keeping tabs on them. Arkady could only trust that she was.

Sounds of frantic activity echoed within the staircase itself, but they were coming from at least a couple dozen floors above them. More than likely, the security officers were heading up to the fifty-first floor, not down in the pursuit of any fleeing criminals. Arkady and Il-Hyeong must have shown up on at least a dozen cameras on their way from the elevator lobby to the staircase, but if the guards weren't already in position, then the bulk of them probably weren't going to make it on time.

Il-Hyeong went in front as the two of them made their way downstairs, the jostling of the case aggravating the pain in Arkady's busted finger. They were past the point of trying to be stealthy, now. If they got mobbed when they got out on the ground floor, then it was all over either way.

At the ground floor landing, the fox and the ferret ducked against the wall to either side of the exit of the stairwell. Arkady nodded to Il-Hyeong, who took the cue, swinging around and kicking the door open. A number of guests shrieked in alarm as the bloodied fox and his gun came into view, but Il-Hyeong called out, "Clear!" and Arkady slunk around the corner to follow.

This portion of the east wing had been set up as a smaller casino area geared toward lower-stakes players who had probably blown all of their investment just getting to Shambhala in the first place. The furnishings were nearly as lavish as those in the other public areas of the building, but the quality of the clientèle was visibly much lower. Two such players, a unkempt coyote and a gal who appeared to be either his wife or girlfriend, had huddled up against the wall, quaking in fear as they covered their heads with their arms at Il-Hyeong's approach. A white female weasel in one of those sleek, black, skimpy and provocative server's uniform walked by them, visibly less perturbed, but content to just stay out of the way.

"This way," Il-Hyeong said, motioning with his gun for Arkady to follow. "They'll have the main entrances blocked off. Our best bet is probably through the east wing kitchen." Arkady remembered what he could of the building's floor plan, but in the urgency of the moment, he decided that Il-Hyeong's first instinct was as good as any.

The swift fox started cutting a path right through the casino floor, with perhaps only half of the customers fleeing at the sight of him. Arkady was slower to keep up with the heavy case weighing him down, and heard the weasel attendant calling out loudly for everyone to just stay calm. The ferret thanked her silently and hobbled up and down the tiered steps between card tables and gaming machines, following in the wake Il-Hyeong had left through the crowd.

Far off to the right, Arkady spotted the gray-and-black uniforms of Shambhala security beginning to pour into the east wing casino. They were far enough away that Arkady and Il-Hyeong could probably make it to the kitchen before they were in reasonable shooting range—assuming, of course, that they'd not take risky shots that had the chance of hitting innocent bystanders.

Il-Hyeong had just about reached the large, swinging double doors to the kitchen when, out from the nearby aisle of slot machines, a black-suited shape dove into view. A solid fist cracked into the fox's face with a loud, bone-jarring sound, and the fox crumbled to the floor, his DKR-8 skittering away from him along the carpet.

"Drop it." The assailant was a short but sturdy black bear, carrying a menacing-looking pistol of his own that Arkady didn't immediately identify. "Drop the case and step away."

The bear wore a fancy tuxedo, which put him in the tier of gamblers that would be gambling on the floors above. He was out of place, and moreover, he definitely wasn't Shambhala security. "Drop it," he repeated, "or I kill you and take it."

Il-Hyeong was still writhing on the floor in pain, the bear's foot firmly planted on his chest. In the time it would take Arkady to drop the case and then draw his gun, the bear would have more than ample time to fire. But if he let the case go now...

The Octavians. The only explanation was that this bear was with the Octavians. If Cibola had had a personal bodyguard, he would have been present for the exchange, not fifty floors away. And if Kentian had just died in the course of helping the Iolite League obtain this case, then Arkady wasn't about to turn it over to the Octavians, of all people—not without a fight.

"Let's not be hasty," Arkady said. He began to lean down to set the case on the floor, taking his time, acting calm in an attempt to buy himself a few more seconds in which to find a window to act.

The bear kept his gun steadily trained on him. "Hurry it up," he growled. "Don't make me have to—"

The muffled sound of silenced pistol fire accompanied the bear's body going instantaneously limp, and he collapsed in a heap, thankfully not falling directly atop Il-Hyeong. The rabbit in the attendant's outfit, the one Arkady had seen when he'd been on his way to join Cibola's card game, walked out from in between the same rows of slot machines, holding her gun up in one paw as she knelt down to help Il-Hyeong up with the other.

"God in Heaven, Ming-Jun," Arkady gasped, joining her to help Il-Hyeong to his feet. "Do you think when you see people running, there might be a problem?"

"I was waiting for Kentian," Ming-Jun snapped, picking up Il-Hyeong's pistol from the floor, slapping it into the fox's paw. "Where the hell is he?"

"He's not coming," Il-Hyeong said, shaking his head, wobbling dizzily. He grabbed Ming-Jun's shoulder for balance, but then quickly pushed his way through the doors into the kitchen. The ferret and the rabbit scampered after him.

Il-Hyeong fired two shots up into the ceiling as he strode into the kitchen. "Clear a path!" he yelled, and the throng of chefs and attendants quickly complied, a number of trays and dishes clattering to the floor in a cacophony.

"I'll get your back," Ming-Jun said, and then the rabbit shoved Arkady from behind to get him between her and the fox. "Security's right behind us."

Luckily, none of the kitchen staff decided to do the stupid thing and attempt to play hero, and by the time that Arkady and the others heard the security detail barging into the kitchen, Il-Hyeong had already led them to the door to the back alley.

2. Elegies

From their hotel room on the twentieth floor of the Central Plateau Grand, Arkady and Ming-Jun could see the sprawling, staggered, and brightly-lit buildings of the city of Seizo, including, of course, the towering skyscraper of Shambhala. Even from a few miles away, the building dominated the skyline. Seizo wasn't quite the titanic megalopolis that cities like Thousand Leaves or Lo Hu were, but it was by no means small, and Shambhala itself still stood among the tallest buildings in the world.

For all of Shambhala's prestige and majesty, however, they hadn't been able to catch up to Arkady's team after they'd gotten out onto the street, and the police hadn't even arrived on scene by the time Ming-Jun had gotten them to the getaway car—likely because Shambhala's execs had been too proud and too interested in saving face to call the Seizo Municipal Police until it was too late.

The team was in the clear, now, but they were still so far from home. They at least had time to rest, in the interim, but it would be a short night's sleep. Shambhala's security forces, local authorities, and whomever Cibola had been working with were all looking for individuals under assumed names and false identities that had been carefully crafted to stand up to a fair amount of scrutiny. In time, they would learn that Kay O'Donnell and Christopher Hamilton had never existed—not in that form, at any rate—but by then, Arkady and the rest would be long gone, with Tomosabaki and Shambhala behind them.

By then, they'd be home. They'd be home, safe with the League, with their comrades. With Pandora.

Ming-Jun had been quick to change out of her casino worker's uniform in favor of casual sweats and a t-shirt, which might have made the rabbit look tomboyish if she didn't look so feminine to start with. What *did* take some of her womanly edge off was the way that she cleaned her gun as she sat at the foot of the bed. She used a Cordellatech Zarna, the same model of pistol that Arkady normally did, and the ferret thought as he watched her with it how lucky he was that she was on *his* side.

She still hasn't explained why she went silent in the middle of the mission, though, has she?

She had fur that was mostly a whitish cream color, with speckles and spots of faint gray that started at the right side of her face and which continued down along her neck and shoulder before disappearing under her shirt. Arkady wasn't sure just how far down that trail of mottled gray traveled, but he'd not been above wondering about it at least once or twice.

"The League's going to make sure they get hold of Kentian's body," Arkady said, killing the silence that had ensued since Ming-Jun had come back from changing her clothes. "The Tomosabaki government shouldn't put up much of a fight on that end."

Ming-Jun didn't look up. "I don't suppose they're going to help us figure out who that bear was."

Arkady shook his head. "No. But he had to be with the Octavians." He looked down at the crude finger splint he'd fashioned out of medical tape from Il-Hyeong's first aid kit. "I doubt there'll be much official evidence to link him back to them, though."

"The Octavians," Ming-Jun said, setting her gun on the nightstand, finally looking back up at Arkady. "I thought they were out of the picture on this."

"I thought so, too," Arkady said. "But there isn't anyone else it could be. Plus, they had cause and motive."

Ming-Jun sighed. "Motive, sure, but how did they find out? We took out their entire cell, and we know for a fact that they didn't get any messages out."

"They must have been working outside the cell beforehand." Arkady saw Ming-Jun's raised eyebrow and shrugged. "I know it's counter to the way that Octavian cells usually operate, but maybe they made an exception in this case. It would be the simplest explanation."

"You don't think it could have just been Cibola? Bringing in insurance, or something?"

"I doubt it." Arkady sat back and replayed the sequence of events out in his head once again. "Cibola brought a gun to the meeting and he panicked. He wouldn't have done that if he had a hired gun in the wings."

At that, Ming-Jun chuckled and shook her head. "I guess most people don't know what to do when they've got a gun pointed in their face," the rabbit said. "Just people like us."

Arkady had no snappy comeback to that: Ming-Jun was absolutely right, of course. People like them were picked for jobs like this one because they knew how to handle the pressure—and they knew how to handle the pressure because they kept getting picked for jobs like this. "I wish they'd let us stay in the city," Ming-Jun said, then. "I'd rather get to investigating Cibola and the others without having to head back, first."

"Our profile is way too high right now, and our cover identities have all been compromised. Besides, we need to guard this and get it home, first," Arkady said, tapping the all-important case with one foot. "After tonight, I'm not letting this thing out of my sight."

Ming-Jun rested her head back on the headboard. "Do you think it's worth it?" the rabbit asked, finally letting her guard down enough to let the ferret see the uncertainty in her eyes.

"That's what Kentian asked," Arkady replied.

"And what did you tell him?"

The ferret didn't want to say that had hadn't had the chance to say one way or the other. "Until we see what's in there, it's hard to say one way or the other, isn't it?"

Ming-Jun looked back at him silently, as if debating how much of that response she was willing to accept under the circumstances. "So open it," she said after a few seconds, nodding toward the case.

"We told Il-Hyeong we'd all see what was in it together," Arkady said. *And I almost don't even care what it is so long as it's safe.*

The digital clock on the nightstand beeped once as it rolled over to midnight. Ming-Jun's eyes flicked back to Arkady's. "Hey," she said. "It's not your fault. What happened to Kentian, I mean."

The ferret nodded. "Yeah, I know," he said. He started to fold his paws together, but he stopped when he felt the splint on his broken finger. That made him settle for drumming the fingers on his other paw restlessly against his knee.

"Can I ask you a question?" he then asked.

"Of course."

Arkady made sure he had her full attention. "Why did you turn your transceiver off while we were inside?"

"Oh." The rabbit sighed, her long ears drooping. "You caught me just as I was about to get a drink order from this fox. He looked shifty, kept looking over at the stairwell that you went through, and so I'd been scoping him out to keep tabs on him." She paused to sigh once again. "You got me on the transceiver just as I was leaning in close to him."

"And you were sure he was going to hear it."

Ming-Jun nodded. Arkady sighed, then, too.

Makes enough sense as an explanation. It's simple and clean—is it almost too clean?—but it also explains why she was still keeping in touch with the security system, and why she still intercepted Cibola's call and routed it through to Il-Hyeong.

It wasn't that Arkady thought she hadn't been doing her job, but she didn't usually get so twitchy while in the field. Then again, what should have been a routine intimidation had turned into bloodshed, and that certainly hadn't been the first time that a situation had exploded and turned around on them with no notice.

Perhaps, Arkady thought to himself, he wanted to put blame on Ming-Jun for what happened to Kentian. After all, if she'd been on the channel like she was supposed to, then he could have...

No, Arkady wouldn't have had any cause to have called Ming-Jun up until after Kentian was already dead. She had been downstairs, working backup, which was exactly where they'd needed her, and she'd pulled through and saved both Arkady and Il-Hyeong when it had counted the most.

"You did a good job tonight," the ferret told her, but she just nodded as if she didn't really put much stock in the words.

A minute or so later, the sound of rushing water came to a stop, which the ferret only noticed due to its having gone away. Ming-Jun had gone back to giving her Zarna another once-over, though it looked more like she was distracting herself than she was actively checking the gun. Shortly after the water had turned off, the louder, more noticeable sound of dryers began to issue forth through the door to the bathroom.

When Il-Hyeong stepped out, he was clad only in a pair of dark gray cargo pants. His fur was still slightly damp from the shower, but he'd done quite a thorough job of clearing that fur of the large amount of blood that had been caked to it after the escape from Shambhala. The long shower appeared to have relaxed him, too, though some of that was likely an active facade to mask his sense of loss.

"So," the fox said, taking a seat on the other bed. "Time to see what the Octavians were willing to drop so much money on." He picked up the case and grunted as he pulled it onto the bed, and both Arkady and Ming-Jun got up and hovered around it.

Il-Hyeong backed off a bit to allow Arkady to move in and unbuckle the sturdy metal clasps holding the case shut, and then the ferret nodded. All three of them put a paw on the front of the case, and after a few silent beats, they lifted it open together.

The interior of the case was divided into two compartments, both sized exactly to fit their contents. In the left compartment was some type of electronic device, built with a crude, light gray casing made of plastic. On the right was a leather-bound book, the cover bearing strange markings that didn't correspond to any code or symbol patterns that Arkady was familiar with.

The ferret carefully took the book in between his paws and lifted it out, only to discover that a second book had been packed underneath it. Handing the first book to Il-Hyeong, Arkady pulled out the second book to find yet a third. The second he passed over to Ming-Jun, and he took the third and final volume for himself.

Now Arkady knew why Cibola and his crew had tried to sell the artifacts off instead of handing them over to the Iolite League: the contents of this case could fetch more money from collectors on the black market than some corporations made in a year.

As Il-Hyeong and Ming-Jun silently flipped through their respective books, Arkady inspected his own. The paper was old and yellowed, but with some delicate handling, it proved to be not nearly as fragile as it looked. The pages were filled with the same mysterious writing that adorned the cover and spine, made up of curious markings that the ferret could not manage to wrap his head around.

The symbols, whatever they were, were ridiculously varied. Some of them were quite simple, made up of just a few linear strokes and dot marks, whereas others were drastically more complicated, seeming almost more like miniature pictures than code markings. Others seemed to be composites of smaller, more simple patterns that were repeated in other characters. Any given page was comprised of more unique symbols than there were letters in the alphabet, but after a cursory check, Arkady did confirm that some of the individual characters did appear more than once.

"What do you think this is?" Il-Hyeong asked in amazement, his muzzle firmly stuck in his own book. "Some kind of code, maybe?"

"Maybe," Arkady agreed. "If it is, though, it's almost unreasonably complicated. And right here we have three whole books full of it."

Ming-Jun was similarly enthralled. "It's beautiful, whatever it is," she said, running a few fingertips along the crispy, dry page to which she'd opened. Her book, it seemed, was printed in a larger, more ornate typeface, but aside from the different proportions and serifs, the characters themselves were clearly of the same sort.

Flipping through his book a bit more, Arkady skimmed to see if there were any pictures, but there didn't appear to be any. All of the pages were intact, though, as near as he could tell, and the binding of the book itself was amazingly well-preserved. It was hard to believe that it could be over four thousand years old, but unless it and the other two books were all forgeries—unbelievably overelaborate forgeries—then it couldn't possibly be any more recent than that.

"I can't wait to see the look on people's faces when we get these back to Château Sainte-Mireille," Il-Hyeong said, his proud smirk sneaking its way into his voice. "Do you think there's anything else back at the library like this?"

"Maybe," Arkady said. "I almost want to say that this all looks... passingly familiar, somehow, but we'll see." In all their time in working for Project Scheherazade, however, they'd never recovered anything like this. What Arkady really hoped was that the amount of text in the three books they had right there would be enough to let them decipher the writing. The Iolite League had some of the best cryptanalysts in the world on staff back at the library, and in theory, with a large enough corpus of text, they would be able to make sense of it.

The ferret stacked the books back into the case, treating them with near-reverence as he made sure that they went back inside in the same order in which they'd been stacked. "Let's see what this is, then," he said, pulling out the ancient electronic device from the case's other compartment.

The device was made of a clunky plastic casing, colored a drab gray-beige. It was marred and dirtied in a few spots, and was definitely not in the same pristine condition as the books. Still, it was intact, at any rate. The top (or what Arkady assumed to be the top, given how it had been stacked in the case) had a clear plastic window, through which a spindle and flywheel were visible. Running parallel were a series of narrow slits that had been carved into the plastic, only partially revealing some more electronics within. At the edge were a series of thick, plastic buttons, labeled in the same indecipherable writing as the books.

"There's something else," Ming-Jun said, reaching into the case. Sure enough, underneath where the ancient electronic gizmo had been was a tiny plastic cassette with two holes in the middle. The rabbit held it up for inspection, and Arkady immediately noticed that the holes were spaced the same distance apart as the flywheel and spindle.

"I think this goes in here," the ferret said, tapping his claw on the plastic window. "Now we just have to figure out which button opens it."

Ming-Jun leaned in to inspect the device. "Let's just try the buttons in order," she said, and before Arkady could stop her, she'd pressed her finger down on the rightmost button. As the ferret cringed, the plastic window popped open, revealing a slot that looked like it was meant to cradle the cassette for insertion.

"Well," Il-Hyeong chuckled. "What do you know?"

The three of them exchanged glances. Figuring out the deeper workings of a device like this was a job for the experts back at the League. Arkady's team was tasked with retrieving the artifacts, not understanding them—but this was an artifact that Kentian had died helping them acquire, and the looks on their faces told them all that they wanted to know just what it was they'd found.

"It looks like this is some kind of magnetic tape in the cassette," Arkady said. "And unless I'm way off base, here, this is an audio playback device." He tapped his fingertip against the series of tiny slits in the plastic case.

"How could it possibly still work, though?" Il-Hyeong asked, furrowing his brow. "Where does it even get its power from?"

Arkady flipped the thing over. There was an obvious plastic hatch that came free with a firm tug of his paw. Inside was some archaic type of battery interface, which had itself been refit with a jury-rigged (and presumably much newer, but still relatively ancient) replacement system that held some type of electrochemical cell in place. "Well, it's got a battery. If it's dead, I don't know where the hell we'll ever find another one."

"Can't hurt to test it out, then," Ming-Jun said. "Did you want to do the honors?"

The ferret popped the battery cover back into place and then set the device back down onto the bed. With far more caution than was probably necessary, he slipped the cassette into the deck and pressed the window closed. Waiting a few more seconds, and seeing that it evidently wasn't going to turn on automatically, the ferret bit his lip. "Any guesses on which of these buttons makes this thing go?" There were half a dozen of them, and if Ming-Jun had already found the one that opened the cassette mechanism, that still left five others to choose from.

"Trial and error?" Il-Hyeong suggested, making Arkady raise an eyebrow. "Hey, it's not like we have any other way to go about it, right? We can't read the buttons, and we have nothing else to test them out with."

Arkady couldn't argue with that. "Okay," he sighed. "Here goes." On a hunch, he picked the leftmost button, but when he pressed it, none of the deck's mechanical components began to move, and the button itself stayed depressed.

"Shit," the fox muttered. "Did you break it?"

"Here, let me see it," Ming-Jun said, trying to pull the deck away from Arkady. "I had some luck with it last time." Her paw hovered over the controls, and again, before Arkady could stop her, she pushed one of the buttons. The button Arkady had pushed popped back up into its original position, and then, the quiet hotel room was filled with music.

If the writing in the books had been beautiful, the sound coming out of this ancient playback device was more gorgeous still, by orders of magnitude. The melody was a little eerie, but at the same time, it was lovely and enchanting; the instruments were hard for Arkady to place, but the plucked strings sounded similar to a mandolin, and it was accompanied by some type of piano or keyboard. Softer woodwinds of some sort made up the harmony in the background.

What took center stage, though—and what captivated Arkady the most—were the vocals. A female voice sang along with the music, sounding so passionate and heartfelt that Arkady couldn't help but swell up with emotion himself despite the fact that he couldn't understand a word she was singing. The ferret doubted that the sounds were even words: the singer sang with a sense of pitch and tonality unlike anything Arkady had ever heard, and though it should have been nothing more than gibberish to him, he felt as though, even without words, he still got the *sense* of what she was trying so hard to convey in her song.

Both Il-Hyeong and Ming-Jun were also silent, and Arkady could see in their eyes that they, too, felt a similar emotional connection to the song. They all looked at each other, but none of them spoke, instead just keeping their ears focused on the music. Il-Hyeong's ears were splayed out to either side, the look on his face bordering on worshipful awe. Ming-Jun appeared on the verge of tears.

The song built up, crescendoed, and then petered out with a delicate, wordless reprise. A quick look at the clock on the nightstand showed that the song had only been about four minutes long, but to Arkady, it felt as if it had been twenty. The cassette clicked to a stop, plunging the room into near silence that was broken only by the sound of three people breathing, almost panting.

With that, Arkady picked up the deck and placed it back into the case, closing and locking it again. He set his paw atop the case itself and steadied himself there as he waited for a moment's dizziness to pass.

Kentian had wanted to know if the contents of the case were worth it. Stricken as he was by the wolf's death, Arkady couldn't bring himself to think, even for a moment, that they weren't.

Seeing the islands of the Deepwater Archipelago coming into view allowed Arkady to finally feel a rush of relief. If anything bad were going to have occurred on their flight from Tomosabaki, it would have happened by now. Once they landed, they would be firmly in the arms of the Iolite League, and no harm would befall them there.

Arkady had insisted that the jet make a direct flight home, without making any stopovers for refueling. The pilot had protested, but he had no choice but to follow the ferret's orders. To fly so far from the Continent—having taken off from a city near its center—made it a stretch, but if the plane were as well-maintained as regulations directed, it could make it. It had meant half a day of nonstop flying, but Arkady wasn't willing to take any unnecessary risks with the contents of the case on the line.

Il-Hyeong and Ming-Jun hadn't been the greatest company in the world, but then, neither had Arkady himself, the ferret was sure. Any of the awe and excitement they'd experienced while perusing the books and listening to the strange song the night before had since faded into nonexistence. They'd worked out how to fast-forward and rewind the tape, but they weren't willing to tinker beyond that. In addition to the team being tired and nervous and on-edge, the energy within the cabin was noticeably wrong, what with only the three of them returning home instead of four.

The fourth seat of the cabin was where Kentian should have been sitting. At this moment, he should have been regaling his teammates with tales of his weeks undercover in Seizo, the various hoops he'd had to jump through in order to ingratiate himself into Cibola's inner circle. He'd have been sharing anecdotes about all the crazy little things that had happened over the course of assuming the role of a whiskey-drinking, ass-grabbing smooth-talker who got to play cards with the Princess of Afortunada while laying the groundwork for a plan to retrieve a case full of artifacts from four thousand years ago.

Instead, the fourth seat was now merely piled with Ming-Jun's surveillance equipment, which had been hastily loaded on board, and the team would never be hearing those anecdotes. None of the agents had dared even speak of Kentian at all since leaving Seizo, and whenever silence settled around the cabin, their intentional avoidance of the subject became apparent.

The wolf had served alongside Arkady for nearly five years. Though that was only half the time that Arkady and Il-Hyeong had been working together, it was more than enough for the ferret to have considered the wolf a friend and not just a colleague. At times, Arkady thought that his superiors sent Kentian along specifically because the two were often at odds with one another (which went along great with the League's position on fostering harmony), but now that his stubborn comrade was gone forever, he wondered how discomfited he'd feel with that comfortable sense of strife removed from the picture.

Arkady looked over at Il-Hyeong, whose attention was directed out one of the jet's windows and at the islands of Deepwater far below. Ten years they'd worked together, and the fox still didn't look a day older than when they'd first met—but then, neither did Arkady. The laity might have thought of the anti-aging gene therapy as a mere job perk; for Arkady and his team, it was a necessity, a way of ensuring that they'd be able to serve the Iolite League for as long as they could, locked forever in the prime of youth, at a physical peak.

Kentian had been the same, of course. He'd had an indelible sense of vigor and energy, and the drive to put it to full effect. Where Il-Hyeong was professional and no-nonsense, and Ming-Jun was quiet and devout, Kentian had brought a higher-level positive energy to the team dynamic. Anti-aging therapy or not, the wolf had *acted* like he'd expected to live forever.

And yet, despite all that energy, all that certainty and ambition, all that talent and devotion and undeniable skill and ability, it had all been snuffed out in less than a second. Two lucky shots from someone who had probably never fired a gun in his life, and years of training and countless missions had meant absolutely nothing.

Arkady bit his lip and closed his eyes, resting his forehead against the cabin wall. He was supposed to be prepared for this. Agents died; as team leader, he knew and understood this. *People* died; as a believer in the Iolite Doctrine, he knew and accepted this. Why, then, was it so hard to wrap his head around now that it had happened?

In three days, Arkady, Il-Hyeong, and Kentian were to have had another medical examination with Dr. Mayflower as part of the augmentation process they were slated to undergo in a few weeks. Now, though, who knew if they'd bother to continue along that route?

With a flick of one ear, Il-Hyeong turned away from the window and looked back at Arkady, and the slight, sad smile on the fox's face made the ferret wonder if his friend hadn't somehow heard his thoughts. The fox got up, then, and walked across the cabin to sit next to the ferret, sighing as he sat down. After sitting in silence for a few seconds, Il-Hyeong reached over to take one of Arkady's paws in his own.

"Hey," the fox said. "He's going to be all right."

Arkady tilted his head. "Who?"

"Kentian," Il-Hyeong replied, the bittersweet smile on his face wavering only in the slightest degree. "He's done his work, and now his reward is that he gets to rest and be with God."

The ferret nodded. "He was a good wolf," he said. "It's a shame he had to go so soon."

"It is," the fox said. "But each of us has our time; this just happened to be Kentian's."

Certainly, there was no higher cause than doing God's work—doing work that benefited the whole of the world, and Kentian had done nothing if not that. The Iolite Doctrine told Arkady to believe that the wolf was in a better place, but he could see from the faint glimmer in Il-Hyeong's eyes that the fox, too, was worried by the chance that he wasn't.

The silence between them then returned, but they stayed seated next to one another. Il-Hyeong kept his paw around Arkady's for a while longer, releasing it after a couple of minutes.

Ming-Jun was still sitting by herself in the other corner of the cabin. Her head was tilted back and her eyes were closed, but Arkady couldn't tell whether she was asleep or not. If she was, he didn't want to wake her; if she wasn't, he didn't want to disturb her all the same. The rabbit hadn't seemed quite so shaken the previous night, but reality had a way of sinking in slowly, at times, Arkady knew.

The line of the horizon through the window disappeared as the plane banked sharply and then began its descent. Most aircraft heading to Deepwater would be headed for the airport on the main island of Stewart. The Iolite League had private jurisdiction over any and all aircraft coming into Château Sainte-Mireille, and so that landing pattern was clear as the jet made its descent. If nothing else, Arkady was glad that he wouldn't need to deal with the hassle of an airport after they reached the ground.

3. The Library of Château Sainte-Mireille

Back in his room within the manorial estate for which the island was named, Arkady lay on his bed, atop the covers, the case from Shambhala beside him. Debriefing on the mission to Tomosabaki wasn't scheduled for a few hours to come, and since he'd done nothing but think on the whole flight back to Château Sainte-Mireille, he wanted to take some time to just relish the relative comfort of his own austere room and vegetate mindlessly. That was easier said than done, though, since there was nowhere on the entire island he could hide from reminders of the things that Kentian had given his life to preserve and protect.

Over ten years ago, now, Arkady had been planning on becoming a monk. He'd been ready and willing to devote himself to that life of quiet piety, to a life where he would uphold the Iolite Doctrine here at the holy Château through contemplation and service. If he'd gone down that route, then right now, he'd actually be showing his age, living a serene and simple yet happy existence at the monastery just outside the grounds proper.

If he'd gone down that route, then someone else would have been chosen for Sahasrara in his stead. Someone else would have been on that mission to Shambhala. Someone else might have gotten out of there with his or her team all still alive.

Here in Deepwater, it was late afternoon, and the sun wouldn't set for several hours to come. Even with all of the lights off, Arkady's room was frustratingly bright. He didn't want to sleep—didn't think he *could* sleep—but the sunlight coming in through the drawn curtains made it too hard to ignore the world outside the window. It was quiet enough, but during daylight hours, there were always Iolite League members out in the manor courtyard, and even if Arkady couldn't hear them, he knew they were there.

Some of the folks outside were people who lived at Château Sainte-Mireille year-round, both penitents and clergy alike. Others were here from overseas, visiting the Château on retreat. Only an elite few knew about Arkady's secret missions, or about the case that Kentian had given his life for, or about the installation built underneath the manor or the hoard of artifacts therein. This was one of the most beautiful, most hallowed places in the world. At the same time, billions of people of dozens of species and cultures—including most members of the Iolite League itself—were blissfully unaware that it was also the gateway to a different world entirely.

Someday it would be different, Arkady told himself. After they'd learned more, after they'd made sure that the world was ready for the elusive truths that they were working to uncover. The world held its mysteries, its secrets, and until they were unlocked, the common folk had to be protected from the misinformation and the half-truths that cropped up along the way.

The Iolite League was an international entity, with membership in the millions. For most of those people, the League represented a spiritual and philosophical ideal: that all people were God's creatures, and that God had made people as different as they were as a means to ensure that they had to embrace what things made them so similar. Life was a sort of test, and it was only in being able to see past the superficial that true peace and harmony could be achieved for the world. The Iolite League strove to help guide people toward that lofty goal, on the individual level and on the group level. It was an uphill battle, but matters of spirituality were not meant to be simple.

It was up to teams like Arkady's to help that process along, by helping to defuse tension where tension shouldn't exist, by helping to solve some of the mysteries presented by the world's fractured history, by helping to foster understanding between people who might otherwise be too stubborn without a stern paw to guide them.

The ferret brought his arms up and lazily draped his forearms over the mask of his eyes. His paws collided with one another in the process, and it was only the dull wince that accompanied the impact that reminded him that his finger was broken. He'd felt so little pain and discomfort from it that he'd forgotten about it completely since before leaving Tomosabaki.

If the outside world was not to be ignored, Arkady could at least get his finger taken care of before it was time for his debriefing. Lingering exhaustion made itself more pronounced as the ferret dragged himself out of bed, and he had to shake off a brief dizzy spell as he walked over to his closet. He'd have enough time to come back to his room before reporting in, he guessed, and so he settled for just throwing a casual overshirt on over the t-shirt he'd been wearing while lying down.

He was ready to walk out the door when he stopped and looked back at the case atop his bed. For several seconds, he considered bringing it along with him, reluctant to let it out of his sight even knowing that it was locked safely in his own room. He chided himself for his anxiety. *You're going to get paranoid if you keep this up*, he told himself. *It's just a case. It's safe where it is.* Forcing himself to be content with that, he locked the door before heading off to see the doctor.

The halls of Château Sainte-Mireille were as ancient as something could be without being pre-civ. Pillars of polished marble that couldn't have been quarried anywhere in Deepwater held up vaulted ceilings lined with tiled mosaics made up of different hues of green and blue. A series of narrow and pointed lancet windows lined one side of the hallway, opening out into the courtyard below, and the vantage from the second floor gave Arkady an excellent look at the dozens of people enjoying the beautiful sunny day. The Iolite League kept a strict regimen of repairing and restoring the manor, priding itself on the fact that they'd kept the structure intact and looking just like it had when it had been built nearly four thousand years ago. While records from that long ago weren't openly available for Arkady's casual perusal, the ferret had seen photographs over a millennium old showing the Château looking quite identical to how it looked today.

The Château hadn't always belonged to the Iolite League, of course, as the League couldn't trace its own origins back much further back than a thousand years. It had clearly been built as some sort of palace, employing architectural and decorative stylings unlike any other building in the world. Some scholars took that as evidence, along with the manor's age, that the Château bridged some gap between pre-civ and the earliest stages of defined history. The genealogists of Clan Spindletree, on the other paw, liked to purport that Château Sainte-Mireille was one of their ancestral holdings, and while their own historical family records were remarkably well-maintained, showing that the raccoons had indeed been in possession of the estate in the period between thirty-five hundred years ago up to when it had been handed over to the Iolite League, there was no concrete evidence as to who might have lived there before then.

Arkady had once asked his friend and colleague Darren Spindletree, one of the librarians, what his personal take on the matter was, but like so many of the other thousands of raccoons who shared his surname, his connection to the great family line was a faint one, and to him, the Château's importance stemmed from it being a holy place, not from it being an artifact belonging to some distant, long-dead relations.

The ferret took the old, rickety elevator down to the ground floor. The mechanism that worked it was old-fashioned, but the manor's caretakers made sure that it was well-maintained and safe. There was no need for anything more modern and advanced to carry handfuls of individuals between a couple of floors, and so the model had intentionally never been updated. Beyond that, Arkady suspected that the maintenance crew made sure to leave the elevator just a little bit rickety on purpose, in order for it to keep its quaint, antiquated edge.

Down on the ground floor, Arkady turned to walk down the central corridor. As with the upstairs, the side leading out to the courtyard was lined with lancet arches large enough for a person to step through. Arkady skirted the perimeter of the courtyard without entering it, still feeling averse to the idea of contact or chatter.

With the courtyard to his right, Arkady passed by the chapel on his left. He spied Ming-Jun inside, the rabbit recognizable from the splotches of gray on the one side of her face. She was facing the altar, the chapel empty save for her. The evening service, held daily for the benefit of pilgrims and residents alike, wouldn't be until sundown, and Arkady suspected that the rabbit was trying to get her prayers in now so that she could avoid the distraction of a crowd and a sermon.

Il-Hyeong, Arkady was willing to wager, was probably at the underground shooting range. He'd grieve and pray in his own time, in his own way. Mostly likely, he would go through training exercises to purge his body of unneeded aggressive tendencies before seeking the solace and counsel of Father Benjamin. On any other day, Arkady might have considered heading down to the range, himself, but his broken finger would have taken much of the fun out of it. Il-Hyeong would probably want to be left alone, besides.

The ferret stood outside the chapel for a few moments more, silently watching Ming-Jun kneel down with her ears back and her head down in supplication. He hadn't had a real conversation with her since the hotel room in Seizo. They'd talked about the mission, the breach in protocol, and had explored the contents of the case together with Il-Hyeong, but they hadn't discussed Kentian or his death. She was clearly deep in prayer, and so disturbing her now probably wasn't the best idea. Besides, Arkady wasn't a priest. He probably wasn't what she needed in terms of spiritual guidance right now.

Despite that, Arkady stayed poised at the doorway of the chapel. The ferret wasn't clergy, it was true, but he was still the leader of Ming-Jun's team, and her teammate—teammate and friend—had just died. Didn't he have a responsibility to her? Just as she had to have faith in God and the Iolite Doctrine that Kentian's soul would be looked after, she had to have faith in Arkady that their team would be safe and secure.

Just as Arkady was about to step into the chapel, a small paw closed down on his shoulder. He turned around to see Father Benjamin, who looked completely casual about having snuck up on him. The ruddy, jovial weasel simply nodded with his head to one side, then walked in that direction, underneath the colonnade, toward one of the corners, away from both the courtyard and the chapel. Arkady followed, checking with one final glance over his shoulder to see that Ming-Jun had at no point looked up from her genuflection.

With the barest flick of his arms, Father Benjamin got the sleeves of his black, violet-trimmed robes to hang free of wrinkles. He then held his arms down in front of himself, crossed at the wrists, and gazed into Arkady's eyes. The weasel was shorter than the ferret, and was also probably younger, if only by a few years, though he of course looked much older. His face put him on the cusp of forty, though he showed it more with the wisdom in his eyes than he did with any graying of the fur at the edges of his snout.

"She's been in there for quite a while, Arkady," he said after a moment of waiting.

Arkady tried to read the weasel's intentions, but the priest might as well have been wearing a mask. "It looks like it. I was just wondering if she—"

"If she needed someone to talk to?" Father Benjamin finished for him. "I'm sure that she does, but that someone isn't you. Not yet."

"If that's the case, Father, why are you out here talking to me?"

Father Benjamin shook his head. "I didn't say that she needed to talk to me, either," he said. "She's talking to who she needs to talk to, and it seems like it's quite the conversation."

The ferret bit his lip and looked back in the direction of the chapel. "I take it you've heard, then?"

"About Mr. McEvoy, yes." Now the weasel finally let some emotion into both his voice and his expression, the tiniest shade of sadness, tempered by his priestly authority. "I was deeply saddened by the news. I know that he was well-loved by his brethren here at the Château."

Arkady felt words catch in his throat before he could speak them, and then a shudder ran down along the length of his body. Though Father Benjamin was Arkady's priest, and was therefore nominally supposed to be his closest confidant, the weasel wasn't a member of Sahasrara— wasn't even aware of the group's existence. "Did they tell you how it happened, Father?" the ferret asked, trying to convey the pretext of being too shaken up to bring himself to break the news on his own.

Father Benjamin nodded, averting his eyes with a dour sigh. "I was spared the particulars that I'm sure I didn't need to hear," he said. "I understand that you and Il-Hyeong were there to see it happen, though. That must have been terrible for you."

What he hadn't needed to hear, Arkady thought sourly. There was no way for his team to hide the fact that they were continually heading afield together, and so their cover story had been that they were ambassadors for the politically-oriented side of the Iolite League. That wouldn't explain why one of them hadn't come back alive from a 'routine' trip to the capital of Tomosabaki, though. What *had* Father Benjamin been told, exactly? Was it cruel to keep him in the dark, or was ignorance truly bliss in this case?

Arkady decided to spare both Father Benjamin and himself any further awkwardness on that front. "I'm... trying not to think about that too much, Father," he said. "Right now, I'm more just trying to come to grips with the fact that he's gone."

At that, the weasel unfolded his arms and set one paw up on Arkady's shoulder. "I know that I don't need to quote basic Scripture to you, Arkady," he said. "I also know that faith can be a hard thing to hold on to when something like this happens." The weasel then released Arkady's shoulder and took one of the ferret's paws in his own, giving it a squeeze. "I'll be here for you to talk to, once you've had time to sort out your feelings, but sorting out those feelings needs to come first before my words will do you any good."

At a momentary loss, Arkady simply nodded. Father Benjamin was right, of course: Arkady was in no state of mind to talk about Kentian's death, but a lot of that had to do with finding a way to express himself to the priest in terms that didn't betray the secrecy of his team and their mission. "Thank you, Father," he said, his mouth running dry. "I'll be sure to come to you soon."

As he turned to walk away, heading back on his way to get his injury looked at, the ferret realized that the paw that Father Benjamin had just squeezed was the one with the broken finger. There had been no pain despite the weasel's firm grip. Flexing his fingers a few times, Arkady felt only a dull twinge on the first couple attempts, followed by a more noticeable spike of discomfort the third time he moved that digit and flexed it harder.

"Arkady," Father Benjamin called out before the ferret could get more than a couple of steps. "She's going to need to talk to you, too, " he said, nodding toward the chapel. "In her own time."

"Yes, Father," Arkady replied, and this time, the weasel nodded his head to let him know that he was okay to walk away.

From a spiritual perspective, Father Benjamin's advice made complete sense, of course: if Arkady was yet to come to terms with the death of his friend, then he could hardly offer a magical solution to Ming-Jun's grief. But again, the priest only knew half the story, and only *could* offer advice from a religious perspective; from Arkady's perspective as a team leader and fellow agent, there were other things that he needed to consider. They'd still need to do their jobs, and duty wouldn't necessarily afford them the luxury of time to grieve or the opportunity to get their feelings and emotions all sorted. Arkady was still going to need to talk to her, and soon, whether either of them were ready or not.

But not now, though. As Arkady walked by the chapel again, he stole another quick look inside and saw that the rabbit was still there, looking as though she hadn't moved a muscle in the meantime. This, at least, she needed to do for herself, and meanwhile, Arkady still had business of his own to take care of.

Halfway down the central corridor, Arkady stopped and faced the grand central arch that led into the courtyard, perpendicular to the hallway that led to the Château's front entrance. This would be the first major sight to greet anyone coming into the Château for the first time: the arch formed a visual frame for the large stone statue in the center of the courtyard, which depicted six figures of indeterminate gender—a wolf, a rabbit, a tiger, a mouse, a fox, and a bat—holding paws and standing in an outward-facing circle. Inscribed along the curve of the arch, in striking, bold capitals, was the motto of the Iolite League: *FOR THE BETTER WORLD.*

It was the definite article in that phrase that gripped Arkady most: there *was* a better world out there that people just needed to find. That was the core of the Iolite Doctrine, and that was what Arkady fought for—and what Kentian had fought for, as well, the ferret told himself. It was in the name of that better world that Arkady did all that he did, and he would pray, later, for the strength and the wisdom to continue to do what was right.

The basement level beneath this section of the Château housed the library. At the foot of the stairs was a podium where library staff sometimes greeted visitors, but it was vacant at the moment. Ancient stone had been kept polished and smooth, illuminated by bright electric brazier-bulbs crafted specifically to give the illusion of firelight. Bookcases lined all four walls and divided the room into a dozen separate aisles, each full of books, periodicals, and small museum-style displays, gathered by the Iolite League from all over the world, from over the last four thousand years of recorded history.

Where old libraries in the larger cities of the world would have such sections languishing under layers of dust, this library beneath the manor was kept fastidiously clean, so that the scores of pilgrims who came from every corner of the world to visit the holy Château Sainte-Mireille could enjoy its historical offerings as well. Every so often, when Arkady wasn't in a rush, he'd stop between a row of bookcases and choose a volume at random from the shelves, flipping through it to get a reminder of how vast the world really was, and of how little one could truly know about all of it. The individual was lowly, after all, but he was part of an immense and beautiful system that operated thanks to the blessings of nature and the grace of God.

Every person of every species had their part to play in the plan, and it was Arkady's part that brought him here. He maneuvered in between the stacks of old and varied tomes, making his way to the far corner of the room. There, at the central reference desk, was Darren Spindletree, who looked up from the heavy, leather-bound volume on his desk and offered the ferret a smile. "Good afternoon, Arkady," the raccoon said, and he made no attempt to stop Arkady as the ferret walked around the desk and down the staircase that was labeled LIBRARY STAFF ONLY.

At the bottom of that staircase was an unmarked wooden door. It was locked, but Arkady had the key in his pocket. Past that door was a narrow corridor, with no pretense of trying to match the Château chambers above. Cool gray steel formed the walls, ceiling, and floor, ending at a lavender-colored blast door emblazoned in gold with a stylized representation of the thousand-petaled lotus, the symbol of Sahasrara.

Arkady stepped up to the door and tapped his paw at the keypad off to the right-hand side. The center of the abstract flower on the door opened up, and the hallway's artificial lighting glinted off of the lens within it. The ferret squared his shoulders and lined his eye up with that hole, and a tiny hum echoed from within the door, followed a moment later by a loudspeaker coming to life.

"Agent Ryswife, Arkady: identity confirmed by retinal scan. Please provide security phrase."

"When your ship has traversed the waters of the ocean, you will reach the fertile shore of the prosperous country," the ferret replied.

With that, the light purple blast door split open at a slight diagonal through the middle, in line with the stylized lotus pattern, and it slid open with hardly any noise at all. The ferret stepped past the steel-framed threshold.

Here was the headquarters of Sahasrara, the proverbial sword of the Iolite League.

Down the hallway to the right were the rooms that stored the artifacts brought back for Project Scheherazade. Those rooms made up the *real* library of Château Sainte-Mireille—a library that would soon benefit from the addition of three new books of strange text and an archaic tape player.

Assisting Project Scheherazade was one of the happier and more noble tasks that Arkady got to do in his service in Sahasrara. The goal of the project was for the Iolite League to gather up as much information on the pre-civ world as possible—to recapture the world's lost stories and make sure that they would never again be lost to time. Here and there, ancient tomes, assorted artifacts, and even fragments of computer data from that period would crop up, and the Iolite League made an open show of wanting to catalog all such material for its archives.

Given the extreme value that such mysterious antiquities held on the black market for wealthy collectors and eccentric aficionados of history, however, it was sometimes necessary for the Iolite League to send in members of Sahasrara to make sure that such lost effects made their way safely back to the library of Château Sainte-Mireille, where they might be used for the benefit of all instead of fueling the greed or the whims of an individual. Besides, some of this lost, ancient information might well be dangerous, and was best kept out of public domain for now, until any risks were properly assessed.

Arkady was not headed to the library now, however. Instead, he took the other branch of the hallway heading to the left, which led to both the Hephaestus Chamber (the only significant addition to headquarters since Arkady had first set foot inside a decade ago) and to his current destination: the laboratory of Dr. Jillian Mayflower.

Before the ferret had even rounded the corner, he could already hear flustered rummaging coming from within. If the world was an ever-changing place, at least the good doctor could be counted on to always stay the same; that thought brought a smile to Arkady's face as he walked in through the door without knocking.

Hopping back and forth between a disheveled desk and one of the room's three computer terminals, the middle-aged kangaroo looked as busy ever. Kangaroos were one of the less populous species, with one of their largest population centers located here in Deepwater—though, like just about everyone else here at the Château, the doctor was another transplant from overseas, brought by her duties to the Iolite League. She didn't show any sign of having seen the ferret enter in the midst of her rummaging, but even so, without even looking up, she called out a cheerful, "Welcome back, Arkady."

"Thank you, Doctor," Arkady replied, folding his paws together and keeping his smile. "It's good to see you again."

The kangaroo punched a long sequence of keystrokes at her terminal, and then, after chewing her lower lip for a few seconds, she left it and finally turned her attention to Arkady, adjusting her glasses after taking her eyes away from the computer screen. "Are you here to check up on Pandora?" she asked. "Not a lot to report, I'm afraid."

Arkady bowed with respect to the kangaroo, and then smiled again. "Not right now. Though I'd like to see you about her later, if you don't mind." The doctor nodded. "Actually, I'm wondering if you have the time to take care of this for me." The ferret held up his paw with the broken finger.

Mayflower shook her head, chuckling. "May as well," she said. "It's not like anything else is getting accomplished around here in the meantime." Again she adjusted her glasses and leaned in to inspect the ferret's fingers, holding his wrist. "You know, I wish more people came back with injuries like yours, Arkady."

When they come back at all. As head of Sahasrara's medical staff, Dr. Mayflower had surely already been notified of Kentian's death; that she wasn't bringing it up around Arkady was either an indication of personal courtesy or of her tendency to hyperfocus on the task at hand. Not wanting to wager on either one, Arkady just let her look at his injury, figuring that she probably had more than enough on her own mind.

"Well, let's check out the break real quick," Dr. Mayflower said. "I should have you back on your feet and ready to go in twenty minutes, though, I think. You have that much time?"

"Plenty," Arkady said, nodding, and he followed Mayflower as she led him across the hall to one of her exam rooms. If there were any other doctors wandering around headquarters this afternoon, they weren't here in the medical ward, it seemed. The kangaroo motioned for Arkady to sit in the exam chair, and then she wheeled over a cart bearing a device that was shaped like a foot-long, metal-and-plastic tube.

Arkady stuck his paw in the tube without the kangaroo needing to prompt him. She pressed a series of buttons on the attached console, and the device began to hum and vibrate. "You know, after the augmentation, you'll never have to go through this again," she said. "I bet you're looking forward to that."

"And I bet you're looking forward to not having to do this for me every other time one of us comes back," the ferret replied.

"At least as far as the three of you go," Mayflower said, and then she frowned. "Well, the two of you, now, I guess." Arkady winced when she pointed that out. The casual lack of sympathy suggested that she'd simply not brought it up before because it had slipped her mind.

The tube stopped its humming, and the doctor said, "Simple, clean fracture. It'll just take ten minutes." She stepped over to the counter and picked up a small metal framework. "All kidding aside, Arkady, be glad that your team doesn't tend to come back with the types of injuries that members of Ajna do. You wouldn't want to see the sorts of things I had to fix back when I worked for them."

As convenient as this whole process was, Arkady had to admit that he was glad that this might be the last time he'd ever have to go through with it. The doctor had a point about Ajna, too: one of the Iolite League's six other secret operations groups, based out of Novoprypiatsk on the far west side of the Continent, they tended to deal with far more violent matters than Sahasrara did. It was almost unheard of for a member of one of the seven branches to be transferred to another—especially not to Sahasrara, which held the highest authority of all—but a medical and scientific genius like Dr. Mayflower was more than worthy of being an exception to that, especially given the critical role she filled for Project Scheherazade.

With the kangaroo sliding the metal frame into place over Arkady's forearm, the ferret tried closing his eyes to cut through the anticipation, but it didn't much help the sharp pain that came when the doctor grabbed his broken finger and forced it into place within the stabilizing unit. A finger, at least, wasn't so bad; when he'd broken his tibia on a mission to Xin-Banzhu a few years earlier, Dr. Mayflower's yanking and tugging had made Arkady wonder how the kangaroo had gotten placed in such a sensitive position. She was good at what she did, of course, but for those moments of intense pain, she didn't rank very high on the ferret's list.

Soon, the ferret's immobilized paw was slipped back into the tube, framework and all. Dr. Mayflower silently entered some more commands into the main console, and this time, instead of the tube beginning to vibrate, it stayed still, humming in a different pitch as a warm tingling sensation began to well up from within Arkady's broken finger. The sensation almost felt like burning, but it was also soothing in some ways, such as how it cut through the residual pain from the doctor's clumsy manhandling.

"So," Dr. Mayflower said, pulling up a chair and taking a seat as the device began to incite the fracture in Arkady's finger to knit at a fantastically accelerated pace, "I don't suppose that your mission to Tomosabaki netted you anything that'll help me out, did it?"

Arkady shook his head. "Just artifacts," he said. "We haven't had any leads on the Pyxis Sequence in months. You know that if I hear anything, you'll be the first to know."

"If they let you tell me," Mayflower replied with a wry smile. "But thanks. I appreciate that."

"They are still looking, I'm sure," Arkady said, feeling much more awake, now, thanks to the increased endorphins now running through his bloodstream.

The kangaroo chuckled again. "Oh, I'm sure they are," she said. "Do you know how much it costs per day to keep the Hephaestus Chamber up and running?"

"No, and neither do you," Arkady said, gently slapping her shoulder with his free paw. "But don't worry. They're not going to just shut the project down. After all, even without the Pyxis Sequence, she's proven incredibly valuable."

Mayflower smiled. "I'm surprised, Arkady," she said. "You don't usually talk about your daughter in those terms."

At that, Arkady felt himself deflate. Yet another spiritual issue on which he couldn't beseech Father Benjamin for counsel. "I'm just trying to put things in perspective," he said. "We knew when we got into this that it was liable to take a long time. But we'll still get it done."

The kangaroo nodded. "No matter how long it takes."

"No matter how long it takes," the ferret repeated. That was, after all, the approach the Iolite League preferred to take with everything.

"Agent Quinn," the tall badger said, turning his attention to the fox, "do you agree with Agent Ryswife's assessment of the situation?"

Il-Hyeong, seated to Arkady's left, looked sharp and severe with his Sahasrara dress uniform on, his paws folded neatly together atop the long, black table behind which they sat. In the dim lighting, the dark violet fabric was indistinguishable from black, with the gold of the epaulets and trim making the light color of his fur stand out even more. Although the uniforms were for official and ceremonial occasions only (which were few and far between for Sahasrara in particular), the fox wore his like it was much more familiar—and he looked more composed and distinguished than Arkady did in his.

With a cool, serious expression befitting a military officer, the fox looked back at the badger and nodded. "I do, sir," he said. "I noticed that Mr. Cibola was armed when he entered the suite, and he was preparing to draw his weapon when Agent Ryswife fired on him in self-defense."

"Using the gun that you yourself had armed him with?" the badger asked.

"That's correct, sir," the fox replied.

The badger hummed to himself; the weasel and gray fox on either side of him were silent and unmoving. Sitting before the Directorate Board was enough to make anyone nervous, even Arkady, and seeing the way the board members carried themselves, the ferret spared a moment to wonder if they didn't spent time practicing their impassive stares and unflappable demeanors. Were those skills that they would look for in Arkady in the hope of granting him such a position of power in a few decades?

"And Agent Devra was not present," the badger stated for the record, looking over at Ming-Jun, who sat to Arkady's right. She didn't look nearly as imperturbable as Il-Hyeong did, and while she still kept a proud bearing, her larger ears betrayed more nervousness. The badger didn't regard her with suspicion, though, and he turned his attention back to Il-Hyeong without asking the rabbit any questions. "And so when Agent Ryswife fired, what did you do?"

Il-Hyeong's composure held. "I drew my backup weapon then, sir," he said. "But Agent Ryswife fired two shots into the contact's chest, and so I assumed that the threat was fully neutralized without my needing to take action."

"And where were you when Mr. Cibola opened fire on Agent McEvoy?"

"I was attempting to break into one of the elevators," Il-Hyeong replied. "Agent Ryswife called for the immediate evacuation of Shambhala, and I agreed that—"

"You didn't check Cibola's body to confirm that he was dead?" It was the gray fox who interrupted.

Il-Hyeong shook his head. "No, sir. Given the situation with Shambhala security, escape was our highest priority, and as I mentioned, I had assumed that being shot twice in the chest had killed him."

The gray fox said nothing, and the badger again took charge of the questions. "Agent Ryswife, you said in your initial report that Agent

Quinn attempted to extricate Agent McEvoy during the withdrawal from Shambhala." Arkady turned to look over at Il-Hyeong to find that the fox was looking back at him, as well. "Do you think that Agent Quinn's actions were in line with escape being the 'highest priority,' given that you had, at that point, called for immediate evacuation?"

Arkady's attention was fully back on the badger, now. Out of the corner of his eye, he thought he could see Il-Hyeong's tail flicking, but it might have just been his imagination. The ferret stiffened and lifted his chin. "Neither of us had been able to confirm the extent of Agent McEvoy's wounds, sir," he said. "It was entirely possible that he was still alive." The fox's tail went still.

The board members all exchanged glances, then nodded curtly, as if they had just had an entire telepathic conversation in the span of a few seconds. "We're still in the process of getting Agent McEvoy's remains back from the Tomosabaki government," the badger said. "We'll conduct our own autopsy and investigation to see if they corroborate the reports we've gotten, but in the meantime, we won't assign a judiciary panel to this matter until we see how the facts line up." The badger then eyed all three agents carefully. "I don't suspect, though, that we'll run into any problems along those lines."

For the first time since they'd entered the room, the weasel spoke up. "Agent Devra, you look as though you have a question."

Arkady turned to look at Ming-Jun, who was leaning forward against the table. "I do, sir," the rabbit said. "I wanted to know when our team can expect to return to Seizo."

The three board members exchanged a look of confusion. "I'm afraid I don't understand, Agent Devra," the weasel replied.

"To follow up on the group Cibola belonged to, sir," Ming-Jun said. "And to pursue leads regarding possible Octavian involvement. Since we did just get back, it should be a simple matter for our team to redeploy after some—"

"Agent Devra," the badger said, cutting in. "Do not presume to know what the activities of your team are slated to entail. Furthermore, any such activities are going to be on hold until the judiciary panel ascertains that Agents Ryswife and Quinn are absolved of any negligence in the death of Agent McEvoy."

The gray fox followed up, as if his remarks had somehow been prepared. "Agent McEvoy's death will already mean a major setback for Project Scheherazade's progress," he said, "especially concerning both Pandora and research into the Pyxis Sequence."

"It's just a formality, Agent Devra," the weasel added. "But the League does have rules, and not even Sahasrara can be held above them."

Arkady could see Ming-Jun deflate, her body seeming to shrink in her chair. She nodded her head, and murmured what sounded like "Yes, sir." The rabbit rarely looked dejected, as she did now, and Arkady was surprised to see that she wasn't more visibly angry. Perhaps, he thought, it was her uniform that was holding up her sense of propriety.

"Agent Ryswife," the badger said. "You have the case that you retrieved in Shambhala?"

"I do, sir." Arkady reached down beside his chair and lifted the case up onto the table with a heavy thud. All attention in the room shifted tangibly. Everyone held their breath, as well, so when the ferret undid the clasps that held the case shut, the sound it made bordered on ominous. Even though they were too far away to possibly see inside, the three board members leaned forward and stretched their necks out eagerly.

Arkady pulled out the three books in a single stack. "These are the books," he stated, setting them on the table. "We'll need to subject them to cryptanalysis and cross-reference other books in the library to see if we don't have any other samples of the script they're written in."

Next, Arkady pulled out the tape deck. "And this is the audio playback device. It's been tampered with; someone fitted it with a relatively more recent battery device, but it works just fine."

"And it came with some type of cassette, as well?" the gray fox asked.

"Yes. That's also here in the case," Arkady replied.

"Play us a sample, if you will, Agent Ryswife," the badger said. The ferret nodded, and withdrew the cassette from the case. He held it up briefly for the board members to take a look at it, and then he inserted it into the tape deck..

The strange tune was starting to become familiar to Arkady; he'd listened to it on the plane a couple of times while figuring out the tape deck's controls. It hadn't lost its effect on him, and even now, in the presence of his superiors, the hauntingly beautiful melody threatened to bring him close to tears. The board members were alert with deep interest, though theirs seemed more academic than emotional. Ming-Jun's head slowly swayed side to side with the music; Il-Hyeong quietly looked down at his own paws.

After having heard the song only a handful of times, Arkady hadn't yet been able to memorize the tonal gibberish that made up the "words," but he wanted badly to understand them. It was all just nonsense on the surface, sure, but the passion had to mean something. The singer *understood* what she was singing, even if she was the only person in the world who did. This woman, whoever she was, perhaps dead for over four millennia, had put a message into this piece of music. Did the books that accompanied the tape have any connection to it, or was the truth behind her song lost forever to the ages?

"All right, that's enough, Agent Ryswife," the badger said, jerking Arkady out of his reverie. The ferret turned the tape player off, the unfinished portion of the song dying out in his mind, since he didn't recall the notes well enough to trace it through to the end.

The three board members stood up. "Please turn the artifacts over to the library," the badger said. "You've done another splendid job, agents," he added, bowing to the three of them as the weasel and fox headed out.

"Thank you, sir," Il-Hyeong side, rising to his feet as well. The badger acknowledged him with another nod, and then left with his peers, leaving the agents alone. Arkady and Ming-Jun remained seated, the rabbit having begun to space out.

The fox sat atop the table, next to the open case. He fidgeted with parts of his uniform, like he wanted to loosen it or undo some of the fastenings, but he left everything on. His tail brushed back and forth, dangling off the other end of the table, hitting silently against the short stack of books. Arkady sat and just watched that tail swish to and fro before the silence finally drove him to say something.

"Come on," the ferret said. "Let's go and turn these things in." He stood up and began to pack the artifacts back into their case, aware that his tail was lashing now.

Ming-Jun fell into step behind him as he headed toward the library, but Il-Hyeong stayed seated atop the table. The rabbit was silent, the ferret barely even able to hear her breathing. It wasn't until she and Arkady were about to round the corner that the fox came trotting up from behind to catch up. "Arkady," he called out. "Wait up."

Arkady stopped, and now that he wasn't moving, he was more aware of just how hard his pulse was running. Il-Hyeong tilted his head as he looked him, but then shrugged it off. "Hey," he said, clapping the ferret on the shoulder. "Thanks. For saying what you said in there."

"I didn't say anything that wasn't true," Arkady replied, and as he went back to walking, he noticed that Ming-Jun hadn't stopped when Il-Hyeong had flagged him down. He thought about trying to catch up with her, but figured it wasn't worth the effort.

"You know what I mean," Il-Hyeong said, walking a little faster so that he could walk at Arkady's side. "You could have dodged a lot of heat for yourself, but you didn't. I really appreciate that."

Arkady thought back to what the board members had been trying to imply. "It's okay," he said. "They'll get Kentian's body, and they'll get Cibola's, and they'll see that our story checks out. We'll be off the hook in no time."

The ferret heard Il-Hyeong's jaw click shut, followed by a sigh of exasperation. Evidently, the fox wasn't going to push the issue. Arkady wanted to feel noble, and he wanted it more knowing that Il-Hyeong had understood why he'd done what he had, but he was too soured by the reality of the situation: the operation had been one colossal screw-up on Arkady's part. Up in that fifty-first floor office in Shambhala, he'd had every advantage on his side. He should have pressed harder, gotten the gun away from Cibola before the raccoon had decided to do something stupid. Everyone should have walked out of that room alive. That had been the plan, and Arkady had been the one to ruin it.

"What's up with Ming?" Il-Hyeong asked.

Arkady looked up again, seeing that the rabbit had further distanced herself from them, moving at a fast clip down the hallway. "She's pissed off," the ferret said, watching her disappear around another corner, down the hallway that lead to the staircase back up to the Château.

"Why? Because you and I are in trouble?"

"Because she knows that, even when we're back on duty, we're not getting sent back to Seizo," Arkady said.

Il-Hyeong stopped in his tracks, prompting Arkady to do the same. "What? You think they're not going to want to look into things?"

"They will," Arkady said, and he began to walk again. "They'll just send a different team."

"What makes you say that?" Il-Hyeong asked, catching up.

"For starters," Arkady explained, "by the time you and I get cleared by the judiciary panel, Cibola's men will have had too much time to bury things and get sorted." Out of the corner of his eye, he saw the fox's ears droop. "Besides, we're assigned to Project Scheherazade; they don't want to send us on some mission that essentially boils down to revenge."

Il-Hyeong scoffed. "Even though we're the most qualified people to handle it?"

"Even though," Arkady said. "To be honest, I'm with Ming-Jun: I'd love to go back there myself and get to the bottom of what happened, but we'll just have to trust that the League will do that for us. There are..." His voice trailed off, and his footsteps slowed.

"There are more important things right now?" Il-Hyeong asked, again resting a paw on the ferret's shoulder.

"Exactly," Arkady said, looking down at the case he was carrying. He looked back up at the fox and mustered half of a smile as he asked, "Do you want to come with me to the library while I drop these off?"

Il-Hyeong smiled back at him, though his was as halfhearted as the ferret's own. "Yeah, sure. May as well finish the job I started, right?

Unlike the library in the Château basement upstairs, Project Scheherazade's library did not leave things out on bookshelves for people to peruse. Not even the members of Sahasrara were allowed to access the artifacts freely. If anyone wanted to see something that Project Scheherazade had in its possession, then they needed to stop by the library's front desk and ask for it specifically.

Working the desk now was Darren Spindletree, apparently having been relieved of upstairs guard duty. The raccoon had been working on Project Scheherazade for nearly as long as Arkady and Il-Hyeong had, before even Ming-Jun had joined their ranks. He wasn't a field agent, though; rather, his job was to help track and catalog the items of interest that teams like Arkady's brought in. Of course, he shared that job with several other people, and Arkady couldn't think that any of them had complete knowledge of the entire archive. Even if they did have some of the contents' catalog information memorized, that still didn't make them privy to the scientists' findings or the historians' analyses.

The librarian's multi-toned fur stood in contrast to the long, sterile-white hallway that led away behind the desk. The walls were lined with compartments, some large and some small, built into the walls themselves, stacked from floor to ceiling. Each compartment housed artifacts, sets of books, or other assorted objects of interest from pre-civ times. Smaller side corridors branched off of the main corridor, but the outlines of the compartments themselves created an optical illusion that made that central hallway seem to go on forever.

"Ah, Arkady," Darren said with a toothy smile, an interest that wasn't just scholarly twinkling in his eye when he spied the case. "They said that you'd gotten some new goodies in Seizo. What do you have for me?"

Arkady dropped the heavy case up onto the catalog desk. "Books," the ferret said. "And some kind of tape player, complete with a cassette. Pre-civ music, it sounds like."

Darren's eyes widened further still. "Ooh! Sounds like the boys'll have some fun with that," he said, unlatching the case. Arkady always did find Darren's voracious interest in such artifacts a marked (and, frankly, disturbing) contrast to the quiet and meek mannerisms he always exhibited while topside. The raccoon clutched the topmost book in his paws and lifted it up and down to test its weight.

"Actually, I was wondering if you know if we had any other books on file that included those same symbols," Arkady asked, pointing to the book's cover. "All three books are full of them."

The raccoon flipped the book open and skimmed through some of the pages. The look of queer excitement in his eyes shifted over to something much more analytical, and he hummed as he stared at the writing. "I want to say I've seen something like this before," he said. "I'll need to look into it, but that's standard practice anyway. Did you want me to call you up if I find something?"

"Please," the ferret said. "I mean, you don't need to rush, but... well, let's just say that I've got a lot invested in the contents of this case."

Darren tilted his head, clearly trying to discern what Arkady meant by that, but he let it go. "No problem," the raccoon said, removing the other books from the case. "Anything from you, Il-Hyeong?" he then asked, turning to the fox.

"Nothing but this," Il-Hyeong said, nodding. "I'll have Arkady keep me in the loop."

"All right, then, agents," Darren said, extracting the tape deck next. "I'm not sure when we'll have a full analysis on these, but... well, you know how that works."

Arkady nodded. "If you can let me know if you've found any other writing samples even before then, though, I still want to know. I'd consider it a big favor."

"Sure thing," the raccoon said. "I'll check with the other guys to see if they don't recall anything off the top of their heads, too." He then placed the artifacts into a plastic tub and carted them off with him down the main hallway and into the archives. They'd end up stored in a temporary sorting drawer while they awaited final analysis and cataloging, after which point they might never again see the light of day if nobody saw reason to dredge them out again—but Arkady was already determined to not let that matter rest.

The artifacts were safe now. If the Octavians really had been pursuing them, then they were out of reach. The League had what it wanted. The League had won again.

Back outside the library, Il-Hyeong stopped Arkady by taking hold of one of his wrists. "Hey. Where are you going after this?"

"I was probably going to just go to bed," Arkady said. "I want to get out of this uniform and get back to a normal sleep schedule if we're going to be here for at least a few more days."

"I want to talk to you," Il-Hyeong said. "Do you have time?"

"Talk about what?"

Il-Hyeong shook his head. "Not here," he said. "Come with me to my room."

"To talk about what?" Arkady asked again, but the fox was already walking off with a purposeful stride.

Il-Hyeong's room wasn't as bare as Arkady's, but the fox didn't exactly keep lavish quarters, either. His walls were covered with abstract art—paintings, crests, and wall-hangings of both religious and of purely artistic nature. He had bookshelves that were packed to the gills, not with ancient tomes of interest, but with more modern books, both academic and fictional. Close friends as they were, Arkady didn't often stop by Il-Hyeong's room, and though he couldn't recall with complete clarity, it looked to him that the fox had redecorated recently.

The ferret pulled up one of Il-Hyeong's chairs and took a seat. "So, what's the deal?" he asked. He'd dropped by his own room and had gotten out of his uniform, but with official business for the evening having all been taken care of, physical and mental exhaustion were much more noticeable.

"I want to ask you something," the fox said, heading over to one of his cabinets. "About Ming."

"What about her?" Arkady asked. He hadn't seen the rabbit since she'd left the debriefing, though he expected she'd either retreated back to her own room, or perhaps to the chapel again for further prayer or guidance.

Il-Hyeong got out a bottle of brandy and poured two glasses. He handed one to the ferret, first, before sitting down and taking a sip of his own. "I know it's still really soon," the fox said, not making eye contact, "but we're going to need to broach the subject sooner than later."

"Broach what subject?" Arkady asked. He swirled his brandy glass around in one paw, but didn't drink from it yet.

"About the augmentation," Il-Hyeong said, looking up now.

The ferret sighed, and did take a long sip of brandy before replying. "What about it?" he asked. "It's got nothing to do with her."

"Doesn't it, though?" Il-Hyeong said. "Now that Kentian is gone, they're probably going to want someone else to take his place."

Arkady could see that Il-Hyeong was serious, but also that he was nervous (and he'd also hesitated slightly before deliberately choosing the word 'gone'). It was a touchy subject, after all, but the fox was right: it *did* need to be broached sooner rather than later. "I don't know that they can just slot someone else in like that," the ferret said.

"You saw Dr. Mayflower today, didn't you?" the fox asked, nodding to Arkady's paw, no sign of any broken finger in the way the ferret held his glass steadily. "Didn't you talk about the augmentation at all?"

"Only in passing," Arkady said. "We didn't go into any details."

Il-Hyeong nodded silently, and took a few more sips from his glass. "You're closer to Ming than I am, though," he said. "Do you think she'd want to take Kentian's place?"

"She hasn't said anything about it," Arkady replied. "I'm not sure what she thinks of it, to be honest."

"Well, after everything that happened today, with the board and all," the fox said, setting his glass down. "Don't you think she might be considering it?"

Swallowing another heavy mouthful of the alcohol, Arkady slouched back in the chair, his tail curling around one of the rear legs. "It's only been a few hours, Il-Hyeong," he said. "Sure, she's probably really pissed off right now, but I don't think that's enough for her to make any rash decisions." He thought again about the attitude the board members had taken with the rabbit. "A decision, I might add, that probably isn't hers to make in the first place."

"Maybe not, but she could at least say that she wants to be considered," the fox replied. "I can't imagine they'd turn her down."

"Like I said, I don't know if it works like that," Arkady said. "They've been prepping things specifically for Kentian for months, now, after all. They might not be able to just put Ming-Jun in in his place."

The fox sighed and nodded. "Probably not," he said. "Still, do you think she could talk to Dr. Mayflower about it? Even if it takes them another few months to get her ready, it'd still be worth it."

"If she wants to do it," Arkady pointed out.

"Of course," Il-Hyeong said, picking up his glass of brandy again. He paused, staring at the glass without sipping from it, and then said, "I think it would be good, though, if all three of us were in it together."

Arkady smiled. "Yeah, I think so, too," the ferret said. "But it's not exactly the simplest choice to make, after all. You know that."

The fox smiled. "Yeah, I know," he said. "Would you talk to her about it, though? Just to see what she thinks, I mean."

"Yeah, I can do that," Arkady said, finishing the rest of his brandy. He then stood up and flicked his tail out. "Hope you don't mind if I get going now, though?"

Il-Hyeong shook his head. "Of course not." Arkady bowed, then, and walked back out into the hallway.

"Oh, hey," Il-Hyeong called after him. Arkady turned around and saw the fox poking his head out from his door. "Thanks again," the fox said. "For everything, you know?"

Arkady nodded, and smiled again. "No problem," he said. "I'll see you tomorrow, okay?"

"Tomorrow," Il-Hyeong said, nodding. "Say another prayer for Kentian, yeah?"

"Of course," Arkady replied, making it a new point to do just that before going to sleep.

4. Pandora

The sun had long since set, but it still felt early. Though Arkady wanted to catch up on sleep in order to get back on track with local time, sleep would not come. He could go back to his room, he thought, but then he'd just end up lying in bed, exhausted yet awake, lost in thought, like he'd been that afternoon.

What could he do that didn't involve having to deal with other people? The matter of secrecy caused guilt to lay too heavily on his chest to speak with Father Benjamin. He could turn back around go back to Il-Hyeong, but right now, the fox was distant, acting like a mere comrade and not like the ferret's best friend. Conversely, Arkady felt like he was too worried for Ming-Jun as her friend, all while wishing he could act more like a supportive comrade-in-arms.

He could stop by and see Pandora, too, he considered. She wouldn't make for much company, but the quiet would do Arkady some good.

But no. If he went to the Hephaestus Chamber, he'd have to deal with Dr. Mayflower or any number of her staff. Plus, that would also mean going back down into headquarters, and he didn't want to go back there for a third time today, especially not in his current state of mind.

A stop by the library might be nice (the public one, not the secret one), but he didn't know if he felt like reading. More accurately, he didn't think that he'd be able to concentrate on reading if he just sat in silence and tried to stare at words. What he *wanted* to read were those books he'd turned over to Darren Spindletree. If he could just make sense of those symbols and crack that maddening code, *then* he'd be willing to put all of his attention on reading what the words said.

Frustration. That's what Arkady could work on. After all, if Ming-Jun was so frustrated that she'd let it ruin her composure, then Arkady couldn't fault himself for needing to work a bit of edge off. Some quick exercise might set his mind right and also help to tire him out.

His first thought was to head on down to the shooting range, but he killed that idea immediately, since that, too, would mean going back into headquarters. Whatever he did, he wanted to just be Arkady Ryswife, the ferret, not Arkady Ryswife, the agent.

The trick was to find something that he could do that didn't tax his brain, but which also wasn't mindless, like running or hitting the weight room. That sort of thing would let his mind wander, and he needed to keep from doing that. As he gazed out onto the dimly-lit courtyard outside the open corridor windows, the perfect idea hit him.

Being an ancient structure, Château Sainte-Mireille had lots of outmoded rooms. Most of those rooms had been repurposed for other things, such as housing the type of equipment that a modern facility would need in order to support the many people who inhabited it. One of the throwbacks to old times that the Iolite League had held on to was the armory—and the practice chamber connected to it. The arms and armor were of historical interest, and so the League had of course held on to those, but only the most spectacular and beautiful items were left out as display pieces; the rest were locked securely in one of the Château's many vaults, freeing up space for the armory to serve functionally.

It had been a long time since Arkady had made a point of keeping up with his sword forms. It was something he used to do frequently, as a means of honing his body and his mind—just a preferred form of exercise, not as a part of any regimented martial training for Sahasrara. Perhaps a quick run-through of some simple practices would be the right note to end his evening on. After all, even after dark, the gymnasiums would be in use, whereas the practice chamber was sure to be empty. Not many people practiced the sword, not that Arkady had ever seen, and so the solitude would be ideal, and going through the motions themselves would allow him to slip into a trance of concentration and muscle memory.

As he approached the practice room Arkady heard the sounds of light physical exertion echoing down the hallway. Closer still, he could hear the sounds of footwork along the room's padded mat, along with the occasional swish of a blade cleaving through the air.

There was humming, too—to the tune of the song from the tape.

The ferret turned the corner and saw that it was Ming-Jun. He hadn't even known that the rabbit practiced the sword, but then, for as much as she was his friend, she did value her privacy. Still, how had it never come up, even in passing? Had it really been *that* long since the ferret had come down here to practice his swordplay instead of heading to the shooting range, with Il-Hyeong or by himself, to practice his aim with pistols and rifles?

You could have gone for a head shot. He was sitting right across the table from you.

He shook his head. He'd come here to get away from thoughts like that.

Ming-Jun hadn't yet noticed Arkady watching from the doorway. She was using what looked like a Kyunjiu broadsword, a blade about an arm's length long with just a slight curve. Judging from the way she moved in short hops and arcing leaps, Arkady guessed that she was using a style that worked to her natural strengths as a rabbit, but it wasn't one that he recognized off the top of his head. From what he could tell, her form was good, certainly not sloppy, even if she didn't quite have the gracefulness of a master, either.

When she reached the end of her form, she stood still and caught her breath, and then one of her ears twitched before she spun around and saw the ferret standing in the doorway. "Arkady," she said, still somewhat short of breath. "I didn't know you were into swordfighting."

"Likewise." Arkady stepped into the room. "You've been doing it long?"

The rabbit nodded. "Since before I joined the League."

"I'm out of practice, myself. I thought I might try to correct that."

It occurred to Arkady that the rabbit might be trying to tone up and get into better shape with a specific goal in mind; namely, that she was interested in the prospect of augmentation after all. He thought again about Il-Hyeong urging him to ask her what her thoughts were on the subject, but without clear information from Dr. Mayflower, was there anything Arkady could even do, other than offend the rabbit by asking or (possibly worse) get her hopes up for nothing?

Ming-Jun ran a paw up through the fur between her ears, brushing her short forelocks out of her eyes. "You up for a little match?" she asked with a fresh grin.

"Oh, God, you'd probably cream me," the ferret said. He was admittedly more excited by the prospect of having an opponent than he was about practicing by himself, though.

Again, the rabbit smiled. "Ah, don't worry, I won't be too rough on you," she said, placing the steely blade back on the rack before heading over to the practice swords. "Mostly I'm interested in seeing what you've got," she added with a wink.

Arkady chuckled at that. "I suppose I can go a round or two."

"What do you use?" Ming-Jun asked.

"I'm mostly saber, myself. Though really, it's been so long since I've picked up anything that the Kyunjiu broadsword is probably just as good, at this point."

Ming-Jun pulled out a pair of practice blades. They were translucent, made of a sturdy, lightweight, shatter-resistant alloy, with a metallic trim that had no sharpness. "Quanyao broadsword, actually," the rabbit said, tossing one of the swords to Arkady. "If you look through some of those dusty old books down in the basement, you'll see that that's what it was originally called."

"Martial history buff, too, huh?" Arkady said, laughing as he moved his wrist around, getting used to the sword's balance and heft and how it felt in his paw. If he was out of practice with the saber, it had been years since he'd even held a broadsword, but he'd be able to manage at least a token match for Ming-Jun's benefit.

Squaring off at her end of the sparring mat, the rabbit looked Arkady in the eye. "Hey, you're full of surprises yourself," she said. Then, she brought her weapon to bear. "Ready?" she asked.

"Ready."

Ming-Jun needed no further word. She sprung forward, using her strong legs to jump halfway across the mat without even getting a running start. Alarmed at her having cleared that distance so fast, Arkady barely managed to dodge away to one side, using his own natural mustelid flexibility to his advantage to twist and contort and then reorient himself. If this was Ming-Jun's idea of going easy on him, he shuddered to think of what she was like when she was playing for keeps.

"So, Arkady, let me ask you something," the rabbit huffed as she delivered a swing that Arkady parried cleanly and then redirected. "If you're okay to talk now, that is," she added, countering with a follow-up backhand swing.

Arkady ducked down and went into a roll, swinging his sword up at the rabbit as he popped up onto his knees. She deflected the blow and hopped back; Arkady had bought himself the time to get back to his feet, but she'd also earned the time to reassert herself for another attack. "Ask away," the ferret grunted as he caught her next swing full-on.

Grinning at him from behind the pair of transparent blades, Ming-Jun bore her weight into her sword, forcing them to lock. "So, Cibola and his cronies had three pre-civ books and a tape recorder," she said. "And after we found out about them, Cibola's group goes running to the Octavians."

"The very reason for putting the mission together in the first place," Arkady replied, throwing Ming-Jun's weight off of him, immediately following up with another swing that went so wide that the rabbit didn't even need to try to parry it.

Ming-Jun took advantage of that opening, too, coming in with a fierce strike of her own that made Arkady fall onto his back as he tried to avoid it. Lying vulnerable and exposed on the mat, the ferret had to block the rabbit's next swing without getting back up. "So," Ming-Jun then said, "we found out about the artifacts first, and approached someone on Cibola's team about them."

"That'd be my guess." Arkady hadn't been told which team on Sahasrara had initially made contact with Cibola's colleagues, and as was likely Ming-Jun's point, he had to wonder why his own team had been in a position where they'd greatly underestimated the situation they'd run into. "You think that we weren't told everything?"

"We're never told everything," Ming-Jun said, stepping back to allow Arkady to get back onto his feet. They squared off again, and Arkady could see that she was getting tired. "But that's not my point. I'm wondering where these folks found those artifacts in the first place."

Arkady tilted his head. "They stole them?" he suggested, leaping forward to make the first strike at Ming-Jun this time around. "They acquired them through some other illicit means? Does it matter?" He was beginning to get a feel for the rabbit's form, and he was pretty sure that, were he up on his practice, he'd be better than her. *Especially once you've gone through with the augmentation.*

Unless, of course, she gets it, too.

"We approached them." Ming-Jun punctuated her remark with a hard swing. "And it was only after we asked for the artifacts that they suddenly panicked and tried to sell them. What does that say to you?"

The ferret felt his ankle twist roughly as he turned aside to dodge Ming-Jun's next blow, feeling the practice blade come within inches of his shoulder. Wincing as he tried to regain proper footing, he turned Ming-Jun's question over in his mind. "That they didn't know the true value of the artifacts before then."

"Precisely," Ming-Jun replied. Her large feet shifted on the mat. Arkady had been paying careful attention to the rabbit's footwork, and he knew where she'd pounce next. As he was bringing his sword up to parry, though, he could see that he'd already fallen for her feint, and he had no time to correct his mistake before Ming-Jun's blunt blade cracked him on the arm.

"Ow. Nice one," Arkady said, rubbing the sore spot with his fingertips. He smiled, and then moved to square off again, but Ming-Jun stayed where she was, her own sword dangling at her side. "You're pretty good," the ferret told her.

"I practice a lot," she said. "If I'd known you were into this, I would've asked you a long time ago to join me."

Arkady brought his sword back to the rack and set it back in place. He saw the sabers resting there as well, and considered challenging Ming-Jun to a match with his own favored weapon, but decided to leave that until next time. "So, Cibola's people didn't know how valuable the artifacts were until after we asked for them," he said, thinking out loud. "What do you think that means?"

"What do *you* think that means?"

With his own question thrown right back at him, Arkady frowned, but thought harder on the subject all the same. "Well, it could mean that they'd had them for a long time and didn't ascribe any particular significance to them," he said. "Or maybe they'd gotten them from someone else who hadn't seen the true value in them, either."

"Both things I've considered," Ming-Jun said. "And in either case, you're left with people who at one point owned those books and tape recorder, but who never stopped to think of their relative value."

"It is all just paper and plastic," Arkady pointed out. "I can see where the uninitiated would take stuff like that for granted."

The rabbit's face broke out into a smile. "Right," she said. "You take something for granted when it's commonplace—when it isn't special."

"But these things *are* special."

"To us, yes," Ming-Jun said. "But what if they weren't special to the people who had them first?"

Arkady again saw Cibola's face in his mind, and remembered the scent of nervousness he'd had on him. He couldn't imagine the raccoon thought of the contents of his case as everyday articles. "Well, then I'd want to know who had them before."

Ming-Jun flashed a playful smirk of triumph as Arkady reached the end of that line of thought. "You, too, huh?"

A good night's sleep with the benefit of a few extra hours had Arkady feeling much better in the morning. Even before he'd dragged his tail out of bed, his mind was feeling clearer, and knowing that he and his team weren't going to be sent out on assignment allowed him added peace of mind. Considering that the Iolite League was all about spiritual harmony between peoples, it was nice to be able to attain a more personal sense of balance with the universe every once and while, too, the ferret thought.

Even after having gotten more sleep than was typical for him, Arkady was still awake early, so he let himself take a long bath instead of a simple shower. One of the benefits of being an agent for Sahasrara was getting a personal bathroom that he didn't need to share with other, transient League members who came to stay at Château Sainte-Mireille for shorter periods. As the ferret soaked in the bathtub, he tried to achieve a minor state of meditation, inwardly telling himself that the bath was cleansing on a symbolic level in addition to a physical one. He wasn't sure how well that little mind trick worked, but he at least managed to space out, which kept him from stressing out.

Once he was clean and dry, Arkady tried to decide whether he wanted to attend late morning services. It was a weekday, and most of the folks who were devout enough to regularly attend weekday services were the sort who'd have gone to the early service at sunrise; the late morning service would be relatively empty, but the ferret wasn't sure that hearing a sermon was what his troubled mind needed. Il-Hyeong would probably chastise him for having such thoughts, and hearing some of the fox's calm objections in his head made him grin. After all, a day of rest like today should be treated like a gift—an opportunity to appreciate nature, friends, family, one's place in the world, and...

Family. Arkady smiled and went to his closet, choosing casual wear instead of the nicer clothes he'd wear to the chapel. If there were a way for him to remind himself of what was important, to remind himself of why he did what he did, then perhaps he'd just stumbled upon in it in that quiet moment of contemplation: when it came down to it, he, Il-Hyeong, Ming-Jun, and all the other members of Sahasrara made up a family. A family that was held together by the oaths they'd sworn to do their secret works.

While he was in the process of pulling his shirt up over his head, the ferret heard his personal comm device chime. Sticking one of his arms out through the sleeve of that shirt, he picked his comm and brought it to his ear just as it, too, poked free of the shirt. "Ryswife," he said.

"Arkady, it's Il-Hyeong. I hope I didn't wake you?"

"Not at all." It was telling that Il-Hyeong was getting in touch with him over the personal comm rather than by phone. "What's going on?"

"I'm downstairs," the fox said. He didn't need to clarify what 'downstairs' actually meant, in this context. "Dr. Mayflower was wondering if you could stop by."

"With regards to what?"

"Something about Pandora," Il-Hyeong said, with just a touch of nervousness in his voice.

Arkady didn't miss that tone, either. "Is something wrong? Did she say?" He was needing to stifle his own instinctual anxiety already.

There was a brief pause on Il-Hyeong's end. "She didn't, no," the fox said. "Though I suspect that if it were that urgent, she'd have gotten in touch with you directly." There was another pause, and then he said, "Still, you might want to get here as soon as you can, just in case."

"I'll be right down," Arkady replied, and then he clicked his comm off. As his nervousness started to grow, the ferret tried to take Il-Hyeong's words to heart. Surely, the fox had a rational point: if this were an emergency, Arkady would have been notified directly. It was strange that Mayflower would ask (or need) Il-Hyeong to inform him at all, really, but if there was even a minor break in protocol, maybe that *did* mean that this was just something more run-of-the-mill, less serious.

Once he was dressed for the warm, sunny weather outside, Arkady took a shortcut through the grassy courtyard on his way to the Sahasrara headquarters. While he didn't stop, he did walk more slowly as he circled the six-species statue, taking time to look at each individual figure, nodding toward it resolutely as he thought about how the Iolite League was, slowly but surely, making a difference in the world. He personally might sometimes be called upon to kill people in the name of the greater good, but there *was* a greater good—the better world—waiting on the other side. The road wasn't an easy one, nor was it supposed to be.

As he passed by the chapel, he spotted Father Benjamin pacing about within. Even from a distance, the tawny-furred weasel exuded that demeanor of a clergyman, that kindly aura of experience and wisdom that suited him well. While Arkady might not have been up for a sermon, he did consider entering the chapel to have some brief words with Father Benjamin, but surely, the weasel was busy planning for the late morning service. Besides, after yesterday's conversation about Kentian and Ming-Jun, the ferret doubted that he could get away with a simple chat. He made a point to stop by after his morning errands, and then moved on.

It was Darren Spindletree who was again watching the staircase that led downstairs to the hidden headquarters. Arkady could see from the twinkle in the raccoon's eye that he'd had quite an enjoyable night poring over the artifacts brought in the day before. Still, the upper library was no place to discuss such top secret matters. The ferret simply nodded, then proceeded to make his way downstairs. He then passed through the door with the thousand-petaled lotus, and then walked straight to the Hephaestus Chamber.

The Hephaestus Chamber was sealed off by another door that was almost identical to the one that led to Sahasrara headquarters itself. Not everyone in Sahasrara had access to the chamber, though: only agents assigned to Project Scheherazade, agents on the medical staff, and, of course, the higher-ups had that privilege. After scanning Arkady's retina and confirming his identity, the door's security system did not prompt him for a code phrase like the main door did. With a faint hiss of hydraulics, the door unlocked and slid open, and then Arkady stepped inside.

A short hallway led to the chamber proper, with a slight downward incline before it opened up into a much larger room. The Hephaestus Chamber itself was shaped like a sphere that had had its top and bottom cut off, roughly twenty-five feet in diameter, with walls that were covered with diagnostics equipment, dozens of separate readout displays, and half a dozen consoles and control panels that were far outside the realm of Arkady's own expertise. There also appeared to be several new systems in place, which prompted the ferret to try to remember when, exactly, he'd come down here last.

It was the centerpiece of the chamber, though, that was the undeniable focus of attention. At the heart of the room was a great, wide cylindrical tube filled with a translucent, pale green fluid, through which tiny bubbles rose slowly. Floating halfway up the tube was a preadolescent ferret girl. An apparatus not unlike a fighter pilot's mask was affixed to her muzzle, covering her nose and mouth completely. Connected to that mask were tubes that led upward and disappeared into the ceiling; a similar fixture was also in place between her legs, with tubes that ran downward. Despite that, her body still bobbed up and down slowly with unfettered buoyancy, and with her eyes closed, her expression looked paradoxically serene.

"Hello, Pandora," Arkady said under his breath as he gazed at her.

"Good morning, Arkady. You look as though you've slept well."

Arkady turned around to see Il-Hyeong standing by the wall, off to one side of the entrance. The fox's arms were folded across his front, his shoulders resting against the wall in between two large diagnostics consoles. Like Arkady, he also seemed to have gone with a more casual look today, sporting an amethyst-purple silk shirt and a loose pair of dark tan pants that cut off midway down the shin. It was unusual for Il-Hyeong to dress down when he was in headquarters, even when just dropping by.

"You're looking better, yourself," Arkady said. "How are you feeling?"

The fox pushed off of the wall and stretched his arms out while wringing his wrists in turn. "Praying helps, so long as I don't dwell on things too long once I'm done," he said with a sad smile. "To be honest,

I'm more impatient about them recovering Kentian's... about recovering Kentian than I am about hearing back about the judiciary panel."

This team is a family, Arkady reminded himself. "We'll have plenty of time to ourselves over the next couple weeks," he told the fox. "Maybe after the funeral, you and I could take the ferry over to Stewart and take a few days to just unwind?"

It took a second, but Il-Hyeong eventually smiled. "I think I might like that," he said. "Getting away from the Château might be just what we need." He paused, then asked, "Would you want to invite Ming?"

Arkady thought again about his uncertainty regarding Ming-Jun's current state of mind: she was grieving over Kentian, as they all were, but she also seemed to be harboring a lot of rage, whether it was directed at the League or the Directorate Board or maybe just the world itself. "If she wants to come," was all he said, though.

Another low-pitched beep sounded from one of the room's many consoles, prompting Arkady to recall where he and Il-Hyeong were, and he was hit by how strange it was to be having a private conversation in such a highly-sensitive area. "Where's Dr. Mayflower?" the ferret asked.

Il-Hyeong shrugged. "I'm not sure," he said. "I'm guessing she's doing whatever it is that made her too busy to ask you to come here herself."

The ferret sighed. "Well, if she knew I was coming, hopefully she won't be long," he said. The fact that *none* of Sahasrara's medical staff were here was definitely out of the ordinary. "So, wait," Arkady then said to Il-Hyeong. "Why are *you* here?"

"Me?" the fox asked. "I don't know, I guess I was just waiting for you." He turned and looked back at the ferret girl floating silently in the tube. "That, and watching her was kind of... soothing, in a way."

Arkady turned and stood shoulder-to-shoulder with the swift fox. The slow, undulating floating and bobbing did have an oddly hypnotic quality to it, much like watching waves lapping at the shore, but when Arkady tried to let himself get taken away by it, the reality of who and what he was looking at broke the spell before it took hold. "If you say so," he said. Perhaps Il-Hyeong's scientific, pattern-oriented mind was more sensitive and susceptible to the sight.

The fox took a step closer to the tube. "She got me thinking," he said. "About what it is we do."

Just as Arkady was about to ask Il-Hyeong what he meant by that, the chamber door opened up behind him. The ferret turned around to see

Jillian Mayflower striding down that short hallway, her lab coat billowing behind her as the portal behind her sealed shut with a pneumatic hiss. Her footsteps bore the heavy tread of impatience.

"Il-Hyeong," she said. "And Arkady. Did they leave the two of you in here by yourselves?"

"It's just the two of us, yes," Arkady replied. "But who is it that would have left us here?"

The kangaroo just shook her head and sighed. "Whole damn department's acting like it's been turned upside-down," she muttered. "Anyway, doesn't matter. I'm here, now."

Exchanging a brief look with the fox, Arkady looked back at Mayflower. "Il-Hyeong said that you needed me for something."

For a second, it looked as though she hadn't even heard him, but the kangaroo then shook her head again and grumbled in exasperation. "Right, yes. Sorry," she said. "The staff's all doing three dozen other things right now, it feels like."

"Is anything the matter?" Il-Hyeong asked.

Mayflower kept talking as she went over to one of the consoles. "Only as much as there ever is," she said. "It's nothing for you two to worry about right now, though."

Arkady stepped closer to her. "So, what *did* you ask me down here for?" he asked, trying to keep his patience reined in, seeing that the doctor had clearly already exhausted most of hers.

"Right," the kangaroo said again, smacking her palm against the side of input station. "I need to take a tissue sample from you, Arkady."

"A tissue sample?" the ferret asked. "What for?"

Dr. Mayflower strode over to one of the medical trays that was set up against one wall. "I just need to run a few simple tests on some of Pandora's cells," she said as she rummaged through the assorted implements at her disposal. "And I need yours to run them against. Just a simple cheek swab is all."

Il-Hyeong shot Arkady another look of confusion, and the ferret just shrugged. "That's all?" Arkady asked. "Doesn't sound like such a big deal to me."

"No, it's not," the kangaroo said, having procured a long, simple probe from her tray. "I just figured it'd be quicker to have Il-Hyeong to tell you to come down here because... well, because channels are a bit slow right now, let's just say."

"You're sure there's not some kind of emergency we need to be worrying about?" Il-Hyeong asked.

At that, Dr. Mayflower snorted. "If there were an emergency right now, I wouldn't be in here with the two of you." She then walked up to Arkady, held up the probe, and said, "You. Muzzle open."

The ferret resisted the urge to roll his eyes, and complied, opening his jaw nice and wide. He nearly coughed a few times as the doctor scraped the probe at the inside of his cheek a few times, but before he came anywhere close to actually gagging, the device withdrew, and the kangaroo placed the implement into a transparent pouch which she then sealed.

"There," Mayflower said as she placed that sealed pouch into small metal storage case. "Now that that's out of the way, since neither of you two seem to have anything better to do right now, did you at least want an update?"

Arkady was willing to look past Dr. Mayflower's unusually brusque behavior in light of any news on Pandora's condition and development. "Do you have one?" he asked.

Mayflower looked up at the ferret floating in the tube. "Right now, she's stable," the kangaroo said. "There are no signs that her growth is continuing, which means that our attempts to freeze her development are still working. I'm not sure that we'll be able to keep that up forever without some degeneration creeping into the equation—that's part of why I wanted that tissue sample for—but for the time being, we're not really worried."

"They'll find more leads on the Pyxis Sequence soon," Arkady said to the doctor as he, too, looked back into the tube. "We have to be close to finding it."

The kangaroo turned away and went back to one of the console stations along the curved outer wall of the chamber. "Or, given another twenty years or so, we can finish reverse engineering it ourselves," she said with a rueful chuckle.

"The Iolite Doctrine teaches patience, does it not?" Il-Hyeong said with a smirk. Dr. Mayflower didn't respond or turn back around, but the ferret was pretty sure that the fox had gotten a smile out of her.

Arkady left the doctor to her work and took another step forward, placing a paw on the glass of the tube. Il-Hyeong stood at his side, saying nothing, touching him softly on the shoulder.

Pandora was the pride and joy of the Iolite League's scientific developments: the world's first synthetic sentient life form. Her brain was effectively an organic supercomputer, capable of both storing and processing vast amounts of data. The hope was that, when she was 'complete,' she would then act as the heart and soul of Project Scheherazade itself, a living and thinking mind to ponder the great mysteries that were programmed into her head. Where raw analytical prowess failed, the potential of imagination and instinct-driven thought might be able to make sense of the scattered bits of information that agents dredged up from the world's past.

She was named after a character that appeared in an ancient story, recorded in both pre-civ texts as well as a few sources from the very beginning of officially-documented history. The story told of the creation of the first woman, created artificially from the earth, imbued with innumerable gifts and talents, entrusted with possession of a mystical box containing hope itself.

It wasn't said specifically what species Pandora was supposed to have been. Even in the most complete literary fragments that Project Scheherazade had collected, it was never stated, and so she very well might not have been a ferret at all; most likely, whoever told or retold the story just imagined her as their own species. Still, the poetic allusion was still fitting enough that it hardly mattered, in that sense, whether she was a ferret or not.

The only reason she was a ferret in *this* case was because her genetic structure was based on Arkady's. Part of it was, at least. Enough of her genetic data was unique that she was closer to being his 'daughter' than a true clone. Her fundamental design involved a (comparatively) simple 'blank' template that needed a gene sample from another individual to fill in the rest of the details, as it were. Arkady had been chosen as the donor for the material mainly due to his key involvement with Project Scheherazade. Other agents had also been considered, with Arkady having ultimately been selected due to his having the 'cleanest' genetic code in terms of potential hereditary disorders and the like.

Arkady looked again at the girl's face, and then at her closed eyes. He realized that he didn't even know what color they were. "Do you think she has dreams?" he asked Il-Hyeong.

The fox turned to look at Arkady. "Dreams?" he asked. "What about?"

Pandora's body had started out as an embryo, and had been raised from there. She had then been put through an accelerated 'childhood,' with her development having been halted at several steps along the way in order to surgically implant the artificial components that were just as much a part of her overall design as what had been generated by her genetic template.

Despite being a marvel of biological science, Pandora was still confined to her tube, unable to wake up. Without a key piece of genetic material—dubbed the 'Pyxis Sequence' by the Iolite League's scientists—full integration between Pandora's artificial and natural parts was not possible. The Pyxis Sequence coded for the neurotransmitters that allowed Pandora's brain to interface with the supercomputer components that had been hardwired into her central nervous system. Without those key chemicals, her mind would not function; she was effectively in a coma until such a time as her brain could be safely 'activated,' allowing her to finally see the light of day.

"About anything. It's just something I wonder, sometimes."

Il-Hyeong turned to face the tank again. "Dr. Mayflower monitors all of her brain activity," he said. "Though I thought she said that her mind wasn't capable of processing that sort of thing."

Arkady again rubbed his paw at the glass, gazing longingly at the young girl trapped behind it. She could be part of the better world—she could be key in making sure that the better world existed in the first place. He wanted that for her, and his hope for her, he knew, would translate into the hope that she would represent for other people, even if only a handful of people would ever be aware that she even existed.

"She's still alive, though," Arkady pointed out. "She's still a person. Aren't dreams more than just random bits of brain activity, anyway?"

Il-Hyeong flicked his tail as he hummed in thought, sounding unsure of himself. Then, his ears pricked up. "You know, I bet you that she'll tell you if you ask her, once she wakes up."

A new smile took over Arkady's face. "I bet you're right," he said. "Unless she's just too embarrassed to tell me."

"If she won't tell you, maybe she'll tell her Uncle Il-Hyeong," the fox said. Even without turning to look at him, Arkady could see his bright expression reflected in the glass.

"Oh, so now you're her uncle?" Arkady returned the playful jab to Il-Hyeong's own shoulder. "And just who said you could do that?"

Il-Hyeong lifted up his snout, preening. "I did," he said, swishing out his tail. "She's going to need a male role model besides her father, after all."

"And just how am I supposed to explain to her why her dear Uncle Il-Hyeong is a fox?"

"Oh, I'm sure that will be simple," Il-Hyeong replied unwaveringly. "The hard part of the discussion will be explaining why her mother is a kangaroo."

Even as he laughed and reveled in his feeling so silly about the whole deal, Arkady did have to take a moment to remind himself that just because he'd supplied his genetic material didn't mean that he got to be the girl's father. Arkady wasn't sure if there was even a concrete plan in place dictating how Pandora was to be raised. There might well be such a plan, one that the top brass simply hadn't shared with Sahasrara yet.

Still, it was fun to imagine what might be. Il-Hyeong probably would make a decent uncle, too.

5. Within the Embrace of the Iolite League

Word had finally come in later that evening: the Iolite League had completed dealings with the Tomosabaki government, and had successfully negotiated the surrender of the remains of Kentian McEvoy. The League was not as successful, however, in getting the government of Ridgecrescent to allow the aircraft that was carrying those remains to be routed through one of their airports.

Instead, the plane (which had already taken off from Seizo by the time Arkady and his team had been informed) would first have to head far south to Corazón, in Afortunada, before refueling and heading back northeast, over the Butterfly Islands, on its way to Stewart in Deepwater. It was a delay of only a few hours beyond what it would have taken if they could have stopped over in Ridgecrescent, instead, but even those few hours were another bitter reminder of the enmity left over from the Butterfly Islands War.

It also meant a few more hours before they could have a funeral, before they could have a burial, before they could have the closure of being able to say goodbye to their friend and move on. It meant a few more hours of Arkady being unable to rest easily, knowing that even after going to sleep and waking up the next morning, he'd still have to be playing this waiting game.

He and Il-Hyeong had done lunch together, with Ming-Jun having joined them for dinner. She hadn't been very talkative, and that was before they'd all gotten the news about the situation with Kentian. The rest of the meal had passed in almost total silence, and none of them, to Arkady's recollection, had actually finished their plate.

Now, Arkady was by himself again. He didn't want to go back to see Pandora, didn't want to practice his saber forms, didn't want to read, didn't want to be alone in his own room—he wanted to just *skip* all this and get back to life as it was supposed to be, as it was 'normal' for him. He wanted to get back to undertaking missions for Sahasrara, back to tracking down leads on the Pyxis Sequence, to digging up their civilization's lost past and forging the Iolite League's path to the better world.

The ferret stood in the upstairs hallway, leaning through one of the lancet windows, arms folded. The sun had set beneath the sea, but the sky still retained a purplish glow that was quickly fading. A few stars had popped into view, and more had probably appeared over the last several minutes, but Arkady's attention wasn't on the sky anymore by then.

Instead, he looked down into the courtyard and at the statue. He looked at the wolf, the rabbit, and the tiger, the faces of which he could see from this angle; the mouse, fox, and bat were facing away from him, though their unique ears and tails still made them easy enough to identify.

"You ever feel left out?" Kentian had asked him once. *"Me, Il-Hyeong and Ming-Jun get our species represented, but not you?"*

Arkady remembered his response clearly: *"How do you think the Spindletrees feel? A statue here in their own ancestral home, and no raccoon?"*

"Guess whoever made it had something against folks with masks on their faces," Kentian had said with a chuckle. *"Speaking of which, do you know who did make it?"*

Arkady didn't know. He'd made a point to find out, so that he'd be able to tell Kentian later. He'd never remembered to ask, though, or to even look it up. How long ago had that been? Three years ago? Four? Kentian would never know, now.

The wolf in the statue didn't look much like Kentian. Oh, it was tall and had a proud bearing, just like Kentian had, but the statue's shoulders were more slender where Kentian's were broad, and the face and muzzle bore softer features where Kentian's had been sharp, angular, and masculine. The statue was supposed to be androgynous, though though the more Arkady looked at it, the more he thought the sculptor had been learning towards more of a male form than a female one. Maybe that was the ferret's own personal bias filling in the blanks, projecting, making him see what wasn't there.

Other Château denizens walked down the hallway behind Arkady, but none of them stopped to engage him. The ferret didn't turn to look, and by sense of smell alone, he couldn't tell who might be there. At one point, he got the scent of fox—red fox, though, so it wasn't Il-Hyeong—but beyond that, all he could tell was that there were two individuals who either didn't know him well enough to say hello, or who knew him well enough to know that he wouldn't want to be bothered.

The pale indigo of the sky turned a much inkier shade, and now more stars did jump out against the backdrop of near-black. A strong breeze carried the scent of sea and shore to Arkady's window. The mixture of salt and sand made the ferret think back to a mission from five years ago, the first actual field mission that Kentian, finally officially Agent McEvoy, had come along on.

There had been an attempted coup d'état in Ezüstpart, a small city-state along the Silver Coast. An Ajna team had been sent in weeks prior in order to help undermine the military usurpers' power base from within; later, League intelligence had caught wind that the Octavians had uncovered that team's activities and were likely planning a strike. Not wanting to spook the Ajna team into giving themselves away, the Directorate Board had decided to not inform Ajna of the intelligence at all, and had instead dispatched a team from Sahasrara—consisting of Agents Ryswife, Quinn, Devra and McEvoy—to take out the Octavians without alerting either their comrades or the Ezüstpart military in the process.

The mission had nothing to do with Project Scheherazade, but there had been a certain logic to using Sahasrara to bail out Ajna without upsetting an already-tenuous situation's careful balance. Before Ming-Jun had even gotten the team's surveillance suite set up in their seaside hotel room, though, Kentian had found himself nearly getting knifed behind a cabana in one of the outdoor resort areas along the beach. It had been just after sunset, and his attacker had apparently been willing to risk being spotted in a public place in order to get a quick takedown.

Kentian had shown masterful skill in subduing his attacker, a black-clad black fox, with nonlethal force, and Il-Hyeong had arrived on scene just in time to deflect any passersby (and authorities) from stumbling across the wolf as he conducted his rough, on-the-spot interrogation. As they soon learned, the black fox was actually a member of the Ajna team; that team had discovered the Octavians' presence all on their own, and had mistakenly taken the Sahasrara agents for the enemy.

The situation was further sorted out over the course of several fruity, tropical drinks, and combining the two teams' intelligence enabled Ming-Jun to track down the Octavian cell within two days. Arkady had gone along with Kentian and Il-Hyeong to the Octavians' hideout (the Ajna team had agreed to stay low and focus on the coup), and the fresh-faced wolf had again proven himself in a live-fire combat situation.

The Iolite League never did learn whether the Octavians had been attempting to disrupt Ajna's efforts to bring down the coup (which they were ultimately successful in doing), or whether they'd simply been gunning for the team for its own sake. Somehow, the Octavian cell had known that Arkady and his team were coming. They had been ready, and had been unwilling to surrender.

That's what it all came down to, in the end, Arkady supposed: they had signed up to be peacemakers, to help in God's work to make the world a better place, and they had known from the start that it was work that sometimes had to get violent. They weren't proud of that fact—nobody was—but it was a reality that they'd accepted. At least, Arkady had thought he'd accepted it; the mission to Shambhala wasn't supposed to have had a single shot fired, but in the end, three people had died in order for the Iolite League to get possession of the case and its contents.

"Whatever's in that case had better be worth this." Those had been Kentian's last words. The last words of a wolf, a creature of God, who had devoted his life to ensuring that such things were worth it.

Arkady pushed away from the windowsill and headed for the old elevator. Now that night had fallen, evening services would have long since let out. The chapel was almost surely empty by now, and that would hopefully grant Arkady the privacy he wanted for the prayers he was planning on offering.

The chapel of Château Sainte-Mireille was smaller than many guests imagined. Though the Château itself was one of the Iolite League's major holy sites, it had been built as a manor, not as a place of worship, and in the interest of preserving living history, the League had never gone and built a larger church on the grounds. Certainly, compared to something like the grandiose Fioletovy Cathedral, where Ajna made its own secret home, the Château's chapel was downright quaint; still, it was usually large enough to suit its purposes, with the only real exceptions being certain holy days when visitors to the island were more frequent.

Tonight, as Arkady had hoped, the chapel was empty, with no sign of even Father Benjamin milling about in back. It was also dark; there was electrical lighting rigged throughout the chapel, but it was turned off, and Arkady had decided to light only the chapel's torchieres and candles for illumination. The indistinguishable mishmash of scents that still lingered in the air were enough to tell the ferret that the evening service had been a busy one. Perhaps the members of the Château community who had known Kentian McEvoy as the individual, not as the secret agent, had come out in force for religious solace as well.

Purple was the dominant color inside the chapel itself. Not just any purple, but a specific, rich shade of purple—calling it "Iolite League purple" was enough to define the exact shade, for most people—it was nearly everywhere, from the ornate trim on the pews, to the altar coverings and wall hangings. A softer shade of purple dominated the few stained glass windows at the back wall of the chapel; with the sun having set, though, all Arkady could see of them was what shone in the dim, flickering torchlight.

The lack of a priest and an assembled congregation did nothing to detract from the feeling of religious weight that hung in the air. If anything, the solitude made Arkady feel even more like he was in a place to be heard one-on-one with God. The ferret understood now how Ming-Jun had been able to spend so many hours in here by herself after returning from Tomosabaki. Perhaps he should have gone ahead with it earlier, himself.

Clasping his paws together, Arkady lowered his head and tried to purge his mind of conscious thought, to start. The quiet helped, and despite the constant barrage of conflicting emotions that he was feeling deep within, he found what he could for some inner peace, and having found that, proceeded to pray.

He spoke his prayers aloud, though very quietly, under his breath, to the point where it probably sounded like an unintelligible hodgepodge of murmured half-syllables. In his mind, the ferret was going over each word carefully, thinking through the prayers verbatim, as chronicled in the ages-old Scripture. Much of it was rote, requiring only the quiet concentration he'd found in order for him to be able to recite the words, but other verses were more obscure, prayers he hadn't had any need to say in years, and those took more effort to dredge up from memory.

Even then, however, it was all still automatic. It was all words he'd simply memorized long ago, and as he went over them now, they started to lose any conscious or tangible meaning. Words, spoken over and over, which were supposed to convey the way that he, as a devout being, felt and believed, but which now might as well have been as empty as the void Arkady was trying to fill by coming here in the first place.

His belief in God and in the Iolite Doctrine both told him to move on. It was like Il-Hyeong had said: Kentian had done his work, and had moved on to his reward. The loss of a friend was a sad thing, but as a servant to the cause, Kentian had done nothing more than what had been expected of him. His comrades in Sahasrara should be *proud* of him for making the ultimate sacrifice in the name of the better world.

But his comrades in Sahasrara hadn't been there. Only Arkady and Il-Hyeong had. Only Arkady and Il-Hyeong had seen what had happened, had borne witness to the shameful truth that Kentian's death had been no great and noble sacrifice, but had instead been nothing but the result of Arkady's poor judgment and ability to think under pressure. He'd gone into that mission to Shambhala expecting no real dangerous resistance from Cibola or anyone else, and he'd let his guard down, gotten sloppy, and one of his subordinates—no, one of his *friends* had paid the price in his stead.

Did Il-Hyeong resent him for that? He'd shown no indication of blaming Arkady for what happened, either at Shambhala or since then, but as the grief passed and the facts set in, would the swift fox decide to blame him, grow to resent him? And Ming-Jun, who hadn't been there, but would only have the accounts of the other two members of her team—what might she think? Was her silence already the result of doubt and uncertainty about the way the mission had all gone down? She'd already gone so far as to scold Arkady in the middle of the action for nearly blowing her cover, so it wouldn't be too much of a stretch for her to doubt the rest of his leadership capabilities after all this.

"Please," the ferret prayed. "Please, forgive me."

He wasn't sure if he was calling out to God, or to Kentian, or to Il-Hyeong and Ming-Jun. He just knew that he was sorry, all while knowing that he could never be sorry enough for what had happened. "I'm sorry," he said aloud, lifting his head to look up toward the front of the chapel, at the altar that was now bare of the normal accoutrements used in an actual service. Candlelight flickered, casting only the shadows of pews and stonework. "I'm sorry."

The flames sprouting from the candles wavered again, but this time, the disturbance was more pronounced. A moment later, Arkady felt the tepid, late-night island breeze sweep through the chapel. The draft whirled on through the chamber, nearly extinguishing some of the candles. As the small flames steadied, the shadow on the wall coalesced into the recognizable, tall-eared silhouette of a rabbit.

"Arkady?" Ming-Jun asked. Her footsteps made barely any sound as she walked up the center aisle. "Where have you been?"

Only then did Arkady turn around, waiting to make sure that he could speak without his voice catching in his throat. "I've been here. Since about..."

He realized that he actually didn't know what time it was, and had no frame of reference for how long he'd been lost in thought and in prayer-by-rote. "Well, for the last good while," he said.

Ming-Jun continued to approach slowly. "You haven't been answering your comm or your phone."

"I left them in my room. I just wanted some quiet. It's been a long day."

The rabbit stopped at a respectful distance, a few rows away. She brought her wrist to her mouth, pressed her comm with her other paw, and said, "I found him, Il-Hyeong." There was no audible reply from the fox, and then Ming-Jun said, "We've been looking everywhere for you."

Arkady got to his feet. "Yeah, well, you've found me," he said. "I didn't wander off or anything. You let the boys downstairs know I'm all right."

Dropping her arms to her sides, Ming-Jun shook her head and stepped out to intercept Arkady as he tried to walk past. "No," she said, resting a paw on his shoulder. "This is... really big news. You need to hear this."

Knowing that this meant top-level Sahasrara business, Arkady didn't want to be too obvious about it in public, but if there was anything the ferret was certain of right now (and he wasn't certain of much, even he would admit), it was that he and Ming-Jun were alone in the chapel. He decided to keep his voice quiet just in case. "Look," he said. "Unless this is about the Pyxis Sequence, I don't want to have to deal with it until tomorrow. Go back and tell them I'll be by in the morning."

Ming-Jun took another step to block Arkady as the ferret attempted to walk past her. "Arkady," she said, eyes locked on his, her tone very serious. "They've given us a new assignment already."

That was enough to stop Arkady in his tracks. "A new assignment?" he repeated out of shock. "Il-Hyeong and I are effectively on probation until the judiciary comes to a decision, and as far as I know, they haven't even started meeting yet. How can we have been given an assignment?"

"Search me," the rabbit said. "All I know is that we're getting a formal rundown as soon as they can get the three of us together."

"It's the middle of the night."

"Well, now you know why Il-Hyeong and I have been searching the grounds for you," Ming-Jun said. "Now come on. Whoever's behind making this call is clearly in a hurry to get the ball rolling."

Arkady followed Ming-Jun as the rabbit left the chapel and started to head for the library. "You're serious about this?" he asked, careful to pitch his voice for her ears only now that they were outside; most of the Château population would be asleep or at least inside by this time of night, but it didn't hurt to be careful. "What have you heard so far?"

"Not much," Ming-Jun admitted. "Only that rumor is that they're sending us off to Ridgecrescent, and that we're due to ship out at the end of the week."

"Ridgecrescent?" Arkady couldn't think of any good reason they'd suddenly be asked to go there, of all places—especially not while on effective suspension from active duty. "And wait, *rumors*?" he asked, placing dubious emphasis on the word. "Rumors from where?"

Ming-Jun rounded the corner and stopped at the door to the upstairs library. "Dr. Mayflower," she said. "And she's actually asked to see you, first."

"Wait," the ferret said, feeling a surge of both panic and excitement, "does that mean that this mission is about the Pyxis Sequence?" He envisioned the kangaroo scientist and her team scurrying about the Hephaestus Chamber, hurrying to get things ready for Pandora's imminent awakening.

"Actually," Ming-Jun said, and only now did she show apprehension about anything that was going on, "it's about the augmentation. They're moving the schedule up."

Arkady stopped again. "By how much?"

"Tomorrow? You've got to be kidding me!"

Dr. Mayflower shook her head. The kangaroo maintained her composure, but she was clearly unnerved by the news that she was delivering. "I've got my team preparing for it now," she said. "Believe me, this is last-minute news to us, as well."

"The augmentation wasn't supposed to happen for another month," Il-Hyeong said, his look of shock and tone of utter disbelief mirroring Arkady's own. "You yourself said that there were still two more rounds of treatments and checkups that we needed to get before we'd be ready for the surgery."

Again, the doctor shook her head, frowning. "They looked at your records and determined that you're ready to go through with it now," she said, looking back and forth between the fox and the ferret without letting her eyes linger for too long on either one of them. "To be frank, I'd prefer to have another month—even two—before moving forward, but you are both still... within acceptable tolerances. I'd have refused outright otherwise."

Arkady called upon his sense of professionalism to stifle the growl he wanted to let out. "So 'they' decided this, did they?" he asked. "Who do they have who's more qualified than you to make that call?"

"Don't confuse 'qualified' with 'authorized.'" Ming-Jun had been sitting in the corner by herself, and she didn't even bother to look up when she chimed in.

The other three all turned their heads and looked at the rabbit, but before Arkady could shoot her a reproving glance, Dr. Mayflower just sighed and chuckled despite herself. "She's exactly right, of course," the kangaroo said. "But don't worry: my team will be ready, and you have my personal assurance that I won't go ahead with anything tomorrow if I don't feel it'd be safe for either one of you."

Arkady clutched at the back of his neck, wringing at his fur and scruff as he stared down at the blank table and tried to make sense of this asinine decision. "We're about to leave on a mission," he said. "A mission that we were just given, one which is apparently of the utmost importance, since they're wanting to brief us in the middle of the night. Why is the augmentation—which isn't even supposed to be happening now—suddenly taking precedence?"

"It isn't," Mayflower replied, her face a mask of professional seriousness. "The mission is still on."

Il-Hyeong interrupted while Arkady was still trying to shut his gaping jaw. "Wait, they told *you* about the mission?"

"They had to," the kangaroo said. "They needed my assurance that you'd still be able to go on it." She seemed to be unaffected by the agents' open disbelief. "The reason they're briefing you in the middle of the night is because they need you in surgery first thing tomorrow morning."

The swift fox let out a barking laugh that was almost a snarl. "Okay, now I *know* this is a joke," he said. "You're going to cut open our chests, arms, and legs, and then stick guns in our paws and send us out to do the good work?"

"That's about the size of it," the doctor said, her expression unwavering. "You'll have the surgery tomorrow. You'll spend the following day in recovery under my supervision, and the day after that, you'll be leaving on your mission."

"That's ridiculous," Arkady said. He was surprised at how level he was able to keep his voice for even those two words. "How are we even supposed to get out of bed for the next week, let alone undertake a covert ops mission?"

Dr. Mayflower got to her feet. "You'll be ready," she said. "Trust me. I know it's hard to believe, but nobody expects you to do anything while you're physically crippled."

"If things even go like they're supposed to," Il-Hyeong muttered.

The kangaroo had been about to turn away, but she stopped and looked back at the fox. "Please, Il-Hyeong," she sighed. "I don't like this any more than you do, but we've all got our jobs to do." She adjusted the glasses over the bridge of her snout. "Now if I were you, I'd make it a point to take it easy until tomorrow."

"Yeah, and go pray with Father Benjamin."

Mayflower just shook her head and then walked off without giving the fox's last snide remark a response.

Il-Hyeong didn't let her get far, though. "Wait," he said. "Hold on one more second."

The doctor turned around with an impatient sigh. "Make it quick," she said. "We both have places we need to be."

Rebuffed, the fox started to let more personal concern show through. "You said we'd be recovering for a full day?" Arkady could see his small, sharp teeth pinch into his lip. "What about Kentian's funeral?"

"Agent McEvoy's funeral arrangements are the purview of Father Benjamin and the other clergy," Mayflower replied. She turned to leave again, but spoke first before walking off. "I would surmise, though, that those arrangements will go on ahead as already scheduled."

6. A Scream in the Dark

"I know you probably won't have time to go over these before tomorrow," Ming-Jun said, handing stuffed envelopes to Arkady and Il-Hyeong, "but given that I'll already be underway by the time you two are even conscious again, we may as well do a quick rundown now." Standard procedure had always involved sending Ming-Jun and Kentian to a site ahead of time if any special advance surveillance preparation was necessary. There had been no mention of providing a replacement for Kentian, and so it looked like Ming-Jun would be heading out all on her own.

Competent or not, Arkady didn't like the idea of the rabbit taking that on by herself without any backup. If anything happened to her because Kentian weren't there to keep her safe, then Arkady would have nobody to blame but himself for that lack of protection.

Arkady's suspicions about what could possibly have been so important as to warrant a last-minute mission being pulled together with such impromptu efficiency were correct: Sahasrara and Project Scheherazade had finally gotten a major lead in their search for the elusive Pyxis Sequence.

The ferret ordinarily would have been elated at that news, but coming together with the news that the dangerously-invasive augmentation procedure was moving forward far ahead of schedule (despite her impassive front, he knew Dr. Mayflower had to be furious as well), fear and anxiety outweighed any joy. The preparatory treatments he and Il-Hyeong had been undergoing weren't minor affairs in their own right, and to be told that the two final arrays of treatments would be skipped entirely in order to move right ahead with the surgery itself sounded like a disaster waiting to happen.

What weighed even more heavily on Arkady, however, was the confirmation that he and Il-Hyeong would indeed be missing Kentian's funeral due to surgery, and Ming-Jun would be on her way to the target site to set up pre-mission surveillance. His last chance to say goodbye to his friend and comrade-in-arms who had died under his command was going to be taken away from him.

Il-Hyeong was still visibly upset by this news, too. He'd tried to protest when they'd been given the orders that confirmed Dr. Mayflower's timeline, and Arkady had urged him to calm down and drop the matter before he earned himself a reprimand.

"For the better world," the swift fox had murmured to Arkady and Ming-Jun as they'd left the briefing room earlier. *"All for the better world."*

The way that Ming-Jun sat on her bed, with her arms behind her, propping herself up, made her look innocent and vulnerable as opposed to competent and deadly. Arkady had been in the rabbit's room no more than half a dozen times since knowing her, and he had a hard time clearly remembering what it had looked like the last time he had. Despite the barely-feminine décor, it still didn't strike him as the room of someone who practiced the broadsword.

The ferret's eyes were on the outside of the unmarked envelope the rabbit had given him, and he heard Il-Hyeong already fishing out his own information packet. "You're going to be Samuel Togen," Ming-Jun said to Arkady, who suddenly had to snap back to attention. "You're an electrical engineer from Chochi-Sankeng, and you're interviewing for a—"

"That's all in here, right?" It was after midnight now. Arkady was tired. They were all tired. The ferret opened up the envelope and dumped some of the papers into his paw, a thin plastic identification card bouncing off of his palm and clattering onto the floor.

Ming-Jun sighed and shook her head. "Yes, but I think we should go over the basics now. I'd feel better if you at least familiarized yourself with this ahead of time, just to make things easier when you need to read up in detail after just having got out of surgery."

"And believe me, I'm looking forward to that," Il-Hyeong said, thumbing through his own papers. "I'm sure that after everything else that's going on, it'll be a picnic to be able to remember all the details of being, ah..."

"Raymond Castille," Ming-Jun finished for him. "You're a postgraduate student from the Technical University of Song Kang, where you study particle physics."

Il-Hyeong tucked his information packet under his arm and looked up. "Well, thank you for picking a field that'll be easy to feign expertise in," he said.

"You don't need to learn that much," Ming-Jun insisted, gesturing to the packet. "The relevant details are all in there; it's just the sort of thing that the customs agents will want to ask when they process your Non-Citizen's Entry Waiver."

"And again, particle physics being something I can clearly fast-talk my way through."

"It's also something the customs agents probably aren't interested in hearing," Arkady pointed out in Ming-Jun's defense. "And I doubt they'd be able to correct you if you did happen to get something wrong."

Ming-Jun nodded. "And it's not like they're going to be giving you a pop quiz," she said. "They'll just basically try to make small talk while they go over your paperwork and stamp a few things."

According to sources, an excellent lead into the Pyxis Sequence had been traced to a company called Fan-Yin Bioinformatics. In fact, if initial data were to be believed, their research teams might have actually unlocked the sequence itself already. That was a long shot, of course, and Arkady's crew knew full well that preliminary information almost never matched up perfectly with reality, but even still, any lead at all was a fantastic leap forward.

The trouble with Fan-Yin Bioinformatics was with its location: the city of Highslope, in the Democratic Republic of Ridgecrescent. Ever since the end of the Butterfly Islands War, Ridgecrescent had begun to adopt more and more xenophobic policies, including making membership in the Iolite League illegal as well banning foreign League members from entering the country. Working around that ban wouldn't be a problem for Sahasrara, but it was still something of a touchy point, even for them. Even though it had happened less than a decade ago, the Iolite League considered the end of the Butterfly Islands War to be the biggest and most tragic failure in their thousand-year history.

The extra bit of workaround that would be necessary made the decision to go ahead and move up the augmentation procedure all the more puzzling than it already was.

"I haven't been to Ridgecrescent since before the war," Il-Hyeong pointed out. "They've really got the whole country gated off like that?"

"That's what everyone's saying," Ming-Jun replied. "It's probably mostly a formality. Still, we are going to need to route you through Song Kang, since if you come directly from Deepwater, suspicion of being affiliated with the Iolite League will no doubt lead to much more scrutiny and cross-checking, and the last thing we need is to blow our best lead on the Pyxis Sequence because one of us got arrested trying to get into the country." The rabbit scrunched up her snout. "Speaking of which, can you do a Kyunjiu accent?"

"More so than I can talk particle physics, at any rate," the fox said. He cleared his throat, tilted his muzzle back, and then spoke with a somewhat exaggerated and mildly condescending tone that would make an aristocrat proud: "There is something to be said about traveling the world being good for something."

The sound of Il-Hyeong's affected voice broke Arkady's forlorn mood for at least long enough to get a smile out of him, and when he saw that Ming-Jun had seen it, he couldn't then try to hide it. "Better than my attempt at an accent would be, for sure," he said.

"You'll have time to practice on the plane," Il-Hyeong said.

"Assuming my vocal cords still work." Arkady still didn't see how he and Il-Hyeong would be in any shape to go on a mission so soon after getting major, body-altering surgery, but if there was one thing that the ferret could say about Jillian Mayflower, it was that she knew how to do her job and was proud of being able to do it. Even she had to realize how ridiculous the prospect sounded, and not knowing why she was so sure of herself was almost more of a mystery to Arkady than the matter of the Pyxis Sequence.

Ming-Jun scooted toward the edge of the bed and planted her feet on the floor as she leaned forward. "All joking aside, you two, I want you to know that I'm really nervous about all this."

It wasn't like Ming-Jun to admit something like that so readily. Arkady shared her sentiment, of course, but hearing her vocalize it kicked his own anxiety into gear. As she said, it was easy for him and Il-Hyeong to bandy about snide remarks about the ridiculousness of the situation, but was there really any surer a sign of fear than trying too hard to make light of something?

"You're nervous?" Il-Hyeong asked. If Arkady hadn't known the fox as well as he did, he would have thought he'd heard a tone of accusation in that question. "I mean, it's not like you're going under the knife with the rest of us."

The rabbit's nostrils widened as she huffed out an anxious breath. "That's not what I mean," she said. "Though to be honest, I *am* worried about you two and your procedure. Not that I don't trust our doctors, or anything."

"What are you nervous about, then?" Arkady asked. He thought back to their sword fight, and wondered if he'd have believed the rabbit showing such sudden vulnerability then.

"There's a lot at stake with this mission," Ming-Jun said. "Even if this isn't the mother lode itself, this could bring us within reach of the Pyxis Sequence. That's years of work for all of us that's finally coming to fruition."

Arkady thought about Pandora, at this very moment still just floating in her silent world within that tube. Obtaining the key to finally wake her from her unbroken sleep meant so much to him, but it also meant a lot to Ming-Jun and Il-Hyeong and even to Kentian—and to a great many people within Sahasrara who had been involved in Pandora's design and development. Even with that huge stake for the Iolite League and the ideals for which it stood, though, did the potential of her waking mean more to anyone than it did to Pandora herself?

So, Ming-Jun was certainly right to be nervous, even afraid, since God knew that Arkady was nervous, too.

"We need to just treat this like any other mission," Arkady said as he tried to let the pieces of the greater puzzle fall into perspective. "Yes, there's a lot on the line for all of us, but we have to focus on the task, not the ramifications."

"That's just the thing," Ming-Jun said, and now her obvious insecurity was growing even more. "Are we going to be able to focus on that?" She looked over at Il-Hyeong, too, to show that it was a question for all of them.

The fox spoke while Arkady was still trying to articulate himself. "Why wouldn't we be able to?"

Arkady saw the abrupt shift on Ming-Jun's face, and he struggled to say something, to say anything that his position of leadership behooved him to, but he was too late.

"Look, Kentian is dead," the rabbit blurted out. "Kentian is dead, and we haven't even had the chance to talk about that with each other, and now you two are being forced into some surgical procedure that'll do who-knows-what, and you're wondering why I think we might not be able to focus on what might be the most important mission of our lives?"

Silence fell over Ming-Jun's room. The rabbit seemed to be patiently awaiting a response, but even though both Arkady and Il-Hyeong were lamely silent, she didn't seem to be lording her superior position over them. Maybe, the ferret thought, that was just because she was right, and all three of them knew it.

Arkady tried to think about how this upcoming mission would feel if Kentian were still along for the ride like he ought to have been. Having him to back up Ming-Jun for the advance maneuvers would take some of the ferret's nervousness away, to be sure, but knowing that this was all for the Pyxis Sequence—hell, he'd still be shaken by those high stakes. Also, there was no way to know for sure that the augmentation procedure wouldn't have still been moved up the way it had even if Kentian were still alive.

"Kentian would be the first person to scoff at the rest of us for acting like this," Arkady said, picturing the way the wolf would probably have thrown his arms up as he feigned disgust at them for being so wishy-washy. In a way, Kentian had always made impatience a virtue. "But you're right," the ferret said to Ming-Jun then. "It's easy for me to say that we need to treat this just like any other mission, when we all know that it isn't."

"You're not exactly helping, Arkady," Ming-Jun said. She tried adding a chuckle for good measure, but it was hard for Arkady to tell whether it was forced or just sarcastic.

The ferret shook his head in response. "At this point, I think I need to correct myself," he said. "We *do* need to worry more about this mission, especially since..." He tried to think of how he wanted to phrase himself, but in the direness of the moment, he decided not to mince words. "Since I messed up last time, and you guys need to be able to count on me when we're out there."

Il-Hyeong was quick to chime in. "Arkady, you didn't—"

"I know what we both said on record," Arkady said. "But the fact remains that I was distracted, and that my attention wasn't where it ought to have been, and we're lucky that the rest of us even got out alive after that." He checked his companions' eyes, then continued. "Now, we don't have a choice about the fact that we're being forced out into the field again, and so the both of you need to be able to count on me as the team leader to keep things together, knowing everything that's on the line here."

From her seat at the end of her bed, Ming-Jun turned her gaze down toward her feet. She hunched over, her elbows on her knees, and her tall ears obscured what small portion of her face that Arkady might have been able to see. "You're still our leader, Arkady," she said. "And maybe you don't believe that we'd still have faith in you, but I do, and I'm sure Il-Hyeong does, too."

Il-Hyeong looked guilty and sheepish at her saying that, but Arkady ignored that. "And what about yourself?" the ferret asked the rabbit. "Do you have faith in yourself?"

The rabbit's head snapped back up. She had obviously been breathing heavily, and her eyes showed faint traces of red. "In myself?" she asked. The way she flinched and straightened out made her look both surprised and affronted. "Why wouldn't I?"

"It's an honest question," Arkady said. "I know I'm worried about you being alone in the field without Kentian, Il-Hyeong or myself to keep an eye on you."

"I'm a professional," the rabbit insisted. "I know how to do my job; I've already given you the benefit of the doubt of believing that you'll still do yours."

"I'm not calling your qualifications into question, Ming-Jun." Arkady grabbed one of her paws and squeezed it in between both of his own. When she tried to yank it away, the ferret still held firm. "I'm letting you know that I'm just worried about you, naturally, both as your leader and as your friend, because as we've all just learned—and it's something we all should have learned a long time ago—things can go wrong out there."

The redness in Ming-Jun's eyes had begun to abate, but the eyes themselves wavered for a moment. Her arm went limp, her attempts to wrest free of Arkady's grip ceasing. "I'm not afraid," she said. Her voice was soft and quiet, but despite the lack of force in her words, Arkady believed them.

"That's fine," the ferret replied. "After all, I'm the leader; it's my job to be afraid for you." With that, he let the rabbit's paw go, and then stood up. He looked at his two companions and nodded. "I know that we can do this."

Il-Hyeong's expression had gone from one of complete bemusement to one of stern resolve. "You know, Arkady, if we do manage to track down the Pyxis Sequence, I hope they do let you look after Pandora." The fox smiled. "You'd make an excellent father."

"You still get to be her uncle," Arkady said, managing to smirk even though he didn't think he had it in him. "Even if you are a fox."

"You'll tell her that's not his fault, though, right?" Ming-Jun said. Her own humor hadn't returned as fully as Il-Hyeong's seemed to have, but it was an improvement nevertheless.

"God chooses what we're born as," Arkady said. "It's up to us to determine who we end up as."

Both the rabbit and the fox smiled, but said nothing. Arkady started to make his way to the door, but he kept his eyes on his companions. "Il-Hyeong, I'll see you bright and early with Dr. Mayflower tomorrow, where we can hopefully enjoy our last few moments of normalcy," the ferret said. "And Ming-Jun, since I might not see you again before you ship out, I just want to wish you good luck, and remind you that I do believe in you."

"Same to you, Arkady," Ming-Jun replied before the ferret could duck out the door. "And hey, even if it's your duty to worry, try not to overachieve in that department, okay?"

"I'm sure he'll do his best," Arkady heard Il-Hyeong say, and it made the ferret chuckle as he finally did slip out into the ornate corridor. He relished the smile that he had as he walked down the hallway towards his own living quarters, thinking himself lucky to have his two friends as part of his crew.

Once he was back in his room and his door was solidly shut behind him, he flopped down onto his bed without even going through his standard nightly routine. He allowed himself to feel the tightness in his chest and the pressure behind his eyes, and he welcomed it. Images of the mission to Shambhala flooded his mind, followed soon thereafter by a series of memories, all jumbled together, all centering on Kentian. Then, for the first time since returning from Tomosabaki, Arkady let himself cry.

He thought of how Kentian would never get to share in the team's celebration on the day that they brought the Pyxis Sequence back to Château Sainte-Mireille. He thought about how Kentian would never get to know Pandora, how he'd never get to hear the song on the tape that they'd gotten from his murderer, and how he'd never get to see the better world that they'd all fought for together.

Arkady was surprised that he was as well-rested as he was the next morning. It had been quite late when he'd gotten to bed, and even then, he'd spent a good while indulging himself in his grief. After waking up, he felt better, if still a little empty, but he tried to assuage that with some heartfelt prayer for Kentian, and for the rest of his teammates.

Il-Hyeong, conversely, was looking rather bleary-eyed. The upside to his lack of enthusiasm was that he likewise lacked the energy to stew in his discontent. He was also very bedraggled, uncharacteristically so, which ordinarily might have been funny if not for the morning's dire circumstances.

The fox and the ferret were in a preparatory area, off in some corner of the medical wing of Sahasrara. Arkady tried to remember if he'd been in this particular room before, but with the way things were outfitted specifically for the upcoming procedure, it was impossible for him to place the room properly in his memory. Dr. Mayflower had been by only briefly, and she'd been so busy calling out orders to the rest of her staff that Arkady wasn't sure if anything she'd said had been intended for him and Il-Hyeong at all. Even if it had, the frantic kangaroo's utterances bordered on the incomprehensible.

"Well, Arkady," Il-Hyeong said, fidgeting with his surgical gown yet again, "even if you and I are completely in the dark, it seems like everyone else besides the two of us knows what's going on. That's got to be a good sign, right?"

Arkady smiled and watched the orderlies and doctors bustle about and drop in and out of the room; he'd stopped trying to sort out what any of them were actually doing a long time ago. "As long as *they* have faith, right?"

Il-Hyeong shook his head, but didn't fully hide his own smile. "I really do wish Kentian were here. He wouldn't put up with not getting answers from these guys."

"They probably think we know more than we do," Arkady said. "And really, I'm not sure how much I want the details anyway."

"I'd feel better if I understood why they expect us to be back on our feet by tomorrow."

The augmentation itself went beyond just the single procedure that they were both about to undergo. The process had been going on for several months, even if they had been thinking of all the steps along the way as 'preparation' for the surgery, since that was undeniably the keystone of the project. Using advances in technology and medicine that the Iolite League had come upon in their development of Pandora, the overall idea was to take those scientific leaps and apply them to other aspects of Sahasrara's workings—especially since the project that had spawned those developments was still stuck in indefinite hiatus.

All told, the true depth of what Arkady and Il-Hyeong were having done to themselves was so maddeningly complex that the ferret wondered how Dr. Mayflower and the rest of the scientific team managed to keep track of it. In general, though, the augmentation was designed to improve the agents' bodies in whatever respects possible: heightening senses, improving reflexes, accelerating the body's natural rate of recovery, streamlining metabolism, and reinforcing the anti-aging treatments that they were already receiving. Today's surgery related to the most complicated aspect of that: a complete overhaul of the peripheral nervous system, with artificial tissue harvested from the same test systems that were used to construct Pandora worked in with their own nerves. Interfacing with the central nervous system, as in Pandora's case, was still impossible, but artificial ganglionic clusters and plexuses would be 'installed' into this new secondary network of nerve tissue, allowing for what Arkady and Il-Hyeong had been told would be "near-seamless integration."

Of course, such near-seamless integration still involved physically going in to 'rewire' the nerves of their arms and legs. The surgical procedure alone was slated to take the better part of the day. Given that, Il-Hyeong's insistence on knowing the nitty-gritty details actually confused Arkady.

Storming back out through the whirlwind of medical personnel, Dr. Mayflower reappeared, her eyes looking as though she'd somehow managed to drink an entire pot of coffee since she'd last been through some minutes prior. Perhaps she had, the ferret thought; there was a very real possibility that she hadn't even slept since she'd met with them the night before.

"We'll be ready to begin shortly," the doctor said, rearranging the first few pages atop her clipboard. "I've just got a few last-minute things to check with the actual equipment. If you two weren't already about to strangle me for this, I'd be afraid that the engineers would get to me first."

"Aw, we wouldn't strangle you," Il-Hyeong said. "You're our only way out of this mess."

Dr. Mayflower tucked her pen in between two of her fingers and motioned with one paw to the parade of technicians drifting about. "Not just me," she pointed out. "This is a group effort in every sense of the word."

"Well, you still get to be *my* hero," the fox said to her, and he again tugged at the edges of his flimsy gown with a look of dissatisfaction.

One of Mayflower's assistants, a slender raccoon with glasses on her muzzle that matched the doctor's own, came up to the kangaroo and said, "We've got the surgery rooms ready. We're just waiting on the lab to finish the final tissue sample checks and then we should be clear to proceed."

"Thank you," Mayflower replied, and with a nod she dismissed the raccoon. The kangaroo then turned back to her charges. "I'll give Dr. Lanither the go-ahead to run the eye exams on you two while I go finish getting the two surgical teams up to speed."

"Eye exams?" Arkady asked. "We just got those two months ago. Don't you still have that on file?"

Mayflower shook her head. "The guys want this done by the book," she said, "and the procedure calls for another small series of before-and-after tests."

"The book also calls for the surgery to not be today," Il-Hyeong pointed out.

At that, the kangaroo just sighed, and when she looked back up she said, "I'll send Dr. Lanither in here shortly. The eye test shouldn't take very long."

"And after that?" Arkady asked.

"After that, then we just need a reflex test, a blood sample, and a lung test."

"And *then* we go in for surgery?"

"And then you go in for surgery," Mayflower confirmed. "Don't worry, Arkady. Within the hour, I hope to have you unconscious."

The ferret smiled. "Because that's the only way you'll get us to shut up?" he asked, sharing a look with Il-Hyeong.

Dr. Mayflower rolled her eyes again, but this time it was playful. "Someone tell Dr. Lanither that Agents Ryswife and Quinn are ready for their eye exams," she called out, disappearing into the throng of busy staff.

Il-Hyeong reached over, squeezed one of Arkady's paws, and then let go. "This is it, then," the fox said. "See you on the other side, buddy."

The last thing that Arkady remembered was staring up at a set of bright lights that washed out the rest of the world surrounding him with its white, impenetrable halo. Then, the white had faded, and the world had gone black. It had been like falling asleep, only it hadn't caught him by surprise.

Then came the blankness. It was as if he were aware that he wasn't dreaming, as if his brain somehow knew that its functions were put on hold while his body was shut down completely. The nothing itself was almost measurable in a way that might have been terrifying if the ferret could have felt terror—or anything at all, for that matter.

The blankness persisted for a time, and then it was replaced by a prickling. Yes, sensation had returned. That prickling started in his toes, and then made its way up his legs, first the right and then the left. At first, it was like he had been sitting cross-legged for a long stretch of time, causing a sensation of pins-and-needles to spread awkwardly along both limbs. Then, that fuzzy prickling got worse, more noticeable and more pronounced, and then it started in his arms, as well.

His eyes refused to open, and he had no voice because he wasn't breathing. There was no air in his lungs; he wasn't even conscious. He was unconscious, but he felt this tingling grow and spread and change from innocuous to aggravating to painful. What had begun as a frustrating ghostlike sensation now felt like fire was raging along the full length of all four of the ferret's limbs, burning just underneath the skin, trying to burst out.

The burning got hotter, more savage, making Arkady's defunct mind panic at its inability to enact even the instinct to pull those limbs from that imaginary fire.

With a wrenching tightness in his chest, the ferret sat bolt upright, his eyes snapping open. They were immediately overwhelmed by light, impossibly bright, cutting out everything but the faintest hints of shapes at any side of his vision. He screamed, he cried out, viciously snarling in a way that made no attempt to articulate the nature of his pain.

"God in Heaven, what the hell is happening to him?" Arkady didn't recognize the voice.

Blurry shapes became grayish-blue outlines. "This is impossible!" another voice cried out. This one was female; Arkady wasn't sure which the former had been. "His vital signs just jumped right off the charts."

The formless mass that was Arkady's vision began to congeal bit by bit. Lowering his head seemed to help. The first voice spoke again. "Well, put him back under," it barked. Male, to be sure. "Quickly! At this rate, his body is going to kill itself."

The ferret's head started to swim. The fires grew weaker. "Dumping thirty units of Hesperidol into his system," a third voice said. Female. "Get those nerve connections turned off right now before they fry themselves."

"We haven't even turned them on yet!" the male voice shouted back. Now, Arkady could see just enough to tell that the darker shape that he was eyeing was his left thigh, cut in half with a half dozen metal devices holding skin and fur out of the way, and another half dozen poking out from the exposed flesh.

"Why is he still conscious?" the first female voice demanded. "Jon, push him back down onto the table. Get him to lie flat."

Now, all sound in the room started to sound as if Arkady's head had been plunged underwater. He could still make out the male voice, though. "No!" it snapped. "Don't touch him! If his nerve connections are live, touching him might overload his entire system."

"Martina, turn down the relative sensitivity on the nerve tuner." It was one of the female voices, but now it was distorted, and Arkady couldn't tell which it was.

The world went from dark to bright again, though this time, the ferret welcomed the whitewash. A voice without a source hit his ears. "But they're still not even connected."

"Do it anyway." Again, Arkady didn't know who had spoken, and he didn't care. He felt well enough to lie down then, and so he did. The air beneath him was like the cushion of his mattress, and though he couldn't manage a real smile on his face, he imagined himself with one, and that was enough to keep him content until everything outside himself did the favor of disappearing.

Arkady awoke, and the world was new again.

He sat up, and saw immediately that he was in a recovery room. It was, blissfully enough, empty, and he felt as if every bad thing that had ever happened to him had all just been a bad dream.

The room was empty, he could see, but it was still noisy. He could hear through the walls not only the thrum of the ventilation system and the heating ducts, but also nearly-distinct murmuring and the sound of footsteps. The scents of at least half a dozen different species—no, exactly seven: ferret, kangaroo, rabbit, raccoon, red fox, gray fox, and weasel—hung in the air. Three of them male, four of them female.

The ferret held up his paw and looked at it. Whereas the walls of the recovery room somehow looked too bright, he now saw that the texture of his own fur was magnitudes more distinct to him than he'd ever seen it look before. He breathed out through his nose, and watched as individual hairs swayed to a degree that should have been imperceptible. His fingers curled up to turn his paw into a little fist, and the tactile sensation of self touching self sent a happy jitter along his arm.

His arm. It had been sliced open in the way one might gut a fish, but there was no pain, no soreness or tenderness. There wasn't even a scar. There was the vague memory in the flesh itself of having been perhaps slightly bruised, but even that was faint, hard to notice even with his increased ability to feel.

There was so much more for Arkady to process, now, in terms of sensory input and things that he could no longer help but notice. It should have been overwhelming, impossible to keep up with, but it wasn't. He had no trouble at all, actually, in sorting out all the different things he was feeling, seeing, and smelling. He could tell that his anesthesia still hadn't even fully worn off, yet, and his mind was still as sharp as a tack.

Arkady heard the sound of beeping from the control panel over by the door, followed by the click of the locking mechanism disengaging.

The door slid open, and the ferret smelled and identified Jillian Mayflower before he turned his head to see her.

The kangaroo looked magnitudes better than she'd looked—well, before the surgery. She also looked far more real, somehow, to Arkady's new eyesight. The uneven patches of coloration in her fur gave her a more natural look, and even while she was still over by the doorway on the other side of the room, the ferret could see the stunning, deep brown color of her eyes. Her shoes clacked against the smooth floor, and though her face maintained its veil of professionalism, Arkady could hear her sigh of relief from halfway across the room.

Everything was so sharply in focus now that the ferret wondered how he could have ever gone through life without realizing just how much of his surroundings he had been missing.

"Welcome back to the land of the living, Arkady," Mayflower said. "How are you feeling?" Even her voice sounded more textured now.

"I feel fine," Arkady replied. "Great, actually." His own voice sounded different to him, too, but in a way he'd somehow been expecting.

Mayflower smiled and pulled up a chair. "I'm glad to hear it," she said. "The operation was a complete success; if the higher-ups wanted this done by the book, I'm happy to let them—and you—know that the nerve integration is registering exactly as we'd expected." A proud smile formed on her snout. "Actually, in some of them, the transfer ratio is even a little better."

The doctor's words knocked something loose from Arkady's memory. "I woke up during the surgery," he said. "It sounded like something went wrong."

From the look on Mayflower's face, Arkady could tell that she'd been expecting—or maybe just hoping—that he'd not mention that. "You did get up, yes," she admitted, turning her eyes down slightly. "It was for less than a minute, though, and it didn't impact the actual surgery or the integration process at all." She studied his face, and Arkady could actually see her pupils dilate and shrink as she scrutinized him. "You're saying that you actually remember that?"

"Vaguely. I'm sort of glad it's not that clear."

The kangaroo scratched at her wrist and chewed her lip. "Our readouts made it look like it was just a freak autonomic nerve response that we hadn't accounted for," she said. "You were clinically brain-dead at the time, and there shouldn't have been any neurological activity at all."

The ferret just shrugged. "I remember it," he said. "That's all I know."

"Hum. Interesting. I suppose if we have time, we should look into that."

"Did it happen to Il-Hyeong, too?" Arkady asked.

Mayflower shook her head. "No, just you," she said. "But like I said, the surgery itself was a complete success, and in the eight hours following that, we haven't picked up any abnormalities in any of your vital systems."

"Eight hours?" The ferret rubbed his head. That sleep had been entirely dreamless. "So, then how long was I out for, total?"

"Not counting the little episode where you sat up on the operating table, twenty-five."

Kentian's funeral had already been held. Ming-Jun was gone.

"And Il-Hyeong and I are getting on a plane to Kyunjiu tomorrow morning?"

The doctor nodded. "Do you think you won't feel well enough to?"

Arkady shook his head. "Actually, I think I'd be well enough to do it now," he said.

With a chuckle, Dr. Mayflower stood up. "You won't be so eager to get on the plane from Kyunjiu to Ridgecrescent once you see how your ears react to the pressure differential at high altitudes," she said, smiling before she turned around to leave.

7. On Hostile Shores

Dr. Mayflower hadn't been kidding. After the single most flavorful breakfast of Arkady's life, the flight from Château Sainte-Mireille to Song Kang had been nothing short of excruciating, reducing both Arkady and Il-Hyeong to little more than quivering, airsick masses for the first several hours. Even after the initial bout of debilitating nausea had passed, it was impossible to not feel the whole world shift with every slight bump and dip of the jet. By the time they landed in Song Kang, both the fox and the ferret were offering up their thanks to God that their flight out to Ridgecrescent wasn't until the following morning.

They got a room in the hotel of Song Kang International Airport, where (in addition to recuperating) they further prepared themselves by going over the details of the identities they would assume for their entry into Ridgecrescent. Those details weren't much more interesting than the high-level overview that Ming-Jun had given them back at the Château, but Arkady and Il-Hyeong were both more than happy to sit in their hotel room, away from the noise and hubbub of Kyunjiu's capital city, eating light, easy meals from hotel room service.

Even after the sickness and headache from the flight had passed, Arkady noticed that Il-Hyeong was much more muted and subdued than usual. True, they were both intentionally trying to keep things low-key, but the fox still seemed to emanate that unusual mood.

"Are you okay?" the ferret asked, looking up from the dossier on the imaginary Samuel Togen, noting that while the fox's eyes were on his own file, he didn't seem to be actually reading it.

Il-Hyeong's large ears, which had been drooped back in lifelessness rather than in concentration, perked back up. "Fine," he replied. "I'm just still getting used to the way this all feels."

"You're not still off-kilter from the flight, are you?" Arkady slid his glass of water across the nightstand between the two beds. "Here."

The fox shook his head. "No thanks," he replied. "I can't help but taste every impurity and contaminant in the stuff. I think they gave us tap water." He snorted out through his nose with what was probably supposed to have been a small laugh.

There was no exaggeration to the fox's claim, though. Here in the hotel room, Arkady could still smell the lingering traces of the room's previous guests—raccoons, a male and a female; both had slept in different beds—even underneath the faint chemical residue of the scent-scrubbers that had tried to eliminate them. The odor of rusted metal wafted in from the heating vent, even when turned down. A businessman in the room next door was arguing over the phone with his secretary. Even a single bite of the food brought up by room service, bland though it should have been by anyone's standards, consisted of more distinct, individual flavors than Arkady had ever been able to differentiate.

"I think I'm starting to get the hang of it," Arkady offered in encouragement. "It shouldn't be more than a day or so, I think, before all this new sensation seems second nature."

Still, the fox just shook his head. "Maybe," he murmured. "I still don't like it. And I'm not looking forward to the flight tomorrow, either."

"Neither am I," the ferret admitted. "Still, after another full night's sleep, I think our bodies will have acclimated further still, and the shock to the system won't be as bad. Who knows, maybe we'll only throw up once or twice."

Il-Hyeong set down his info packet and looked over at Arkady. "A full night's sleep, huh?" he asked. "I'll be lucky if I can stay asleep for ten minutes at a stretch in this place." He motioned with a single finger, making a jabbing motion toward the ceiling.

"It's not *that* noisy," Arkady said. "And you've slept next to airports before. There shouldn't be too much air traffic overnight."

"You don't have these," the swift fox pointed out, batting himself on one ear. "Just sitting here is like standing on the middle of a transit tube platform during rush hour. And every time one of those planes does land, I can feel the vibrations all the way through my skull."

Arkady hadn't thought of what the increased sensitivity to hearing would be like for someone whose range of hearing was already much better than his own. "Is it really that bad?" the ferret asked. "Dr. Mayflower said that we should adjust before too long."

"Maybe I will," Il-Hyeong said. He snorted again. "Really, I guess I'll have to, won't I?"

"Well, you and I are the only two people to ever go through this," Arkady said. "We've only got each other if we want to talk about it, so... well, do you want to talk about it?"

The fox shook his head and then lay back down on the bed, setting his paws underneath his head. "What's there to talk about?" he said. "Our whole perception of the world has been changed. Even if it were reversible—which I'm sure it isn't—I don't think we could go back to the way things were, knowing what we know now."

"Is that so bad, though?" Arkady asked. "Just think of it as a low-level form of enlightenment. Now your eyes are open to things that you didn't know were there before." A chuckle escaped his throat. "And your ears, and your fingertips, and your taste buds."

"Yeah," Il-Hyeong replied, suddenly much quieter; without Arkady's advanced hearing, he might not have even heard him. "It just feels wrong, though. Off. I... I don't like it."

The ferret got up from his bed and walked past Il-Hyeong's. "Like you already said, there's no going back," he said to the fox as he went for the minibar. "So we may as well embrace it and move forward."

Arkady heard Il-Hyeong sit back up behind him. "Because it's just going to be that easy?"

"We'll get through it together," the ferret said, pulling out a small bottle of brandy. He grabbed two glasses with his other paw.

"Very reassuring," the fox said dryly. "You're the one who's actually going to be able to get some sleep tonight."

The glasses clinked together as Arkady set them down on the table, and he poured the brandy. "Il-Hyeong, tomorrow, you and I are going to fly to Ridgecrescent, and we're going to meet with Ming-Jun," he said. "We're going to put our plan into action, we're going to get the Pyxis Sequence, and we're going to head back to Château Sainte-Mireille successful, where we can give Dr. Mayflower the good news and prepare for Pandora's birthday." The ferret held out one of the brandies for Il-Hyeong.

The fox took it, and though he looked unconvinced, Arkady could see signs that he was at least close to an uneasy half-smile. "It's going to go just like that?" the fox asked, bringing the brandy closer to his muzzle, not yet sipping. "We go in, we win, and we come home heroes, like clockwork?"

"Of course," Arkady proclaimed, drawing himself to his full height and holding up his glass. "I'm the leader, and that's my promise to you."

At last, a brief but honest laugh escaped Il-Hyeong's muzzle. "Well, here's to guaranteed success, then," he said, raising his own glass before taking a long sip. Arkady joined him, and then it was his turn to laugh when he saw the wide-eyed, twisted-up expression on the swift fox's face. "God in Heaven, that's good," he gasped. "Strong as hell, but good."

"See, there's a silver lining to everything, Il-Hyeong," Arkady said. "One of those being, apparently, that even bottom shelf stuff tastes like the good stuff, now."

"Imagine how the good stuff must taste, then," the fox said, smirking as he took yet another sip of that strong, flavorful brandy.

The second flight had been markedly better than the first, but that only meant that Arkady and Il-Hyeong were able to last longer in between bouts of vomiting. Judging from the way things were going, Arkady was hoping that by the time they finished their mission and were on their way back to Deepwater, they'd only throw up maybe once or twice en route.

Il-Hyeong had recovered enough of his sense of humor to make his dealings with the Ridgecrescent customs agents something to be proud of. His Kyunjiu accent really was quite good, Arkady had to admit, and after the fox played the part of the haughty physicist, the ferret found his own stint as Samuel Togen the engineer something of a disappointment in terms of making for a story worth telling to folks back at Château Sainte-Mireille.

After being processed through the airport, the two agents were set loose into the national capital of Thousand Leaves, the largest city in the world.

Both the fox and the ferret had been through Thousand Leaves before, back before the Butterfly Islands War, and even then the city had been an assault on the senses. The city was bounded by mountains and the sea, and it was divided into three separate tiers, the new layers having been constructed atop the existing city at points in the past when space had run out but population and industry continued to grow. The only way to build was up, and though Ridgecrescent was a small nation, they did pride themselves on their technological prowess—and what better way to show that off than by turning their capital into a living symbol of all they were capable of?

Grandstanding or not, Thousand Leaves was impressive, and rightly so. It was teeming with people; Ridgecrescent's government had taken a turn for the tight-lipped after the war, but recent estimates put the city's total population at around seventy million. Standing in front of Skyline Central Station, located on the topmost layer of the city, Arkady felt like he could hear all seventy million of them bustling about below. He thought that he could smell about half of them, too, with the other half being blocked out by the stench of industry, automobiles, and the overall unnatural, offensive reek of the urban landscape.

The ferret couldn't help but wonder how many of those people in the massive city below had belonged to the Iolite League before the federal government had made affiliation with it a criminal offense. Surely, many of the devout had left for the more welcoming shores of a dozen other countries, but many more had probably had no choice but to stay behind. Arkady watched the faces of the crowd, and he comforted himself with the thought that most of those people still upheld the Iolite Doctrine in private, practicing their faith even if, for the time being, they could not be with their brethren across the globe.

More important than the political lines was the fact that most of the people here and across the rest of Ridgecrescent still believed in God, even if the Iolite League didn't figure into their worship. They were good people, by and large, even if they themselves sometimes forgot it. Even among the masses who hadn't found religion, the bulk of them were still good people, and Arkady had to remember that it was for *all* of these people that he did what he did in the name of Project Scheherazade.

Across the platform, a family of weasels dragged around a few too many pieces of luggage. Further down, a raccoon shared a brief but loving kiss with a vixen. A well-dressed tiger businessman kept his attention on his newspaper, tail flicking with agitation that his face didn't show. The people here were just like the people anywhere else. A weasel was a weasel before he was a citizen of Ridgecrescent.

From beside him, Arkady heard Il-Hyeong let out the quietest of sighs, which mere days before would have been inaudible. The ferret turned to see the dusty-furred fox gazing out over the glittering metropolis, the first traces of neon illumination just coming on as evening approached. Il-Hyeong didn't turn to look back at Arkady, but he still said, "How can I be surrounded by so many people and feel so disconnected from all of them?"

"You just need to remember why we're here," the ferret replied. He started to reach out to place a paw on the fox's shoulder, but stopped himself. "Remember what we're fighting for."

"I know," the fox said. He continued to stare blankly out over the three-layered city. "I just don't like it here, standing amidst this many people, knowing that so many of them would scorn me if they could tell just by looking at me that I wasn't really one of them."

Arkady looked past the tops of the distant buildings, at the spot where the cloud-tinged, orange flourish of sunset was starting to form. "But you are one of them. Even if—especially if they don't realize that."

"How can an entire country embrace xenophobia on such a wide scale so quickly?" Il-Hyeong asked.

"Someday, it won't matter anymore," Arkady said. "They'll remember that a fox is still a fox and a ferret is still a ferret, no matter what silly accent he speaks with."

Il-Hyeong's smile was harder to hide with his face still in profile. "I'm sure you have a point there, Mr. Togen," he said, again affecting his fake Kyunjiu accent. "It's just hard to see with all of these buildings and people in the way."

Arkady tried to remember if Kentian had ever been to Thousand Leaves. The team hadn't been on a mission to Ridgecrescent since before Kentian had joined up. Before Sahasrara, had the wolf ever had the chance to see the world's largest city with his own eyes? Yet another detail of Kentian's life that had never come up in conversation. Arkady could probably check his file when he got home, but that wouldn't really *tell* him anything.

If the wolf had been here, what had he thought? Had he been awed and humbled by what was a physical manifestation of all that civilization was capable of when people worked together, or had he felt apart and alienated like Il-Hyeong now did?

"Well, let's get going, then," Arkady said, taking Il-Hyeong's paw in his own. "We've got ourselves a train to catch, and it's taking us away from all of this."

The fox tore himself away from his thinking and fell into step beside Arkady. Though they didn't continue to hold paws in the crowd, they did walk close to one another, and the ferret could feel that, even if the fox wasn't connected to the other seventy million people out there, the two of them were at least connected to each other.

In truth, the city of Highslope wasn't a huge change of pace from the metropolitan whirlwind of Thousand Leaves. It was nowhere near as large and sprawling as the capital, but it was still quite a bit larger and more hectic than even the largest cities in Deepwater. The train trip out to the western half of Ridgecrescent had been a pleasant escape from that uproar, but given the country's relatively small size, that escape had only lasted a couple of hours.

It was nightfall by the time the agents got there, and the bustle of the evening crowd had begun. They remained focused, however, heading directly to a downtown apartment rented out to one Miss Tokiko Akitoshi.

Ming-Jun greeted the fox and the ferret with a big, expectant smile. She still had a listening device hooked up into one of her large ears, though it didn't appear to be active. A skimpy sleeveless top, some type of undershirt that Arkady didn't know the name of, clung to the rabbit's torso. Below that she wore what looked like a pair of men's gym shorts; the ferret didn't dare wonder where she'd gotten them. "You guys made it," she called out happily, face awash with obvious relief as she ushered her fellow agents into the apartment before double-bolting the door behind them. "In one piece, even."

"That part is debatable," Il-Hyeong said, promptly falling down on a tiny patch of sofa that wasn't covered with scattered pieces of inoperative surveillance equipment. "I think I lost a fair part of myself just before landing in Song Kang."

"Oh, that part wasn't so bad," Arkady said, seating himself on a hassock that he wheeled into the uncluttered center of what appeared to have been the living room. "Taking off from Château Sainte-Mireille was far worse."

On the opposite wall, over the sofa, Arkady saw a Kyunjiu—no, Quanyao broadsword, a real one, hanging on display. He wondered why the rabbit would have brought such a decorative item to an apartment she'd only be living in for a week at most.

Ming-Jun took a seat at her desk and rested her chin in her paws, watching her two male comrades with bright, interested eyes. "So, what's it like?" she asked. "Other than nauseating, I mean."

"I'm not sure explaining it would really do it justice," Arkady said. "Dr. Mayflower had a questionnaire that she insisted on running through after the surgery, but at the time, I think I was still in so much disbelief that my answers probably didn't make any sense. I'm not sure they'd make sense *now*.""

"You know how if a radiator has been running for a long time, you don't notice it?" Il-Hyeong asked the rabbit. "But then it suddenly turns off, and then you can't help but notice it?" He waved a paw around at the room. "Imagine being unable to not notice things, all the time."

That was a strangely apt way to put it, Arkady thought. He suspected that the fox was still on the irritated side, but he'd hopefully get past that soon. They'd both agreed that the train ride was much smoother than either of the flights had been, and had induced barely any nausea at all, by comparison.

"And what about the memory module?" Ming-Jun asked. She tapped the side of her head.

"Haven't really had a chance to test it out, yet," Il-Hyeong said. "I don't think enough time has passed for things to have slipped that deep past the natural ability to recall them."

"Though they did say that they pre-installed them with the full text of Scripture," Arkady added.

Ming-Jun's eyes lit up. "Oh, really?" Her lips drew up into a mischievous smirk on her snout. "Book of Sirius, chapter twelve, verse thirty-two."

"*And the Wolf saw that size alone did not make his dogs superior to the ocelots,*" Arkady recited from the banks of that artificial memory, "*and with his men routed, he looked toward the sky and the moon, and he conceded that it was cleverness that had won the day for the Feline nation.*" It was one of many Scriptural verses that was cited in support of one of the Iolite Doctrine's chief tenets: that all species had their strengths and their weaknesses, and that it was in working with those differences, not against them, that people would find their way to harmony.

"No fair," Il-Hyeong said in chuckled protest. "Pick something from a book that Arkady hasn't already memorized." The ferret tried to kick the fox lightly in the shin, but he was too far away.

The rabbit visibly mulled things over for a few seconds, and she scratched at her ear where the listening device was situated. "Well, I have to admit, I was expecting you two to look a whole lot worse than you do," she said. "Guess the doc made good on her promise after all. Not quite sure how she did it, though."

"You're not the only one," Arkady replied. "So, what's the situation been like on your end?"

"You really want to go over that?" Ming-Jun asked with a chuckle. "You sure you wouldn't rather just get right to sleep and let me catch you up in the morning?"

Il-Hyeong started unlacing his boots. "As tired as I am, I don't think my brain is ready for sleep," the fox said. "I think that talking shop might be just the distraction my mind needs right now."

"All right, very well, then," Ming-Jun said, turning back around in her chair to face the computer terminal laid out on her desktop. "If you want to gather around the monitor, I can show what I have set up."

As she went about inputting commands into her program window, Ming-Jun started to hum under her breath. After only a couple of bars, Arkady recognized the tune as that of the song from the tape. Almost subconsciously, Arkady started humming along, keeping his own voice to himself, and it was with the contrast of his own humming with Ming-

Jun's that the ferret noticed that the rabbit was doing more than just keeping up the tune. She was mimicking the actual sounds—the would-be singing—from the song, and from what Arkady could remember, she was doing an okay job of it.

The monitor displayed a satellite map of the northwest section of Highslope. Overlaid atop the satellite imagery was a highly-contrasted grid that showed the major roadways, with more details filled in in the areas immediately around Fan-Yin Bioinformatics and the team's apartment. Ming-Jun pressed a button on the keyboard, and the less-detailed road map disappeared; at the same time, a series of red squares popped up, forming a loose hexagonal perimeter a few blocks around the Fan-Yin central building. The rabbit pointed to those and said, "This is where I've already wired up both cameras and listening devices. The neighborhood itself seems pretty tame, less busy than I was expecting, which is good for us."

"How does security look?" Arkady asked.

Ming-Jun tapped another key, and the map zoomed in on Fan-Yin. The satellite image went away and was replaced by a line schematic of the area. "It's a little tighter than it should be," the rabbit said, and a series of blue arrows started to trace paths around the main building. "I suspected that they'd probably stepped things up as a specific precaution, so I hacked my way into some not-strictly-public records, and sure enough, they just added to their security details earlier this week."

"Before or after you got to town?" Arkady asked.

"Before," the rabbit replied. "A couple of days earlier, just after the weekend. There's no listed reason as to why they hired additional security, but I don't think we need to do too much guesswork."

Hanging over her shoulder like he was, Arkady couldn't help but notice the rabbit's scent. She'd been hard at work setting up equipment for the last few hours, the ferret could tell, but it wasn't an unpleasant scent at all. His sense of professionalism kicked back in hard, then, and he physically shook his head to ward off the distracting thoughts inside of it.

"You think they know we're coming?" Il-Hyeong asked.

Ming-Jun shook her head, and the display zeroed in on one of the model patrols. "I don't see how they could," she said. "And while they've stepped up security, it's not to a degree that suggests they're expecting an elite covert ops mission."

The swift fox chuckled. "Maybe they just can't afford anything better."

"That'd be nice, wouldn't it?" the rabbit said with a smile. "But no, I think we're safe. From what I can tell, the company is planning on making a 'big announcement' soon, and the industry is looking at them pretty closely. I think we've just landed square in the middle of legitimate business."

"So should we still strike now?" Arkady asked, making mental notes about the locations and markings on Ming-Jun's security map. "Or do we wait for this announcement to happen first?"

"Well, 'soon' could mean tomorrow, or it could mean halfway through next week," Ming-Jun said. "So not only would waiting be inadvisable, but I honestly don't think that breaking in there and getting what we need is going to be much of an issue, even with all the increased security."

Arkady stood up and looked around the room as he paced. They certainly had a lot of equipment at their disposal, and if there was ever a time to use it, the window to grab the Pyxis Sequence was it. "All right," the ferret announced, turning back around to face the fox and the rabbit. "We'll take one more day to scope out the area, first. Il-Hyeong and I will case the area to familiarize ourselves with it on foot. Ming-Jun, I want you to keep checking the records for anything else related to this upcoming announcement or about this new security detail. If nothing crops up by late evening, I want to hit them tomorrow night."

Il-Hyeong's shoulders straightened out, and his tail went still. "Works for me," he says. "The sooner we finish up and get the hell out of here, the better."

The ferret turned to Ming-Jun. "Is that enough time for you to finish what you need to do?" he asked her.

"Of course," she replied. "I've had a few days' lead time already; there are a few more places I want to poke, and a few more trackers that I want to set in place, but nothing that will take longer than the rest of tonight and tomorrow."

"Speaking of tomorrow," Il-Hyeong then began. He stood up, and the too-clear sound of his joints cracking and popping made Arkady wince. "I'm still absolutely exhausted because the last good sleep I had was when I was drugged into unconsciousness. Ming, do you mind if I set up some of your sound dampers in the other room?"

The rabbit blinked, and Arkady thought she looked slightly offended. "That's mission equipment, Il-Hyeong," she said, sounding like a schoolteacher pointing out classroom rules to a student. Sometimes, even Arkady forgot that he and his team were older than they looked.

"My being well-rested is crucial to this mission," the fox pointed out, smirking. "Besides, it's not like you're going to need them until tomorrow, anyway—if you even need them at all—so what's the harm?"

Ming-Jun sighed and shook her head. "Fine," she said, typing a few keystrokes to turn off her security display of Fan-Yin. "But you're on your own setting them up. I've been wiring things up all day long, and I am *done*."

The fox headed over to Ming-Jun's pile of high-tech goodies and started to rummage. "Fine by me," he said. "So long as you don't try to disconnect them before I've woken up."

As she was pulling out a pair of pants from a still mostly-unpacked garment bag, Ming-Jun stopped and looked back at the fox. "You're setting them up right now? Don't you at least want to get dinner first?"

"I'm not sure how hungry I am," Il-Hyeong replied, finding the first unit in the set of sound dampers he was looking for.

"Yeah, but who knows when the next time we'll be able to come back to Ridgecrescent is?" the rabbit pointed out, slinging the pants over one shoulder. "Let's take in some of the local color while we can."

Il-Hyeong didn't take his attention away from his task at hand. "Just go on ahead without me," he said, checking the underside of the unit. "I'll be fine here. I really just need sleep more than anything else."

Before Ming-Jun could protest the fox's unwillingness further, Arkady brushed a paw against one of hers. "It's okay," he said. "He's not up for it. If he needs his sleep, he needs his sleep."

The rabbit looked up at the ferret, and she wrinkled her nose a little. "He'll be fine," Arkady said more quietly, though still within definite range of the fox's improved hearing. "It's safe here. Let's just you and I grab dinner before the good restaurants all close, shall we, Tokiko?"

With a chuckle, Ming-Jun tapped Arkady on the nose. "Why, Mr. Togen, I'd be delighted to. Let's go see what this lovely city has to offer, then, shall we?"

Arkady exchanged another glance with Il-Hyeong, but the fox just nodded and picked up another sound damper unit.

Ming-Jun had left Arkady alone with Il-Hyeong when she went to go get changed, but the fox and the ferret had not said anything further to each other. Nor had there been the need, really. Arkady empathized with his comrade's difficulties in adjusting; it wasn't exactly easy on him, either, but unlike the fox, he *was* hungry.

After the rabbit had come back into the living room, the other two agents remained similarly speechless. Arkady had no idea where Ming-Jun had gotten the flowing, sky blue silk top that looked like a cross between a tailed jacket and a vest ("These are all the rage in Jung Sim Weon right now," she'd insisted), but it somehow managed to bring out her more feminine features to an almost startling degree despite not being all that girly a garment. It definitely made her stand out, and not just due to the more sober fashion standards of western Ridgecrescent, that was for sure.

Arkady felt underdressed next to her, but since he hadn't packed formalwear in with his mission gear, he had to settle for a simple black and tan ensemble with a collared shirt and long pants. Il-Hyeong had probably packed something slightly nicer for himself, just in case, but the fox's body type was all wrong for Arkady to be borrowing clothes from him. The ferret decided not to fret over it, though, and he knew that the looks that he and Ming-Jun got from the people of Highslope had more to do with the rabbit herself than any sort of mismatch in clothing between the two of them.

Since Ming-Jun had already thoroughly mapped the area around her apartment (in her head as well as in her surveillance system), she had a few restaurant ideas in mind already. At Arkady's insistence, they'd stopped at one of the more mid-range choices, an unassuming but acceptable eatery called North Point that overlooked the wide river that separated Highslope from its twin city, Holygate. He let Ming-Jun sit facing the wide window that actually faced the river, and he just scoped out the restaurant's interior, seeing little that concerned him from a professional, mission-related standpoint.

Over her entrée salad, Ming-Jun stared wistfully out at the river, over Arkady's shoulder. She kept up her part of the conversation, at least, keeping the ferret filled in on what her last couple of days setting up in Highslope had been like, and assuring him that even without Kentian as backup, she'd not had too difficult a time in getting her job done in preparation for her teammates. "Compared to Shambhala, the overall security in the area is almost laughable," she insisted, but Arkady was sure that the job wasn't as easy as all that.

"Are you okay with our timetable?" Arkady asked, washing down a mouthful of food with a big sip of beer before inspecting the drink's rich, amber color in the faint light of the restaurant. "I know you haven't gotten to see exactly what Il-Hyeong and I are now capable of, and I want to know if you question our competence."

"Your competence? Never," Ming-Jun said, setting her fork and knife down. "The uncertainty factor has me a little wary, but if anyone can do this job, it's the three of us."

The three of us. It hadn't been "the three of them" in years. It felt weird to think that the three of them even constituted a full team. Arkady and Il-Hyeong were, at least in theory, now worth more than ordinary agents, but despite what strict resource management directives might say, their team still wasn't "whole" in its current state—not to Arkady's point of view. Ming-Jun still professed her confidence in their abilities, and so the ferret wasn't going to call that into question. Not at the risk of demoralizing her.

"Let's change the subject, then," Arkady suggested. "Let me ask you a question."

Ming-Jun nodded while swallowing back a mouthful of ice water. "Of course."

"What does '*yī qī yī huì*' mean?"

The rabbit nearly choked on her next sip of water, coughing and sputtering for a few seconds before the look on her face darkened. At first, her expression was one of utter shock, but it soon shifted over to something approaching anger for just a moment before she tried to mask that, as well. "Excuse me?" she asked.

Her reaction—and the intensity of it—both surprised and unsettled Arkady. "I'm just curious," he asked. "I mean, if you even know. But you sing along with it like you know what it's supposed to mean."

"I don't know what you're talking about," Ming-Jun said. One of her paws reached for her fork, dropping it immediately after picking it up, her eyes never even looking toward it.

The ferret reached out to take that paw, but she yanked it back and hid it under the table. "Hey, look, I'm not accusing you of anything," Arkady said. "I honestly just want to know." If she really did know more about those sounds from the tape, those syllables that came so close to sounding like words, he didn't just want to know, he *needed* to know.

"Arkady, please, I swear to God, I had never heard that song before we first listened to it together," the rabbit said. Her eyes flicked past both of Arkady's shoulders in turn, as if seeking potential escape routes. "And I agree with you, it's a beautiful song, and it's just... it's just been stuck in my head, and that's all."

Yī qī yī huì was the part of the song where Arkady had noticed Ming-Jun's voice crack subtly. It was only because of that distinct vocalization that the ferret had managed to pick out the sounds and memorize them at all. "I'm not saying you necessarily knew the song before you heard it," he said. "But that still doesn't—"

"Arkady, please," Ming-Jun repeated, both her palms hitting flat against the table as she got halfway out of her chair. "Not here. Not now."

The ferret remained seated. He found himself fascinated that Ming-Jun was reacting the way she was. When he'd asked, he'd been expecting her to say something about how she was just repeating the sounds as she heard them—and really, even if that had been a lie, it would have been the obvious lie to tell to cover her tracks. For her to be getting so defensive *meant* something, but instead of Arkady feeling betrayed or upset or even confused that Ming-Jun could possibly be keeping such a secret from him, he was excited and intrigued.

"Okay, so not here and now," he agreed. "Is there a time and place that would work better for you?"

Ignoring Arkady's words, Ming-Jun finished getting up and stormed out of the restaurant. Though she hadn't been particularly loud in her altercation with Arkady, it looked as though the entire restaurant now had their eyes on her as she made a line for the front door. Perhaps her exotic clothing was the cause of more undue attention after all. Arkady turned around in his chair but still didn't get up until the rabbit was almost to the door.

Once Ming-Jun had actually slipped outside, Arkady finally got up to follow, leaving a wad of Ridgecrescent dees that would more than cover the cost of the half-eaten meal. The crowd of diners seemed less interested in the spectacle, now, and so the ferret had a clear path to the door. Outside, Ming-Jun was tromping off in a direction that wasn't back toward the apartment.

Arkady opened his mouth to shout after her, but caught himself before inadvertently blurting her real name out at the top of his lungs. "Tokiko, wait up!" he called out to her. She wasn't running, so he only needed to maintain a brisk jog in order to catch up to her. She made no attempt to outpace him, but she did make him catch up to her.

"We're here in this country to do a job," the rabbit said without turning to look at him. "Let's focus on that first, all right?"

Arkady considered grabbing for her paw again but decided against it. "I fully plan to." He slowed so that his strides matched hers. "And I promise not to interrogate you, either. I just want to know one thing."

Abruptly, Ming-Jun came to a stop. The tail-like flaps of her top fluttered slowly in the nighttime breeze. Her eyes fixed on Arkady's face, and they were cold and distant. The ferret was suddenly less excited and intrigued. "I already told you, we can't do this. Not here."

"Is this going to have any effect on the mission?"

"Of course not. Don't be ridiculous."

"You don't need to tell me what it means," Arkady said, and at that, Ming-Jun started to walk away again. "I just need to know if it means *something*."

Ming-Jun was silent and continued to pace along, but a few steps later, she stopped and turned back around. "Yes," she called back. She almost sounded like she was in pain, like she'd just taken a strong blow to the chest. "Yes, it does."

With Arkady staying put, Ming-Jun resumed walking down the street, away from him. If she needed to blow off some steam, then Arkady was willing to let her go and do that now, rather than have it become a problem during the infiltration. She knew the area better than he did, after all, and he knew that she'd find her way back eventually.

Arkady took a circuitous route back to base, sticking to side roads that led back to the main thoroughfares between North Point and Ms. Akitoshi's apartment. He didn't seriously think he was being followed, but it paid to stick to procedure. Out in the hallway, there were no fresh traces of either Ming-Jun's scent or of the light perfume she'd worn out to dinner, so he wasn't surprised when he opened the front door and found the main room vacant and the rabbit's computer station empty.

She'd come back, he knew. If nothing else, Ming-Jun was devoted to the mission and to the Iolite League. If she really was keeping secrets from Sahasrara that were important to the scope of Project Scheherazade, then he'd make sure that she wasn't going to keep them for long. He had meant it when he'd told her that he didn't plan to interrogate her, and so he hoped that it wouldn't come down to having someone with more authority in the organization doing it in his stead.

How can she know? How can she possibly know? Where could she have possibly run across anything like that before?

The ferret sighed, and he was about to let his weight drop onto the sofa when the door to the bedroom suddenly flew open. His accelerated reflexes kicked in, and he dropped to the floor and went into a roll, catching the silhouette in the doorway out of the corner of his eye. The familiar shape of a gun was visible through the shadows, and while still crouched low against the floor, the ferret reached under his pants leg and pulled out his single-shot backup pistol.

Before Arkady had his gun up to bear, though, a rough voice barked out, "Drop it!" Almost without conscious thought, Arkady kept hold of his gun and aimed, instinct telling him that his augmented body would be quicker, and that he'd get his shot off before the invader did. He sighted along the short barrel of the pistol and aimed right for his target's head, and then dropped the weapon with a start when he saw that it was Il-Hyeong.

"God in Heaven, you scared me out of my wits," Arkady gasped, coming just short of yelling at the fox, who was still holding up his gun. There was nervousness on the vulpine's face, though, and his paws and arms shook for several seconds before he, too, let his gun down.

"Oh, God, sorry, Arkady. Sorry." Il-Hyeong slouched slowly into the room, stuffing his DKR-7 into the back of his pants after switching the safety back on. "I heard the door open and I... I could smell you, but I just... I didn't recognize your scent."

Arkady could smell Il-Hyeong from where he was, and he could tell that the fox was scared and on alert, but he still smelled like Il-Hyeong. Well, mostly. It wasn't quite the same as he remembered it, or thought he remembered it, but then, it wasn't as if his sense of smell hadn't been muddled up beyond reason over the last few days. Perhaps to a fox, the difference was even more distinct, to the point of affecting recognizability?

"Well, I appreciate your warning before shooting," Arkady said, clambering to his feet, then dusting himself off. He dropped his tiny pistol onto an end table and went back to the couch where he'd been about to sit before, sinking into it and letting out his tensely-held breath.

Behind the couch, Il-Hyeong continued to hover. Arkady could hear the fox's breathing, restless and shallow. "Where's Ming?" he asked. His bare feet padded against the floor as he paced.

"Out clearing her head," the ferret replied. *Probably something we could all do right now, it seems.*

"Ah," the fox replied noncommittally. He drifted over to the side of the couch, and he looked like he wanted to sit down, but he kept standing, awkwardly. "Think we need to call things off?"

Arkady looked up. "Call what off?"

"You know," Il-Hyeong said. "The mission."

"Don't be ridiculous," the ferret said. "Why would we do that?"

Il-Hyeong motioned around the room with an empty paw. "Look at us," he said. "Ming's off God knows where, I almost just shot you, and if either of us gets any sleep tonight, it'll be a miracle."

"It's not as bad as all that," Arkady insisted. "Ming-Jun's just going for a walk. She'll be back here any minute." He hoped that those words didn't sound like a complete lie. "Trust me, if I thought that she wasn't capable of handling her duties, I wouldn't let her stay on the mission."

"And what about me?"

"I wouldn't send you out into the field if I didn't think you were fit for duty, either."

The fox sniffed out through his nose, the tone of it bitter and harsh. "And maybe we'll just feel better in the morning?" he asked.

"I know you, Il-Hyeong," Arkady said, standing up and walking toward the unadorned, barely-furnished kitchenette. He turned on the tap at the sink and started to pour himself a glass of cold water. "And I know that if I *did* tell you that you were to stay behind while I went on to Fan-Yin by myself, you'd stay behind."

"True. But I'd also try to convince you to stay behind as well," the fox said.

Arkady drained half of the glass with a single swallow, then wiped the back of his paw on his mouth. "It's not going to come down to that, though," he said. "Because I know that despite all of this... this second-guessing that you're doing, when it comes down to staring duty in the eye, you'll be able to pull it together. You're a professional, and I've never seen you not come through for me or for anyone else on this team." *And you were the one who still at least tried to save Kentian after I'd left him for dead*, he added to himself.

Pulling the gun from the back of his pants, Il-Hyeong held it up and then released the magazine, letting it fall into his other paw. "Let's just make sure I don't shoot Ming when *she* comes in, first," he said. "Because without her, there isn't going to be a mission."

"Stop being so overdramatic," Arkady rasped as he finished off his water on his second sip. It really did taste awfully of chemicals and impurities, as Il-Hyeong had mentioned before, but it was only now that the ferret could fully appreciate it. Could he order the fox to stop the histrionics?

Il-Hyeong's ears skewed to either side. "If you want to treat me like a professional, then you need to take me seriously," he said. He sounded mad, but composed, and Arkady felt a tinge of guilt over the fact that he was slightly relieved that the fox's anger was at least keeping him from falling apart.

"I am taking you seriously," the ferret replied. "And that's exactly why I'm not ordering you to shut up and get to bed. I know you're having problems, and I know all three of us are beyond scared that we'll screw this job up, at this point, but we're *better* than this."

"Is that why Ming's out there on the streets instead of sitting there at her security console where she belongs?" the fox asked as Arkady walked past.

The ferret stopped in his tracks. "Agent Devra is away from her post because I'm allowing it," he snapped. "In the meantime, if you're that concerned about her security console—and seeing as you're so keen to point out that you can't sleep—you're free to cover for her until she gets back."

"That's not what this is about and you know it," Il-Hyeong retorted.

"It's not?" the ferret said. "Then stop trying to tell me and Ming-Jun how to do our jobs and concentrate on doing your own."

Arkady turned and started off toward the bedroom, then. "I'm *trying*, Arkady," the fox pleaded. "But something's not right about this, and I know you're sensing it, too."

When he got to the door, the ferret braced himself against the door frame and looked back over his shoulder. "If something is wrong, then that just means we need to be extra careful, doesn't it?"

There was no further comeback from Il-Hyeong, and so Arkady slipped into the bedroom. He set up the small sleeping bag he'd brought with him and got cozy on the floor next to the bed where Ming-Jun would be sleeping. For a long time, he lay awake, staring at the ceiling, able to analyze the grooves and patterns in the plaster even in the near-total darkness.

Through the walls—whether because they were flimsy or because his ears were just that good now—Arkady could hear Il-Hyeong typing away at Ming-Jun's computer station. He doubted that the fox was really all that keen to do the rabbit's job so much as he was just loath to lie in the quiet, awkward darkness with the ferret. Even so, the soft clacking of keys continued for a good while, and so Arkady contented himself with knowing that the fox was at least channeling his frustration into his work.

Ming-Jun still hadn't returned to the apartment by the time that Arkady finally fell asleep close to an hour later.

8. Tinderbox

"West entrance is clear." Il-Hyeong's voice cracked softly as it came in through Arkady's earpiece, mixed with wind. "Area appears normal."

Arkady peered through his binoculars and zeroed in on the south entrance. There was a lone security guard, who looked to be a bear from this distance, slouched against the wall with all the pride and alertness of a bored rent-a-cop. "South entrance shows one mark," the ferret said into his transceiver.

"Plans call for two," the fox replied.

"Probably in taking a leak," Arkady said. "We'll give him five. Even if he does show up, these guys don't look like much to worry about."

The wind died down enough for Il-Hyeong's quiet chuckle to register in his microphone. "How wonderful the job market in Ridgecrescent must be if people are so eager to take positions like this," he said.

"Ming-Jun, how does traffic look?" Arkady asked. He set down his binoculars and scanned his surroundings with the naked eye from his perch atop a small office building. Even in a commercial district like this, many of the buildings of Highslope were still lit up even though it was after midnight. Sounds of activity still drifted up from below, too, even if they were muted compared to daytime. Fan-Yin Bioinformatics, though, was nicely lifeless save for the two security guards Arkady and Il-Hyeong were tracking.

The rabbit took a moment to respond. "Pretty typical for this time of night," she replied. "There's some construction about a mile north of your position, but it's nothing that should affect any escape routes."

Ming-Jun had come back during the night, while Arkady was asleep and while Il-Hyeong was still awake at the computer station. Earlier that day, they'd all been cordial enough with one another, if perhaps a bit more professional and businesslike than usual. Now that the time to strike at their target had come, though, the ferret was calm with relief, sensing no residual ill will between his teammates that might jeopardize the mission.

"Patrol has rounded north side of the building," Il-Hyeong reported. "Looks just as bored as before, too." Arkady checked his watch again. That kept the average time for the patrol to walk around all four sides of the building at just over seventeen minutes. Fan-Yin's stepped-up security really didn't amount to much more than a token show.

"All right," Arkady said. "If the second guard hasn't come back to the south entrance by the time the patrol next rounds the southeast corner, we take the west entrance." As he was saying that, the first guard lit up a cigarette. The ferret just smiled and shook his head.

"I'm activating the visual feed, now," Il-Hyeong announced. "Ming, is that coming through on your end?"

"Crystal clear," Ming-Jun replied. "Well, not crystal, but static is at a minimum and the motion blur isn't too bad. Arkady, go ahead and switch yours on for me." As directed, the ferret reached up and flicked the tiny switch on the back curve of the earpiece, activating the tiny camera that was built onto the earpiece frame. "Good," the rabbit said. "Little to no interference that I'm detecting so far. What's your time to ground?"

Arkady was already walking toward the fire escape. "About two minutes from here to the ground, and another four to clear the area between here and the Fan-Yin perimeter."

"I'm at about three and three," Il-Hyeong said. "I'll reconfirm visual on the patrol once I've got my feet on the ground, and that'll determine which side we sync up on."

"Roger that," Arkady said. "Ming-Jun, keep this channel open just in case anything on the network happens and you need to fill us in."

"Already on it," Ming-Jun said. Arkady heard typing on the other end. "Network seems pretty dead, but better safe than sorry."

With those assurances, Arkady began his descent. His footwear was padded with soft, flexible soles that muffled his footsteps while still allowing for his feet to bend. Although he wasn't particularly worried about alerting anyone inside this insignificant office building (which, as far as he could tell, was empty at this time of night anyway), he'd be running a lot faster once he got into the Fan-Yin facility. For now, he had the luxury of a few minutes' time, and so he used it to make sure he stayed quiet, just on the off-chance that some random passerby happened to spot him and called the police to report a prowler.

There was a soft whine inside Arkady's ear as the electronics came to life again. "Hey, Arkady." It was Ming-Jun. "I've got you on an isolated channel, here."

By now, Arkady was still just under halfway down the side of the building. "Is everything all right?" Ming-Jun didn't sound particularly worried, which made the ferret all the more curious.

"Look, about last night," the rabbit said. Arkady came to a stop partway down one of the miniature flights of stairs. "I didn't mean to be so... so unprofessional. I just..." While she hesitated, Arkady remained still on his steps. "It's called *Zhōngwén*."

The tonality of Ming-Jun's voice changed entirely when she said the strange word. The first half of it was high and steady, and the second half started at a lower pitch, but then rose higher. "What's called that?" he asked. He played with the sound in his mind. It was intriguingly alien.

"That's the name of the language from the tape and the books," the rabbit said. "*Zhōngwén*," she repeated, and indeed, the tonal quality of the word resembled that of the singing that had so captivated Arkady.

"What do you mean, 'language?'" Arkady said as he resumed his climb down the fire escape. "It doesn't sound or look anything *like* Language."

"That because it's not the same Language. It's another language."

Arkady actually chuckled. "Now you're being silly," he chided. "How can there be another language aside from Language?"

"You've heard it yourself," Ming-Jun said. "You've seen the writing with your own eyes. It's still all words—it's just an entirely different set of words, that's all."

After he dropped down to the next landing on the fire escape, the ferret stopped again. He scanned the alleyway below, but there was no movement in the shadows, no sound other than the noise of late-night traffic a few blocks away. "So, what, someone went through the trouble to come up with a code for every single word we have?" he asked the rabbit.

"No, I didn't say that at all," Ming-Jun said. There were traces of exasperation in her voice, but Arkady could tell that she was earnestly trying to get him to understand. "It's not 'Language' like you or most people know it at all." She paused as if to let the magnitude of that statement sink in. "It's completely different. Completely separate."

Recalling the myriad of symbols from the books they'd reclaimed in Shambhala, Arkady wondered what made more sense: the unbelievable idea that someone came up with a code so astronomically elaborate, or the idea that a whole other 'language' existed beyond the one that everyone else spoke. "So where did this 'Zhongwen' come from?" Arkady asked, now just a few stories from the alley.

"You're not saying it right," Ming-Jun said, and Arkady swore that he heard a chuckle that she'd tried hard to disguise. "*Zhōngwén*. The tones are important. And it's been around at least as long as history has.

We don't know where it 'came from' any more than we know where much else originally came from."

Someday that will change. It'll change through the success of Project Scheherazade.

"Who's this 'we,' then?" Arkady asked. He looked down past the railing of the final landing. There was a drop of about eight feet, but the ferret would be able to make it easily.

A sigh came in through the earpiece. "Look, it's... complicated," Ming-Jun said. "I need to have a talk with you—off the record—before we head back to the Château."

"Of course," Arkady said, and to stanch his violent curiosity for at least a moment, he swung down onto the tiny ladder beneath him and then dropped down onto the ground below. His feet hit the pavement flat and even, and with his superior sense of balance, he managed to let his legs buckle just enough to avoid any painful shock upon impact. "Although I do have to say, if any of this goes counter to the League's—"

"Arkady, just promise me that we can talk about this off the record, first," Ming-Jun interrupted. "After we're done with Fan-Yin. Please."

If what Ming-Jun was saying was true—and it was a bit too far out there to believe that she could possibly be making all of it up—then that meant that she might be the best key to deciphering what was in those books they'd reclaimed in Tomosabaki. It could mean the biggest pre-civ breakthrough of all time. Surely, Arkady could bend the rules a little for that, couldn't he? After all, it *was* Ming-Jun, and...

Think about how much we'd have to teach Pandora. Think of all the wonderful mysteries of the world that she'll be privy to once we unlock this portal to our lost past. That's what we're here for.

"I promise," the ferret said.

"And please, don't tell Il-Hyeong anything about this, either," Ming-Jun said. "Not until after I've had the chance to talk to you, first."

"I promise that, too," Arkady said. He wasn't sure that the scientifically-minded Il-Hyeong would even be willing to believe something so crazy without empirical proof.

The other end of the line was quiet for several seconds, and in the meantime, Arkady checked and double-checked the equipment he had on his person before he started to head down along the alley in the direction of the Fan-Yin facility. "Thank you, Arkady," Ming-Jun said, then. "And I see you're approaching the street."

"Check on Il-Hyeong for me," he said. "I want to know where I'm headed."

"I'll re-open full communications in just a moment," the rabbit said softly. "And Arkady?"

"Yes?"

"*Zhù nǐ hǎo yùn*," Ming-Jun said. "That means 'good luck.'"

Another electronic whine sounded in Arkady's ear, and with that, he was able to hear Il-Hyeong's breathing on the other end. It sounded like the fox was still making his way down to the street on his front, and so Arkady broke into a light jog, clearing the dimly-lit section of concrete between the building he'd been spying from and the likewise nondescript office building across the way.

Zhōngwén. Yī qī yī huì. Zhù nǐ hǎo yùn. Words that were not Language, and yet which conveyed meaning all the same. Could the Iolite League really have missed something like that?

The scents and sounds of the city were still overwhelming, even at night. Years of automobile exhaust had imbued a permanent stink into pavement; industrial contaminants from the river were carried in on the breeze; from every angle came the sounds of automobiles, of a distant nightclub, of vermin crawling through trash in the alleyways.

If he concentrated on the task at hand, though (*focus on the mission—the mission, not the song and the books*), Arkady could block out most of the sensory assault. Several blocks remained between his present location and the Fan-Yin perimeter, but he had more than enough time to get into position before he and Il-Hyeong checked back with one another again.

"Police rotorcopter incoming from the north," Ming-Jun called out. "Il-Hyeong, it should buzz you a few hundred yards to your northwest. Hold your current position."

Il-Hyeong acknowledged quickly. Arkady looked up, but there were too many buildings in the way to get a visual on the rotorcopter in question, and the way that so many other sounds echoed off of walls to reach his oversensitive ears made it impossible to make out any distant aircraft. He made the decision to keep moving, and Ming-Jun said nothing to get him to stop. When the ferret reached the next street corner, though, he stopped and brought his paw to his ear. "All clear?" he asked.

"Just about," Il-Hyeong replied. Behind his voice, Arkady could make out the dull sound of the 'copter's whirling blades through the communication link. "Seems to be sweeping toward downtown, away from the industrial district. Just a standard patrol would be my guess."

"There's nothing on any of the police channels," Ming-Jun confirmed. "Go ahead and keep moving, Il-Hyeong."

Arkady peered around the corner of the building and looked down the street. He had a decent line of sight to the Fan-Yin building, now, but he couldn't clearly see the south entrance to see whether the second guard had returned yet or not. He jogged further down the street, but still the entrance did not come into view. No matter. Il-Hyeong still had a few seconds of lost time to make up for, and a quick glance at his wristwatch told the ferret that he was still well within the four minutes he'd budgeted himself to get into position.

The comm channel was all silence while Arkady finished making his way to the perimeter. A second guard had indeed rejoined the first, he saw, but at his current distance, he couldn't tell what species it was. He didn't dare pull his binoculars out, either, where he stood a much greater chance of being seen. Besides, if all went as planned, it wouldn't matter what species the guards were.

"Two marks at the south entrance," the ferret said into his microphone. "Il-Hyeong, do you have visual on the patrol?"

"Coming down the west face of the facility," the fox replied. "Proceeding at his nice, lazy pace. Doesn't seem to be doing much of anything. Barely even waving his flashlight."

It was ironic that the key to such a groundbreaking scientific breakthrough lay within the walls of a building so casually defended. Then again, Arkady reminded himself, the world of Sahasrara was a world that lay beneath the surface, a world that the people with the power and authority could keep out of sight from the masses simply by never drawing attention to it, since nobody knew enough to bother looking.

Almost nobody, Arkady said to himself. He closed his eyes and envisioned Pandora, living in a world outside of that prison of a tube, her eyes open, a smile on her muzzle. Someday very soon, now, the people of the world would be one step closer to knowing some of those truths that lay hidden beneath their feet—once they were ready, and the people of Sahasrara would work in secret to ensure that they were ready.

"Okay, Arkady, I'm going to rendezvous with you at the southern edge," Il-Hyeong said as the guard on patrol wandered around the corner into Arkady's field of vision.

"Roger that," the ferret said. "As soon as the patrol drops out of sight again, we make for the entrance." Silence again, then. Arkady went over his equipment again as thoroughly as he could without drawing undue attention to himself. It was only a matter of minutes, now.

From off to Arkady's left, Il-Hyeong appeared from the shadows. He waved a paw, and it was very jarring to see him at a distance yet hear his voice so close up through the earpiece: "I see you now. Any change in status?"

"None visible," Arkady reported, taking another glance over toward the lazy guards. "Looks like getting into the building really is going to be the least of our worries."

"Just like the plan," Il-Hyeong reported, snickering under his breath. "Just like *any* of our plans, really." Arkady shared in the laugh, then.

For the next couple minutes, the fox and the ferret watched as the third guard wandered around the southeast corner and disappeared into the shadows, the faint beam of his flashlight pointing away from them. Arkady and Il-Hyeong exchanged looks, and then Arkady spoke into his microphone again. "Everything clear on your end, Ming-Jun?"

"You are good to go, boys," the rabbit responded. "Now go find us the grand prize." Il-Hyeong's slender snout broke out into a triumphant grin, and Arkady waved over to the fox, motioning for him to follow.

The two agents came together, and were halfway across the Fan-Yin Bioinformatics parking lot before either of the guards even bothered to look up and notice them. The one on the left—the bear that Arkady had spied from the building earlier—lifted his head and drew up to his full height. The approaching agents were still only at hollering distance, and so Arkady held one arm up high and waved a paw, acknowledging the guard's attention.

The other guard looked up, then, too; he was some type of grayish feline, but Arkady couldn't quite tell what type from this distance. The ferret broke into a slight trot, with Il-Hyeong in step aside and behind him. Though it was impossible to discern facial expressions from so far away, body language told Arkady that the two guards were confused, but probably too happy at having their boredom disrupted to be very worried.

"Hey!" the ferret called out as he got closer. "Either of you guys got the access card for the building?" He laid on the Kyunjiu accent nice and thick.

"Who the heck are you?" the bear asked. He had tried to force some gruffness into his voice, but as far as Arkady was concerned, he failed rather miserably.

Arkady stuck one of his paws into his pants pocket and began fishing around. "My name's Sam Togen," he said, and with his other paw, he motioned toward the building. "I work here. I just need to swing on up to my lab and grab my laptop. Left it here earlier."

The bear looked fully unconvinced, and he exchanged reaffirming glances with his feline partner. "Uh-huh," the guard said, nodding noncommittally. "And where's your own access card, Mr. Togen?"

Flattening his ears, Arkady turned around and flashed a guilty look at Il-Hyeong before facing the security guards again. "Aw, come on," the ferret said, waving a paw and flicking his tail. "Me and my buddy here were just... y'know, checking out the town tonight, and I just want to run upstairs before catching the tube back to Holygate."

"You don't sound like you're from around here," the bear asked. "Where are you from, if I may ask?"

"What, you mean, like, originally?" Arkady asked. The cat was starting to step in closer, too. "I'm from Chochi-Sankeng. Well, okay, so if you want to get technical, I'm *originally* from this small town outside of Lo Hu called—"

"Can I see some I.D., sir?" the bear said, gruffly clearing his throat. He was close enough now that Arkady could smell that he was as lazy with his hygiene as he was when it came to standing by the door.

Arkady muttered to himself as his paws fished through his pants pockets, going through the front left and rear left before dipping into the front right, where he actually kept his wallet. "Here you are," he said, fumbling with the wallet as he moved to flash his fake identification card.

While the bear was leaned in to look at it, Arkady saw Il-Hyeong move as a flash in his peripheral vision. The swift fox pulled out a tiny syringe from his back pocket, then jumped for the cat. In less then a second, he had the feline in a headlock, the syringe already sinking into the side of his neck.

As the bear started to turn toward his fellow guard, Arkady dropped his wallet and snatched him by the wrist. In the time it took the bear to let out a growl of shock and alarm, Arkady had pulled out a syringe of his own, which he jabbed hard into the bear's thick forearm. As he pressed the plunger to inject the bear full of the syringe's contents, Arkady saw Il-Hyeong release the cat, who then crumpled to the ground in a limp, motionless heap. Moments later, the bear collapsed as well.

Arkady knelt down to inspect the guards, picking up his wallet in the process. He checked the bear's pulse at his throat. The syringes' payload was small, but it would keep the guards unconscious for a few hours at the very least. The ferret plucked up both empty syringes, set them alongside one another on the pavement, then ground them both up under his foot.

"You know, if there's one thing to come out of the Butterfly Islands War," Il-Hyeong said as he helped Arkady back to his feet, "it's that playing the 'stupid foreigner' card is actually a viable tactic here in Ridgecrescent." The ferret didn't find the subject in question one warranting humor, though, and so he frowned in disapproval before dusting off his paws on the sides of his pants.

"Nice headlock," he said to Il-Hyeong as the fox reached into the back of his pants to draw his DKR-7. "Now for the hard part." The ferret drew his own Cordellatech Zarna and approached the card reader by the door. "Ming-Jun, do you have the access code ready?"

"Sure do," the rabbit responded. Arkady reached into his rear pocket and pulled out the mocked-up access card that Ming-Jun had made and swiped it through the slot on the reader. The red light on the device turned to amber, and then, after Arkady punched in the code as Ming-Jun read it off, it changed to green.

Il-Hyeong's ears perked at the sound of the door's mechanized lock clicking open, and holding his gun up, he grabbed the door handle with his free paw and pulled it open. The door itself was made of glass, but the fox remained vigilant and cautious nonetheless, in case some new danger were to make itself known. "Clear," he said, bracing the door open with his foot, allowing Arkady to take point.

The main corridor led to the reception desk, empty at this time of night, the display monitors behind it—doubtlessly used to show a repeating reel of company info—turned off. The lobby wasn't terribly spacious, but it branched off into two hallways that went off to the left and right behind the reception desk. Arkady had memorized the floor plan beforehand, and so he was already taking the path to the right when Ming-Jun told him to do so.

Beyond the next door lay various offices belonging to the senior scientist staff, and in that area, there was a decent chance that there would also be one or two members of the internal security team. It would still be a few minutes before the patrol guard outside discovered his colleagues' unconscious bodies by the front entrance, and so Arkady and Il-Hyeong could avoid immediate suspicion if they ran into another guard on the inside—for at least long enough to incapacitate him, as well. By the time the alarm was raised, the two agents would hopefully have made their way up to the third floor, where the genetics laboratories were located.

After opening that door, however, Arkady breathed a sigh of relief, seeing the area empty. He paused to listen, but heard no approaching footsteps, either, and so he motioned with a paw for Il-Hyeong to follow as he pattered quickly down the next hallway, heading for the stairwell at the far end.

"Stop," Il-Hyeong whispered to Arkady as he scooted up alongside him. "Listen."

Stopping and listening again, Arkady shook his head. "Is someone coming? I don't hear anything," he said, knowing Il-Hyeong's hearing was still better than his.

"Exactly," the fox replied. "I don't hear anyone moving around upstairs, either."

Arkady looked up toward the ceiling, almost as if he'd been expecting he'd be able to see through it. "So?" he asked. "Maybe the guards are just standing post like the ones outside. We're not exactly dealing with the cream of the crop, here."

Il-Hyeong hummed, shut his eyes for a second, and then started walking again. "All right. I still don't like this, though."

Was it really all too easy, though? Arkady had to wonder. Government installations and high-class private establishments were in a completely different league than a standard, run-of-the-mill biotech company office. The prize might have been something extraordinary, but that didn't change the fact that the place they were breaking into wasn't someplace that would boast top-notch infiltration countermeasures.

The stairwell was chilly. Sound would have echoed nicely if Arkady and Il-Hyeong had been making any noise. There were security cameras, but Ming-Jun would have already taken care of those. Arkady couldn't afford any extra worry, now—not when every step brought him and Il-Hyeong that much closer to their grand goal.

When they reached the second floor landing, Arkady saw Il-Hyeong's ears twitch. From down below came the faintest sound of a soft, mechanical click. "Okay, now *that* I did hear," the ferret said.

"They locked the door," Il-Hyeong said. A quick glance at the doorway out into the second floor showed that it too was locked, the small, red light on the access panel blinking. "They know we're here."

Arkady looked back down the stairway. There was only the one door that led back to the ground floor. "Well, if they know we're here, then let's not disappoint them." He started to walk up the stairs to the third floor.

"Wait, you're serious?" Il-Hyeong asked.

"If we can't go back, then the only way out is through," Arkady replied. He took the steps two at a time until he reached the third floor landing, and this next door showed no such blinking red light.

Il-Hyeong checked his DKR-7 and then gave Arkady a look. "You really want to do this?"

"Arkady," Ming-Jun interjected via the earpiece, "if you're thinking of calling this off, there should be an emergency fire exit at the top of the stairwell. If you just head—"

"I'm not calling it off," the ferret said. "We're not aborting this mission until we've got proof that what we came for isn't here."

"Even if it's a trap?" Il-Hyeong asked.

"I'm sure it's a trap, now," Arkady replied. "But that doesn't mean that they're not guarding what we've come to get. If there's a still chance we can get it, then we have to take it."

Neither Il-Hyeong nor Ming-Jun said anything right away. They both knew that if they backed out of this opportunity, they wouldn't get a second chance. Not with Fan-Yin Bioinformatics, at any rate. If they did let the Pyxis Sequence slip through their fingers, there was no telling when they'd ever make any headway on the project again—and there was no telling what someone else might do if they were in possession of that all-important data.

Once more, Il-Hyeong readied his gun. "If we're going in, we're going in together," he told the ferret. "Let's go do what we were sent to do."

Arkady met Il-Hyeong's steely gaze and nodded. He clicked off the safety on his Zarna and reached for the door panel with his left paw. The fox took up position on the other side of the door. Arkady did a silent three-count in his head, and then he pressed the button to unlatch the door.

The door swung inward, and immediately, a hail of gunfire pounded through the open doorway and into the wall of the stairwell. The barrage was quick, but intense—a chorus of high-end assault rifles. Amateurs, firing before they even had a visual on their targets, giving away their position. Well-armed amateurs, perhaps, but amateurs nonetheless.

A single voice cut through the resounding echo, quick and sharp. Arkady's ears were ringing from the gunfire, which made the voice tough to make out, but the single word that had reached his ears sounded like a curse.

In the ensuing silence, Il-Hyeong and Arkady nodded to each other simultaneously.

Arkady was first to swing around into the doorway. At first glance, he spotted at least seven individuals. Over to the right was a laboratory bench that must have been pushed over when—no, he'd think about those details later. For now, his attention had to remain on the people who were shooting at him. Time seemed to slow down for the ferret as he went to duck back behind cover, hoping to get at least one shot off before the people holding position had a chance to return fire.

He got off three. It felt as if he had all the time in the world to select his target, aim his weapon, and pull the trigger. A red fox, a ferret like himself, and a young coyote. Head, chest, head again. They were still falling when Arkady pressed his back against the wall, out of view of the doorway.

In the wake of the volley of gunfire that had been too late to catch Arkady, Il-Hyeong swung in behind him, firing rapidly with his own pistol before ducking back as well.

Now, Arkady had a spare moment to process what he'd just seen and done.

There were definitely more than seven people in the room; another half dozen or so were perched in the wings on either side. The seven who'd been lined up and taking aim had, in fact, been armed with assault rifles, and they all wore matching, slate blue uniforms. Neither the uniforms nor the insignia thereupon matched those worn by the security detail hired by Fan-Yin Bioinformatics, however. Arkady considered the possibility that they might have been Octavians, but that still didn't explain the uniforms, either. Hired by the Octavians, perhaps? No way to know for sure without learning more.

If Il-Hyeong had killed even two more of the opposing force with the four shots he'd fired, that still left two more of the initial group standing. From the way the lights and shadows played on the walls, Arkady could tell that not all seven had been taken out in their initial attack. As the ferret thought that, Il-Hyeong popped out from around the door and fired twice more before slipping back behind cover. The fox then flashed a single digit to Arkady with his free paw. Six down. One and however many more to go.

Arkady thought he might be able to use his new sense of smell to determine how many of them were left, but he immediately regretted the deep sniff he took. All he got was the stench of gunpowder, blood, and less pleasant scents of death. He relied on the endorphin rush of combat to fight back the onset of nausea.

"Ming-Jun, can you run a check on the insignia on those uniforms?" he asked.

There was a second's delay before the rabbit replied: "You were both moving way too fast for the camera to catch that level of detail."

"Then we take them out now and figure out who they are after," Il-Hyeong said.

Arkady spun back into the doorway. Six of the initial targets had indeed gone down, leaving just one set of ears peeking out from behind a lab bench that had been shoved aside for cover. For a moment, Arkady just stood there, having no clear shot to take, until someone further down the hallway barked out a single-syllable order. The ferret couldn't make the word out, partially deafened as he was by gunfire, but the ears behind the bench flicked at the command and then began to rise.

It was as if Arkady was watching events play out in slow motion. This was almost a cruel parody of what a gunfight should be, he thought, but instincts still guided him so that, as his would-be attacker's head popped into view—it was another fox, like the one he'd killed seconds before—it was horrifyingly easy for the ferret to just pull the trigger on his Zarna, leaving him to wait in his time-dilated perceptions until he saw that he'd once again gotten a clean head shot.

The body crumpled and dropped out of view behind the lab bench, and the hallway was again silent.

Il-Hyeong looked at Arkady, and the ferret just nodded. They would have a respite of at least a few seconds, now, and when Arkady took a deep breath, he wondered when the last time he'd taken one was. He could feel the warmth radiating from his pistol, could still smell that he and his partner had just killed seven people, and he knew that they'd need to kill more before the night was through.

After the agents' display of their expert marksmanship, these defenders, whoever they were, wouldn't be dumb enough to send another wave out after them. They'd wait for Arkady and Il-Hyeong to come to them, and since inside was exactly where the fox and the ferret needed to be, there was no choice but to do just that.

If they just rushed in with guns blazing, what would happen? Surely, their reflexes weren't good enough to let them dodge bullets, but...

Before a coherent plan of action could take shape in Arkady's head, the whole stairwell shook as a quick boom echoed from down below. A small explosive charge had just gone off, the ferret realized, and as that dawned on him, he heard the patter of rushed footsteps. "Upstairs!" called a rough voice.

"Well, fuck," Il-Hyeong muttered. "The only way out is through, huh?" Arkady bristled as the fox threw his own words back at him, but there was no time to dwell on the point. Il-Hyeong was already rushing into the hallway.

"Ming-Jun," Arkady barked. "We've got some new friends coming up from the first floor. Can you tell us how many?"

"Newcomers?" The rabbit was obviously confused. "Arkady, I'm showing the first floor totally clear."

The footsteps from the stairway were getting closer now, so Arkady took off on the heels of Il-Hyeong. "That's impossible," the ferret said. "There was just an explosion. I can hear them in the stairwell right now."

"The stairwell's clear, too, Arkady. I don't know what to tell—"

Ming-Jun kept talking, but Arkady tuned out her voice entirely. A slender female cacomistle stood in the left-branching hallway, dressed in the same sort of uniform as the others, but she had no rifle; instead, her only weapon appeared to be a pistol of some sort that she wore at the hip. From a tactical standpoint, Arkady thought it would be prudent to take her out, even if she was in no position to defend herself, but in the split-second hesitation he felt at taking aim at a woman who wasn't properly armed, the cacomistle motioned with her paw, and four more of the more well-armed uniformed men rushed out, blocking her from view. Arkady fired twice as he dove to the right, behind one of the lab benches, and he could tell from the cry of pain he heard as he landed that he'd hit at least one of them.

The familiar sound of Il-Hyeong's DKR-7 echoed from off to Arkady's left, and the ferret looked over his shoulder to see the swift fox duck behind a supply locker. More of the mysterious troopers had clustered into position at the right-hand hallway, too, he now knew. Whoever these people were, they were coordinated enough to have laid a decent trap, but what came next? Were they just planning to throw lives away until their pincer tactic overwhelmed the intruders?

The footsteps from back in the stairwell had stopped. Arkady could tell that the newcomers hadn't yet gotten as far as the third floor landing, though. "Who the hell are they firing at?" asked a deep voice, presumably the one who'd yelled before.

"Internal security?" suggested another, higher-pitched voice. "Look, we need to get them before they reach whatever the hell they're looking for."

Arkady felt relief and confusion at the same time. Did these people really not realize why they'd come here? They'd been waiting for them, and surely, with the Pyxis Sequence, they—

"Ming-Jun, I've got at least two targets in the stairwell we entered through," he said. "Can you confirm?"

In the moments before Ming-Jun answered, Arkady heard Il-Hyeong on the other side of the corridor, muttering quickly under his breath. "Please, God, please," the fox prayed. "Please, don't make us have to kill all of these people." His voice was soaked through with regret and anxiety. Even as his words trailed off, a few footsteps sounded at the right branch of the hallway, and the fox popped out from cover long enough to fire two more bullets. Two more empty thumping sounds followed.

"Negative, Arkady," Ming-Jun replied after what had to have been only seconds, but which had felt so much longer. "Stairwell shows empty."

"Then you're seeing it wrong," the ferret snarled. He could smell intruders in the stairwell, finally, too: strongest—and the first he could clearly identify—was mustelid, like himself. There were others, he could tell, but he couldn't bring himself to try to smell more through the gore and carnage. If Ming-Jun didn't have an accurate report about what was going on in the stairwell, though, then Arkady and Il-Hyeong couldn't risk going back. There would be no aborting the mission.

Sounding unperturbed by Arkady's reprimand, Ming-Jun said, "Arkady, look down at one of those bodies for a second if you can." For the moment, the two sets of defenders waiting in the wings weren't rushing out to the slaughter, so the ferret had moments to spare. He kept his paw at the back of his ear to steady the communications mount, and he leaned in to allow the camera to 'peer' at one of the soldiers he had already felled.

A spray of covering fire from an assault rifle chewed a line of holes in the wall over by Il-Hyeong. Back from the stairway came the sound of a metallic pin being pulled, followed by an aerosol hiss.

"Arkady," Ming-Jun said, her voice sounding more urgent. Before she could finish her warning, though, an arm reached in through the door from the stairwell, lobbing a canister grenade that left a trail of smoke in its wake. It overshot Arkady and Il-Hyeong's position by several feet before it began to billow forth a thick cloud of smoke closer to the intersection of the hallways.

The opportunity was clear: whether it was intentional or not (and he doubted that it was), Arkady needed to take it. He got up from behind the lab bench and ran, motioning urgently for Il-Hyeong to follow. The fox fired a few shots back toward the stairwell before following.

Arkady dove through the smoke, its noxious scent burning in his nose. After even such brief exposure the onset of nausea was making him stumble as he ran. Behind him, he heard Il-Hyeong cough and choke. *Fight it*, the ferret told himself. *This is nothing.* To his own great surprise, the wave of nausea, intense as it was, began to rapidly recede. A quick glance back at Il-Hyeong showed that the fox was no worse off, either.

The report of a large-barreled handgun—it couldn't have been the pistol Arkady had seen on the cacomistle's hip—echoed down the hallway, and then the assault rifles joined back in as well. The ferret ducked aside, and as the bullets again pounded the walls and windows, he thought that there was less gunfire than there ought to have been.

Listening harder, Arkady realized two things: there were strained sounds of several people retching back within that cloud of gas (which was already dispersing rapidly), and also, as much assault rifle fire was being aimed *away* from Il-Hyeong and Arkady as was being aimed towards them.

Another rapid-fire rifle chimed in, then, but it was quite clearly of a lower caliber and different make than the others. Arkady scurried behind another locker, and nobody seemed to be following him. He'd lost sight of Il-Hyeong for the moment. The higher-pitched voice yelled at the far end of the hall: "Shit! How many of these guys are there?"

Il-Hyeong came back into view from within a shallow alcove within the corridor. One of the uniformed troops, a rifle-wielding skunk, charged out of the thinning smoke, raising a fanatical battle cry. Il-Hyeong pointed his DKR-7 and pulled the trigger, but the magazine was empty. Arkady saw that the fox didn't even miss a beat as he reversed his hold on his weapon and leapt forward.

The skunk saw Il-Hyeong coming—he'd been looking in the fox's direction even before he jumped out of cover—but Il-Hyeong was unfairly faster than him. With a shallow hop, the fox skipped in past the rifle as the skunk brought it up, and he delivered a solid blow to the skunk's head with the grip of his pistol. The skunk staggered. Il-Hyeong released the pistol, and while it was still falling to the floor, he grabbed the skunk's head in both paws and yanked him down, bringing up his knee to meet the skunk's face. The skunk's neck snapped backward at an unnatural angle, and when Il-Hyeong released him, he dropped motionless to the floor. The fox then picked up the assault rifle and fired a quick burst into the corridor intersection before diving back into the shallow alcove in which he'd been hiding before, kicking his dropped DKR-7 into it along with him.

The fox unleashed another volley of covering fire for himself, and then he bent down and picked up his discarded pistol, released the empty magazine and slapped in a new one. By now, the gas from the grenade had all but vanished, and several people were still coughing and sputtering. There were half a dozen chemicals that Arkady could think of, off the top of his head, that would have such quick-acting effects. All of them would have had a much more extreme effect on Il-Hyeong and himself after even a brief exposure, though.

"Arkady! Il-Hyeong!" Ming-Jun's voice pulled Arkady's attention aside so roughly that the ferret almost lost balance. "Do you still read me?" From the sound of her voice, she'd been trying to get the other agents' attention for a while.

"I hear you, Ming," said Il-Hyeong, his voice sounding clearer through the earpiece than it did from across the hallway. "What's going on?"

More panic. "Both of you, whatever you do, do *not* head back to the apartment when you get out of there."

"What?" Arkady snapped, loud enough to have in all likelihood given away his position. "Why?"

"Just trust me," the rabbit urged. "It's not going to be safe here. I'll radio back to you when I find someplace else for us to rendezvous."

"Agent Devra, explain your—" A bullet hit the wall less than a foot from Arkady's head, cutting off his order. He saw the large handgun he'd heard earlier, pointing at him from the other side of the hallway intersection, in the paws of an enormous white wolf. He was crouching, so the ferret couldn't tell exactly how tall he was, but with his broad shoulders and massive head, he looked like he could have ripped one of the security doors off of its hinges with just his arms.

The wolf was wearing a dark flak jacket, and Arkady had to wonder where the giant lupine had found one that fit him. Dressed in similar body armor, green to match the green uniform-like top he wore, was a weasel, taking up position on the other side of the hallway from the wolf. He was the one who carried the other rifle, a modified Duhamel Allemande A-17.

Hugging the wall, the weasel swung his weapon around the corner and fired down the hallway, into the side corridor that the cacomistle woman had disappeared down before. The wolf, though, was still taking potshots at Arkady. "Ming-Jun," the ferret murmured into the earpiece. "The wolf and weasel. Have you gotten a clear look at either of them?"

"Let me check," the rabbit responded. "Maybe." It was difficult to hear over all the gunfire and occasional shouting, but it sounded like she was moving around the apartment.

"If you can isolate either of their faces, check the Ridgecrescent federal archives," the ferret ordered. He had no idea who the hell these newcomers were, and no idea whose side they were on, but his gut was telling him that they'd find an answer there, first.

The weasel was pulling back around the corner to move back into position across from the wolf. He'd left his back exposed for a few seconds, and across the way from him, Arkady noticed movement. It was Il-Hyeong again, his DKR-7 back at the ready.

"Il-Hyeong, don't!" the ferret shouted. Il-Hyeong's ear twitched— clearly, he'd heard—but he didn't stop. He fired twice at the weasel, once clipping him in the shoulder.

The weasel yelped in pain and dropped his rifle, but Il-Hyeong still had his gun up. "Agent Quinn, I am *ordering* you to stand down!" Arkady barked, but the fox fired twice more, catching the weasel in the side both times. The weasel dropped to the floor, in the middle of the hallway, eyes wide open. Those last two bullets had clearly penetrated a thinner section of his flak jacket. Blood was pooling all around him, but he was still visibly breathing.

"What the hell are you doing, Il-Hyeong?" the ferret demanded, tackling the fox against the opposite wall, barely avoiding another spray of gunfire from both the pistol-wielding wolf and the first group of soldiers. "I gave you an order not to fire," he snarled. He'd never known Il-Hyeong to lose his cool in a combat situation, or to flagrantly ignore a direct order.

"They're firing on us," the fox spat back, throwing off Arkady's grip and checking his pistol again. "That makes them the enemy, and a threat to the mission."

"We need to figure out who these people are, first."

"No," Il-Hyeong retorted, his eyes narrowing with anger. "First and foremost, we need to find the Pyxis Sequence, like you say."

Arkady motioned toward the hallway, riddled with bodies. "Don't you get it, Il-Hyeong? There *is* no Pyxis Sequence! Not here."

"Maybe not," the fox said. "But are you really going to leave without checking first? These people are here for something."

"They're here for *us*," Arkady said. "And yes, if it means we get out of here alive so that we can figure out just what the hell is going on, then we *are* going to leave without checking first."

Il-Hyeong paused to fire a few more shots into the fray. "What's the matter, Arkady?" he asked. "A few minutes ago, you were do-or-die, 'the only way out is through.'"

"And a few minutes ago, you were begging to not have to kill these people," Arkady said. "So when I give you an order *not* to, I expect you to follow it."

That dull fire continued to burn in Il-Hyeong's eyes. They'd been through combat together before, but Arkady hadn't ever seen this look on the fox's face. "No matter which way we go, there are people standing between us and the door," he said. "We're going to have to go through them one way or the other."

Arkady nodded. "Right, then," he said. "We're getting out of here. Split up, and then we reconvene as per standard protocols. Got it?"

Il-Hyeong slapped a fresh magazine into his gun. "Got it," he said. "I'll take the right, you take the left?"

"No," Arkady said. "I take right. Now go."

The fox didn't question that order, jumping free from his hiding place and blasting away with his pistol as he barged on through the set of double doors that might have, if this hadn't all just been some elaborate trap from the start, led to the laboratory proper. Arkady slipped out to the right as guns trained on Il-Hyeong's previous position, buying the ferret a precious half-second to land himself behind new cover before they aimed at him again.

A few dozen feet away, the weasel still lay dying. For one moment, Arkady wanted more than anything, more than even finding the Pyxis Sequence at this point, to run out and get him out of there, but the ferret would be cut down before he even got close. There was nothing to be done for the weasel now. The hallway behind Arkady was clear, so he started to backpedal, keeping his eyes on the direction of the soldiers, ready to fire as soon as another of them showed their vulnerable head.

Arkady reached another access stairwell. He pounded the keypad with his paw and the lock clicked open. A quick look down the staircase showed it to be clear, as near as he could see. He took once last glance down the corridor, over to where he'd last seen Il-Hyeong, and then went through the door.

The ferret sensed movement from above just in time to dive out of the way. The white wolf from before landed in front of him with a tremendous thud, keeping his balance as he held up his huge handgun level with Arkady's head.

"Drop your weapon, and state your name and business," the wolf growled. "This building is under the protection of the Iolite League."

9. Soldier of Fortune

Arkady was smacked with a sense of such ridiculous disbelief that he actually laughed. "The Iolite League?" He saw the wolf's snout wrinkle. It was almost hilarious, in a way, that these people had chosen the exact wrong cover I.D. for their operation.

As huge as the wolf had looked back in the main hallway when he'd been hunkered down on one knee, Arkady had underestimated just how massive he really was: easily seven feet tall, and so broad at the shoulders that he looked like he could get struck by a small car and make the car regret it. The wolf's pelt was, as far as Arkady could tell, a uniform white, but his eyes were a deep brown and not the reddish-pink that signified albinism. Not that anyone could mistake this wolf for someone who had grown up as a weak and secluded albino whelp. Even augmented, Arkady would probably have his limbs snapped like toothpicks if he tried to go toe-to-toe with this hulking lupine.

Arkady would need to recompose himself before he gave away any hint of his allegiance, so he decidedly to play along with the preposterous charade set before him, working with the mocking laugh he'd already accidentally let out. "The Iolite League has no jurisdiction in Ridgecrescent."

"No?" the wolf growled. "I don't see how that changes the fact that I've got a gun to your head."

This was true. What was also true was that the ferret's reflexes likely made that matter a non-issue, but the wolf didn't need to know that. Holding up both paws, Arkady let his pistol hang from his middle finger, dangling in surrender. As the wolf reached out to take it, Arkady knew that he was quick enough that he could swing his gun back into firing position and score a shot on either the wolf's head or chest before his captor had the chance to react, but coming along quietly would probably be his best way out of the building. Later, his superior physical prowess would allow for him to make escape at a more opportune time.

"Cordellatech," the wolf noted as he claimed Arkady's pistol. He ended the word with a dismissive snort.

Arkady eyed the wolf's own weapon. "Duhamel," he replied, recognizing the oversized Furukawa model. He didn't know anyone who used one, personally, mainly because the average person would be hard-pressed to even wrap their fingers around the grip. In this case, though, size meant power, and the Furukawa could put a hole clear through someone's chest even after passing through the standard-issue body armor used by most modern-day police forces.

If the wolf cared to further discuss the makers of their respective firearms, he didn't show it. Without another word, he snatched the earpiece off of Arkady's head and crushed his paw around it, snapping it in half and breaking off Arkady's line of contact with his teammates. He hoped that Ming-Jun had at least been able to get a good enough look through the unit's camera to get an I.D. on this wolf, since that could prove invaluable in tracking certain parties down later, after Arkady had made his escape.

Thinking of escape, Arkady thought of Il-Hyeong. Surely, the fox was already well on his way to making it out of the building by now, wasn't he? He'd taken out the weasel who was the wolf's companion (against Arkady's orders, the ferret reminded himself), and he'd already proven himself more than capable of fending off the crew of defenders who'd holed themselves up here. But how many more of them were there? Had Il-Hyeong escaped down one hallway only to run into a few dozen more men with assault rifles? The fox wouldn't be able to take on that many.

Tapping Arkady on the shoulder with the barrel of his gun, the white wolf turned the ferret around. Arkady complied, and when the wolf told him, "Put your paws behind your back," he was already doing so. A pair of electronic cuffs slid into place and contracted around his wrists. The wolf jabbed the muzzle of his gun between Arkady's shoulder blades and growled, "Walk. Down the stairs. Quickly."

Whoever it was the wolf worked for, they wanted Arkady alive, then. That definitely put him in a different camp than the people who had ambushed him and Il-Hyeong. The Octavians would have taken more obvious delight in apprehending him, and any one of them would have slashed his own throat before even pretending to be associated with the Iolite League.

As Arkady descended the staircase, he could hear additional sounds of panic and chaos from the hallway they'd left behind. If Sahasrara had completely fouled up this operation, then at least they weren't the only ones. That being the case, it only made Arkady that much more painfully curious about who this wolf and this weasel really were. If only the augmentation could have given him the powers of unparalleled insight, or at least a psychic connection with Ming-Jun.

"So, what interest does the Iolite League have with this building?" Arkady asked as he and the wolf rounded the second floor landing.

Arkady got another tap on the back with the wolf's gun. "Keep moving."

Just because Arkady didn't hear anyone following them didn't mean that it wasn't prudent to hurry. Although being taken prisoner wasn't the ideal circumstance for it, the ferret very badly wanted to get out of the building and to leave it far behind him. Counting footsteps, he could tell that the wolf was taking the stairs two at a time as he rushed them both down the stairwell.

When they got to the first floor, Arkady started to turn down the hallway that led back toward the lobby, but the wolf growled, "This way," and forced him down the maintenance corridor instead. Arkady resisted the urge to curse under his breath; he'd wanted to see with his own eyes that the ground floor doorway to the other stairwell had, in fact, been blasted open with some kind of explosive, but he'd just have to believe what he'd heard instead of what Ming-Jun's cameras had seen.

The wolf stepped out in front of him when they got to the maintenance exit. He pushed open the door with one paw and kept his gun trained on Arkady with the other. "Get into the back seat," the wolf said, motioning with his gun, and Arkady had to actually lean over to look past the wolf's big frame and see the dark, unmarked van idling just outside.

Arkady was about to protest that he couldn't open the door with his paws cuffed behind his back, but the door swung open on its own. The wolf stepped in behind him and hovered, and so he wasted no further time in complying, climbing into the back seat and shimmying all the way over to the far side. His captor slammed the door shut behind him and then circled around the back of the van.

The back seat was sectioned off by a reinforced transparent divider similar to ones used in police cruisers and taxicabs. Arkady guessed that it was both bulletproof and shatterproof, though a summary inspection of the seal that kept it in place showed that he could probably kick it out of place if he got the leverage to deliver a few solid blows with both feet. There were no locks on in the inside of the doors in the back seat, either. Either this really was a refurbished and retrofitted law enforcement vehicle, or these guys were actually law enforcement, though Arkady rather doubted the latter.

A mouse sat in the driver's seat. He was short enough that Arkady didn't see him at first, his head not even coming up past the top of the seat. His fur was a mix of dirty browns and grays that didn't at all match the young, almost innocent face he had. Like the wolf and the weasel, he wore some sort of green jacket, but there was no way for Arkady to see the front of it to check for any additional evidence of badges or other insignia.

The wolf came around and climbed into the passenger seat. The mouse looked up at him, and only then did he actually start to show Arkady any attention, trying to get a look at the ferret out of the corner of his eye. "Where's Jenkins?" he asked the wolf.

"We'll give him two more minutes," the wolf said. His own attention was kept forward, away from Arkady and away from the Fan-Yin building as well.

Arkady closed his eyes. "I think he's dead," he said. *Dead because my man disobeyed direct orders*, he thought to himself, seeing the scene of Il-Hyeong gunning down the weasel play out in his head again in the same slow-motion detail in which he'd first seen it. "I'm sorry," he added. Why in God's name hadn't Il-Hyeong listened to him? Why had he fired and continued to fire on someone who wasn't an immediate threat to either of them?

The wolf didn't turn around. "We'll give him two minutes," he repeated, though this time, he sounded more resigned.

Sniffing about, Arkady was able to catch only traces of personal scents, even with his keen sense of smell. This group had obviously taken the precaution to hide those scents—and, by extension, their number—but the cleansing wasn't perfect. Even so, the van yielded only the scents of mouse and wolf, which he could smell now, and weasel, whom he could only assume was the aforementioned Jenkins.

The interior of the van was otherwise unremarkable. There was no equipment stored in the far back, behind where Arkady was seated, and there were no identifying markings of any sort. It wasn't as if Arkady had ever been arrested in Ridgecrescent and then coincidentally been thrown into a van instead of a cruiser, and so he had no mental reference for comparison, but if this were a military vehicle, he'd have expected more equipment space, and if these guys were paramilitary, well, things weren't disheveled enough for that to be the case.

"Those folks upstairs with the uniforms," Arkady said. "I take it you're not with them?"

"Uniforms?" the mouse asked. "What's—"

The wolf interrupted the mouse to snap at Arkady. "Enough with the questions." He went back to staring out the windshield. "Another minute and a half," he said, this time to the mouse. "Then we go." He brought a paw to his forehead and rubbed at his temples.

The mouse quite clearly was not a fan of that idea. Arkady could smell his fear through the tiny holes in the divider that allowed for captor and captive to speak to one another. The mouse probably believed Arkady's statement that the weasel was dead. The wolf probably believed it, too, the ferret thought; he was probably just better at hiding it.

"You don't need to be harsh with me," Arkady said, then. "After all, you and I really aren't as different as we may appear on the outside."

"I told you to shut up, okay?" the wolf growled. This time, he didn't even bother to turn his head.

The response made Arkady sigh. *"The different species of this world are not as different as they may appear on the outside."* That was the opening verse of Chapter One of the Book of Alexandretta, and moreover, also one of the chief tenets of the Iolite Doctrine. If this wolf had really been a member of the Iolite League, he'd have immediately recognized Arkady's attempt at a shibboleth. As unlikely as the odds were that wolf really had been with the League, it was still a disappointment to confirm that he wasn't.

The next minute passed in silence. Finally, with a grunt, the wolf slumped back in the passenger seat. "Drive," he said. Without question, the mouse grabbed hold of the gear shifter, and they sped from the Fan-Yin Bioinformatics parking lot as quickly as they could without leaving the screech of tires in their wake.

The drive from Fan-Yin Bioinformatics was uneventful. Arkady had been sure that the getaway van would be pursued by whoever else had holed themselves up to defend the Fan-Yin labs, and the mouse had only proven himself to be an adequate and thoroughly unexceptional driver. Arkady was fully prepared to start offering his captors evasion tactics, but at this time of night, hardly anyone lingered in the rear-view mirror for more than a block or so along the urban streets.

Unfortunately, Arkady was mostly familiar with the parts of Highslope in the vicinity of the Fan-Yin building and Ming-Jun's apartment, and so of course, the mouse ended up driving in an entirely different direction. Highslope was a modern city, but it was also an old city, which meant that its street layout made little to no logical sense by modern standards. As a result, the van's path curved and turned so much that Arkady eventually lost track of which direction they were even headed, and heightened senses didn't grant the ferret the magical ability to determine his bearing relative to some other arbitrary spatial position.

The van eventually pulled to a stop in front of a row house, one in a series of identical, dilapidated brick houses packed together along a street a few blocks away from the closest major downtown thoroughfare. If they were going to hold him here, then Arkady was at least relieved that he wasn't going to be stashed in some abandoned boathouse or in a shack at the outskirts of town.

The mouse stopped the van, but he didn't park, and the wolf got out while the gas was still running. He opened up the rear passenger's-side door and pulled Arkady out by the shoulder. He started to march the ferret toward the front steps, but the mouse unrolled the passenger's-side window and called out, "Hey, hold on."

Standing out on the sidewalk in plain view probably wasn't the best place for Arkady to be while bound in a set of cuffs, at least if—as the ferret assumed—these guys didn't want to risk a scene. The wolf's grunt of impatience did more than just reflect that very sentiment. "What?" he snapped, pivoting back around on one foot, setting himself back down with a heavy thump.

Arkady could see in fine enough detail to notice the quick ripple in the mouse's fur as he swallowed the lump in his throat. "Should... should I go back for Jenkins?" he asked the wolf.

The wolf looked away, and he didn't answer for several seconds. "No," he eventually said. "If he got out of there, he'll make his own way back."

"All right," the mouse replied with a weak nod. "I'll be in touch."

"Yeah," the wolf said. "Later." He turned back around, and before the van had even started to drive off, he was back to urging Arkady up the front steps of the old brick building.

The wolf marched Arkady straight to a cluttered spare room. He grabbed an old steel folding chair that was resting against the wall, snapped it open with a one strong flick of the wrist, then plunked it down in the center of the room. He shoved Arkady down into it, then proceeded to handcuff him to the metal frame. "If I hear you banging around in here," the wolf warned, "I'm going to come in and knock you out." Before closing the door, he also removed the doorknob.

After that, there was silence, save for the sound of the occasional vehicle driving down the street just outside. If the wolf was doing anything elsewhere in the apartment, it wasn't something that made any noise.

Given the militant nature of the operation (and subsequent abduction), Arkady figured that the wolf would observe military protocol and wait for his weasel comrade's return. It was just as likely, the ferret wagered, that the wolf knew full well that no one was actually coming back.

Were Il-Hyeong and Ming-Jun doing the same thing right now—waiting for Arkady, hoping against hope that the wait wasn't in vain? How long would they wait for him to come back before mounting a rescue effort? And they *would* mount a rescue effort, the ferret was sure, even if the smart thing to do would be to get back to Château Sainte-Mireille as soon as possible to report on the sheer disaster that the mission had degenerated into. They wouldn't do that, though. They'd come for him, because they'd already lost Kentian, and because they didn't have their leader to order them not to.

The last thought made Arkady chuckle through his nose. It was probably the first sound he'd made in the last two hours or so.

He could only guess at how much time had actually passed. Did his augmented senses make it easier to track the passage of time, or did they distort his perceptions of it from what he was used to?

One thing he could discern clearly was that this wolf didn't live in this apartment. The only traces of his scent here were superficial ones. In fact, no scents had really pervaded or sunken into the furniture other than the dusty, slightly rank smells of an aging, under-maintained home. Had the apartment served as a safehouse for years, or had it only just recently been picked for the purpose since nobody else was using it?

Outside the spare room door, Arkady could now hear the wolf's occasional pacing. The floorboards were old enough (or perhaps the wolf was just heavy enough) that the creaking was noticeable, even on the other side of the apartment, but at no point did Arkady hear the wolf using a phone or trying to contact anyone via radio. His patience in the midst of the unknown was admirable. Il-Hyeong certainly wouldn't have lasted this long under a veil of silence.

Only minutes later, Arkady heard the front door slam. After that, there was total quiet throughout the apartment. There had been no obvious signal that the ferret could detect, so he had no idea where the wolf could be going, unprompted, at this dead hour of the night. Perhaps there had been a standing agreement, like some prearranged rendezvous point. Again, Arkady imagined his own teammates drawing up detailed plans involving a search and rescue at that very moment.

If the wolf really had left him alone, then now was the perfect time for Arkady to try to mount an escape. He could probably stand the pain of breaking his wrist in order to slip out of the cuffs, and then just hope that he retained the manual dexterity to pick a lock on a door that had no doorknob. Of course, this also assumed that the opening he'd been so handily given wasn't all just a ploy to see if Arkady wouldn't mount such an escape attempt when given the opportunity.

It wasn't the chance that it might all be a trap that convinced the ferret not to go for it, though—it was the fact that he was still determined to figure out who these people were and what they were doing at Fan-Yin Bioinformatics on the same night as his team. The mouse had seemed legitimately surprised by the mention of people in uniforms; did that mean that the wolf and his team knew more, or did that mean they were just as much in the dark as Arkady?

Arkady would wait it out. If his lupine captor (or any of his associates) came back, he would do what he could to try to learn more about him. If Ming-Jun and Il-Hyeong succeeded in rescuing him before that, then that would mean, by extension, that they'd learned something on their own, and that was just as good.

Not even an hour later, Arkady heard heavy, plodding footsteps coming up the stairs, ones that couldn't belong to anyone other than the wolf. It sounded like he was alone, and given the slight clumsiness to the gait, it appeared that he really had left the apartment and gone somewhere before coming back. The footsteps kept coming closer until they stopped in front of the door to the spare room.

The door jiggled for a few seconds before it flung open, the wolf's gun already up in one paw, pointing at Arkady in case the ferret had gotten free of his bonds, or was otherwise ready to try to pull off some desperate gambit. The wolf smiled wryly when he saw that his captive was still obediently cuffed to the chair. Clicking his tongue, he then lowered his gun and withdrew a bulky handheld device from his jacket pocket.

Its make wasn't something that Arkady recognized. It was boxy, with a smallish screen and only the most basic of visible control inputs, so it didn't appear to be any kind of elaborate torture device. Besides, this wolf seemed more like the type who would prefer to beat information out of his hostages rather than try to coerce it out with more subtle ways of inflicting pain.

"All right, then, little sharpshooter," the wolf said, roughly grabbing Arkady's cheek with his free paw. "Let's figure out who you are, shall we?" His claws pinched in at the side of the ferret's muzzle, and he yanked free a few stray furs.

The furs were deposited into a small compartment at one end of the wolf's mysterious device. The machine sprung to life at the press of a button, and it let out a low-grade whining and humming as it went to work. Arkady could hear that whatever it was doing involved some type of mechanical components as well as electronic ones. It could be some kind of medical scanner, he theorized, or a similar device.

The wolf pressed a few more buttons, and then waited. The internal components of the device stopped moving, but the electrical hum was still present, and the wolf's eyes were still on the screen. After a few seconds, Arkady noticed that his eyes were moving left to right, left to right, as if reading. Shortly after, the wolf grinned and then looked back up.

"Samuel Togen, huh?" he said. "You're a bit far from home, Mr. Togen, wouldn't you say?"

"Farther than I'd like to be, that's for sure."

The wolf let his arm hang at his side, but he didn't set the device down. "Didn't anyone tell you that the people of Ridgecrescent are none too fond of people like you spending time here, causing trouble?"

"I'd be more than happy to go home, then, if that's what you'd like."

With a quick snort, the wolf bent downward, bringing himself closer to eye level with the ferret. "What I'd like to know, frankly, is how a—what does it say you are, an electrical engineer?—gets so good at firing a gun," he said. "That, and I'd like to know how somehow loses their Kyunjiu accent within a week of relocating." Arkady could smell alcohol on the wolf's breath, now. He hadn't been drinking much, but he'd been drinking something strong. It smelled like some sort of whiskey.

"Well, like you said, there's a big pressure to fit in with the locals around here."

"That there is," the wolf agreed. He started to pace in a circle around the chair, his gaze locked on Arkady the whole time. "Only problem is that you don't exactly sound like you're from Ridgecrescent, either."

"I've already admitted that I'm not."

"But what sort of accent *am* I hearing, then, hmm?" the wolf asked as he pulled up another chair and sat himself down in front of the ferret. Even when he stooped over, he made Arkady feel small. "It's starting to sound a lot like you're from Deepwater. The people of Ridgecrescent don't much care for folk from Deepwater."

"I didn't think they cared much for anyone."

"Deepwater even less so." The wolf flashed him a satisfied grin.

Arkady hadn't ever thought of his accent as particularly strong, but if someone knew what to listen for, his was certainly placeable. "And do the people you're working for really care where it is I'm from?" he asked, putting on an exaggerated Kyunjiu accent with the full intent of it sounding fake.

"No," the wolf said, "but it might change how valuable you are to... certain parties." He gave the ferret another appraising look. He was staying wary, Arkady realized. Smart.

"If the objective was to neutralize me, you would have done so already," Arkady said. "But I can't imagine that you were simply sent out to capture me and then auction me off to the highest bidder. That makes even less sense."

The wolf laughed. "That would be convenient, wouldn't it?" he said. "But no. It just changes the equation to know that I might have a spy from Deepwater on my paws, here. The Ridgecrescent government would be very interested in hearing about that."

"Why not turn me over to the Iolite League?" Arkady asked. "After all, if they're the ones you're working for, isn't that what should come next?"

Arkady expected the wolf to flinch when he called his bluff, but his captor didn't miss a beat. "Ridgecrescent might pay more. Enough to make up the difference in failing to pull through on the job for the Iolite League."

"I notice you're not using 'we' whenever you refer to Ridgecrescent," Arkady replied. "And you *do* sound like you're from here. Why is that?"

"I don't think it matters where I'm from if the government will still pay out a handsome reward for turning in a spy," the wolf said. "After all, trying to sabotage federal research projects is something they'd understandably be a bit upset about."

A connection between Fan-Yin Bioinformatics and the Ridgecrescent federal government? *That* was a new piece of information. Arkady smiled inwardly as he filed that tidbit away. "Did you fight in the Butterfly Islands War?" he asked.

There was a slight change in the wolf's demeanor: he pulled out of his slouch a little, and his expression got more guarded. "What, you think this is about government loyalty or something?" he sneered. "If I do turn you over to them, it's because I expect to get paid. Nothing more, nothing less."

"But you still fought in the Butterfly Islands War," Arkady said. "Which would make you ex-military, I'm guessing, since otherwise, this would be a government sanctioned job."

"Well, look who thinks he's smart." The wolf's snout twisted up with an angry scowl. "Where are you getting that from, electrical engineer?"

Arkady tilted his head back and made a show of appraising the wolf in much the same way the wolf had done to him. "For starters," he began, "I'd guess you're somewhere in the neighborhood of thirty or so, which would make you the right age to have been on the front lines down there. Second, your group strikes me as being some kind of mercenary company, but you personally act like you're following military-type protocols."

He smiled back into the wolf's scowl. "Also, you gave quite a mighty sneer to my Zarna when you took it from me, and Cordellatech manufactured most of the weapons used by the Afortunada military during the war. The fact that you're using a Duhamel might just be a coincidence, though, since their weapons are so pervasive and—"

Arkady's triumphant deduction was cut short by a big fist catching him right in the side of the face. He should have seen it coming. Even with excellent reflexes, it wasn't as if he had anyplace to dodge. The wolf hit hard, and the ferret's vision went dim for several moments, the flimsy metal chair lifting off of one leg for just a second before settling back down. "How professional do you think I am now?" the wolf growled.

"Ouch," the ferret grumbled. His tongue poked around the inside of his mouth, checking to make sure that none of his teeth had been knocked out. At least he was recovering from the blow quickly. "Guess I hit something of a nerve."

"Oh, the boys in the basement of the Capitol Spire are going to *love* torturing information out of you," the wolf said, his paw grabbing hold of Arkady's jaw, forcing it shut and holding the ferret's head back. "There's nothing better than a prisoner who loves to mouth off and who practically *begs* for you to hurt him." He held the ferret back like that for a few seconds longer, then yanked his paw away.

Gasping for breath a few times, Arkady looked back up at the wolf. "You're not working for the Iolite League," he said, sounding weaker than he'd meant to. "The Iolite League doesn't hire mercenaries."

"You sound awful sure of that, Mr. Togen," the wolf said as he got to his feet. "I have to wonder how you can be so convinced of something and still be wrong."

"So prove it, then," Arkady said.

"I don't need to prove anything to you," the wolf said with a chuckle. "I just need to turn you in and get my money."

Arkady curled his tail around one of the legs of his chair. "But you're still asking me questions."

"I need to be able to convince the government why you're valuable, don't I?"

"Yes, but you should already know that," Arkady said. "After all, you knew where we would be, and you knew when we'd be there, and..." His words trailed off as his train of thought continued along its current path.

Then, Arkady started to laugh.

"Oh my God, you don't know *why* we were there, do you?" He continued his chuckling, turning his disbelief into mockery that he directed at his captor. "You were hired for a job, told to stop us, and now what? One of your teammates gets killed, you run into resistance you weren't expecting, and now you're trying to salvage the whole botched deal by figuring out if anyone will pay you for some electrical engineer you kidnapped?"

The wolf delivered a swift kick to the underside of Arkady's chair, sending it flying over onto its back and causing the ferret's head to hit the hard floor with a dull crack. "Look, ferret, if you keep treating this like it's a joke, I'm going to make sure that you stop laughing."

Arkady's head was swimming dizzily again. "Was Jenkins the one who made the deal?" he asked. "Is there no way for you to get paid now that he's dead?"

The wolf stepped onto Arkady's chest, his giant boot pressing down against the ferret's ribcage. "Is that how you want things to be?" the wolf asked, putting more weight behind his foot, making it nearly impossible for the ferret to breathe. "Because if that's the case, then that makes you pretty useless to me after all, doesn't it?"

Without any breath, Arkady could barely speak, but he forced the words out regardless. "What about the men in the uniforms?" he rasped. He wanted to keep his eyes wide so that the wolf could see into them, but with the way the wolf was pushing down with his foot, Arkady didn't have a choice *but* for his eyes to bulge open wide.

"What, you think you're worth money to them, too?" The wolf shifted more of his weight onto Arkady's chest.

It wouldn't take much effort on the wolf's part to crack some of Arkady's ribs, the ferret realized, and so the ferret knew he needed to cut to the chase. "It was a trap," he said, exaggerating the movements of his jaw in order to form that last word.

Now the wolf's expression changed just slightly, revealing restrained interest. "What for?" he asked.

"Don't know," Arkady replied. His eyesight was dimming, and it was getting even harder to talk, but he didn't feel any closer to passing out. "They... were waiting."

"For you?" the wolf asked. His paw started to move toward his pistol.

"Or maybe you." It hadn't occurred to Arkady until just then that that was a real, distinct possibility. He decided to run with it. "Th-think about it."

The wolf did appear to think about it. He let his weight back off of his foot and then stepped off the ferret entirely, though he still loomed over him and was ready to grab for his gun. "I'm listening," he said.

"You were hired to show up there," the ferret said. The rush of getting a full breath of air into his lungs was almost painful. "At least someone knew that you were going to be there tonight."

"Only because we knew *you'd* be there. That doesn't prove anything."

Arkady nodded. "Exactly. Maybe we were the bait for the trap."

"And who would want to trap us?" The wolf was beginning to look less convinced. "We're just hired guns."

Another admission. Excellent. "Hey, you'd know better than I would. I just thought you might—"

"Plus, it was *your* man who killed Jenkins, wasn't it?" More than before, the form looming above Arkady seemed like a solid wall of white wolf that might come crashing down at any second. "You're doing a bad job of making a case for yourself, Mr. Togen."

"Wait, hold on," Arkady said. It didn't look like the wolf was ready to draw his gun just yet, but the ferret wanted to put the brakes on that before it started. "You saw that the two of us were already fighting upstairs before you and Jenkins showed up."

Arkady could see that the wolf was taking the time to process the information as it was fed to him. That possibly meant that the wolf and the weasel hadn't been expecting to walk into a firefight, and that the wolf was therefore trying to determine what ramifications that actually had. "And yet you still opened fire on us," the wolf pointed out simply.

"I..." Arkady wanted to say, *"I ordered him not to,"* but not only would that feel like too little, too late, it would also fail to serve his purpose in trying to convince the wolf that he wasn't an enemy. "I don't know why he fired on your man."

"You don't seem to know a lot of things," the wolf replied, and then he started to wander around the room aimlessly. "You also don't seem to know who those people were," he added. "I believe that much."

There was something about this wolf that was starting to take the edge off of Arkady's well-warranted anxiety. Maybe it was the fact that he was so well-spoken when he could have gotten away with acting more brutish. Maybe it was the look he'd had in his eyes when Arkady had mentioned the Butterfly Islands (and before the wolf had struck him, of course). Maybe it was just the fact that ferret was cuffed to a chair and had no other choice, but Arkady wanted to like him for some reason. "Doesn't that just make me useless all over again?" he asked.

The wolf stepped back up to the knocked-over chair and squatted above Arkady. "Let me make you a deal," he said. "You tell me what it was you were looking for back there, and I'll let you out of those cuffs."

"What?" This wolf had a pretty good track record of making Arkady sputter in disbelief.

Grinning, the wolf pulled a tiny key out from one of his jacket pockets. "I want to know what the Iolite League was sure you'd try to steal," he said, "and I want to know what's so valuable that four fireteams are needed to protect it."

Whoever the wolf was really working for, Arkady no longer doubted that the wolf at least *thought* it was the Iolite League. If Arkady just cooperated long enough, he might be able to figure out, based on what the wolf was after, who had really hired him and his team.

"It was a genetic sequence," Arkady said. "And no, just to confirm, we weren't expecting that level of resistance."

"What's this genetic sequence do?"

Arkady eyed the glimmer of the wolf's key out of the corner of his eye. "It's a cure for a disease," he said. That wasn't strictly true, but if one thought of Pandora as a brain-dead young girl, there was an element of truth to it. "We think that's what it is, at least. Assuming it was ever actually there in the first place."

The wolf considered that for a bit. He didn't appear to like that answer, but nor did he look skeptical. "That doesn't make a lot of sense," he grumbled. "Someone seems pretty intent on making sure people stay sick, if that's the case." Arkady's fib might cause his entire story to unravel, he realized—but then, it also didn't make a lot of sense that anyone would want so badly to keep the Iolite League from activating Pandora. Hell, nobody else should even *know* about Pandora.

Now was time for Arkady to play his real ace in the hole. "We were hired by—" He intentionally cut himself off, clicking his jaw shut and letting the barest hint of nervousness show through in his eyes.

"Talk," the wolf demanded. "If you want out of those cuffs, I want to know who you're working for, first."

The ferret chewed on his lower lip for several seconds, playing up a nonexistent debate within his head. "I'm just a hired gun," he stressed. "Hired by the Octavians."

"Who the fuck are the Octavians?"

A very small part of Arkady had been hoping that, in working for an underworld mercenary outfit, this wolf would have come across some mention of the Octavians, though it wasn't surprising that he hadn't. "We're—*They're* a secret society," Arkady blurted out, faking another slip of the tongue, "dedicated to undermining the Iolite League's leeching grip on society."

The wolf stared down at Arkady, and the look on his face made the ferret imagine that his captor was trying to decide whether that was the most ridiculous thing he'd ever heard, or whether it made some absurd amount of sense. "A cure for a disease," the wolf repeated dubiously. "You're sure it wasn't some chemical superweapon instead?"

Arkady snorted. "Yeah, because *that's* something Deepwater would love to have in its arsenal after the Butterfly Islands War."

"Well, it doesn't make a whole lot of sense that the Iolite League would keep someone from getting hold of some kind of remedy."

"No, it doesn't, does it?" Arkady snipped. "Unless you consider that the Iolite League would want to hoard the cure for themselves so that they can 'discover' it later on, stopping the epidemic just in time, earning all the glory and converting countless more people to their cause."

The wolf sighed and shook his head in frustration. Then, to Arkady's amazement, he flipped the chair onto its side and started to unlock the cuffs.

"Wait, so you're actually letting me go?" the ferret asked.

"I said I'd let you out of your cuffs," the wolf replied. "Whether you want to go, well, that's up to you."

Arkady sat up on the floor and rubbed his paws and wrists together, resisting the urge to groan with relief as proper circulation started to return to his arms. "You're not afraid I'm going to try to, like, bring an end to you and all your works?"

The wolf actually chuckled. "Nice try on the reverse psychology, trying to get me to think you're not just a hired gun," he said. "But these 'Octavians' of yours sound like a bunch of crackpots, and—no offense, but—you don't sound like a crackpot."

Maybe Arkady could grow to like this wolf after all.

"Well, it sounds like your employers sent you on a job, woefully unprepared for what you'd run into," the wolf said, standing back up, "so it seems to me like we both have an interest in figuring out just who this third party was. Unless you want to just walk away from that."

Walk away, forget all about it, call it a wash and head back to the Château. That was probably the smart course of action right now. "And you'd just trust me to help you?" Arkady asked.

"Of course not," the wolf said with a chuckle. "But with Jenkins dead, there's a spot open in the job, and if you don't trust me, I think you'd at least trust the promise of vast sums of money."

"This isn't about money," Arkady said, and again, he thought of Pandora, floating in silence with the mask over her face. It then occurred to him that if he did sign up with this wolf's team, that could get him a step closer to finding out who had actually hired him, and therefore a step closer to finding out who knew that Arkady and Il-Hyeong were going to be at Fan-Yin Bioinformatics that night.

It was a stupid idea, he knew. Moreover, the mission had already been a failure and he had no orders to pursue things any further. Plus, he'd lost track of both of his teammates, and if what Ming-Jun said was to be believed, they no longer even had their base of operations.

Still, if he was ever going to track down the Pyxis Sequence, this wolf might be his only shot.

"Okay. Let me... let me think about it. I need to regroup with my team and see what information and resources we still have."

The wolf leaned up against the wall. "I will point out that you did kill one of my teammates," he said, his voice still calm and level. "If you walk out that door and I run into you again in the course of finishing my job, I'm not going to make the mistake of stopping to consider that we're actually on the same side."

"I'll come back," Arkady insisted. "Or I'll at least let you know, one way or the other. It's the least I can do in return for your actually letting me go."

"Fine." The wolf pushed off the wall and wandered back out into the living room. "If you want your gun back, though, you're going to have to come back and get it yourself."

Arkady followed the wolf out into the living room. He had a clear shot for the door if he wanted to just try running for it. Instead, he turned to the wolf and offered a paw. "Hey," he said. "Honestly, if you don't hear from me, then you have full permission to open fire on me when next we meet."

The wolf stood there for a second, then shook Arkady's paw; Arkady held his grip for longer than necessary. "You're a strange fellow, ferret," he said. Before Arkady could turn away, he added, "One more condition, though."

"And what's that?"

"If we do end up working together on this, I want to know how a kid your age knows so much about the Butterfly Islands War."

10. Fear of God

Highslope was a busy enough city that Arkady was able to find a taxi without much trouble. Once he got into the cab and gave the driver the address, he slumped back in the seat and let out a sigh that carried with it the pent-up tension from the last several hours.

The driver, a scruffy, mixed-breed feline, looked at Arkady via the rear-view mirror. "Rough night?" he asked.

"You don't know the half of it," the ferret replied. Ordinarily, he might have allowed himself a clever grin, but he was too tired to even want to muster one. He wasn't so much physically tired, even though he knew he ought to be, but mentally, he was exhausted.

Another bungled mission. Not only had the Fan-Yin job been a catastrophic blunder, Arkady still had no clear means of getting in touch with either his teammates or with the Iolite League. Service to Sahasrara demanded someone with better capabilities than he possessed.

The cabbie made a few attempts at small talk, but Arkady's halfhearted replies (or perhaps the ferret's Deepwater accent) caused him to soon give up, and the rest of the drive was marked by silence. It was just as well.

Arkady got out at the building where the Tokiko Akitoshi apartment was. He paid the driver, and then just stood on the sidewalk for several minutes, looking up at the building. Ming-Jun had specifically warned him to stay away, but he had nowhere else to go—to help find his comrades or, he thought grimly, nowhere else to look for clues as to what happened.

Having halfway expected to see smoke and fire pouring out of the apartment, Arkady was still only barely consoled by the lack of any visible sign of disturbance. Ming-Jun had claimed that their makeshift home base wasn't going to be safe anymore. Somehow, their location must have been compromised. But how, and to what end? Who had found them out, and what had they done—or tried to do—to Ming-Jun and their operation?

Ming-Jun had also said that she'd radio back when she found a suitable location to meet back up. She'd know by now (*if she's still alive*, Arkady added grimly) that his radio contact had been broken, which would necessitate some other way of passing along the message.

Dangerous and stupid though it may be, the first and most logical place for Arkady to check was the apartment.

As a simple precaution, Arkady took the stairs instead of the elevator. It might be a stretch to believe that such specific traps were waiting for him and him alone, but if the people opposing him were as well-connected as the League, it wasn't entirely beyond the realm of possibility. Besides, taking the stairs allowed him more time to compose himself, to mentally run down the list of things that might await him once he got to his destination.

When he got to his floor, Arkady paused and took stock of what he could observe. He sniffed the air for traces of gunpowder, or even signs that a large group of individuals had come through, both of which he'd have been able to detect even without his augmented senses. The ferret picked up neither. He walked down the hallway until he was within sight of the door to the apartment. It hadn't been kicked in or smashed down. It was closed, though. Someone might be waiting on the other side.

Arkady trotted down the rest of the hallway and stopped just to one side of the door. He wished that he still had even his single-shot backup pistol. That way, he'd at least be able to give himself the tiniest bit of insurance if there were people inside waiting for him. If there were, he'd still have no choice but to run, and he wasn't sure that he'd be able to run far enough or fast enough for it to matter.

The ferret stood and listened at the door to see if he could hear any milling about or patient breathing. All he heard was the low, droning buzz of the hallway lighting. Just to be sure, he waited a few seconds longer, but there was still nothing. Could he trust his augmented hearing to pick up such faint sounds, or would he just nervously imagine them for his trying too hard? Holding his breath, he reached out one paw and jiggled the doorknob.

The door did not erupt into a cloud of splinters and debris. Also, the door was unlocked. The ferret tightened his grip, turned the knob, and pushed the door open. Again, no waiting gunmen opened fire.

"Tokiko?" Arkady called out. "Are you in there?" Ming-Jun's scent still lingered in the air, but it didn't smell like she was still present. Il-Hyeong's scent, as well as his own, were there as well, albeit fainter, along with the indistinguishable background mishmash of more than half a dozen other species from this floor of the building. "Tokiko?" the ferret asked again.

When no response came, Arkady finally swung around to take a look in through the doorway, ready to duck back and bolt if some elaborately-hidden ambush really was still waiting for him. What he saw, though, was that the apartment was empty, and certainly not in the state that he'd left it.

Ming-Jun's computer equipment was in ruins. Her monitors had been smashed in, the cases ripped open and the innards destroyed, and even her desk looked to have been torched in places. Other pieces of equipment were strewn about the floor, most of it badly damaged, as well. Aside from that, it didn't appear as if the apartment itself had been ransacked, and with the exception of the damage to the hardware, there was no further sign that there had been any struggle: no overturned furniture, no bullet holes in the wall, no signs of blood...

Blood. Arkady closed his eyes and breathed deeply again. He tried as hard as he could to pick up the scent of the one thing he hoped he wouldn't find, and he let his breath out as a sigh of relief when he failed.

He considered whether Ming-Jun had wrecked her own equipment before taking off, but that wasn't likely. Even in a frenzied rush, Arkady knew that Ming-Jun could have wiped her databases and rendered her computer systems forever inoperable with just a few keystrokes, so it had to have been someone else. Who, then, had come and done this?

Moreover, why hadn't they stolen the equipment instead of destroying it? Whoever knew of the Sahasrara team's presence here would surely also have to know the incalculable value of the data the Iolite League's special ops would have on hand. Why waste that?

There were too many unanswered questions. Arkady couldn't take any more of them. He was all alone, abandoned in a country that didn't want him, with no friends, nobody to trust, and presumably, someone out there had a bullet with his name on it.

Samuel Togen, if he were real, would at least have the luxury of getting on the next flight out and retreating to his old home back in Chochi-Sankeng; Arkady Ryswife had a botched mission that he had no feasible hope of salvaging, and teammates whom he didn't know he could ever find.

The ferret stumbled through the rest of the apartment, looking for any other glaring clues. Even with his advanced perception, his mind was becoming less able to process input by the moment. It was entirely possible that his body didn't even require sleep anymore, but right now, his mind definitely did.

He found himself in the bathroom, staring into the dirty mirror. The dark mask of fur on his face made his eyes appear too small and somehow distant. His eyes themselves were flat and dull, without a spark, the brown pupils looking like they'd had a few layers of color washed out of them. He couldn't even remember seeing himself look like this, not even after the most intense of missions, not even after Kentian had died.

The emptiness in his eyes then reminded him of the look on Kentian's face after he'd been shot. The wolf's lifeless eyes had been much the same, peering straight forward, but not looking at anything. Everything behind those eyes had just stopped.

How long could Arkady go without blinking? He looked deeper into the mirror and just stared at himself. His dead eyes didn't waver, didn't so much as twitch as he maintained perfect focus. He concentrated on keeping his eyelids open, resisting the urge to blink them shut.

Whenever he felt instinct to blink ready to take over, though, he felt a thin layer of liquid seep down and coat his eyeballs again, eliminating the need to close his eyes, allowing him to keep his perfect, steady stare.

With a grunt and a curse, Arkady tore his gaze away from the ferret in the mirror, and then hung his head off to one side, holding his eyes shut. He concentrated hard in order to purge the image that felt as if it had burned itself into his retinas, and when he opened his eyes again, he made sure to blink consciously for a few intervals until his body got back into the habit.

If giving up were even an option now, would he want to take it? Would he be able to count himself lucky and just thank God that he managed to survive, and that he'd be able to go back to Château Sainte-Mireille with his life intact, if nothing else?

No. Doing nothing was the one thing he'd never be able to do. He thought back to when he'd been ready to enter into life at the Château monastery, when a wise and noble rabbit deacon had asked him if a bright and promising young fellow of integrity, who was ready to devote his life to his faith, might not want to try something else, try a different path, one that was more active, that might have a far greater impact in furthering the cause of the League and spreading the word and wisdom of the Iolite Doctrine.

Il-Hyeong and Ming-Jun both had taken that same vow, had made the same solemn decision to devote themselves to the difficult and arduous path of an agent of Sahasrara. Sahasrara, the seventh chakra, which symbolized the oneness of an individual's mind with the greater cosmic truth of the universe. The tangible world was one of crude matter and flesh, filled with imperfect people of dozens of different species, who didn't look alike or act alike and yet who still possessed souls that transcended all of those base, unimportant particulars of physical existence. Peace and understanding were realities that could be achieved in the mortal realm if people were willing to look closely enough at the world to see that their lives, and the lives of everyone else around them, were all intertwined within the same beautiful framework that was the whole of creation.

Arkady and his teammates had all sworn to work toward that ideal. It might not happen in their lifetime, or their grandchildren's lifetimes or Pandora's lifetime, but each thing they did, they did for that hope of enlightenment. For the better world.

No, Arkady could not give up—not on his teammates, nor on that dream for a world his daughter could grow up in and help forge. Neither could he simply throw himself headlong into an uncertain situation and waste his own life in an act of desperation. He needed to collect himself, to gain the perspective he needed, to find a way to come at this problem.

For the immediate future, that meant getting to sleep.

The ferret dragged himself out of the bathroom, then paced around the living room some more. He wanted to sleep, but just wanting it didn't make him any less antsy. The sight of Ming-Jun's wrecked equipment made him even less inclined to get to bed and let his guard down, but he knew that he'd be useless to his cause if he didn't rest. That wasn't just something they'd gone over repeatedly in training; it was common sense. Why was common sense so hard for him to accept lately, though?

He certainly couldn't sleep here, he knew. He needed to find someplace else. With the apartment compromised, he'd be safer sleeping in some random alleyway. God willing, he'd be able to find something a little better than *that*, but he'd take what he could get.

As Arkady went over his mental checklist of the area, he stopped in the living room, noticing something that had escaped his notice the night before: the wall over the sofa was bare.

Having not spent much time in the apartment before the mission, it hadn't been immediately obvious to Arkady why that would be unusual, but then he remembered what had been so unusual about the wall in the first place: Ming-Jun's Quanyao broadsword. It was gone.

If Ming-Jun had been in the apartment when it had been raided and she'd still had time to grab the broadsword, there would certainly have been more signs of a battle having taken place. If she'd fled the apartment before anyone else had gotten there, why would she have taken the sword and left everything else?

Arkady looked over at the doorway to the room where Il-Hyeong had slept the night before. The sound dampers the fox had set up were still in place. *Peace and quiet*, the ferret thought. That's what he needed. Peace and quiet.

Leaving the apartment, Arkady made his way back toward the staircase, once more avoiding the elevator, just in case. Securing legitimate accommodations in this part of town at this time of night would be difficult, and even if he did manage to find a hotel or motel to check into, there was no telling for sure whether his Samuel Togen identity was still secure; it was entirely possible that whoever had found the apartment was also keeping their eyes peeled for any activity under the agents' assumed names.

Sleeping in an alley or on some park bench carried with it the risk of being discovered, as well, though it was more likely that he'd be found by the local authorities, first—and being picked up as a foreign indigent and getting deported was preferable to taking a bullet in the head while he slept.

Arkady's sleep was fitful. He dreamt of Château Sainte-Mireille and of the sterile corridors hidden beneath its hallowed ground. He dreamt of Pandora, floating lifelessly in the center of the Hephaestus Chamber, mask over her snout, sleeping the same kind of fitful sleep. Her eyes were closed: just as Arkady could go without shutting his eyes, so too could Pandora go without opening hers. He wanted her eyes to open. He wanted to smash his way into that glass tank, to tear the mask from his daughter's face, and to peel back her eyes with his own fingers so that she could awake and see the world.

Was Pandora ready to see this world, though? And was Arkady ready to see into Pandora's eyes if it meant that he might see the same lifeless brown gaze that he'd seen in his own?

"Arkady." The voice was calm and soft, accompanied by an equally soft yet insistent shaking of the ferret's shoulder. "Arkady, come on. Wake up."

The ferret opened his bleary eyes and saw Il-Hyeong squatting over him. Almost immediately, the rest of Arkady's senses kicked in as his body jolted to full wakefulness, and the next thing he noticed was the scent of blood that lingered on the fox.

Arkady's eyes focused next, and it looked as though Il-Hyeong had had about as pleasant a night as Arkady's. The fox's fur was unkempt, his eyes showed an all-too-familiar deadness, and a huge patch of his shirt was soaked through with dark, dried red that coated the whole left side of the front, which he'd at least tried to conceal with a dark gray windbreaker that he certainly hadn't worn along on the mission. At the fox's hip was his trusty DKR-7, and Arkady's nose picked up traces of gunpowder residue.

Underneath all that was the scent of city and nearby garbage. With bleary eyes, the ferret looked around the dingy bus station alcove he'd taken refuge inside. It was only a few blocks away from the apartment, but he'd hoped it wasn't too obvious a place for any would-be pursuers to look.

"What time is it?" Arkady asked as he sat up. It didn't feel like he'd slept long at all, but with the way he'd felt before going to sleep, he wouldn't have been surprised if he'd slept for days and still felt like this upon waking up.

"Couple hours past sunrise," Il-Hyeong replied.

With his eyes adjusted, now, Arkady took another look at the bloodstained fox and at the dirty alcove around them both. "How did you find me?"

Il-Hyeong tapped his own nose with a fingertip. "Tracked you from the apartment," he explained. "I'm impressed with how well this thing works, now." He cracked a smile that lasted only a second, then went wholly serious again. "Where's Ming-Jun?"

Arkady shook his head. "Not here," he said. "No sign of her." He remembered how the wolf had destroyed his communications device, and then looked hopefully at Il-Hyeong. "Did she relay a new rendezvous point to you?"

Il-Hyeong pulled his own earpiece out from his pocket and twiddled it back and forth. "Her end of the line went dead before I got out of Fan-Yin," he said. "From the look of things back at the apartment, I'm really hoping she has some other plan for getting in touch with us."

The fact that there hadn't been any traces of blood or signs of a larger struggle didn't mean that Ming-Jun still wasn't in danger—or that she wasn't already dead—and Arkady realized now, as he was faced with Il-Hyeong, that he'd been trying not to acknowledge those as eventualities. From the way she'd sounded the last time he'd heard her voice, it was clear that she knew something about what was going on, and that, at least in theory, she was more prepared for whatever was going to happen to her. Without knowing what that *something* was, though, Arkady and Il-Hyeong couldn't take anything for granted.

"She's trained for this sort of thing. She knows what she's doing," Arkady said as he dragged himself to his feet and started dusting off his soiled clothes. "If there's a way for her to get in touch with us, she'll find it."

"I hope you're right," Il-Hyeong said, and then Arkady heard the sound of the fox checking his gun.

Arkady finished brushing off his pants on and then turned back to see what Il-Hyeong was doing. Before Arkady could ask, the fox holstered his weapon, hid it from sight, and said, "In the meantime, I think you'll like the lead we have to follow."

"A lead?" Arkady noticed the smallest of smirks on his fellow agent's face. "Did you find something out back there?"

"Let's not spoil the surprise right now," Il-Hyeong said, and just as Arkady opened his mouth to snap an order to just come out and say what he knew, the fox motioned with a single finger to the stream of early-morning commuters who were beginning to mill on by en route to the bus station building proper.

So, Arkady kept his mouth shut and nodded to Il-Hyeong in acknowledgment of his wordless message. "Should we get going, then?" he asked, when it was clear that the passersby really were just that.

"The sooner the better," Il-Hyeong said. "Is that all you're bringing?" he then asked, looking fixedly at Arkady's bare hip.

The ferret grimaced. "It's all I've got." He didn't know where he'd even begin to explain why his gun was gone, let alone where it had gone.

With a hum, the fox paused, and then secretively checked his own gun a second time. "It'll have to do," he said. "We might not get another crack at this." With that, he slipped over towards a narrow side street.

"Where are we going?" Arkady asked as he started to follow.

"Back to the apartment," Il-Hyeong said. "I've got my car stashed there."

Arkady hurried his step. "Car? Where did you get a car?"

"It's a long story."

"Tell me what you can along the way, then," Arkady said. "In the meantime, if we're on our way back to the apartment, we could probably both stand to change our clothes."

Il-Hyeong sounded hesitant. "I don't want to have to linger at the scene too long," he said, but Arkady could hear the fox sniff at the scent of blood that clung to him, and then wrinkle his snout. "So let's just be as quick as we can about it."

"You stole a car?" Arkady had been surprised enough to see that Il-Hyeong had gotten hold of a vehicle, but he was even more shocked that the fox had the keys and hadn't just hotwired it.

Il-Hyeong kept his eyes on the road. "I'll give it back," he said. "Eventually. Right now, we need it more." Despite having changed his clothes, the stench of blood still clung to him.

"That doesn't give us the right to just steal things."

"This is a life-or-death situation, Arkady. I'm willing to overlook a minor transgression or two if it means finding Ming-Jun and getting home alive."

Arkady had seen Il-Hyeong's shirt after the fox had changed out of it, the red-black stains having soaked through both sides of it. That at least meant that the blood wasn't his, and while that was reassuring in a way, it didn't make the sight itself any less gruesome.

Although Arkady didn't disagree with the fox's rationale, the idea of conducting League business in a stolen automobile still rubbed him the wrong way. "I don't know if breaking the local laws is really going to help our image with the locals," he murmured.

"I can live with 'Raymond Castille' taking a black mark on his record," Il-Hyeong replied with a snort. "Besides, with the number of cars that get stolen every day in a city this size, I'm not too worried about having to make a high-speed getaway from the local authorities."

"You promise you're giving it back, though, right?" Arkady asked.

As he rounded a bend, Il-Hyeong took a moment to look over at Arkady. "And what if I'd taken this from the people who attacked us?" he asked. "Would you be so concerned about where it came from then?"

Arkady knew that extenuating circumstances made the matter of theft less subject to a clear cut 'right and wrong' judgment, but he didn't like the way that Il-Hyeong seemed so dismissive about it. "Don't worry," the fox said before Arkady could get another word in, his gaze turning back to the road. "Once we're done using it, we can make sure that the police get it back to the rightful owner, okay?" He sighed and shook his head. "Is *this* really what you want to waste energy worrying about?"

The ferret didn't want to dignify that with a response. It wasn't like Il-Hyeong to be so flippant and, frankly, borderline insubordinate. Extenuating circumstances, Arkady reminded himself. Ming-Jun was missing, and after the death of Kentian (*Ming-Jun might be dead already.*), there was reason to be nervous.

Like Il-Hyeong was insisting, Arkady should be willing to overlook a mild transgression, given the nature of what they were dealing with. They'd find Ming-Jun, they'd figure out what was going on, and before they knew it, they'd be back at Château Sainte-Mireille, enjoying the comforts of home and the Iolite League.

Why *was* he so anxious about something as inconsequential as a stolen car? Less than twelve hours previous, he and Il-Hyeong were killing people they didn't even know. After that, Arkady himself had been held captive by yet another unknown quantity. And now he was getting squeamish over a boosted automobile. Had his faith in his own leadership abilities degraded to the point where he had to grasp at straws just to prove to himself that he could still be assertive, could still retain control of the situation?

"So, what's this lead of yours?" Arkady asked, resisting the urge to open up the glove box and sift through the contents looking for clues about the car's owner.

A grin appeared on Il-Hyeong's muzzle. "You want to know who the people who attacked us at Fan-Yin are?"

The fox's expression grew more and more proud and assured. "Il-Hyeong, where are we going?" the ferret asked, worried.

"Let's just say that I found a place to stash a few things that I managed to grab on my escape from Fan-Yin," Il-Hyeong said. They were headed in the general vicinity of the Fan-Yin building now, Arkady realized. "The question is whether you and I can't get at the clues we need."

Arkady could tell that the fox was on to something big, and it was making him nervous. "Oh my God, Il-Hyeong, did you capture one of them?"

"Two of them," Il-Hyeong said. He looked altogether too pleased with himself, Arkady thought. "That'll teach them to chase after their quarry too far."

"How did you do it?" Arkady asked.

"Hey, twenty-on-one, the odds are in their favor; two-on-one, the odds are in mine."

"And where exactly are you keeping them?" the ferret asked. That Il-Hyeong had managed to take prisoners was a huge boon to their cause, he had to admit, but it wasn't like the team had a secure place to hold them.

Il-Hyeong tapped at the side window with one claw. "Just up through here," he said, taking the next turn down a trash-laden side street. "Trust me, even if they could yell, nobody around here would be able to hear them."

The car passed through a run-down portion of the industrial sector, several blocks away from where Fan-Yin Bioinformatics was located. The next block was rowed with buildings that appeared to be abandoned, and Il-Hyeong slowed down and stopped the car outside one of them.

"In through here," the fox said, taking Arkady in through a side door that had been propped open with a rock. The door led to a tight stairwell that they took down into the basement, and from there, Il-Hyeong continued to lead Arkady down past row after row of storage aisles until they came to a door that had been barred shut from the outside by an old steel rod.

Il-Hyeong yanked the bar out of place and then pulled the door open. The room within was dark, but even though Arkady could see only the outlines of figures, he could smell the odor of bodily waste and hear dull groaning. The fox reached a paw inside, fished around on the wall, and then flicked a switch, causing the old overhead lighting to crackle and flicker a few times before it came on and stayed on.

Arkady instantly recognized the slate blue uniforms on the two men bound and on their knees in the center of the room. Both captives were feline. The larger of the two, both taller and stockier, was a black panther, and the other was a younger-looking, tawny-furred cougar. The latter looked like he'd been asleep (or passed out) until Il-Hyeong had opened the door, and his eyes still showed the signs of the hope that had been dashed when he saw that rescue had not arrived.

There were so many questions that Arkady wanted to ask Il-Hyeong, but he couldn't show uncertainty and confusion on his part—not in front of prisoners that they'd need to interrogate. *So much for reasserting leadership*, he thought to himself. He didn't know enough about the situation to act on his own, however, and so he kept his mouth shut and tried to look dispassionate as he walked around the room, assessing the prisoners and their circumstance.

Both of the cats had their paws bound behind their backs with cuffs, cuffs that were of the same make that the wolf had slapped on Arkady only hours before. Il-Hyeong must have gotten them off of Jenkins, the ferret realized. Both prisoners also looked haggard and worn out. The panther had a kink in his tail where it appeared to have been snapped, and flecks of dried blood liberally dotted one of the cougar's cheeks.

With nothing to say that wouldn't give away his ignorance of the situation, Arkady remained silent and took up position in one of the corners, folding his arms across his midsection as Il-Hyeong stepped into the room.

The fox made a show of checking his gun in front of the prisoners, and with his attention still on his firearm, he said, "So, now that we're well-rested, let's answer some questions."

Arkady noticed the cougar wince and hold his eyes shut. Not only was he smaller than his comrade, but he was clearly meeker and more afraid. The panther appeared more resolute, simply staring back at Il-Hyeong without any fear on his face. Transfixed by that expression of simple defiance, Arkady noticed that one side of his face had been scratched deeply by a set of claws. Again, probably Il-Hyeong's doing.

"Now, it seems a bit unfair to me that you knew what we were up to," the fox said, pacing back and forth between the two prisoners. "Let's even things out. Why don't you tell me a little bit more about who you are and what you were doing?"

Neither captive had any response. They didn't even look to one another to assure their mutual silence. The cougar still looked like the more timid of the two, but Il-Hyeong walked up to the panther, instead, the fox's gun dangling casually at his side.

"You," Il-Hyeong said, tapping the panther on the forehead with a single finger. "What's the name of your little organization? Whose insignia is this?" He pointed dismissively to the emblem on the panther's uniform.

As members of Sahasrara, Arkady and Il-Hyeong had both been given training in interrogation techniques. Arkady was confused as to why Il-Hyeong had started with the panther. Conventional wisdom declared that, if handling a group of captives, it was better to start with the captive that was most likely to let information slip: an otherwise weak-willed prisoner could become emboldened by seeing their stronger comrade hold up to threats and questioning; conversely, a prisoner's resolve might break by seeing a more vulnerable cohort crack under pressure.

True to expectations, the cougar looked relieved that his vulpine captor had not started with him, and the panther's expression remained resolute. "I will tell you nothing," the panther snarled at the fox, his exhaustion adding an unexpected layer of menace to his voice.

Il-Hyeong sighed. "Of course you won't," he said, his voice dripping with disappointment. "That's because you lack the proper motivation." The very next moment, Il-Hyeong brought his gun up and fired right between the panther's eyes, causing his head to snap back as a spray of bright red painted the wall behind him.

The cougar turned his head aside a fraction of a second too late to be spared the sight, and his eyes scrunched up like those of a wounded kitten as he cried out, "*Tiān a!*" Arkady let out a brief shout as well, muffled by the echo of the gunshot in close quarters, the suddenness of it all having caught him entirely off-guard.

The ferret's reflexes had kicked in all too late. He'd seen Il-Hyeong lift up his weapon, watched him take aim, but he hadn't expected that the fox would ever actually pull the trigger.

Il-Hyeong hadn't done so much as blink. With no change of expression on his face, he turned his attention to the cougar and brought his gun up again. Arkady was frozen, knowing that he couldn't possible act in time to stop the fox from firing again, and so he watched helplessly, making no attempt to even brace himself for what he'd see.

This time, however, Il-Hyeong didn't fire. Instead, he merely pressed the barrel of his pistol right up against the cougar's forehead, and Arkady could smell the feline's fur being singed by the still-hot metal. "How about you?" Il-Hyeong asked the cougar. "Do you have any problems with motivation?"

The cougar's body shook with weak sobs, and Arkady could see the first signs of tears pooling up in his eyes. "*Qiúqiú nǐ, bù yào shā wǒ,*" he whined, his eyelids still held firmly shut. "Please... please don't kill me."

"Then talk," Il-Hyeong said with a tone that mocked an attempt at being soothing. "Who are you, and what do you want?"

Zhōngwén. The words themselves may as well have been gibberish, but even when forced through a choked-out plea, the tones of the syllables were still unmistakable.

Arkady wanted to leap across the room and tackle Il-Hyeong to the ground, breaking the fox's wrist if he had to, so long as it meant getting the gun away from him. To exhibit such senseless cruelty, to brutally murder an unarmed and defenseless living being—none of this was anything that the Il-Hyeong he knew would ever do. As the cougar began to simper and spill forth words, though, Arkady knew that he had no choice but to let the interrogation continue, so that the horrible damage already done would at least not have been for nothing.

"We're called the Carmine Order," the cougar said. His chest still heaved with panicked breathing and frightened sobs, and he still refused to open his eyes. "And we... we just came to protect ourselves."

"Several dozen heavily-armed men worrying about protecting themselves from two people who aren't even out to get you?" Il-Hyeong asked. "Now, something about that doesn't sound right to me."

"I swear!" the cougar cried. "They... they told us where to set up. They said that's where you'd be, and that we needed to take you out. They said it was... was self-defense."

Il-Hyeong leaned forward. "Who's 'they'?" he asked.

"I don't know," the cougar replied, and when Il-Hyeong pressed his gun harder against the feline's head, he stammered, "I don't have names, honest! They're just... they're the elders. They're the ones who are in charge."

"In charge of what?"

"In charge of protecting ourselves," the cougar said. He was going to end up hyperventilating at this rate, Arkady feared. "Protecting our way of life. They... they know what's best for us."

Il-Hyeong snorted. "Your way of life? What, so you're a bunch of Ridgecrescent nationalists?"

The cougar tried to shake his head. "No. We're... no, I... please, I... I can't..."

"Look, if this conversation is uncomfortable for you, we can end it right here," Il-Hyeong said, tapping the cougar on the head with the barrel of his gun.

That made the cougar's eyes open, finally. They were full of both tears and abject terror, but even still, he sniffled and shook his head in weak defiance.

Arkady saw Il-Hyeong's trigger finger begin to tense up. "What do you know about Ming-Jun Devra?" the ferret called out.

Both the cougar and Il-Hyeong snapped their heads to the side, both flashing looks of confusion at Arkady. The cougar again shook his head as he gasped for air. "I don't know any Ming-Jun," he said. "I swear, I don't. We were only there to wait for you, honest."

Arkady scrutinized the look on the captive's face. He hadn't reacted with any sort of alarm at Ming-Jun's name in particular. "Who's the cacomistle?" the ferret asked without segue. "The woman who was with you. You know who I mean."

"That's..." With another nudge from Il-Hyeong's gun, the cougar squeezed his eyes shut again. "Kuai!" he yelled. "She works for Kuai. He'd be the one who put her in charge of the operation."

Il-Hyeong smiled approvingly at Arkady, but Arkady felt no joy at dragging information out of a man whose life was dangling from a thread—a thread that Il-Hyeong could and probably would cut at any moment. "And what was the scope of this operation?" the fox followed up with.

"I told you already," the cougar said. "We were there to wait for you. A fox and a ferret, she said. We were supposed to kill you because you were a threat to our way of life."

"How did you know we were going to be there?" Il-Hyeong asked.

"I don't know," he said. "Nobody told me, I swear. I'm just a soldier."

"Soldiers fight in wars," Il-Hyeong said, using the barrel of his gun to 'caress' the cougar's cheeks. "Is there some war going on that we should know about?"

The cougar began to cry again, tears matting down the fur at the edges of his muzzle. He started to shake his head again and began to murmur incomprehensible things under his breath. "I don't think he knows anything else," Arkady said to Il-Hyeong. "Come on. He's given us the leads we need. Let's go."

"And what do you want to do with him?" Il-Hyeong asked. "Leave him here to starve to death?"

"Of course not," Arkady replied. "But we can—"

"Don't even try to say that we can let him go," Il-Hyeong said. "You know that's not an option."

"Why not?" Arkady asked. "What could he have possibly learned about us that this Carmine Order doesn't already know?"

"I really don't want to find out," Il-Hyeong replied. "And neither should you. You're smarter than that, Arkady."

Now the cougar's muttering got more intelligible, to the point where Arkady recognized it as frantic praying. The ferret opened his mouth to say something, but found himself at a loss for words. He needed to think of something, and he'd never felt more put on the spot to act. He'd ordered Il-Hyeong once before not to kill a man, and Il-Hyeong didn't listen. Here, a man was rushing to make his peace with God, while Arkady's own partner—the same fox who had been praying to God just the night before to not have to kill people—was all too willing to snuff out that man's life.

"Come on," Arkady said. "We can't just kill him."

Il-Hyeong, still facing Arkady, nonchalantly lifted his gun again and fired sideways, twice, both bullets striking the cougar in the chest. The feline slumped and then toppled over onto his side, blood forming a dark pool in front of him, his paws still bound behind his back.

Both cats now lay dead. The scent of blood in the air grew thicker, until it was almost cloying, but Arkady couldn't even build up the urge to retch. All he could do was stare at Il-Hyeong, the fox as still and as motionless as the two feline bodies bleeding silently onto the cold floor.

11. Severed Lifeline

"What the hell is wrong with you?" Arkady screamed. He kept looking back and forth between the fox and the dead cougar, between the fox and the dead panther. He wanted to take a swing at Il-Hyeong; he wanted to drop to his knees and cry; he wanted to wake back up at Château Sainte-Mireille and have Father Benjamin or Ming-Jun or Kentian tell him that this whole week had been some awful dream.

Holstering his gun, Il-Hyeong went to remove the cuffs from the pair of dead prisoners. "You said it yourself," the fox replied. "He probably didn't know anything else. We were done with him."

"You murdered these two people!" the ferret snarled. "They were helpless, unarmed, and you just executed them without—"

"Without what?" Il-Hyeong snapped back, looking back up at Arkady. "Without a trial? What were we supposed to do? Bring them back to Château Sainte-Mireille? Give them over to the police?"

Arkady started to pace around the room as anxiety and nausea took him over. This couldn't be happening. Il-Hyeong could not have just done what he had. "I... I don't know!" The ferret went to punch the wall, stopping his fist before it actually collided, likely sparing himself the pain of a few broken bones. "But you didn't have to kill them," he said, taking a deep breath, pulling forth some semblance of composure.

"And if we let them go, then what?" Il-Hyeong asked. He didn't quite get into Arkady's face, but he was close. "Do you honestly think that either of these men wouldn't have tried to kill us at the first opportunity, if not now, then the next time we ran afoul of this Carmine Order?"

The ferret wrung his paws. "We don't know that for sure."

Il-Hyeong ignored him. "Or who's to say that they'd even be welcomed back? How do you think a fanatical group like this would treat traitors, Arkady? You think letting them have their 'trial' with their own people was a better idea?"

"That doesn't give you the right to just *kill* them!"

"Arkady, if this was back at Fan-Yin, and both of these men were holding guns, then you would have killed them without a second thought. Don't try to hide behind some illusion of moral superiority."

Again, Arkady felt his fists clench on instinct, knowing that trying to deck his partner would be a mistake he'd never get to correct. "That's different," he insisted, hearing his overdefensiveness in his voice. "These people weren't attacking us; they were at our mercy."

"They *did* attack us, and this *was* merciful," the fox said, getting back to his task of retrieving his equipment. "If they were good people, then God will forgive them."

"That's your justification for this?" Arkady asked. "Where in any of the Scriptures does it say—"

"Hey, look, do you think I *like* having to do this?" Il-Hyeong snapped as he got back to his feet, motioning to the two bodies with a paw. "Of course I don't. But we're in danger, here. These people have told us that they consider us 'a threat to their way of life,' and they've shown unmistakably that they have the resources and desire to see us dead. These aren't people that we're going to reason with, and every minute that we waste trying is another minute that we leave Ming-Jun in danger, wherever the hell she is right now."

Il-Hyeong's argument made logical sense, Arkady had to admit, but that didn't make the fox right. There was a line, and the fox had crossed it, and Arkady didn't and couldn't understand why. "I want to find Ming-Jun, too," the ferret said with a sigh. "So let's get back to it, okay?"

The fox turned out the light and walked back out into the basement. "Let's," he agreed. "Any thoughts on where to check next?"

The two of them had the name of the group who had tried to kill them, as well as the name of the man who'd organized the attempt on their life—and who had possibly set the trap involving the Pyxis Sequence in the first place. Il-Hyeong may have committed abhorrent sin, but he'd helped to get them a great deal of information that they desperately needed.

"The mercenary," Arkady said. "The white wolf we ran into at Fan-Yin. I know where he is." He turned and started to leave, trusting Il-Hyeong to follow. More than anything, the ferret just wanted to be out of the building, to be away from the bodies of the two men who had died for nothing.

As expected, Il-Hyeong fell into step behind him, then tried to overtake him. "The mercenary?" the fox asked. "What, do you have prisoners stashed away in an abandoned building, too?"

Arkady shook his head, continuing to walk. "I know where he's staying." He didn't have to see Il-Hyeong's face to register the fox's surprise. "I think we can make a trade with him."

"A trade of what?" Il-Hyeong asked. "Wait, you're not talking about trading information, are you? Because if you're thinking about exchanging Iolite League secrets with someone who tried to *kill* us, then—"

"He wasn't trying to kill us." *Not like some people.* "He claims that he was hired by the Iolite League."

"Well he's lying, of course."

"Of course," Arkady repeated. "But I think *he* at least thinks he's been hired by the Iolite League. I want to find out who's pretending to be us."

Il-Hyeong grunted. "What, did the two of you leave Fan-Yin together and grab a cup of coffee?"

"Yeah, something like that." Since Il-Hyeong couldn't see his face, it wasn't worth Arkady's effort to roll his eyes. "Look, all I know is that I'm pretty sure that we can get some information out of him if we're willing to do a little give and take." The ferret placed his paw onto the handle to the door that led outside. "Plus, he has my gun."

The swift fox's flat expression went even flatter. "So you got all buddy-buddy with someone who tried to kill us, *and* you let him keep your weapon? Well, lead on, Mr. Ryswife." He made a grandiose, exaggerated gestured towards the door.

Wanting even more to roll his eyes at the fox, now, Arkady just pushed the door open. "Look, we don't know where or how to find this Kuai person right now, so this is the best lead we have." He stopped short of adding, *'because you killed our other two sources of information.'*

As soon as Arkady stepped back outside, a small section of the concrete wall next to his head seemed to explode, showering the side of his face with bits of pulverized matter. At once, his too-keen reflexes kicked in; he could still see the smoky wisps of what had once been solid wall drifting off into the air. He calculated the trajectory of impact in his head, his line of sight following along as he went over invisible numbers in his mind, and found himself looking at the top floor of another building on the opposite side of the abandoned industrial park.

"Sniper!" he called out, trusting Il-Hyeong to duck back behind the door on command. For Arkady, taking the time to double-back on himself might give the shooter more time to get a bead on him, and he couldn't be sure what the rate of fire was on the weapon that was targeting him. There was probably a sizable margin of error in his off-the-cuff threat assessment, but the most obvious "safe" move for him was to dive behind the car, the one that Il-Hyeong had stolen.

A dull *plunk* echoed through the deserted parking zone as a second bullet pierced the body of the car. Going by the sound of the impact and what he'd seen of the building before he had to take cover, Arkady was getting closer to narrowing down just which window the shooter was firing from, though given where he and Il-Hyeong were pinned down, it was unlikely that such information would do them very much good. Even assuming they survived long enough to get out of their current crisis and thereafter circle back around here for clues, there was no guaranteeing that whoever was behind this wasn't skilled enough or practiced enough to do a good job of covering their tracks. This definitely didn't have the mark of an amateur job.

At a full sprint from his current position, Arkady estimated that he could make it around the corner of the building across the way in under ten seconds—perhaps in eight or even seven, if he really pushed himself. Even if the shooter were among the best snipers Arkady had known, there was a reasonable chance that he'd have difficulty hitting a small target running at full speed (and whoever it was had missed Arkady when he'd been relatively still). Making the shot wouldn't be impossible, though, and even then, the ferret was gambling that they—whoever this 'they' was—didn't have other snipers set up in other buildings covering any escape routes.

The sound of another bullet smashing into the concrete wall of the building behind him made Arkady turn his head, and he had no time to shout any orders to Il-Hyeong, who had already sprung off of one foot, diving into a roll that then landed him behind cover with the ferret.

"What the *hell* are you thinking?" Arkady snapped. Glass shattered and tinkled as the car's rear windshield was shot out.

"I thought he still had a bead on you," Il-Hyeong replied. "Besides, he still missed." The fox's voice didn't show any signs of exertion or tension.

Arkady scanned the area for visual cues, like light glinting off of other weapons that might be taking aim at them. "Well, now that you're no longer within the safety of a building that might have *another way out*, do you have any bright ideas on where to go from here?"

Il-Hyeong was unfazed by his superior's edged remark. "One of us makes a run for the corner over there," he said, pointing to the spot where Arkady had considered dashing toward before. "While the sniper wastes a shot trying to hit one of us, the other heads around back here," he added, nodding down the length of the building they were pinned against. Making a run for that corner meant leaving one's back exposed to the shooter for several seconds, with nowhere to dodge or hide behind in the meantime, but if the shooter *were* distracted—

"I don't like it," Arkady said, shaking his head. "Too risky. We're good, but we're not invincible."

"We're something close to it," Il-Hyeong replied. "Besides, I don't think this guy's the best shot in the world, anyway."

"Are you willing to risk your life on that?"

The fox grinned coldly. "If you like, I can be the one who runs out first in order to draw fire."

If Il-Hyeong's newfound lack of respect of life had translated into a death wish, then Arkady's problems with his fellow agent were going to extend beyond their present predicament. For the time being, getting the two of them out of there alive was still the ferret's foremost concern, and though it might matter little by now, he was still at least technically in charge. "No," he said, more firmly this time. "There has to be a less risky way to get out of this. We just need to look and—"

Both the fox and the ferret went quiet and still at the sound of an automobile engine. It was such a mundane sound, but the lack of any traffic from blocks around their current position made it stand out. It got louder—definitely getting closer—and changed pitch and tone, indicating the vehicle itself slowing down, turning corners, and speeding up again.

"We have to run, Arkady," Il-Hyeong insisted. "Now."

The closer the sound got to them, the more obvious it was that they were dealing with a van or truck and not a smaller car of some sort. Arkady didn't want to agree to Il-Hyeong's plan, but the fox was right in that they couldn't stay where they were, and there simply wasn't enough time to think of a better course of action. "Fine," the ferret conceded. "But I go first."

And so he did. Starting from a crouch, he broke into a run and sprinted catercorner across the way. The sound of the approaching vehicle got much louder as it rounded another corner, and the ferret didn't need to turn and look to know that it was coming along the roadway leading to the intersection he was crossing, perpendicular to the sniper's line of fire. He heard another bullet strike the pavement harmlessly several feet to one side of him, and by then he just needed a little more push to get around the corner and out of view.

Knowing that he had no hope outrunning a motor vehicle outright, and that his only option would be to dodge down side-paths or into one of the numerous empty buildings, Arkady afforded himself the chance to turn around and check on Il-Hyeong. The fox was partway across the intersection already, his pistol gripped in one paw as his arms swung back and forth in excellent sprinting form. "Go!" he shouted upon seeing that Arkady had stopped on his account, even momentarily.

Then, what was supposed to have been the ferret's brief spot-check turned into his standing there for another second or two as he stared in disbelief at the van—the very familiar van—barreling down the street towards them.

Arkady took cover behind the short staircase that led up to the boarded-up front doors of the building he'd run up to. When he saw the appalled and confused look on Il-Hyeong's face, he hurriedly waved the fox closer. Now Il-Hyeong must have been overwhelmed with curiosity, because he spun around to look behind himself, too, then quickly started to pull his pistol up for a shot. Thinking of how he'd been too slow to say anything last time, Arkady called out, "Hold your fire!" without regard to the possibility of giving away his position.

Il-Hyeong complied, but didn't look happy, and though he lowered his gun, he still gripped it in both paws, one finger still on the trigger. "What the hell is going on, Arkady?" he snarled, holding position in the middle of the street, standing in the way of the van as if to challenge it. Arkady was less worried about the van hitting the fox than he was about Il-Hyeong standing right out in the open in the line of potential sniper fire, and the ferret again wondered if the fox's defiance was such that he'd hold onto his frustrations at the expense of his own life.

The van screeched to a halt after it cleared the intersection. The driver cut the wheel sharply to the right, causing it to spin out with the driver's-side door facing Arkady and Il-Hyeong. The front window rolled down, and out popped the mouse's head that the ferret had been hoping to see. "Get in!" he chirped at the duo, his demeanor frantic and his voice urgent.

Arkady started to move closer to the van, but he hadn't even taken a step when Il-Hyeong had the gun trained on him, instead. "Nobody's going anywhere until someone tells me what's going on," he growled. A quick glance told Arkady that the safety on the fox's pistol was, in fact, off.

"He's with the mercenaries," Arkady said. "We can—"

"Look, just hurry up and get in!" the mouse shouted to Arkady. He lacked any sort of grit or toughness that a hired gun ought to have; how he ended up in a mercenary group with the likes of the wolf and Jenkins was beyond Arkady's ability to guess.

Il-Hyeong motioned with his gun for Arkady to approach the van. "Fuck it. We can talk about it on the way. Get in the van."

The ferret complied, feeling relief that Il-Hyeong was willing to go along with this (and would presumably do so without shooting anyone else). Once Arkady was inside, he made space for Il-Hyeong, who in a single motion hopped inside and pulled the door shut behind him. He was in the process of bringing his gun up to the back of the mouse's head when he noticed the bulletproof divider in place. "Arkady, you had better know what the fuck you're doing," he said without even turning to look at the ferret.

Wasting no time, the mouse started to wheel the van around, doubling-back the way he'd come. "Not that way," Arkady urged, slapping his paws on the bulletproof glass to emphasize his words. "They've got a shooter in place."

Now Il-Hyeong did look at Arkady, sideways, flashing him a one-eyed glance of accusation, but the ferret ignored it. "Damn it," the mouse snapped, tugging the steering wheel sharply in order to swing the van around before it could roll out back into the intersection. "Boots was afraid that might be the case."

"'Boots?'" asked Arkady and Il-Hyeong simultaneously.

The mouse shook his head, but kept both paws firmly on the wheel. "Sorry. The Sarge, I mean," he said. "He told me you were in deep shit and that I needed to bail you out ASAP." His eyes flicked into view in the rear-view mirror, alighting on Il-Hyeong. "Didn't mention you weren't alone, though."

"And how'd this 'Sarge' of yours know where to find us?" Il-Hyeong asked. His free paw fidgeted, gripping at the fabric of his own pants and at the seat.

The eyes that had popped up into the rear-view mirror were facing straight ahead, now, but the mouse kept his paws firmly on the steering wheel. "Didn't say how," he said. "Just told me where to go." He pressed harder on the gas, the van's rumbling engine echoing through the deserted industrial sector.

Arkady froze. How could the wolf have possibly known that this attack was going to happen? The simplest way would be if he were somehow behind it, of course—but if that were the case, why send rescue? It could all be some ploy to engender trust, but that seemed overly elaborate, and moreover, not the wolf's style. So long as it had resulted in his tail being pulled out of the fire, did Arkady have any right to complain?

Looking less amused by the moment was Il-Hyeong; even his scent was changing to show his irritation, now—something the fox was usually better at keeping in check. An ordinary person couldn't really be faulted for that under the circumstances, but Arkady was nervous about the fox losing his cool, as given what had happened in the last—damn, it had to have been less than fifteen minutes since the execution of the Carmine Order prisoners. Life-or-death situations had a strange time-dilating effect to start with, and given Arkady's unique ability to sense minute things, the slowed-down passage of time was exacerbated (maybe that also explained the more rapid increase in Il-Hyeong's agitation?).

"Where are you taking us?" Il-Hyeong asked. His fur bristled momentarily before he visibly settled in a forced state of calm.

The driver took a sharp right and slammed harder on the gas, getting onto the roadway that led from the industrial complex to the more populated section of Highslope, where there would hopefully be less risk of a public attempt on their lives. "Back to the Sarge's safehouse," the mouse replied, "and from there, presumably to someplace else."

"And could you let us know who and what we're running from?" the fox asked.

"Boots didn't say." The mouse showed no signs of relief, even as he watched the buildings behind them get smaller and smaller in the rear-view mirror. "He just said to get you and—"

The sound of the van's windshield shattering apart didn't do enough to muffle the sickening, wet thump that echoed through the vehicle as the mouse's head smacked back into the divider between the front and back seats, a grotesquely symmetrical red splatter painting it. The divider now looked like a morbid stained-glass window, the spray of blood interrupted by the spiderweb pattern that radiated out from the circular breakpoint where a rifle round was still lodged, just inches from Il-Hyeong's face and muzzle. The van began to swerve, and it slowed down some, but didn't stop.

Arkady's own shout made him unable to determine exactly which expletive Il-Hyeong barked out. As the van careened to the left, heading toward the highway barrier, the ferret slouched down in his seat, drew up his legs, and kicked with both feet at the ruined divider. The first kick dislodged it, and a second kick popped it out entirely, allowing Arkady to slip his way into the front seat.

"Arkady, get the fuck down!" Il-Hyeong shouted, but the ferret was already keeping low, his slinky form allowing him to almost spill over the seats. Arkady muttered a quick prayer as he pulled the mouse's body over into the passenger's seat, trying not to notice how much or how little was left of his head. With the driver's seat at least mostly clear, the ferret slumped down into the tight space where his legs should go, paws gripping the steering wheel as his feet awkwardly positioned themselves by the accelerator and brake pedal, respectively. Down as far as he was, he couldn't see over the van's dashboard.

"Steer for me," he yelled back to Il-Hyeong as he tried to course-correct by feel alone, to realign themselves with the roadway before they ended up smashing into the concrete barrier. He pushed the gas pedal all the way to the floor.

"Fuck! This is fucking crazy, Arkady," Il-Hyeong replied. The ferret heard him scoot over toward the middle of the back seat. "Okay, more to the left. You're cutting too hard to the—shit, more to the right again."

The swerving would hopefully make them less of an easy target, Arkady was wagering, though it did cut down on their speed. Part of the trick would be making sure that the bulky van didn't tip over with all the back-and-forth. In Arkady's previous ride in it, it had seemed like a reliable enough vehicle, but there was no time to test its limits with an unacceptable risk of failure.

"How far are we from the overpass?" the ferret asked.

"Overpass? What overpass?"

"There was an overpass that we crossed on our way in," Arkady pointed out. "Can you see it from where we are?"

Il-Hyeong growled. "No, I—wait, no, I see it." He slid across the back seat to counterbalance Arkady's steering, and the ferret was glad that the fox could still follow along with the unspoken plan. "Except it's not an overpass; it's a bridge."

"Over the river?"

"Yeah, over the—"

"Great. How far?"

"Eighty yards? Maybe a hundred?"

That was close enough for Arkady to risk it. He straightened the van out, cutting at a shallow angle to the right. Again, he pushed the accelerator to the floor and held still. "Arkady," Il-Hyeong warned. "Arkady, we're heading right for the—"

"Grab hold of the back seat!" Arkady shouted, and a second later, the van smashed through the guard rail and soared out into the air.

They felt the illusion of free-fall for about a second and a half, and then the van plunged into the narrow tributary, landing on its right side. Il-Hyeong was flung against the right-side door, but his hold on the back seat seemed to dampen the impact, as far as Arkady could hear. Arkady himself remained wedged tightly in the small gap between the seat and dashboard, managed to avoid being dislodged by the impact.

The vehicle was hardly water-tight, and it began to flood even with the bullet hole in the windshield still above the water line. Wresting himself free of his tight, safe space, Arkady looked into the back seat at the banged-up (but otherwise no worse for the wear) Il-Hyeong. "So," he said to the fox. "You want to see how long we're able to hold our breaths, now?" He thumped on his chest with a closed fist.

Il-Hyeong had already accused Arkady of being crazy once, and though he didn't say it again, his eyes said it for him. His only reply was to open up the passenger's-side door (now effectively the 'bottom' door), kicking at the slide handle with one foot, causing the van to sink several more feet all at once as a fresh influx of water rushed in.

"Downstream, as far as you can," Arkady ordered while there was still enough room to keep his head above water. "Go."

The fox dove first, disappearing through the open door at the bottom of the van and into the murky waters beyond. Arkady followed after him, slipping past the mouse's now-floating corpse, but even only a handful of seconds behind, the pollution in the water made it impossible to see the fox. The chemical cloudiness stung the ferret's eyes only briefly, though, and then the sensation was like an afterthought.

Seeing through the water was now merely like trying to peer through a thick fog. There were shapes, indistinct ones, some moving and others not, none of them obviously Il-Hyeong. Having given the fox his orders, Arkady turned himself downstream. The current was fairly strong, but he wished it were stronger, to allow him to cover more distance in a shorter period of time. Still, hopefully the augmentation of their bodies would allow him and Il-Hyeong to hold their breaths for at least ten minutes—which was merely a guess, but an educated one—without having to surface, by which point any pursuers would either still be searching nearer the van site, or have simply assumed that they'd already drowned.

For now, then, all Arkady could do was to swim along with the river, trusting that they could avoid pursuit and detection by staying underwater for as long as possible. That, and he needed to trust that Il-Hyeong was still following along with the plan. Arkady recognized that the fox had doubts that were legitimate, and while those doubts concerned Arkady himself, he still placed his faith in Il-Hyeong.

At least, he could place his faith in Il-Hyeong for the time being. The fox might not understand what Arkady was asking of him, and he might not hold his own safety in high regard anymore, but he wouldn't place Ming-Jun's safety in jeopardy, not if he could avoid it.

If Arkady could trust Il-Hyeong with anything, he could trust him with that.

12. Turning the Tables

Ming-Jun had always been a great deep cover operative. Her communications expertise and well-traveled youth made her well-adapted to readily taking on mannerisms and personalities that would let her sink more easily into different cover identities as situation or location dictated. Rabbits also tended to draw less attention in general from the rest of the populace, their natural demeanor being quieter and more reserved than that of most other species.

That aptitude was part of why she was usually sent in to do advance setup for longer missions. For any mission that necessitated establishing a base of operations for any real length of time, it was almost always preferable to try to blend in than it was to try to hide outright. Kentian had originally been assigned to go along with her simply so that she wouldn't have to risk going out into the field alone, but she and the wolf rapidly developed a good working rapport, and the arrangement of pairing them together had stuck.

There had been one mission a couple years ago, in Song Kang, where the two of them had pretended to be a married couple. The logic had been that, amongst the modern-minded, well-socialized urbanites of Kyunjiu's capital, such an arrangement would bring with it little fanfare; instead of merely tolerating such an odd couple, though, the neighborhood had almost instantly gravitated towards them, treating them like minor celebrities as far as pleasant gossip and the local social scene was concerned. As a result, the two had needed to play along with the charade longer and more intently than initially anticipated, but they'd still gotten the job done in the end.

Arkady had never gotten a straight answer out of Kentian as to just how far things had gone in order to maintain the illusion, and the ferret knew better than to ask Ming-Jun. The wolf and the rabbit had continued to exchange playful jabs for at least a couple of months after the mission had finished, though.

Ming-Jun was a master at hiding in plain sight, at fading into the local surroundings and keeping a low profile. If she had some advance warning that people had been coming for the apartment—coming for her—then she'd have gotten a head start. She had the skills to disappear at will, if she needed to.

Surely, she'd have found a way to keep herself safe while this business with hired mercenaries and mysterious fanatical groups blew over, right?

The apartment where the wolf—the one that the mouse had called 'Sarge'—had held Arkady the day before was less than a block away, now. Neither Il-Hyeong's fur nor Arkady's own were fully dry, but at least they'd mostly rid themselves of that 'fresh out of the river' smell.

Before the fox and the ferret had even made it a mile from the riverbank where they'd crawled back onto land, they realized that the stench of contaminated river water wasn't going to help them escape notice from passersby, even the normal masses who didn't have their sense of smell artificially enhanced. They picked up a bottle of shampoo at a corner store and managed to get at least somewhat clean by washing up in the dingy showers at a run-down bus depot. There weren't much in the way of drying amenities, however, and so the pair had to content themselves with being damp and thereby only affecting the olfactory senses of anyone they happened to stand directly next to.

There hadn't been any signs of trouble on the long walk to the apartment. Having taken a taxi or bus might very well have placed innocents in danger, and while it didn't appear that pursuers were still on their immediate trail, the other upside to walking was that it gave Arkady an opportunity to think about what had gone wrong and what he ought to do next.

"Hold up," the ferret said, physically blocking Il-Hyeong's path with his forearm. "Before we head on up inside, I want to ask you something."

Il-Hyeong narrowed his eyes impatiently. "We can't linger out here on the street, Arkady," he said. "Let's just get inside. Whatever it is can wait."

"No, it can't wait," Arkady said. "If this Sarge is still waiting for us inside that apartment, then I need to know something first."

With the fur between his ears still matted and damp, the fox looked almost comical with his expression of annoyance, but there was nothing funny about the circumstance. "All right, fine. What?"

Arkady wanted to bite his lip. He didn't expect Il-Hyeong to provide a straight answer, but even if it was too late to salvage the mission he'd blown, he needed to assert his leadership now, at least for his own sake. "What's gotten into you? Ever since last night at Fan-Yin, it's like you don't care about what you do or what happens to you."

The fox shifted his weight to one side, appearing both bored and annoyed. "What the hell is that supposed to mean?"

"You're shooting first instead of asking questions. You're putting yourself in danger without regard to any risk involved."

"In case you hadn't noticed, Arkady," Il-Hyeong pointed out, "we're both in plenty of danger without having to put ourselves in it."

"That's not what I meant," the ferret sighed. "What I meant is—"

"Is what?" Il-Hyeong briefly brought a finger up to jab in Arkady's face. "That we blew our fucking mission and that our main concern right now is to find Ming-Jun and get the fuck out of here?"

Reprimanding Il-Hyeong for being insubordinate wasn't going to help things. "Yes, that's exactly it," Arkady said, traces of cynicism slipping into his voice beyond his intentions. "And in order to do that, we need to—"

"We need to hurry the fuck up and do whatever it takes to find these people and find Ming-Jun before they kill her—assuming they haven't already."

Il-Hyeong glanced downward at the sound of knuckles cracking as Arkady balled his paw into a tight, hard fist. "She's not dead," the ferret snapped. "If they wanted her dead, they would have killed her in the apartment." (*Say that with enough authority and you might have an easier time believing it.*) "We'll find her, and we'll find her as soon as we can, but there's a right way and a wrong way to do it."

"Don't preach to me like you're suddenly Father Benjamin," Il-Hyeong said. He nearly spat in Arkady's face as the words came out. "The 'right' way to do this is the *fast* way, and you full well know it."

"*Fast*, yes," Arkady agreed. "That doesn't mean stealing cars and jumping in front of moving vans and *executing* unarmed prisoners."

Il-Hyeong grunted and barreled his way past Arkady. "We're past the point of moral culpability, Agent Ryswife," he shot back. "Sahasrara taught you how to point a gun at someone and kill them just as well as they did me."

As his colleague—his colleague and friend—continued to storm off in the direction of the wolf's apartment, Arkady tried and failed to find the words he needed. Assuming that they (*all three of us*) got back to Château Sainte-Mireille safely after this was all done, the ferret would need to inform his own superiors of "Agent Quinn's unacceptable and insubordinate behavior while on-mission," but more importantly, he'd need to figure out just what had shaken his friend so badly to get him to act this way.

But that would have to wait. Il-Hyeong was correct about one thing: the right way to do this was the fast way, and so Arkady followed after him, hoping (and yet still doubting) that his own example as leader might help the fox keep the Iolite Doctrine in mind when carrying out their task.

Walking up the stairs to the apartment was a surreal experience. When Arkady had last been here, as a prisoner, he'd been expecting Il-Hyeong and Ming-Jun to storm the place, setting him free after gunning down his captor in a precise, by-the-book surgical strike on an enemy-occupied position. Now, as it turned out, he was returning because he needed to trade information for information, in the hopes that something he learned would help him find a woman who he'd previously thought would be coming to *his* rescue.

He and Il-Hyeong stood outside the apartment door now. The fox was silent, waiting closer to the staircase, and he nodded for Arkady to keep going when the ferret looked back at him. No sound came from within the apartment itself, but based on the strong scent coming through the beat-up door, Arkady was betting that the wolf was home.

God, Arkady wished that he had Kentian with him right now. Kentian would be able to strike some kind of rapport with this other wolf, all while putting up a strong face, making his determination a tangible thing. Meanwhile, Il-Hyeong could remain back downstairs, alone, unhindered, keeping watch; he could maintain that personal bit of control while performing an important task and keeping everyone else out of trouble.

How would this all go down, then? Would the wolf uphold the deal that he'd made with Arkady not a full day before, or would he turn hostile when he learned that his driver—Arkady realized he'd never gotten the mouse's name—had been killed in a misguided rescue attempt?

Only one way to find out, the ferret told himself, and he sucked in a deep breath before gently rapping his paw against the door.

Almost immediately, the wolf's familiar voice barked back, "Northbound along Horizon Boulevard."

Arkady turned and looked back at Il-Hyeong, who just shook his head. *Shit.* This had to be some kind of code phrase trigger that had been prearranged.

There was no way around it, though—no alternative other than coming clean. "Listen, uh, 'Boots,' you have to open up," Arkady said. "There's been a—"

The door flew open, and stooped within the door frame was the hulking mercenary himself. One paw was ready at the huge Duhamel Furukawa he had strapped to his thigh. When his eyes settled on Arkady, his lip curled back, exposing some teeth, but there was no sound to his snarl. "Inside. Now," he demanded. He then looked past the ferret and saw Il-Hyeong. "You too."

The large wolf stepped back to allow the two agents entrance. Arkady went in first, and only once he was fully inside did Il-Hyeong follow. Once the wolf closed the door behind them, the fox snapped into action.

Moving faster than his 'host' could hope to react to, Il-Hyeong had his DKR-7 up under the wolf's muzzle and against his throat within a second of the door latching shut. "All right, big guy, first things first," he said. His voice was dark and cold, just like his eyes.

Arkady saw Il-Hyeong murdering those men in the basement all over again. "God in Heaven," he cried out. "Are you—"

Il-Hyeong wasn't listening. "Give him his gun back," he demanded of the wolf. "Right now. Hurry it on up."

Even though the fox had to lean up onto his toes in order to keep his pistol pressed in place against the wolf's neck, the wolf wasn't taking any chances. He didn't say anything as he reached back behind himself with one arm and, with the careful slowness of someone who had been held at gunpoint before, showed an exaggeratedly-spread paw that he stuck into the waistband at the back of his pants. He withdrew Arkady's sleek Cordellatech Zarna, which looked comically tiny in that huge paw of his, holding the barrel in between two thick fingers, offering the grip to the ferret.

Arkady took it. He couldn't show an apologetic look to the wolf while also flashing a displeased glare at Il-Hyeong at the same time, and so instead, he just kept his expression as neutral as he could manage. The wolf released his hold on the Zarna once Arkady had a solid hold on it. To the ferret's surprise, the gun was still loaded.

"Good." Il-Hyeong took his gun away from the wolf's throat, but before stepping back, he took the liberty of pulling the wolf's own weapon from its holster and dropping it onto the floor, kicking in into the corner. "Now, let's hear what you know, shall we?"

The look on the wolf's face suggested to Arkady that he was thinking that he might be able to endure a bullet or two from Il-Hyeong's DKR-7 in the time it would take to reach out with one of his enormous paws and wring the fox's neck. Were Il-Hyeong not the engineered super-soldier he now was, Arkady might have even put his money on the wolf being able to pull it off.

There wasn't time to see whether things would turn violent or not, though. Arkady was sick of not being able to properly hedge his bets, and so he did something he never thought he'd do.

Arkady pulled his gun on Il-Hyeong.

"Agent," he snapped in a tone that actually managed to draw the fox's attention to him. "You will holster your weapon immediately."

"We *just* went over this," Il-Hyeong said. He hadn't lowered his gun. "If we—"

"Agent, that is an *order*. I am *not* going to tell you again. Holster your weapon."

Arkady honestly wasn't sure whether it was Il-Hyeong's face or the wolf's which was registering more shock, and at this point, he didn't care. The fox's whiskers twitched along with a quick huff from his nose, and then he flicked his pistol's safety back on before stuffing it into the back of his pants, by his tail.

As Arkady lowered his own weapon (while still keeping it held in his paw), the wolf cleared his throat. "So, who the hell told you to call me 'Boots,' huh?" he asked. "And where's Carson?"

"Is Carson the mouse?" Arkady asked.

The wolf nodded, and Arkady bit his lip. Evidently, that was answer enough. "Shit," he grunted. "No wonder it took you so long to get here. I was hoping maybe you'd just been forced to lay low."

"So you're really the one who sent him to get us?" Il-Hyeong asked. Arkady wanted to tell the fox to shut up and to leave all the talking to him, but after the spectacle they'd just allowed to play out in front of the wolf, the ferret didn't want to give any further credence to the idea that the two of them weren't doing such a good job at working together. It might be too little, too late, but it would be something.

"You knew enough to come here," the wolf responded. Now that the heat of the moment had died down some, Arkady noticed the scent of whiskey on the wolf's breath, again. It smelled like a different variety of whiskey, this time.

Without being able to brandish his gun around like some trigger-happy punk, Il-Hyeong afforded some more space between himself and the wolf. "Why bail us out?" he asked. "And moreover, how did you even know we were in need of 'rescuing' in the first place?" The threat in the fox's voice even *sounded* weaker now that he didn't have his fingers on a weapon.

Offering a resigned look to both Arkady and Il-Hyeong, the wolf grabbed a chair from the kitchen set and sat down in it. "Well, since you have me at a bit of a disadvantage," he said, looking no less imposing when seated, "I guess I'll offer some information up first, as per my part of our bargain." His eyes went right to Arkady with the words *'our bargain.'* "My contact with the Iolite League told me that you had been followed to the old industrial complex by the river and that people would be waiting to kill you on your way out."

Arkady saw Il-Hyeong's paw twitch as he started to reach for his gun, stopping himself on his own. "The Iolite League isn't welcome in Ridgecrescent," Il-Hyeong pointed out. "You expect us to believe that they've got spies here in the country?"

The wolf grinned. "*You're* both here," he said. "Or did you mean spies other than the two of you?"

"You're taking stabs in the dark," the fox laughed (Arkady recognized the laughter as forced). "You have no idea who we are."

A satisfied expression played out across the wolf's face, and his lips curled up, but before he could counter Il-Hyeong's own boldfaced bluff, Arkady interjected with, "The soldiers we ran into back at Fan-Yin were with a group called the Carmine Order."

Hateful glances from Il-Hyeong were something that Arkady was beginning to get used to today, and he ignored this most recent one. The wolf, on the other hand, smiled an honest and friendly smile. "Thank you," he said. "See? Now we're one for one." His attention was directed toward Il-Hyeong.

"That means it's your turn again," the fox said. "Who's this supposed Iolite League contact of yours?"

The wolf lounged back in the chair now, appearing quite a bit more relaxed. "Oh, if we're doing an even exchange, then I need to know that you have something else worthwhile to tell me in return. You already told me the one big thing I wanted to know."

"Come on, Arkady. Just let me shoot him in the shoulder or something." The way Il-Hyeong said it made it sound like their camaraderie hadn't been fractured as badly as it really had. "One bullet. He can take it."

The wolf was in the middle of rolling his eyes, resulting in a rather awkward expression when he stopped midway through at Arkady saying, "The Butterfly Islands War." The ferret waited for the wolf to recover his composure before continuing. "You said you wanted to know what I knew about back then."

"What the fuck is all this?" Il-Hyeong asked. "Now suddenly you're in the business of selling classified military secrets in exchange for tenuous leads?"

It was Arkady who had the wolf's full interest, though. "I tell you the name, I get to ask you one question," he said. "Does that work for you?"

"Deal," Arkady replied. He didn't wait for Il-Hyeong to voice his disapproval.

Readjusting himself so that he was sitting nice and upright in the tiny chair, the wolf held his ears perked and upright. "Lederle," he said. "I don't know his first name."

Arkady didn't know any 'Lederle' that had connections with Sahasrara, but the Iolite League itself was a world-spanning organization with countless members, and just because Arkady didn't know who somebody was didn't mean that they weren't somebody important. It was also possible that 'Lederle' was just some code name, too. As Il-Hyeong had said, it was a tenuous lead, but it was still a lead. "All right," Arkady said. "What's your question?"

The wolf looked Arkady right in the eye. "Where were you when you saw the Pillar of Light?"

Answering that, of course, carried the admission that Arkady had seen the Pillar of Light with his own eyes, but there was little point in hiding that from this wolf. "I was in Deepwater," he said. "One of the smaller islands near Stewart." A true statement, by itself, and there was also no need to specify that he'd been at Château Sainte-Mireille.

"And what did you think when you saw it?"

"You said *one* question."

"Lederle told me that your real name is Arkady Ryswife," the wolf said. "And that his is Il-Hyeong Quinn. There. Does that earn me a second question?"

Arkady heard Il-Hyeong mutter "Oh, fucking *God*" under his breath. The ferret actually sympathized with the fox on that one. "Okay, then," he said. "I guess it does." Arkady's cover story about working for the Octavians was blown by this point, but that was probably immaterial now, anyway.

Whoever this 'Lederle' was, he knew the identities of two Sahasrara agents, and the same did not hold true in reverse. Arkady considered whether it could have been someone with one of the other secret operations groups, like Ajna or Vishuddha, but no group was privy to information on any group that outranked them, and Sahasrara was at the top of the ladder. Moreover, if another group had an active presence in Ridgecrescent, Sahasrara would have known about that, too.

"So," the wolf said after a moment. "What *did* you think?"

"About the Pillar of Light?" Arkady asked. "I thought it was the most terrible thing I'd ever seen in my life."

For the next half a minute, the wolf just sat there in silence, occasionally nodding his head, visibly deep in thought. He seemed removed from time itself, and if it weren't for the sounds of the water pipes and heating vents echoing through the structure of the building, Arkady might have believed that the world had stopped for a brief moment. That semblance of stillness was broken when the wolf looked back up, met Arkady in the eye, and responded with a simple, "All right."

The wolf started to rise from his chair, then, but Il-Hyeong stepped forward. "Hold it," the fox snapped. "Who said we were done with you? Sit the hell back down." Poised halfway between sitting and standing, the wolf curled his snout with a growl, appearing ready to leap or bite or even try for a swipe with his claws.

"Let him up, Il-Hyeong," Arkady said. The ferret's eyes had already alighted on a shelf in the back room, past the kitchen, and to the device resting on it. He stayed to make sure that Il-Hyeong complied with his order, and didn't complain when Il-Hyeong took the precaution of resting his paw on his gun.

Nodding to Arkady, Il-Hyeong asked the wolf, "You want to tell us some more about this Lederle of yours?"

"I've never met him," the wolf said. "Spoke to him on the phone today, yeah, but other than that, it was Jenkins who had the most direct contact with him."

"What species is he?"

"Never seen him," the wolf repeated. "Didn't really come up over the phone, either."

Il-Hyeong continued to press. "What connection does he have with the Iolite League?" Already knowing that the fox's line of questioning with the wolf was just going to result in a lot of pointless back and forth, Arkady walked around the back of them and strolled into the next room before either of them could hassle him. There was some commotion behind him once he was out of sight, but he figured that Il-Hyeong was more than motivated enough to keep the wolf held in place.

Resting on the shelf he'd seen through the door was the handheld device that the wolf had used to identify the ferret as "Samuel Togen" during their last encounter. He inspected the interface briefly, and finding that it appeared simple enough to operate without instructions, he walked back out to where Il-Hyeong currently had the wolf held in a painful-looking wristlock.

"Keep him still a moment," Arkady told the fox. He then reached up and grabbed at the scruff of the wolf's neck, tugging at the pelt and then checking his fingers to confirm that he'd pulled some thick, white furs free. The wolf let out a grunt as he watched Arkady insert the furs into the tiny compartment at the lower end of the device.

Arkady initialized the analyzing cycle, and watched in astonishment at how quickly the device actually did its work. It appeared that it chemically deconstructed the fur itself, then scanned the genetic material obtained from the follicle cells and cross-referenced the results with some type of database. Given the speed with which the data was being processed, the database had to be self-contained within the unit itself; not even Ridgecrescent technology could establish a connection to a remote access point and scan through so many data points so quickly.

In under half a minute, the machine was ready to display its results. The first several lines appeared to be some kind of genetic shorthand that Arkady didn't understand. The ferret thought of Dr. Mayflower then, figuring that this was the sort of thing that she'd be quite familiar with in her work on Pandora—and then Arkady thought to commit this string of numbers and letters to the memory module that had been installed in him during the augmentation process.

The ferret felt his fingers twitch in what even to him were barely-perceptible movements, in some kind of autonomic pattern that he just somehow *knew* as the module directed his brain to write an eidetic snapshot to the artificial memory bank. His eyes stung in the next moment as he blinked, and then his fingers went still.

The rest of the genetic analysis report was much more mundane in nature, and Arkady proceeded to read it aloud for Il-Hyeong's benefit, as well. "Vasilis Berzeviczy," he said. "Age thirty-one. Former Sergeant First Class in the JDR military; honorable discharge."

The wolf—Ex-Sergeant Berzeviczy—looked more embarrassed that he'd made such a clumsy slip-up than he looked angry. For someone of his size, even the slightest tilting back of the ears conveyed quite a bit of self-deprecation.

"'Vasilis Berzeviczy,' huh?" Arkady said as he set the device down on a nearby counter top. "I can see why people call you 'Boots.'"

"Yeah, 'Boots,'" Il-Hyeong repeated with a chuckle. "Let's get back to business. How do we get in touch with this Lederle person?"

Boots sighed and rubbed at his temples with his paw. "Look, I don't know, all right?" he grumbled. He wasn't afraid, Arkady could tell; it was more like he was just frustrated that things were going as shakily as they were. Arkady still believed that the wolf's attempts to help them were sincere, and while Il-Hyeong's more cautious tack was probably the by-the-book way to handle things (especially since they were cut off from headquarters), the ferret still wished that the fox would ease up.

"I want you to think real hard about this, Boots," Il-Hyeong said. He seemed to take pleasure in using that name. "We appreciate that you're 'going out of the way' to help us so selflessly and all—" Arkady didn't know if he'd merely imagined the sidelong glance the fox shot him. "—but I hope you'll understand that it would be an even bigger help if we were able to talk to your buddy and corroborate things for ourselves."

"I don't contact him," Boots said. "He contacts me."

Il-Hyeong shook his head. "Wrong answer." He reinforced his grip on the wolf's right wrist and braced himself, getting ready to twist. "You want to try one more time?"

"The only reason he even gets in touch with me is because *you* killed the person he's *supposed* to be in con—"

Boots' words were cut short by a shout of agony as Il-Hyeong pulled up on the wolf's wrist with one paw and pressed hard towards his elbow with the other. Underneath that cry, there was a dull *snap*, and Arkady could see the wolf's limb twist sideways at an unnatural angle as one of the two bones in his forearm broke. The wolf's first instinct was to lash out at his attacker, but Il-Hyeong moved with enhanced quickness and kicked sideways into the wolf's right knee, bringing him down on that side.

"Now," Il-Hyeong demanded, snatching up Boots' left arm into a full-on armlock, holding at the wrist and shoulder, "let me ask you one more time how to get in touch with Lederle."

Arkady should have known that Il-Hyeong was still just as dangerous without his weapon drawn. As much as he wanted to stop the fox, wanted to order him off again, he'd already risked compromising the mission more than once in this very room, and if Il-Hyeong was able to get results, abhorrent though the methods may be, it might be within Arkady's reasonable duty to allow this to happen. So long as the fox didn't step over the line and kill their prisoner (*again*, Arkady thought), the ferret needed to let this happen. *For Ming-Jun. For the better world.*

Though his face was twisted up and his snout was gaping in a rictus of pain, Boots made no sound of discomfort following his initial cry. "He's gone into hiding." The wolf clenched his jaw as he spoke, putting the pain aside like the well-trained soldier that he was. "I swear that I don't know where he is now."

"Where was he before he went into hiding?" Arkady cut in. He wasn't yet completely willing to let Il-Hyeong take full charge of the situation.

Boots shook his head. "I'm not sure," he said. "I have no idea who he is or what he does. Jenkins just said that we were hired to repel the intruders that'd be coming to Fan-Yin that night."

It definitely sounded, based on both that admission and the previous conversation that Arkady had had with Boots, that the 'intruders' that Jenkins' team was hired to defend against were the Sahasrara strike team and not the men from the Carmine Order, but there was no way to be sure. After all, if this 'Lederle' really was connected to the Iolite League, why would he hire a mercenary team to keep other members of the Iolite League out? More importantly, why would he then order the same team to *rescue* them afterwards? It didn't add up.

"You really, honestly promise that you don't have a way to get in touch with Lederle?" Arkady asked. Boots nodded. "You swear to God?" the ferret asked, more intently. Boots nodded again.

Il-Hyeong tugged on Boots' arm, not hard enough to cause any injury, but enough to get the wolf's attention. "Think you'd mind asking for us the next time he decides to check in with you? After all, he's going to want to make sure that you succeeded in rescuing us for him, right?"

The wolf's endorphins must have begun to kick in, because he was showing less visible pain. "I'll be sure to tell him that you *really* want to get in touch with him," he said, glaring up at Il-Hyeong. "I can't promise that he'll be amenable to that, though."

"That's all we can ask," Arkady said, making sure to speak before the fox could. "Come on, Il-Hyeong. Let him go."

For a few seconds, it looked as if Il-Hyeong were going to break Boots' other arm anyway, but he let the captured limb go and then strolled away, pulling out his gun and giving it a cursory inspection as he left his back turned to the wolf, tail waving about as if to mock him. Boots didn't rise to the bait, though, and in fact was only just beginning to become outwardly concerned that his forearm had a severe break. "If you're not going to kill me, then," the wolf said, "would you mind getting out of my apartment and letting me drag myself to the hospital?"

"Your van's at the bottom of the river right now," Il-Hyeong said without turning around. "Hope you've got money for a cab."

Arkady withheld a sigh. So long as the fox was actually calming down, he could let a snide comment slide. "I hear that you guys have pretty good hospitals here in Ridgecrescent," he said. "Hopefully you'll be back in top shape soon."

Boots grunted out through his nose. "Thanks," he murmured, rubbing his right shoulder with his left paw, then testing out his right knee, the one Il-Hyeong had kicked pretty hard; there didn't seem to be any real damage. "Guess this'll teach me to fuck with a peace-loving, philosophically-bound organization like the Iolite League, huh?"

"Size alone does not make dogs superior to ocelots," Il-Hyeong quipped, paraphrasing Scripture. "Or foxes." He didn't look at Boots as he walked past, waiting for Arkady by the front door.

With his own back turned to Il-Hyeong, Arkady went to flash Boots a sympathetic look, but then stopped himself. "Wait," he said. "One last thing." The wolf rolled his eyes, but Arkady ignored his exasperation, deeming it fully understandable.

"Does the name 'Kuai' mean anything to you?"

Boots' eyebrows went up in recognition that he didn't try to hide. "Kuai?" he asked. "Kuai's small time. Likes to think that he and his boys actually amount to something approaching 'organized crime' out in these parts, but really, it just boils down to nobody bothering to fuck with him because he ain't worth the time to fuck with."

Arkady took a step closer. "What else do you know about him?"

"Why, you think *he's* involved in this?" Boots asked, and then he laughed. "Kid, Kuai might be a number of things—a thug, an egotist, and a pain in the ass—but one thing he isn't is a criminal mastermind."

"You let us worry about that," Arkady said. If Boots hadn't seen that cacomistle who was at Fan-Yin on the night of the raid, the one who purportedly worked for Kuai, it was probably better to keep that information a secret—for Boots' own good, really, at this point. "Do you know anything?"

Boots leaned with his good shoulder up against the wall. "Dianjiang Gardens," he said. "It's in Holygate. Try checking there."

"Will do." Arkady looked back at Il-Hyeong, who already had one foot out in the hallway. "I'll leave you to it, then," he said to Boots before turning to join back up with the fox.

The ferret was just about to close the door behind him when Boots called out, "Hey, Arkady."

Arkady peeked his head back in through the partially-open door. "Yeah?"

The wolf looked him right in the eye with neither humor nor enmity. "That one was for free."

At that, Arkady actually smiled. "Thanks, Boots," he said. "Good luck with the arm."

"So," Il-Hyeong asked, breaking the long silence that had begun when he and Arkady had boarded the intercity transit tube from Hightown to Holygate. "Think we'll ever actually hear back from our friend Sergeant Berzeviczy?"

"Maybe not," Arkady said. He didn't think it was necessary to add that the wolf might have had more incentive to cooperate if the fox hadn't broken his arm. "Though if there really is a Lederle, I do think Boots will tell him we came around, in one way or another."

Il-Hyeong huffed out through his nostrils. "I still think that it was a mistake to leave him alive," he said, but before Arkady could chide him, he added, "but hey, if he calls the cavalry on us, at least the bad guys'll be coming to us instead of us having to track them down."

When it came to tracking people down, Arkady and Il-Hyeong were both heading off into the unknown again already. There was no 'Dianjiang Gardens' in the battered phone book they'd found in a phone booth near Boots' apartment. A quick call to directory assistance got them a phone number that just went directly to an ambiguous answering machine, though a second call at least got them an address.

Still, they didn't know exactly *where* they were going, and they didn't know how Kuai or the Carmine Order were involved. Il-Hyeong had said (twice already) that Boots might well have just sent them walking straight into a trap, but when he didn't have any better ideas on places to check next while they waited for potential contact from Lederle, he conceded to Arkady's plan.

"What do you think they're after?" Arkady muttered under his breath so that the hum of the transit tube would drown out his words for anybody but Il-Hyeong; they were sitting far off by themselves already, but the extra precaution couldn't hurt. "The Carmine Order, I mean. Just how the hell are they involved in all of this?"

Il-Hyeong looked forward, out the opposite window, as the transit tube began to cross the river that separated Hightown from Holygate. "It could be the Octavians," he suggested in a low murmur of his own. "Maybe trying to catch us off our guard on enemy soil?"

"You know, I tried convincing Boots that I worked for the Octavians."

The swift fox snorted out a little chuckle. "And what did he think of that?"

"He seemed to find the very notion of their existence pretty ridiculous," Arkady said. "Maybe we should offer him a job once all this is done."

Il-Hyeong let out a slow sigh. "If the Octavians *are* involved with all this," he said, "they sure wouldn't skimp on putting whatever top operatives they could on the mission."

"That doesn't explain—" Arkady was almost late in stopping himself from saying, *"how they speak Zhōngwén."* "—the sort of fanaticism that they showed in the name of the Carmine Order. If a member of the Octavians were looking death in the eye, they'd admit their allegiance proudly."

The fox hummed. "True," he conceded. "I'm still not convinced that Berzeviczy and the Order aren't related somehow, though, in any event." There was a loud rush as the transit tube reached the other bank of the river and then dipped into an underground tunnel.

"Well, if we show up at Dianjiang Gardens and immediately get perforated by a hail of bullets, that'll answer that pretty handily," Arkady said. He didn't want to believe that that could possibly be the case, but it was an eventuality that, all joking aside, he needed to seriously consider.

The transit tube pulled into the Holygate Riverfront Station. The doors of Arkady's car hissed open. Only one passenger, a middle-aged vixen, disembarked. No one else got on.

"This still doesn't make sense, Arkady," Il-Hyeong said over the chime that sounded as the doors slid closed. "Why go through so much trouble to try and kill us?"

"Maybe that's not what they're after."

"People have been shooting at us for two days," the fox pointed out. *"Someone's* trying to kill us."

"And someone wants to keep us alive." Arkady thought again about Boots' claims about whom he was purportedly working for. "What if it really *is* the Iolite League?" he asked Il-Hyeong.

The fox shook his head dismissively, with almost too much vehemence. "Can't be," he insisted. "That makes even less sense. We're here on a secret mission of utmost importance with no way to get back in touch with headquarters, in what's essentially enemy territory. If they had a way to get in touch with us, they'd have done it by now." His eyes fixed down at the floor of the transit tube. "Especially if they have Ming-Jun," he added, voice quieter.

Arkady withheld a sigh. So many clues and leads, which might or might not be legitimate, and yet still nothing that was pointing them back clearly to Ming-Jun. Nothing overt, at any rate. Nothing except for the one secret she'd shared with him. "We might still hear from Boots," the ferret said. "If this Lederle of his really did go into hiding—"

"Yeah, that's convenient, isn't it?" Il-Hyeong said. "Someone from the 'Iolite League' sticks his neck out to save our asses, and then magically disappears again as soon as we need to get our own word in? Come on."

Arkady shook his head, but really, the only thing he knew that Il-Hyeong didn't was the Carmine Order's connection to *Zhōngwén*. Was it worth betraying Ming-Jun's trust to set Il-Hyeong's fears at ease? The fox's paranoia could be an asset, as long as Arkady could keep the violent outbursts in check, after all.

"If it's not actually the Iolite League—and I'm doubting that it is," Arkady said, "I still don't think it's the Carmine Order."

Once more, the transit tube began to slow down as it entered the next station. "Well," Il-Hyeong said, checking the transit map, "we've only got three more stops before we get to find out."

13. The Teahouse at Dianjiang Gardens

Holygate didn't look terribly different from Highslope: both cities had skylines dominated by marvels of Ridgecrescent architecture, and given their proximity to one another, it was apparent that city planners had kept a mutual aesthetic in mind when expanding both outwards and upwards. Though both paled in comparison to the titanic, exceptional wonder of Thousand Leaves, they were still on par with most every other top-class metropolis in the world.

Of course, despite the uniformity the two cities shared with each other, it wasn't as if either of them displayed buildings of only a single architectural style. Even with the variety of styles and designs typical of major cities, however, the buildings of Dianjiang Gardens stood out amidst the modern structures of Holygate.

Nestled in one of the older sections of Holygate's downtown area, Dianjiang Gardens had to be some sort of local landmark, Arkady reasoned, if only a minor one. It was set off by itself, a group of three buildings on its own miniature city block. The tallest of these was only six stories tall, dwarfed by the nearby downtown high-rises. That they hadn't been demolished to make room for the surrounding shopping centers and office parks was itself very telling of how important they were.

All three buildings were small, tiered towers, octagonal in shape, with large, almost exaggerated eaves that sloped out at each floor. The eaves were a bright crimson, and even as the sky was darkening as sunset made way for dusk, the vibrance of the red paint was still impressive. The walls of the building itself were a dull green, a few shades darker than olive, with a woodwork trim that was a dirtier red than the eaves. Each floor had large windows on the four sides that faced the cardinal directions, and arch-shaped cuts in the stonework that gave the illusion of windows on the sides in between.

None of the buildings themselves bore any signage. Instead, a free-standing sign identifying the cluster as "Dianjiang Gardens" was set up nearer the street corner. The sign was, even at first glance, obviously much newer than any of the buildings, and Arkady smirked, wondering if any Holygate locals would even need such a sign to tell them what they were looking at.

The twilight sky's remaining blush began to fade by the moment into a darkness that would never reach "true dark" due to the amount of light pollution. Arkady looked over at Il-Hyeong, and the fox nodded back to him. They had holstered their weapons out of sight; drawing them would take extra time that might mean the difference between life and death, but Arkady was hoping that whatever transpired here this evening wouldn't need to come to violence.

Il-Hyeong let Arkady step out onto the crosswalk first. The staggered, tiered layout of the buildings made them loom more impressively the closer the ferret got to them, even if they were so much shorter than any of the other buildings within sight. Then, before those jagged-looking towers could take on an even more daunting presence, the calming scent of sumptuous cooking overwhelmed Arkady's nostrils.

The aroma conjured up a strange wave of nostalgia, even though the smell itself was not familiar in the least. It made Arkady think of his own childhood, before Château Sainte-Mireille and long before Project Scheherazade. He was reminded of old-fashioned home cooking, warm and friendly, with the paradox that his nostrils were being assaulted by spices and oils unlike anything he had ever smelled before, richer and bolder than that of any cuisine he had ever eaten. The aroma pervaded his senses, bordering on intoxicating. If the average passerby could smell only a fraction of what Arkady could, then the ferret couldn't understand how there wasn't a line out the door to get inside.

As Arkady got closer to the tallest building, the one nearest the street corner, he could now see that there was, in fact, a garden here at Dianjiang Gardens, nestled within the triangle described by the three structures. It wasn't large, and without the benefit of direct light, it was hard to make details without wandering into it, but there were definitely some exotic botanicals of some sort in there; not even the scents of the crowded downtown nor the luxurious smell of unfamiliar food could drown that out entirely.

The door to that nearest building was open, with the entryway framed in a glow of light that Arkady imagined was inviting him inside. What was actually drawing him in, of course, was a combination of those lovely smells along with the chatter of conversation that got more distinct the closer he got. Far from the den of iniquity that he had been expecting, the atmosphere greeting him now was one of foreign temptation, and he wanted to experience it.

Stepping in through the front door, the rest of the city of Holygate behind him seemed to disappear—a trick of acoustics, perhaps, or maybe just an illusion created by boisterous din inside. While there wasn't a line leading out around the block, the ground floor of building was nevertheless a packed-to-the-gills restaurant, with a great many of the tables seating large parties of six or eight or more, all of them conversing loudly and animatedly.

There was an empty stand just inside the entryway, and no sooner had Arkady noticed it than a hostess appeared seemingly out of nowhere. She was young, a cat of indeterminate breeding (Ridgecrescent seemed to have more than its share of her ilk, Arkady noted), and she radiated a rare kind of professionalism that in no way detracted from her geniality or her good looks. She wore an outfit that reminded the ferret of an even more elaborate version of what Ming-Jun had worn on the night that they'd gone out to eat at North Point.

The night she disappeared the first time. The night before she came back and then disappeared again for good.

"Welcome to Dianjiang Gardens," the pretty cat said with a quick but humble bow. "Would you like a table at the restaurant?"

Arkady scanned the restaurant area. There was no visible way to get upstairs, despite the building being several stories tall. "How long is the wait?" he asked.

"Half an hour to an hour," the hostess replied. "Though we do have seating available in the tearoom upstairs."

Arkady turned to look back at Il-Hyeong. The fox merely nodded. "The tearoom sounds lovely," the ferret told the hostess.

"Wonderful," the cat said with another bow. "Please follow me."

Despite the restaurant floor being a constant shuffle of movement of both diners and staff, the feline hostess seemed to have a sixth sense that let her dodge through just the right openings that would allow her and her two customers through with the minimum of fuss. As he followed her, Arkady examined the back of her outfit.

It was a deep red, probably a shade that matched the eaves of the building, with an embroidered trim of gold. The pattern stitched into the back was as intricate as it was beautiful: a frame of stylized, flower-like latticework that surrounded a much more detailed and much more realistic floral depiction within. The gold stitching reflected the light very well from certain angles, though it didn't seem to be metallic itself.

A brief look around showed that the other wait staff, at least the females, wore similar outfits, but none of them were identical. Were the designs handmade, then? If so, then whoever had done the embroidering was quite accomplished indeed.

To Arkady's surprise, the hostess lead him and Il-Hyeong into the kitchen. She didn't hesitate at all, and as soon as the swinging double doors opened toward the ferret, both the scent and the sizzle of fragrant, high-quality oils assaulted his nose and ears in a way that would have been pleasant if it hadn't been so unexpected. As he walked passed the busy cooking stations and oblivious-looking chefs, he felt an uncomfortable tingle, recalling that the last time he'd been through a restaurant kitchen like this was during his team's escape from Shambhala, not nearly as long ago as it now felt.

At the far end of the cramped kitchen was another door, this one leading to a narrow stairwell. None of the kitchen staff were the least bit perturbed by customers being dragged through their area, so Arkady could only conclude that being led through here wasn't anything out of the ordinary, unusual and suspicious though it may seem to him. Again, the hostess continued without delay, as if expecting Arkady and Il-Hyeong to know what they were doing. It was all that they could do, then, to fake it as best they could.

Both the staircase walls and the stairs themselves were made of stone. There was a faint, musty smell that probably came with sheer age, but the stairwell itself was clean. The hostess got off at the second floor landing and pushed her way through the curtained entryway.

Arkady and Il-Hyeong followed. Almost no sound from downstairs echoed up to reach them now, save what little clattering could be heard from the kitchen immediately behind them. That lack of racket helped to accentuate what was already a far more intimate setting.

Instead of the crowded restaurant tables of the floor below, there were half a dozen smaller tables in this room. The tables themselves were low to the floor, with patrons sitting on cushions instead of chairs. None of the tables were large enough to accommodate more than four individuals, and all of the tables were occupied.

The feline hostess didn't even give any of the tables—or Arkady or Il-Hyeong, for that matter—a second glance. She kept right on walking, right on up to the far wall, where a firmly-pressed paw pushed the wall itself aside, revealing it to be nothing more than a painted, sliding wooden partition, beyond which was another room much like the first.

This second room had two empty tables. The hostess led the fox and the ferret to one of these, and she bowed to them once more as they sat atop the cushions. "Enjoy, sirs," the cat said, her first words since inviting her customers to follow her, and she then departed with just as much efficiency, heading back towards the staircase.

"Well," Il-Hyeong said with his tail curling out of sight beneath the table. "*This* certainly isn't what I was expecting."

"That's putting it lightly," Arkady agreed. He looked around the room, noting that none of the other customers had so much as looked up since they'd come in. "Well, if anyone *is* watching for us, I can't imagine they haven't seen us by now."

The sliding door opposite of the one they'd entered through opened up, and a middle-aged male feline, speckled gray with large-framed glasses atop his muzzle, came in. He bore a tray with an ornamented teapot and a pair of cups without handles, setting all three pieces down onto Arkady and Il-Hyeong's table without a word. Arkady thanked him, but he just nodded, and departed without another word, keeping himself hunched as if holding his head low would place him beneath notice even in plain view.

The tea itself smelled lovely. Arkady could tell that it still needed to steep, but probably for not much longer. Even Il-Hyeong cracked a smile like Arkady hadn't seen on the fox in days, his whiskers dancing for a moment as he took a deep whiff. The invigorating scent of tea had always been nice, even before the augmentation, and it seemed its effects were enhanced in kind.

Neither the hostess nor the tea server had left them menus. The other customers had small plates and bowls cluttering their own tables, though, so the tearoom had to serve food, as well. The tearoom did have an air of exclusivity and almost secretiveness to it, even if the hostess hadn't kept its existence hidden, per se; it was like the place was only for people who were "in the know." Were diners simply supposed to "know" what was available to order?

Not for the first time since Arkady's arrival, Dianjiang Gardens exhibited its supernatural quality to pick up on his questions and answer them as soon as they crossed his mind. The wall through which the stooping cat had come opened yet again, this time revealing a younger vixen who pushed a wheeled cart with her. She wore a version of the red vestment that the hostess wore, only fancier and more restrictive of movement.

The vixen and her cart stopped at the first table on her right. The older (married?) mongoose couple who sat there inspected the cart's offerings, and with a series of hand motions, the man selected three small dishes, which the fox set on the table for them. She collected no money, but she did pull out a pad reminiscent of the ones most waiters and waitresses used, and she tagged it three times with a self-inking rubber stamp. Then she moved on to the next table, where a lone, elderly wolf sat, and he waved her along without so much as looking at the cart.

Il-Hyeong started to pour the tea as the cart came up to their table next. "Gentlemen," the vixen said in a voice pitched only for them. She didn't describe or even introduce what any of the various dishes on her cart were.

Were it not for the augmentation giving Arkady the ability to distinguish between so many different scents at once, he would have had no idea what comprised any of the dishes he was looking at. They all looked so completely alien, even to him, an agent of Sahasrara who had traveled the world over countless times. While they were unfamiliar and even imposing, the smells coming from them were beyond inviting. The ferret could tell that the sets of curiously-shaped dumplings were stuffed with various meats and seafood, that the sauces were made of mixtures of vinegar and chili oil and fermented soybeans, and that the lot of it was seasoned with spices so rare that they defied immediate recognition.

Arkady let his nose guide him as he selected four dishes, pointing at each in turn: a plate of steamed buns, two small baskets of dumplings, and something that looked like a thin, fried omelet stuffed with seafood and vegetables, which looked so bizarre that he couldn't help but order it. The vixen silently set the dishes atop the table, and then she stamped her pad thrice with one of her stamps, then once more with another. With a bow, she left him and Il-Hyeong to eat.

Il-Hyeong's eyebrows were still raised from when he'd seen Arkady order the omelet-looking thing. "Are you sure this stuff is safe to eat?" the fox asked.

"Everyone else is eating it," Arkady replied, already reaching for one of the steamed buns. "Besides, I'm starving. When was the last time you ate, anyway?"

"Before the mission." Something approaching a chuckle had crept into the fox's voice. "It would seem that we don't need to eat anymore. At least, not as much."

With Il-Hyeong pointing that out, Arkady realized that his hunger was psychological, but not physical. "Well, *I'm* eating," the ferret said, and then he took a good-sized bite from the steamed bun that was warming his paw. He chewed slowly. The texture was doughier and more elastic than any other bread that he'd ever eaten, but it was still a pleasant texture, and it felt so good just to be doing something so mundane and commonplace as *eating* that he went so far as to let out a small sigh as he swallowed.

"See, now you're making me jealous," Il-Hyeong said. Not to be outdone, he plucked one of the tiny dumplings in between two fingers and popped it whole into his muzzle. His eyes rolled partway up into the back of his head as he ate it, then shuddered as his fur bristled all over for a moment. "Oh, God, that *is* good."

And so, the two agents ate, venturing together into this strange, unexplored culinary frontier together. Two whole days' worth of tension, of anxiety, of strife melted away over the course of those minutes, their current predicament set aside for the time being as they let down their carefully-groomed sense of duty and conviction to just enjoy themselves for the first time in what had been far, far too long.

The strange omelet, Arkady discovered, tasted as unusual as it looked and smelled. He couldn't decide whether he liked it or not; Il-Hyeong was more confidently indifferent. The real hit, both agents agreed, were the seafood dumplings, which carried a more complex and more satisfying flavor than the vegetable-filled ones.

The tea itself was splendid, as well. Its aroma was similar to a variety that Arkady had had many years ago on Kenéle, in the Butterfly Islands, but the taste itself was rather different. The older feline had come by and refilled the pot once already, and Arkady and Il-Hyeong were happily making their way through that second pot when they were interrupted by yet another member of the restaurant staff.

A slender cacomistle stood by the table—the same cacomistle who had been at Fan-Yin Bioinformatics, the one who had apparently been leading the uniformed troops of the Carmine Order.

She wasn't tall, but still she seemed to loom. Her poise was impeccable, the entirety of her long, ringed tail hidden from sight within silky folds of her red gown. Her paws were likewise hidden by keeping her arms folded so that one draping sleeve was tucked into the other. If anything else was hidden there, Arkady couldn't see it.

She bowed, but only with her head. "Gentlemen," she said in a voice that made her sound around forty, while her face made her look closer to thirty. "Pardon the interruption."

"Not at all," Arkady said. The severe look in the cacomistle's eyes told him that she knew exactly who he was, and that she knew that he recognized her, as well.

She wasted no further time on perfunctory apologies, but her air of obeisance remained. "The proprietor has asked if the two of you would care to take tea with him," she said. Though her tone did nothing to betray it, it was clear that this was not a request.

The proprietor. Kuai? That the cacomistle was here was enough to back up Boots' claim that Dianjiang Gardens was connected to that mysterious name, along with tacitly validating the executed prisoner's claim that the cacomistle worked for him.

Il-Hyeong shifted where he sat, muscles tensing under his clothing and fur. He looked at Arkady without a word, and the ferret didn't need to be a mind-reader to know what the fox was thinking: *This is it.*

"We would be honored," Arkady replied. He tried to mimic the formal bowing style that the teahouse staff had been employing, but whether he'd gotten it wrong, or whether the cacomistle was unimpressed or uninterested, he did not get a reaction. It was hard not to think of her as "the enemy," even though he still had no idea who her people really were or what they were after.

"Please, follow me." The cacomistle took a step back, but kept her eyes on both agents. Some of the other clientèle present were paying attention now, too, but none openly stared. Arkady motioned for Il-Hyeong to stand up first, before checking the gun tucked in by his tail, using the sitting cushion as a convenient excuse to have his paws move back there as he, too, got to his feet.

The cacomistle led them out of the tearoom and back to the staircase. Her flowing tail remained curled neatly within her robe, never once dipping down more than a single step behind her where it might become a tripping hazard in the narrow stairwell. In these closer confines, Arkady could now smell the fragrance of lavender from his guide, naturally floral as opposed to artificially chemical.

Noise coming from the floors that they climbed past got quieter and quieter with each story, solid doors barring the way instead of hanging curtains. At the sixth and topmost floor, the three of them came to a large set of wooden doors, with gilded handles molded in the shape of flowers. The cacomistle grabbed hold of a heavy iron knocker in her delicate paw, then knocked only once.

A full five seconds passed, and then, without any obvious prompt, the cacomistle announced, "It's Jenfei."

Both doors swung inward, revealing a large, spacious hall lit by torches and braziers. For a moment, Arkady thought that the doors had open via some automated mechanism, until the two attendants stepped out into view from behind them. One was male, a swift fox like Il-Hyeong; the other was female, a mongrel canine of some sort who kept her eyes fixed down at the area of the floorboards immediately around her sandaled feet.

The cacomistle—Jenfei—nodded to the pair of attendants, who bowed to her before ushering themselves out through a small door off to the left, disappearing into what looked to be a service corridor. Jenfei then folded her sleeves into one another again, and, without bothering to remind Arkady and Il-Hyeong to follow, escorted them into the hall.

At the rear of the hall hung a scroll that was nearly as tall as the wall itself. On it was painted a symbol that reminded Arkady of the strange, complex characters that the *Zhōngwén* texts were written in, only rendered in a more fluid, calligraphic style. A moment later, the ferret realized where he knew this particular symbol from: the insignia worn by the men from the Carmine Order was a highly-stylized version of what was written on this scroll.

A tall raccoon sat alone at the sole table set back by that wall, dressed in the sort of flowing, formal garb that the rest of the staff at Dianjiang Gardens wore. In contrast to the crimson of the wait staff, his was a pale, shimmering green, and while it was less robe-like than those other garments, it was still somehow more ceremonious, if not ostentatious.

As Arkady and Il-Hyeong approached, led by Jenfei, the raccoon looked up from the cup of tea upon which he was (at least pretending to be) fixated. He wore spectacles, ones of a distinctly archaic style. With a grin, he set down his teacup, adjusted his glasses, and inspected his two guests with understated mirthful curiosity.

"Thank you, Jenfei," the raccoon said. "You may go back about your business." His voice was a surprising contrast to his stature, a steady baritone. He spoke with a rich, cultured accent, but it was not one of Ridgecrescent; if Arkady had to guess, he'd have said either southern Kyunjiu or possibly the southwestern part of Jung Sim Weon.

Jenfei bowed to the raccoon. "Of course, sir," she said, and then she moved like a ghost down the hall and around the corner, out of sight.

Arkady, Il-Hyeong, and the raccoon were all alone together, now.

"Mr. Kuai, I take it," Arkady said with a nod of his head that he was careful to ensure was not as deep or as respectful as the bows he'd seen the others in the establishment exchange.

The raccoon nodded. *"Kuài Jiāngzhào,"* he said, his syllables carefully enunciated with the peculiar *Zhōngwén* tones that Arkady was coming to recognize all too well. "Though you may find it simpler to call me Jiangzhao Kuai," he added, this time dropping the tonality from his name in addition to inverting the order. "I promise I will not take offense."

There had to be some cultural significance to the way Kuai styled his name. The feline Aléu of the Butterfly Islands had the custom of placing surname before given name, but they were a unique case in that their society had been isolated from the modern world until relatively recently, and had retained their strong sense of nationalistic individuality. Kuai was certainly not Aléu, and moreover, Arkady knew that Ridgecrescent high society would find it exceedingly awkward for someone to adopt such a foreign manner of address.

"Well, Mr. Kuai," Arkady repeated, "thank you very much for your invitation to join you. To what do we owe the honor?"

Kuai had his own place at the table set, but his was the only one. "Please, sit," the raccoon offered first. "I'd like very much for the two of you to be comfortable and to feel at home."

Next to Arkady, Il-Hyeong let out a low, throaty noise that the ferret was sure Kuai couldn't hear. When Kuai did then look at Il-Hyeong, however, the fox responded with a neat and polite, "Thank you," as he took a seat upon one of the cushions on the floor by the raccoon's table. Arkady sat as well, taking careful note of Kuai's sitting posture, determining how easy it would be for the raccoon to pull out a concealed weapon or to lunge across the table in some display of bravado and stupidity. A gun, the ferret decided, would be the only real threat, and he'd put money on himself to get off a shot of his own before the raccoon even got a weapon into firing position.

It didn't seem to be Kuai's intention to just kill them, though—or, at the very least, he seemed to want something else from the agents, first. "Are you still hungry?" the raccoon asked. "I realize that I called you up here while you were still eating, so please, if there's anything you would like, do not hesitate to ask."

"No thanks," Il-Hyeong said. "And you didn't answer his question," he added with a nod towards Arkady.

Kuai looked disappointed. "Some tea, at least," he offered. He sounded for all the world like a legitimate host who might take deep personal offense at a refusal.

"Tea would be lovely," Arkady replied, before Il-Hyeong could rebuff the raccoon again. "And yes, you haven't answered my question. Why have you brought us here?"

Before answering, Kuai picked up his own teacup and took a long sip, eyes closed as if in unconcerned contemplation, as if he were enjoying a moment alone to himself. Then, just as casually, he opened his eyes again, and called out in a voice loud enough to be heard in the next room without his having to shout. "*Xiǎotù*, some tea for our guests!" There was no response, but Arkady did not doubt that the request was being heeded.

"So," the raccoon said, as if he hadn't been the one to interrupt himself, "why have I brought you here, you ask?" He chuckled a chuckle that would have sounded friendly and jovial were he someone else. "As I see it, the two of you are the ones who decided to come here of your own accord." He then set down his teacup, but neither his posture nor his tone of voice changed. "Unless you expect me to feign belief that your visit to Dianjiang Gardens this evening is a mere coincidence, which I can surely do, but which will likely result in neither of us getting the answers we want from the other."

A stony silence fell over the table. Arkady was nonplussed; Kuai was nonchalant. The raccoon took another sip of tea while he waited for either of the agents to respond. "All right, then," Arkady admitted. "Yes, we came here looking for you."

Kuai held on to his teacup. "Ideally, I would have preferred advance notice that I would be hosting such esteemed guests from such a prestigious organization as the Iolite League," he said. "I assure you I would have planned accordingly. Still, given your group's... status here within Ridgecrescent's borders, I can see where there may have been difficulties, and above all else, I am flattered that you would seek my hospitality." He cleared his throat, then spoke up again. "Speaking of which: *Xiǎotù*, where *is* that tea?"

"Your hospitality has been very impressive so far," Arkady said, trying to mask his annoyance at Kuai's insistence that they drop all pretense while continuing with more pretense of his own. This was Kuai's home turf, though, and that gave the raccoon the advantage, so Arkady and Il-Hyeong would need to play along for now. "I'll admit that this was not the reception I was expecting."

For the first time, the raccoon looked proud of himself. "Dianjiang Gardens is delighted to provide a unique culinary experience," he said. "Ours is a very ancient style of cuisine, and this is the only place in Ridgecrescent where one can enjoy it. Perhaps that may change, someday, but for now, we are glad to be where we are, to provide the unique experience that we provide."

"But surely running an eatery isn't all you do, Mr. Kuai." Arkady let teeth show through his grin. "I get the impression that your own interests are pretty far-reaching, Going from what I've seen and heard, that is."

"Ah, yes, well," Kuai murmured, pausing to take another long sip of tea, draining his cup. "Speaking of interests, Mr. Ryswife, can I assume that you yourself have a vested interest in history?"

"We do," Arkady replied, nodding sideways to Il-Hyeong, pointedly including the fox in his response. "For instance, I can't help but assume that Dianjiang Gardens itself is some type of historical landmark in this city."

Kuai's proud grin grew even prouder. "Sadly, we lack official documentation that proves it," he said, "but we are quite sure that these buildings date back to pre-civ times." His posture relaxed, then. "Oh, it wasn't always a restaurant and teahouse, of course, but having been brought up from downstairs, I'm sure you must have already pieced that together just from the building's design and layout."

"Upkeep and renovation must be very expensive for such an ancient and important historical site," Il-Hyeong chimed in. "Your restaurant must turn quite a profit."

"People are happy to pay a premium to eat food that they can't get anywhere else in the country." The raccoon's beaming smile had turned into a smirk. "Which reminds me, you needn't worry about your bill from earlier this evening; consider it taken care of." Then he sighed. "But no, you're quite right in assuming that the restaurant itself does not generate enough revenue to cover costs. One of the other buildings does also host a small—but, I assure you, impressive—museum that might be of particular interest to gentlemen like yourselves. Perhaps later, a private tour can be arranged."

Arkady smiled. He was starting to actively enjoy this little dance that they'd begun. "Being from Château Sainte-Mireille myself, I still find it a *little* hard to believe that such an enterprise can support what is obviously a remarkably well-maintained set of buildings as old as these. Then again, my knowledge of Ridgecrescent property values and the like is a bit limited, so perhaps I'm entirely off-base."

"You flatter us, Mr. Ryswife," Kuai replied. "I assure you that our history is our most germane interest, and maintaining that would not be possible without the addition of private contributions from those who share that interest."

Boots had said that Kuai was "small time." If the Carmine Order did have a criminal element to it (and Arkady couldn't rationalize a way that it didn't), was Dianjiang Gardens itself such a money sink that the organization itself didn't prosper beyond these small boundaries? Was Boots merely wrong about what he knew? Or was Kuai really just interested in being a restaurateur who occasionally ordered his wait staff to conduct armed raids of biotechnology facilities?

Or, Arkady wondered, was Kuai just a small part of a much larger web, one which didn't hinge on Sahasrara showing him undue respect or, if it came down to it, mercy? Perhaps that was thinking too much like Il-Hyeong (*is the augmentation really letting us rationalize this sort of thing?*), but if Kuai was just another obstacle and not the key to the rest of this mystery, did the situation warrant wasting as little time on him as possible—and removing him as a potential hindering factor?

"So, we both share an interest in history," Arkady said. He wasn't ready to make a decision about Kuai just yet. The last time he'd made a snap judgment to kill the man sitting across the table from him, not only had he taken a life, but he'd wasted that of his own comrade and friend in the process. "Where does that leave us, then?"

Kuai looked disappointed, like there was something he'd hoped Arkady or Il-Hyeong would have figured out by now. "That depends on you, I suppose," he said, and then his ears pricked at the soft sound of footsteps from the back hallway.

Arkady recognized Ming-Jun's scent before he even set eyes on her: it was wrapped up in a cover of jasmine and something else he couldn't identify, but it was unmistakably her. Il-Hyeong stiffened; clearly, he'd noticed, too.

She then stepped into view, the white-and-gray rabbit looking as elegant as Arkady had ever seen her. She was clad in the same manner of dress as the Dianjiang Gardens staff, but like Kuai, she was not in uniform. Her body-length robe was the startling red-purple of amaranth blossoms, trimmed with a silver-and-gold weave that glittered in the room's ample firelight. Atop her head, circling her brow and wrapping once around her right ear, was a wreath of tiny blue flowers. She kept her body posture rigid and perfect as she came up from behind Kuai, bearing an ornamental silver tray with a large, clay teapot and two cups that matched the one that Kuai had been drinking from.

"Ah, *Xiǎotù*, thank you," the raccoon muttered without ceremony. He motioned to the table without even looking at her.

As Ming-Jun approached, she didn't make eye contact with either of her teammates. Was this merely the humble deference that went with her role, here? Was she trying to hide any hints of recognition with the other agents in front of Kuai? Or was she ashamed, ashamed of having committed an unforgivable betrayal, unable to look her former companions in the eye?

Arkady didn't try to get her attention as she circled the table, either. If she were still loyal to the Iolite League's cause, then she'd done a masterful job of infiltrating enemy ranks. If, though (and Arkady was afraid to consider this the more likely explanation), she'd been in cahoots with Kuai and the Carmine Order all along, then calling down suspicion here, in the Order's sanctum, would bring no good.

Ming-Jun poured for the guests before pouring for Kuai. As she leaned over the table to fill Arkady's teacup, she murmured under her breath, *"He doesn't have it."* The ferret's eyes snapped up to her face, but she was neatly expressionless—though it was worth noting that Kuai could not have seen her lips move, given the angle at which her head was bowed. Il-Hyeong's ears also twitched in Arkady's peripheral vision.

Of course, Ming-Jun would know that her teammates could hear things that Kuai could not. What did she *mean*, though? Why take the risk of saying anything at all if she weren't going to say something more immediately helpful—or even more immediately reassuring?

Il-Hyeong's face had twisted up in anger, but Arkady saw him quickly turn that into feigned surprise at the smell of the tea, his nose wrinkling at what was a legitimately unusual odor even compared to the other tea they'd been served downstairs earlier. Arkady sniffed at the tea, as well, noting that at least part of the jasmine scent he'd noticed earlier came from the tea itself, though most of it was still centered on Ming-Jun.

Once Kuai's teacup was filled, the raccoon nodded, and the rabbit left the teapot on the table before turning and taking the tray with her as she left. Kuai held up his cup in a small, wordless toast, then drank. Arkady and Il-Hyeong followed suit, which seemed to satisfy their inscrutable host.

"Now, then," Kuai said, steam still rising up from the cup, passing in front of his face, fogging up his glasses. "Given this shared interest of ours, I was hoping we might be able to help each other out."

"How so?" Il-Hyeong asked.

Kuai removed his glasses and wiped them clean with a small cloth he'd produced from somewhere on his person before putting them back on. "I understand that the Iolite League has recently come into possession of a set of three books," he said. "Pre-civ books, to be specific. May I correctly assume that you know the books of which I speak?"

Arkady failed to hide his reaction when Kuai said that. He bit his lip, struck with both surprise and a feeling of stupidity. This couldn't all really just boil down to some secretive history buff wanting to get his paws on a set of books, surely! The connection between Kuai, the Carmine Order, and this bizarre *Zhōngwén* language was an obvious one, but that didn't explain the team of armed troops or their presence at Fan-Yin Bioinformatics the other night.

"The Iolite League collects a lot of old books," Arkady said. "We have quite an extensive library."

The raccoon's smile took on a toothy edge that was neither coy nor playful. "Again, I'll assume that you *do* know the books in question, and I'll come out and say it: I want them."

Il-Hyeong began to respond with, "Out of the—", but Arkady talked over him, and Kuai seemed to hear only the ferret's words. "I don't have the personal authority to make such a deal on the Iolite League's behalf," Arkady said, "but if you'd tell me what you're offering in exchange, I could certainly bring the matter to their attention."

"You're an agent in the field, though, are you not?" Kuai said. "I'm guessing that means you must have some degree of authority in making on-the-spot decisions."

"This hardly seems like a critical matter," Arkady replied. "Surely, as a point of historical interest, the Iolite League would be willing to at least entertain a discussion as to how much these books might be worth."

Kuai shook his head. "The books themselves may not be critical, true," he said. "What *is* critical, though, I assume, is the matter of this Dr. Lederle you're trying to find, yes?" His tongue came out and slid over his teeth, his eyebrows arching higher.

"All right," Il-Hyeong snapped, abruptly rising to his feet. "I've had about enough of this."

Outwardly surprised, Kuai leaned back, resting back onto one paw. "Mr. Quinn, please, if you're concerned about—"

"No," Il-Hyeong said, surprising Arkady with the way that a single word got Kuai to flinch, the raccoon looking the most vulnerable he had since their arrival. "I'm not going to sit here and let you dictate the terms of some 'gentlemanly agreement' while you smugly make the point that you've got us at a tremendous disadvantage."

Now, Kuai just looked angry. "If you're willing to jeopardize your own mission over some—"

"Over some books full of nothing but gibberish?" Il-Hyeong countered. "Seems like a pretty sweet, pretty innocuous deal, doesn't it?" He reached into the back of his pants, pulled out his DKR-7, and undid the safety. "I'll take my chances."

Arkady got ready to throw up a paw to stop the fox, but instead of bringing the gun up to fire at Kuai, Il-Hyeong turned on his heels and stormed off toward the staircase, his tail flicking angrily behind him. Kuai was again reduced to stunned silence. The mixed-breed canine girl who had been among the pair to open the door for Jenfei showed her head through the entryway to the side corridor, then barked in alarm and ducked out of view when she saw the fox's gun.

The swift fox pulled the heavy wooden door open, slipped through, and let it slam shut behind him. As the loud noise echoed through the hall, the resulting draft caused the firelight to flicker, and a moment later, Ming-Jun reappeared from the back corridor. "*Kuài-shīfu?*" she asked, cocking her head.

"It's all right, *Xiǎotù*," Kuai said as he recomposed himself, paws flattening out the creases in his sleeves. "One of our guests apparently wasn't feeling well. Please, bring out something for us to eat, would you?" The rabbit gave a curt nod and disappeared again.

Awkwardness lingered after both Il-Hyeong's and Ming-Jun's departures, with Arkady not knowing what to say, and with Kuai not offering anything of his own. If Kuai was putting on some elaborate act, it had to be coming precariously close to falling apart. In the meantime, it was going to be at least a minute or two before Ming-Jun came back with food, so someone had to break the silence.

"My associate does have a point, Mr. Kuai," Arkady said. "The Iolite League does not take kindly to being threatened or blackmailed. I'm sure you'll have heard, from the other night, just how capable we are when pressed."

The wind had been taken out of Kuai's sails, clearly. "Just so," he said. His paws fidgeted with his clothing and the tea implements, like he really did have a concealed weapon on his person and was itching to find reasons to not use it. "The point remains, though, that each of us has something the other wants, and that the simplest solution, I'm sure you'll agree, is to come to terms for a mutual exchange."

Arkady grinned. Whether it had been Il-Hyeong's intention or not, the fox's outburst and subsequent refusal to negotiate had made Kuai nervous and off-balance. The ferret might have been left on his own, now, but he could turn this to his advantage—especially if Ming-Jun was telling the truth about Kuai not actually having what they needed (*because she has to still be trustworthy, right?*). "That sounds like it could be a solution. Tell me exactly what you're offering, and I'll see what I can do."

Kuai put his game face back on. "Like I said, I do know that you're trying to track down Dr. Lederle," he said. "Jenfei and the others in my employ can attest to that much."

Ming-Jun chose that moment to reappear. She carried what appeared to be the same tray as before, but this time it was loaded up with two baskets of the seafood dumplings that smelled the same as the ones Arkady and Il-Hyeong had enjoyed downstairs. As she bent over to set them on the table, she again subvocalized for Arkady's benefit: *"If this all goes wrong, there's an antique shop on Heliotrope Way."* She took the tops of the baskets with her as she gathered up Il-Hyeong's abandoned teacup.

If Ming-Jun's intention was to be enigmatic and the very opposite of reassuring, she was certainly succeeding. It wasn't as if Arkady could ask for clarification in Kuai's presence, though, and so he had to trust that she'd chosen her words deliberately and carefully, for a specific reason.

"If this all goes wrong." Arkady wondered how—or even *if*—they could go more wrong than they already had.

"Give me one day," the ferret offered, making sure to answer while Ming-Jun was still in earshot, hoping that she'd pick up on it. His obvious attention, however, was on Kuai. "Shall I meet you back here?"

Kuai appeared to give the question some thought. Ming-Jun lingered behind him for a few more seconds, but he didn't seem to notice. Before he answered, the rabbit slipped back into the corridor.

"No," Kuai said finally. "Come here tomorrow evening, and tell the hostess downstairs that you have a reservation under the name 'Ryswife.' Someone will tell you where to meet me then."

Twenty-four hours wasn't enough time to fly to Deepwater and back—unless flying direct, of course, but that was unfeasible, and Kuai would know that. Perhaps that meant that Kuai thought the books were here in Ridgecrescent. That, or he was expecting that Arkady would answer the Carmine Order's bluff with a counter-bluff, which would surely end in violence.

If it had to come to that, Arkady and Il-Hyeong could handle it. Over the course of the next day, then, they had to find whatever leads they could, to prepare for the eventuality that Kuai would simply have to end up dead as a matter of course.

"Until tomorrow evening, then," Arkady said, picking up a single dumpling with his fingers and popping it into his muzzle as he stood, wasting little time in chewing it. "And thank you again, Mr. Kuai, for your hospitality."

"Tomorrow, Mr. Ryswife," Kuai replied. "I hope we'll be able to help each other."

"As you say, Mr. Kuai, the simplest solution here is the obvious one."

Kuai nodded, and began to clean up his place setting. He made no further pleasantries for a farewell, and so Arkady took that as his sign to leave. As he reached the stairwell, the ferret considered rushing back in, gunning down Kuai, and making a run for it with Ming-Jun, but with a sigh, he admitted to himself that he needed to consider that, despite dropping the little hints she had, she wasn't entirely on the Iolite League's side anymore.

He hoped as hard as anything that he was wrong about that, and he resolved that, should the opportunity arise, he wouldn't be letting Jiangzhao Kuai keep his precious little *Xiǎotù* by the time this was all over.

14. The Iolite Doctrine

Outside, it was like the magic of Dianjiang Gardens had faded. That ambient mystique and allure were gone entirely, and in their place was nothing but cold night and the smell of food that was odd and unfamiliar instead of enticing. Home may as well have been on the other side of the world for how far away it felt right now.

Arkady thought about how there was a very real possibility that he'd never again set foot back in Deepwater, never again walk the ancient halls of Château Sainte-Mireille. His conscience wouldn't allow him to give up on his quest, now. So many things depended on the mission—depended on Arkady himself: Ming-Jun's safety and well-being; Pandora's chance at life; Il-Hyeong.

Il-Hyeong. Had his outburst up in Kuai's sanctum been for real, or had he simply been improvising, attempting some brilliant gambit to throw Kuai off-balance so that Arkady could gain the upper hand in their discussion? It was so hard to tell, now, just what was making Il-Hyeong tick. Regardless of how this all turned out, Arkady knew that his duty to Sahasrara obligated him to go to the Directorate Board with a report of his comrade's actions during the mission. That might forever ruin Il-Hyeong's standing in the Iolite League—might mean the end of 'Agent Quinn'—but part of that might be for the best, in the end, if the fox really had lost sight of their cause.

Before Arkady could cast his own judgment on that, he needed to *find* Il-Hyeong, first, and then they needed to finish the mission. Neither one of them would be leaving Ridgecrescent until the Pyxis Sequence and Ming-Jun were secure.

After putting a few dozen paces between Dianjiang Gardens and himself, Arkady could read more smells in the air without the strange foreign food pervading everything. In the busy downtown of Holygate, there were of course more individual smells than the ferret could ever hope to count, but with his enhanced senses, maybe he wouldn't have to. Maybe if he concentrated hard enough, he could just sift through them.

Standing there on the sidewalk, he took a few deep, cleansing breaths, acclimating to the cold air as it filled his nostrils, his mouth and his lungs. He closed his eyes and let his sense of time slow down, putting all of his focus onto what he could smell. Il-Hyeong's scent was one that he should know almost as well as his own; if he could pick it up, he could tell where the fox had gone.

The nighttime breeze shifted, and with it came a myriad of new scents—among them the familiar musk of swift fox that Arkady sought. The ferret opened his eyes, breathed again, and got a sense of which direction the wind had come. Somewhere through the crowd, in that direction, he'd find Il-Hyeong.

The smells of vehicle exhaust faded as Arkady rounded the corner into a narrower side street, but those odors were soon replaced by those of garbage and waste. Even so, traces of Il-Hyeong lingered, and the ferret followed them. The fox must have been quite angry, he knew, for his scent to be so clear and acrid, even now. That much, at least, answered one of Arkady's many questions.

From a nearby shadowy alleyway, the ferret heard a low sigh. "Well, what now, Arkady? Where do we go from here?"

Arkady leaned his back up against the wall, right by the corner. Il-Hyeong still didn't emerge. "We're not giving him what he wants," Arkady said. "We've got to beat him at his own game."

"Can we beat him?" the fox asked. "Is it even worth trying?"

Was it worth it? God, what *had* happened to the Il-Hyeong that Arkady had always known? "He's given us a full day," the ferret said. "That's more than enough time for us to get to the bottom of what he and the Carmine Order are up to, if we play our cards right."

"What cards?" Il-Hyeong demanded, and only then did he step out from the alley so that he could look the ferret in the eye. "What cards, Arkady?" he repeated. "We've been played for fools this entire time. The only thing that's ever been waiting for us here in Ridgecrescent is a trap."

"Well, we can't just leave. Not without Ming-Jun."

"Ming-Jun betrayed us, Arkady," Il-Hyeong said. His fingers tightened to form a fist at his side. He looked as though he wanted to punch the nearest wall. "You have to realize that."

Arkady shook his head. "No," he said. "No, I'm not ready to believe that just yet."

"She was pouring tea for their fucking *leader*!" the fox snapped. "She didn't just wander in off the street and get a part-time job doing that."

This could be a life-or-death situation for Ming-Jun, Arkady knew. She'd confided in him the existence of *Zhōngwén*, but hadn't mentioned the secret culture that apparently existed along with it. Why leave that out if it meant potentially confusing her as one of the enemy? She wasn't stupid; she had to have had a reason.

Without knowing that reason, though, Arkady couldn't break that confidence to Il-Hyeong—especially since he knew that the fox would never buy into the ferret's reasoning if he had no explanation to back it up.

"I don't know how she ended up with Kuai," Arkady said (and that much was true, too). "Maybe she's a plant. Maybe she's a double agent. I don't know, but I—"

"But you what? But you still trust her anyway?"

"Yes, as a matter of fact, I do," Arkady said. When Il-Hyeong gave him an angry, dubious look, he continued. "Look, if she'd been leading us into a trap back at Fan-Yin on purpose, we'd be dead right now. She knows what we're capable of; she'd have been able to help the Carmine Order set up a better ambush than that."

Il-Hyeong sighed. "If she had an inside line to the Carmine Order all along, why not tell us from the beginning? Why not use *that* to get us access to this Pyxis Sequence—which, by the way, I'm still not convinced even exists, at this point."

"I don't know, all right?" Arkady knew that part of his insistence was due to his not wanting to believe that she really had double-crossed them, but any way he looked at it, things didn't add up right to form a simple betrayal. "I'm trusting her because my gut is telling me that I have to, okay?"

"Because your gut has done so much good for us on this mission already?"

Arkady could have just let the fox go right there. Was it a bad sign, he asked himself, that he put more faith in Ming-Jun right now than he did in Il-Hyeong? "I can't believe you'd just give up on her like that," the ferret said. "You refused to give up on Kentian until you knew for sure that it was too late."

As soon as the words were out of his mouth, Arkady could tell that he'd hit Il-Hyeong pretty hard; at the same time, the sting of those words cut back into Arkady himself. What would Ming-Jun think about Arkady using and twisting Kentian's memory like that? What would Kentian have thought?

For several seconds, the fox was silent. Then, he said, "You realize that this could get all three of us killed."

"I thought you weren't afraid of dying."

"That doesn't mean I want to die for nothing," the fox said. "Which we all still might."

"One day," Arkady said. "One day to get to the bottom of all of this. And if what we uncover leads us to the fact that there is no Pyxis Sequence or that Ming-Jun really is working for the other side, then we'll... we'll do what we have to, as the situation calls for it."

Il-Hyeong pulled out his gun, gave it a quick check, and then concealed it again. "I want to say that I hope you're right about this, but if you're wrong, I guess we'll both know it soon enough."

"Come on," Arkady said, already starting to walk again. "Let's get out of the cold, first, and find someplace else to talk."

The nightclub had actually been Il-Hyeong's idea. Arkady had to ask the fox twice to make sure that he was serious, and even then, the ferret had a hard time believing it.

Still, Il-Hyeong had made good points. The ambient noise would mask their voices very well, lowering the chances of anyone eavesdropping while their own enhanced hearing let them speak to each other with relative ease. It would also be warm, they could keep to themselves without drawing undue suspicion, and they could linger for a while without anyone complaining of loitering.

Plus, the fox pointed out to seal the deal, they could both probably use a drink.

Ridgecrescent's popular music wasn't entirely to Arkady's taste. Il-Hyeong actually seemed to like it a fair bit more, which surprised the ferret even more than the fox suggesting the nightclub in the first place. Maybe the tension and seriousness of the possibly-botched mission had gotten so high that Il-Hyeong simply *had* to find some outlet to unwind, and casually bopping his head and tilting his ears in time with the music was the bare minimum he was willing to allow himself.

Arkady had intended for his glass of brandy to last him the entire conversation, but evidently, *his* tension had been ratcheted up too high, as well. Before he and Il-Hyeong had finished ascertaining their relative privacy, the ferret had moved on to a second. Arkady wasn't even sure if he *could* become intoxicated after the augmentation, but two wasn't too many for him, he knew, and the relaxation came more from the act of drinking itself more than it did from alcohol.

"All right," Arkady said, licking his lips after his first sip of his second brandy. "Let's look at where we are and what we've got at our disposal."

"You said Kuai's giving us a day to come up with the books he wants," Il-Hyeong said. "There's no way we can actually get them."

"No, but I was never planning on that," Arkady said.

Il-Hyeong was still on his first drink, and he'd barely touched it. "Was there an 'or else' stipulated in this agreement at all?"

"Not explicitly. But they *have* been trying to kill us."

"And so they're going to back off for a day to let us get our shit together?" the fox asked, raising an eyebrow. "What's to stop us from just leaving?"

Arkady thought again of the way Kuai's voice lilted whenever he'd said the name *Xiǎotù*. "They do have Ming-Jun," he said. "Maybe they know she's a double agent, and they paraded her out in front of us so we'd know we have something to come back for."

Il-Hyeong's muzzle twisted up in a bitter expression that had nothing to do with the brandy. "If they know as much about the Iolite League's inner workings as they seem to want to represent, then they should know that we don't brook betrayal."

Even just thinking about that possibility felt like legitimizing it too much. *Rule everything else out, first,* Arkady told himself. "If they did know of her connection to us, then they'd also have to realize that letting us see her would be a huge risk. Do we think they're really willing to go that far?"

"We know they're willing to try to kill us to stop us," Il-Hyeong pointed out. "Why suddenly decide that we're more valuable alive? What's so important about these books that they'd change their minds?"

"We did find our way right to their leader," Arkady pointed out. "Or at least one of their leaders. It could just be self-preservation on their part, at this point."

"They need us for something," Il-Hyeong said. "There was no reason not to kill us when they had the chance."

Arkady considered that. "Perhaps after having tried and failed so many times, they've decided to think better of attempting again?"

"If that's the case," Il-Hyeong said, "we still don't know why they were so intent on trying to kill us in the first place." He cracked his knuckles, leaned back in his chair, and did another quick, cursory check to make sure there were no eavesdroppers. "They had to have had a pretty good reason, seeing as they knew who we were and we didn't— hell, still *don't* really know who they are."

Arkady recalled the way that Ming-Jun had panicked over the line when they'd been raiding Fan-Yin. She'd been spooked, all right, and she wanted the team to disperse as fast as possible. It was obvious, in hindsight, that she had to have known at least something about what the Carmine Order was doing—well, perhaps not what they were *doing*, but at least who they *were*.

"Well," the ferret said, running past events over in his head as he tuned out the pounding dance beat, "Kuai did say that he knew we were after—"

When Arkady didn't finish his sentence, Il-Hyeong took another cautious look around. "Something wrong?" the fox asked, his hackles raised and his tail going still.

Arkady shook his head, and then he smiled. Il-Hyeong's ears tilted back in modest annoyance. "What is it, then?" the fox asked.

"Dr. Lederle," Arkady said. He could feel his grin splitting, growing wider.

By contrast, Il-Hyeong's frown of frustration was also getting more prominent. "Right, Sergeant Berzeviczy's so-called 'Iolite League' contact," he said. "The one who, the more I think of it, the more I'm convinced doesn't exist. What about him?"

"That's just it," Arkady said. "That's what Kuai said we were here for."

"A contact with the Iolite League?" Il-Hyeong looked no less confused.

"No," the ferret replied. He was actually on the verge of giggling now. "He specifically said *Doctor* Lederle." He leaned in over the table, bringing his snout closer to the fox's. "Doctor," he repeated once more, triumphantly.

Il-Hyeong sniffed at Arkady, and—as if contenting himself with that—again rested back in his chair. "I don't follow," he admitted.

"Neither did I," the ferret explained. "Not until just now. God in Heaven, I can't believe I didn't make the connection before!"

The fox rapped his claws on the small table. "Are you going to tell me what this connection is," he asked, "or do I have to threaten to shoot someone again?"

His moment of elation was such that Arkady was willing to let the fox's snide attempt at a joke go without reprimand. "After you left, up in Kuai's room, he told me that Jenfei and his other cronies knew we were looking for Lederle." He picked up his glass of brandy, but didn't sip yet. "But think about it: *we* didn't even know we were looking for Lederle until just earlier today. And when were Jenfei and her squad waiting for us?"

In the following moments, it was like Arkady could see all the gears inside Il-Hyeong's head click into place, one by one, the fox's eyes widening steadily in disbelief as he, too, put the pieces together and made the connections. "Oh, you've got to be fucking kidding me," the fox said, his voice a mixture of exasperation and relief.

"So," Arkady said, pausing just long enough to sip from his brandy before setting it back down, "want to finish up here and find a network terminal? Because I'll bet you fifty dees that Fan-Yin's public site will list a 'Lederle' on staff."

Il-Hyeong stood up from his chair. "Tell you what," he said, pulling out his wallet. "Let's skip the bet, and I'll just pay for your drinks now."

For the first time in what might as well have been forever, Arkady Ryswife and Il-Hyeong Quinn smiled at one another.

Ethan Lederle.

One quick after-hours trip to the nearest public library (involving what was, as a strict matter of legal technicality, breaking and entering) was all it took to get that simple bit of information.

It took only slightly more effort for Il-Hyeong to hack into the municipal database and pull up what was, after all, a matter of public record. Not only had they confirmed that Dr. Lederle was, in fact, a real person, but they now also knew that he was a red panda, thirty-nine years old, and lived in Westchurch, one of the outlying suburbs of Holygate.

They also had his phone number, as well as his home address.

Arkady rested with his back against a public phone booth, flicking a half-dee coin chit from paw to paw. It was getting past the point of being pretty late, but Holygate was a busy enough city that the streets weren't deserted, by any means. Still, the crowds were thinning out, and nobody took undue notice of the fox and the ferret standing there on the sidewalk.

"You realize that this might all be part of some trap that Kuai is laying for us," Il-Hyeong pointed out.

"Maybe." And Arkady had considered that, too. "But really, I don't think Kuai is dumb enough to try to bait us with information that isn't even secret. I honestly think he thought we already knew all of this."

Il-Hyeong shook his head despite himself, chuckling. "So basically, our own ignorance has saved our tails this time?"

"Looks that way, doesn't it?" Arkady said, snatching the half-dee chit out of the air one last time, holding it fast in his paw as he slipped on into the phone booth.

Il-Hyeong leaned his head into the booth as well. "So you're really just going to call a cab and drive right on up to his house?" he asked.

Arkady already had the receiver in his free paw. "I can't really think of a better way to get there. Can you?" he said. "He's almost certainly at home, probably asleep at this time of night."

"That's not what I meant," the fox said. "I'm asking whether we really just want to rush into this without knowing what we're getting into."

"I don't see that we have a lot of choice," the ferret said. "Besides, I'd rather take my chance with a sleeping scientist than with another few fireteams who're all carrying assault rifles with our names on them."

Il-Hyeong took a deep breath, but then just nodded, saying nothing as he withdrew from the phone booth, giving Arkady his space as the ferret dropped the half-dee into the coin slot and began to dial.

It took the better part of an hour and a fair chunk of change to get to the suburbs by taxi. Still, at this time of night, the buses were no longer running, and the transit tubes didn't even go out that far, so taking a cab was the only real way to get there—short of stealing another car, which Arkady had ruled out before Il-Hyeong could even suggest it.

To be on the safe side (or at least what passed for it, now), Arkady had the cab driver drop them off one block over from where they were actually going, and so it was only a brisk, dead-of-night walk to get to their destination: a gated-off condominium in a fairly well-to-do neighborhood, the surrounding area lit mostly only by streetlights and the moon. Arkady walked up to the gate, and rested one paw atop the box that controlled the intercom system.

"You're not going to buzz him awake in the middle of the night and ask to be invited inside," Il-Hyeong said before the ferret had even begun to do anything.

"That's exactly what I'm going to do," Arkady replied.

"Instead of, say, just breaking in and getting the drop on him before he runs off?" Il-Hyeong asked. The fox motioned with both arms. "Because look around you," he said. "There aren't any witnesses here to see us. We've already broken into one building tonight, and this one is going to be a whole lot easier."

Arkady started to go through the list of names on the intercom display. "If he's really Berzevicy's contact, maybe he's inclined to help us," he replied.

"That's awfully cavalier and optimistic of you."

"I want to make a show of good faith."

"If he *is* this purported contact," the fox said, "he's probably going to get in touch with Berzeviczy as soon as you're done talking."

"I'm counting on it," Arkady said. "Hopefully he tells Lederle that we're legit and convinces him to stay put." He highlighted Lederle's name on the list, then pressed down the call button.

Il-Hyeong opened his muzzle to speak, but went silent as soon as he saw Arkady's finger pressed onto the button. The ferret knew what the fox was going to say, anyway: *or Boots might warn Lederle to get out of there.*

Well, Arkady was going to have to trust *someone* if he was going to salvage this mission, and if the only thing he had left was his own gut, then so be it.

After Arkady buzzed the fourth time, the intercom finally sprung to life. "Hello?"

The voice belonged to a middle-aged male. Ridgecrescent accent, somewhere from the east or north. Tired, but not the sort of tired that came from having just been woken up.

"Good evening," Arkady responded. "Sorry to call on you at such an hour. Is this Ethan Lederle, by any chance?"

There was a brief pause. "Who wants to know?" The voice was more collected, now.

"I am but a humble messenger," Arkady said. "Surely you can see that I alone pose no threat to you." As breathing came through the speaker, the ferret held his own breath anxiously, hoping for a very specific response in kind.

After another few seconds, the man on the other end said, "The threat posed by a lone individual is nevertheless still a threat; but speak, messenger, and tell me what you have been sent to tell me."

He hadn't gotten the wording exactly right, but his rejoinder still completed the exchange from Chapter Six of the Book of Sirius, where the wolf messenger met with the Ocelot on the night before the Battle of Two Rivers. Whoever was on the line was, if nothing else, someone who knew his Scripture.

"My name is Arkady," the ferret said, and he let his Deepwater accent come through in full. "Dr. Lederle, I urgently need to speak with you."

Another pause. Then, "I don't know anyone named Arkady. What's this about?" The response carried the tacit admission that it was, in fact, Dr. Lederle on the other end.

"It's in regard to what happened the other night," Arkady said. He let that sink in for a moment or two. "I trust you know what I'm talking about."

The intercom was dead and quiet for several long seconds. Arkady was about to order Il-Hyeong to circle around back to check to see if the doctor was trying to make a break for it when the speaker came back on. "Give me a minute to get dressed." Arkady heard Lederle try and fail to mask an anxious sigh. "I suppose I should put on some tea."

The condominium smelled faintly of incense. Even without a more advanced sense of smell, that much would be noticeable to anyone who came by. That alone didn't mean much, of course, but taken in context, the scent took on something of a different meaning. The décor didn't give much away, either, though Arkady suspected that was on purpose.

No, it was only the subtle things that gave Ethan Lederle away, and even then, if one weren't looking, it was debatable whether even those few things would be obvious or indeed even noticeable at all. For almost all purposes, the red panda's dwelling simply indicated that he was a well-to-do member of the Holygate area community, one who enjoyed an above-average standard of living and who didn't trouble himself with too many excess trappings.

Not including the lingering hint of incense, the first thing Arkady noticed was the slight preponderance of purple in living room—not in all things, but just slightly in favor, like in the purple trim in the carpet, the blue and violet drapes, the faint indigo glass vase that was currently filled with lavender blossoms. Again, this wouldn't be unusual, at least not to anyone who hadn't—at least at some point in their life—been a member of the Iolite League.

True to his promise, Lederle had a pot of tea brewing when Arkady and Il-Hyeong were let inside. The red panda looked weary and nervous, but even then, he received the two agents into his home with a very quiet, "Be welcome here, friends."

Those words, which Arkady had heard Father Benjamin use time and again to begin services in the chapel at Château Sainte-Mireille, were probably more for Lederle's own benefit than any further attempt to establish identity; by this point, anyone who wanted to feign knowledge of the Iolite League might risk beating the point into the ground, but the nervousness that Arkady saw in the red panda's eyes wasn't the same fear that he'd come to know in individuals who were waiting for the right moment to turn the tables or spring some other trap. No, more likely was the probability that Lederle feared some kind of undercover operation to expose his true allegiance. Religious affiliation with the League didn't (insofar as the League itself was concerned) have any political stipulations associated with it, but the government of Ridgecrescent didn't see things that way. Arkady knew that Lederle had every reason to fear such repercussions, and so the ferret set out at once to better put the doctor at ease.

"I appreciate your meeting with us on such short notice, doctor, and at such a late hour," Arkady said. "I know that you're putting yourself at risk just by seeing us."

The red panda took out a cloth to wipe his glasses, which had fogged up in the course of moving the steaming teapot over to the kitchen counter. "The greater risk would be to do nothing," he replied, fidgeting as he put more of his obvious attention on getting out a set of nice teacups. "Besides, if I weren't prepared for risk, I wouldn't have stayed behind."

Il-Hyeong started to ask a follow-up question, but Arkady help up a paw to silence him, then watched as Lederle got the sugar from his cupboard and the milk from his refrigerator. The red panda's breathing was still heavy, and his body language practically screamed how ill at ease he was. Il-Hyeong took the opportunity to pace around the living room and nearby hallway, checking for any yet-unnoticed threats as Arkady remained close to the kitchen counter.

Red pandas were one of the world's rarer species. Even world traveler Arkady had only ever seen a few, and Lederle was the first to whom he'd ever actually spoken. The mask of pale fur around his face and eyes was like a photonegative version of Arkady's own. His ringed tail was far bushier than Arkady's—and it would have been bushier still if it weren't in the bedraggled state it was, as sure a sign of sleepless nights as his dark, sunken eyes, which currently strained to look as bright as possible from behind a pair of broad-rimmed glasses.

"Milk and sugar?" he offered as he poured three cups of tea, one after the other.

"Please," Arkady replied. In actuality, he preferred his without sugar, but he wanted to observe his host (and contact) as much as he could before the conversation began in earnest. His sensitive nose picked up no hint or trace of poison having been added to the brew.

Il-Hyeong came back from the side hallway. "Not for me, thanks," he said before giving Arkady a quick nod to let the ferret know that the condominium was clear and secure.

With a polite smile, Lederle added both milk and sugar to two of the cups. He slid the third over to Il-Hyeong, first, then took one of the others for himself. "This will probably keep me up all night," he said. "Not that I expect I'd've gotten much sleep, anyway."

"Again, we appreciate it," Arkady said. He took a testing sip of his tea. Still too hot.

"I'd appreciate knowing what you know," the red panda said. "Or, well, what you might be able to tell me." He blew across the surface of his own tea, then said, "I'm assuming you're from...?"

Il-Hyeong filled in the blank. "The Château, yes," he said. "We arrived just before the attack."

"Not in time enough to prevent it, then," Lederle said with a sigh. Again, he blew on his tea.

"So you knew it was coming?" Arkady asked. Lederle just gave a solemn nod.

Here, then, was one of the biggest questions Arkady had to face: if the research on the Pyxis Sequence was critical to the Iolite League, and Dr. Lederle himself was with the Iolite League, why had Sahasrara been sent in to obtain the data by force?

Had the people in charge of Project Scheherazade known that this so-called Carmine Order was going to attack when they did? If so, why not inform Arkady and his team in advance? Why also not inform them of Dr. Lederle's existence, or his usefulness as a potential contact? Why the secrecy?

Why didn't any of this add up, still?

"Doctor," Arkady said, "before we tell you what we know, we need to know what it is you're doing here." He took a sip of tea, ignoring the heat. "Not because we don't trust you; we just need to be sure." It was a poor excuse, he knew, but if Lederle and his research were legitimate, then they didn't need or want excuses—they needed openness and honesty.

Lederle leaned against the counter and sighed again. He closed his eyes, took several breaths, then opened them again. "Very well," he said. "If you are just here to kill me, I've made my peace. I've done what God needs me to do."

To Arkady's side, Il-Hyeong tensed up. The ferret didn't try to get him to stand down.

"First off," Lederle said, "I'm going to guess that you're with the Project. Is that a fair assumption?"

Arkady nodded. "We are."

"I guess I'm not surprised they sent you, then," the red panda said. "Given the way things have been going in Ridgecrescent over the last few years, I imagine that the League was afraid that the data would never make it out of the country."

"Do you think your work has been compromised by the government?" the ferret asked.

"Compromised? No," Lederle said with a wry chuckle. "I'm as much in charge of my own research as I've ever been, going all the way back to... well, even before this whole mess with the war created this xenophobic panic, we were still working in relative secrecy, of course. But I'm guessing you know all that."

"Of course," Arkady lied. If scientists at Fan-Yin Bioinformatics had been working in secret, then it was a secret that Sahasrara wasn't in on, but in the interests of learning what he needed to learn, the ferret wasn't going to let Dr. Lederle know that.

Lederle sipped at his own tea for a while, his long tail sliding into view for a few moments before disappearing behind the counter again. "To answer what I'm sure will be your next question," he said, "it was the League who warned me of the attempted raid."

"A spy here in Ridgecrescent?" Il-Hyeong asked.

The red panda swallowed a tight lump in his throat. "If you really are with the Project, then you know what they want you to know about who else is on the job."

"Whoever it was," Il-Hyeong said, "it wasn't anyone capable of delivering any assistance, though, was it?"

"What makes you say that?" Lederle asked.

"Berzeviczy," the swift fox said. "Why hire his team if you had League protection looking out for you?"

Lederle hung his head. He looked both humiliated and frustrated. His tea swirled in his cup as his paws wobbled from side to side. "The League can't operate openly here," he murmured. "Even if you're not who you claim to be, I'm sure that you've got to know at least that much."

What was more apparent than anything else, now, was that Ethan Lederle was a man who felt abandoned. That, or he was the world's greatest actor, because only the world's greatest actor could so honestly radiate that internal conflict between faith and a realization that something had gone terribly wrong and he'd been left to fend for himself.

"You mentioned staying behind," Arkady said. "A little while ago, I mean. What did you mean by that?"

Lederle looked up, and his expression took on an edge of pride, pride that, despite everything else, remained unwounded. "My family," he said, his voice carrying that same pride. "When the government made adherence to the Iolite Doctrine illegal, I couldn't ask them to give that up."

"So they left you, too?" Il-Hyeong asked.

The red panda shook his head. "I sent them away," he declared.

"To where?" Arkady asked.

"To Xin-Banzhu," Lederle said. "Right near..." He stopped, cleared his throat, then adjusted his glasses. "Well, it doesn't matter where, exactly, does it? What matters is that they're someplace where they can be safe and happy and worship as they like, and as soon as I'm done with this, I'm going to wash my hands of Project Semiramis forever and go to be with them."

That unfamiliar name sent Arkady's mind right off its mental rails. He didn't want to betray his ignorance *or* his surprise, but one or both of those things must have shown, because Lederle looked nervously at the ferret, and then at the fox before reaching for the cutlery drawer and grabbing for a knife. Here was a man definitely dedicated to his cause, and if someone, somewhere were trying to mislead Arkady and his team, then the deception didn't lie with Ethan Lederle.

"Hold on," Arkady said, holding up both paws, one for Lederle and the other for Il-Hyeong. The last thing anyone needed, he told himself, was for this to get violent. "Project Semiramis, you just said." He leveled his eyes at the red panda. "What do you mean by that?"

"You said you were *with* the Project!" Lederle growled, both paws clutching clumsily at the small steak knife he'd snatched from his drawer. "Tell me who really sent you!" He took a step back, still brandishing the knife at Arkady and Il-Hyeong before his muzzle twisted into an even more determined glare as he brought the knife's blade up against his own throat.

Il-Hyeong dropped his teacup and had his DKR-7 at the ready almost instantly. Arkady was about to order the fox to lower his weapon before noticing that he was aiming right at Lederle's arm, finger already on the trigger. *Quick thinking*, the ferret had to concede, even as he continued to hold up both of his own paws in a gesture of peace. "Easy, doctor," he urged. "Just calm down. We're with the Iolite League. I promise you that."

The knife's edge started to make a furrow in the fur of Lederle's throat, but Arkady couldn't see (nor could he smell, he realized) any blood yet. "I'll do it," the red panda said, his voice catching in his throat as his paw started to shake. "I'll do it, and everything I know will die with me."

"I've got a clear shot, Arkady," Il-Hyeong said, quietly enough that Arkady knew Lederle couldn't hear.

Arkady murmured back in that same subvocal tone. "Not yet," he said, and then he raised his voice back to a normal, very level speaking tone. "Doctor, please. The Iolite League needs to know what you know." He took a small step forward. "Sahasrara needs to know what you know."

"Sahasrara?" For just a moment, the paw holding the knife wavered and fell a few inches away. The red panda then reaffirmed his grip on the handle, but his grip on his conviction had obviously weakened more. "Sahasrara?" he repeated. "What happened to Ajna?"

The last fleeting doubts Arkady had about Dr. Lederle's allegience flickered away completely in that instant. Sahasrara, the sword of the Iolite League; Ajna, the shotgun, striking sure and final. Less subtle, but results were results, and moreover, its very existence was every bit as much a secret at Sahasrara's.

"We're with Sahasrara," Arkady said. "Project Scheherazade."

Lederle shook his head, moving the knife away from his neck as he did so. "I don't know what that is," he said. "I've been working at the behest of Ajna for over a decade on Project Semiramis. But you say you don't know what *that* is."

"We know Ajna," Il-Hyeong said. "But I've never heard of this 'Semiramis' thing, either. What's it about?"

Slumping against the wall of the kitchen, Lederle sighed and chewed his lip. "I'm not sure I can say, now," he said. "The people at Ajna made it very clear that even other members of the Iolite League weren't going to know what we were trying to do, here. I realize that may sound strange."

"Well, we outrank Ajna," Arkady said. That was true, but he knew that Ajna would be none too happy to learn that Sahasrara had stepped on their toes like this. Of course, if Ajna had any secret projects, Sahasrara should have known about them. "If you want," the ferret offered, "we can take you back the Château with us, under our protection. How does that sound?"

"I still don't understand," Lederle said. "Why isn't Ajna coming to claim their research themselves? Why didn't they send anyone if the League knew the attack was coming?"

Arkady shook his head. "I don't know," he replied. "I don't know, but I promise you, I'm going to find out, but I need your help." He took another step forward and offered a paw.

The red panda looked at Arkady's paw, but he didn't take it; instead, he just clutched the knife harder, now holding it at his side. "I don't know," he said, the words nearly a whisper. "I don't know who to trust anymore."

Oh, God, you don't know the half of it, Arkady thought.

"Does the word 'Pyxis' mean anything to you?" Il-Hyeong asked.

Lederle started to bring the knife up again, but this time, he stopped halfway. "How do you know about that?" he asked. How his paws were trembling; if he tried to hold the knife to his throat again, he was probably going to end up cutting himself by accident.

"We told you," Arkady said. "We're with Sahasrara. We—"

"That still doesn't explain anything!" the doctor said. Il-Hyeong readied his pistol again, but the red panda either didn't notice, or he was paying the fox no heed. "And it doesn't prove anything, either, because whoever else attacked Fan-Yin knew something about my research, too." Then the red panda's eyes widened as if in horrified revelation. "Oh, God, you *are* with them, aren't you?"

Arkady could see Il-Hyeong's finger beginning to tense as it slid along the trigger of his DKR-7. The fox would be able to stop Lederle from posing a threat to himself, Arkady knew, but the doctor wouldn't come clean with any more info after he'd been shot—not until it was too late, at any rate, and Arkady didn't want it to come to that.

"Okay, let's see if I can make this simple," the ferret said, interposing himself between Il-Hyeong and Lederle. "Doctor, your work involves genetics, right?" The red panda nodded. "Do you have access to your lab?"

"I might," Lederle said. "But you can threaten me all you like, and I won't—"

"No one's going to threaten anyone," Arkady said. "You're going to want to take me there."

"And what makes you so sure of that?"

"Because I'm Pandora's father," Arkady said. "And if you take me to your lab, I can prove it."

At this ungodly hour, there were few other vehicles on the road. The highway ran along the river, and from there, the skylines of both Highslope and Holygate were clearly visible. Both were only partially illuminated against the black backdrop of the night sky, but even now, there was enough bustle that the cityscapes looked eerily alive, but in a state of mere torpor.

Arkady sat in the passenger's seat, his pistol resting in his lap. The weapon's state of readiness had less to do with the prospect that Lederle might still try to double-cross them, and more to do with the possibility that someone might still be tracking the lot of them. In the back seat sat Il-Hyeong, his own gun likewise drawn, his attention on the currently dull surroundings outside.

Dr. Lederle tried fiddling with the radio. Within minutes of leaving home, however, he'd turned it off, plunging the car ride into an awkward silence, punctuated only by the occasional pointed question. "Are you the only Iolite League member on your research team?" Arkady asked at one point.

"Of course not," Lederle replied. "Though you'll understand if I don't divulge their identities to you right away." Arkady had just nodded at that.

The doctor's car, much like his home and his manner of dress, indicated a standard of living that was more than just comfortable. Not rich, by any means, but well-to-do, past the sort of level of contentment that most of urban Ridgecrescent enjoyed, to Arkady's perceptions. It was with a delayed aftertaste of bitterness that the ferret realized that Lederle could likely afford such comforts only because he no longer had his family to look after.

"So, Pandora's still around, then?" Lederle asked as the buildings of Holygate rapidly began to loom closer. "Still the original?"

"Still the one they based off of me," Arkady replied. As he gazed out the window, watching lights whip by too quickly for normal people to see, he thought about how long ago it really was that Pandora had been 'born,' living—no, subsisting in a state of non-life for all these years.

Lederle cleared his throat anxiously. "So you claim," he said. "Whoever sent you could have known well enough to send any ferret along, in that event."

"You've been working on the project," Il-Hyeong said, "and yet Arkady's name doesn't ring a bell?"

The red panda shook his head. "It's not as if we've been working with Pandora herself. Just data. Just the things we need to know to crack the code that makes her brain work with the rest of her components." He gave Arkady a sideways glance. "The name of whoever happened to contribute the genetic foundation isn't consequential to that."

To hear the doctor talk about the girl Arkady thought of as his daughter like she was just some machine was unnerving, but to a scientist's perspective, that's what she had to be, after all. It didn't matter to someone in Lederle's position that this girl in a tank, half a world a way, had to have come from someone else's flesh and blood. None of that was Lederle's fault, of course, and it didn't make the doctor a bad person, not by any stretch. Probably it was better that he was more clinically removed from the subject.

If only Arkady could achieve that same level of detachment, he mused in dejection.

"Hey, doc," Il-Hyeong said, his head turning to the left to look first beside and then behind the car. "You missed the turnoff for the bridge."

"I'm not taking the bridge," Lederle said.

"Well, then how are we going to get to Fan-Yin?"

"I'm not taking you to Fan-Yin."

Arkady could hear the safety on Il-Hyeong's gun being switched off. "You mind telling me why not?" the fox asked.

Lederle was doing everything he could to maintain composure, Arkady could tell; moreover, the red panda seemed to be getting better at it, finally. "Because," the doctor replied calmly, "that's not where the lab we need to go is."

When Arkady and Il-Hyeong both stopped to look at one another, the red panda let out a brief, wry chuckle. "Well, honestly," he continued. "If I had suspicion that people were going to be after our work, I wasn't going to just leave it behind, now, was I?"

It was a good thing, Arkady thought, that Lederle could be so clever, even if he was definitely in way over his head. By extension, it was a shame that the League—or perhaps just Ajna?—hadn't done its own due diligence in looking out for him. Arkady still meant to get to the bottom of that, first thing after this mission had finally resolved itself.

And after we get Ming-Jun back, he added.

"So, where *are* we going, then?" Il-Hyeong asked.

"You'll see," Lederle replied. "It's one of our auxiliary testing facilities."

Il-Hyeong reset the safety on his gun and set it on the seat beside him. "So, you took your top secret research and you hid it someplace where your company already has ties? Did it not occur to you that that wasn't going to buy you a whole lot of time, in the long run?"

"Well," Lederle said, "if you are from the Iolite League, like you say, then I'd say it's bought me just enough, now, hasn't it?"

"FY-SES," the large, unlit sign read. "It stands for 'Fan-Yin Scientific Engineering Services,'" Lederle had explained as he was parking the car.

The building itself looked like it might well have fit in at the industrial park in Highslope where Il-Hyeong had kept (and then executed) the prisoners from the Carmine Order. It was in slightly better shape than that, but not by much. Evidently, Fan-Yin proper didn't believe in spreading the wealth to its satellite holdings.

"So, what all goes on here, then?" Arkady asked as Dr. Lederle swiped his badge at the front door's sensor. The internal lock disengaged with a hollow click, but the red panda still had to manually unlock the nighttime security lock with an old-fashioned key. Automated sensors of some type caused the run of lighting to turn on as he stepped inside. He beckoned the pair of agents to follow.

"A lot what you might call the 'grunt work' of the scientific process gets carried out here," Lederle explained as he led the way down the hall. "That's a gross oversimplification, of course, but things like large-scale assays and other rigorous processes that require high bandwidth but otherwise less direct technical involvement are done here."

"How long is verifying Arkady's claim going to take?" Il-Hyeong asked. Arkady noticed that the fox was putting up a front of appearing less on-alert than the ferret could tell he really was.

Lederle bypassed the elevators and went instead directly to the nearby stairwell. "Less than an hour, hopefully. Most of that time will actually be me reverse-engineering data based on Pandora's genetic sequence that I have on file here, since I don't have an actual tissue sample to work with."

The stairway brought back memories of the raid on Fan-Yin. On reflex, Arkady checked his gun. He remembered Ming-Jun, assuring him repeatedly over his headset, that the coast was clear and that she wasn't seeing any intruder activity. Further reason, the ferret told himself, to never take his situation for granted.

"And if it turns out that I'm not lying," Arkady asked, "what next? Will you come back to Deepwater with us along with your research?"

"When you put it that way, it sounds almost rash. Still, given that people are probably out to kill me, 'rash' is better than 'stupid.'"

"We'll find a way to work it out," Arkady said. They'd exited the stairwell on the second floor, another set of lights activating automatically as they walked into the hallway. "*I* know that I'm not lying, at least."

Lederle stopped, turned to look at the ferret, and smiled. "I'm really hoping you're not," he said. He'd gone suddenly quiet and solemn. "I've been pouring years of my life into this, and now that things have ended up where they are now, I... well, I'll just be glad when it's all behind me."

"Xin-Banzhu is a lovely country," Arkady said as he clapped a paw on the doctor's shoulder. "I'm sure you'll like it there."

"Thank you," the red panda murmured. He then gently shrugged his arm free and walked just a few feet more to the next door, over on the right, and pulled out his keys again. There was some rattling and fumbling, and then the door pushed open.

Inside, it was dark, and no lights sprung to life on their own this time. Lederle went straight to work, turning on a series of computers and other devices, the room soon filled with the humming of machinery warming up. He then checked to make sure that all the blinds were drawn.

The room itself appeared to be a small-scale laboratory, not unlike the ones located beneath the basement of Château Sainte-Mireille. Dr. Mayflower's equipment was far more elaborate than the setup in here, of course, but that wasn't really a fair comparison. The general feel of the place was still far more upscale than a look at the building from the outside had indicated. Would this all be enough for Arkady to finish making his case to this wayward member of the Iolite League?

"You mentioned that you'd moved your research here," Il-Hyeong said as he pulled out a chair for himself. "Does that include the Pyxis Sequence itself?"

"It includes what I need to bring back with me," Lederle replied. He flicked on a few additional monitors, then got a syringe ready. "There's nothing for you to take without my mind to make sense of it for you."

Really, Arkady couldn't blame the doctor for his paranoia. At this point, they were both so very close to the things they'd been seeking, and hopefully they'd be able to come to the acceptance that those things were one and the same. "Again, we appreciate the risks you're taking by even dealing with us," the ferret said. "Now, what do you need me to do?"

"Well, first, I'd like to take a blood sample," Lederle said, indicating the syringe. "I could use fur, but that would be less reliable and take more work, and I think we're all in something of a hurry, yes?"

Arkady holstered his pistol and then rolled back his sleeve before offering his arm to the red panda. "By all means," he said. "I've got nothing to hide."

Lederle didn't have the bedside manner that a medical doctor would (but then, neither did Dr. Mayflower, thought Arkady), and he wasn't too gentle or careful in obtaining the blood sample. Still, given the trials and troubles Arkady had been through even just since coming to Ridgecrescent, a not-so-tender poke with a needle was the least of his worries.

With the syringe soon filled, Lederle deposited the contents into a small transparent cylinder, then drew a small portion of that sample and placed a single drop onto a microscope slide. He checked the instrument panel on the large device over on the far wall (its purpose beyond Arkady's ability to guess), and then went back to the microscope to examine the slide.

The red panda let out a quizzical hum as he peered through the microscope, and he chewed his lip after he sat back up. "Well, you certainly *seem* healthy enough," he said. "I'll just run your sample, here, and the results from that shouldn't take more than ten or fifteen minutes." He went back to the large machine again, this time bringing the cylindrical tube with the rest of Arkady's blood sample with him.

The device, Arkady then began to realize, was much like the handheld scanner that he'd seen and used in Boots' apartment. Doubtless it was vastly more complex, but it had a similar loading mechanism for inserting the sample, and the attached monitor was likely where the results would be displayed once the analysis cycle was complete.

With that underway, Dr. Lederle sat down at one of the room's many computer terminals and began to type rapidly. "I'm sorry if this is going to be boring," he said, attention wholly on the computer monitor. "I'm afraid that there's not much you can really do at this point but wait."

"What are you doing there?" Il-Hyeong asked, stepping in beside the red panda, watching the monitor over his shoulder.

"What I'm doing here," the doctor explained, "is I'm going to go through my on-file genetic information and try to extrapolate the pointers I'll need to match against the sample I've taken from your comrade, here."

Arkady walked over to the microscope, looking in through it as he listened to Il-Hyeong and Dr. Lederle speak. "It must be difficult," he heard the fox say, "working with a subject you don't actually have access to."

The blood sample that Arkady looked at didn't appear remarkable in any way, but then, he was hardly qualified to know much about what he was looking at. "I won't lie; it's been pretty tough, at times," Lederle replied. "It looks like we were still able to pull it off, though, in the long run."

"And so this here is Pandora's actual genetic information?" Arkady looked up and saw Il-Hyeong pointing at the computer display. "You wouldn't just be able to use this to create a Pandora of your own?"

"Genetics doesn't work that way," Lederle said, not bothering to mask his amused chuckle. "This is basically just a blueprint, but just because I handed you a set of blueprints doesn't mean that you could make a building."

"And this here, then," Il-Hyeong asked, tapping a claw at a section of the monitor. "This here indicates the Pyxis Sequence?"

Again Lederle chuckled. "Just a tiny fraction thereof," he said. "It goes on like this for pages and pages." Arkady took a few steps closer to get a look, himself. Seeing his daughter reduced to a sequence of genetic data displayed on a computer screen filled him with an eerie sense of unease that he couldn't really rationalize.

"Pages and pages, huh?" Il-Hyeong hummed. "In genetics terms, how long is that?"

"I'm not sure how to give you a frame of reference," Lederle replied. "Essentially, it's code for a whole series of neurotransmitters, if you didn't already know that bit of specifics, but without a background in biochemistry, I'm not sure what good it would do to try and compare the size of that to something else."

That Lederle was seemingly so blasé about having the Pyxis Sequence itself told Arkady that the doctor had either already made up his mind about being able to trust these mysterious agents from Sahasrara, or else he'd resigned himself to the fact that the information would just be forced out of him later, anyway.

"But you *have* worked the code itself out, then?" the swift fox asked, peering more intently at the monitor, now. "If we are going to be bringing you back to Deepwater when all this is over, the busywork has been completed?"

Lederle nodded. "That's the theory," he said. "It's like the world's biggest subcellular jigsaw puzzle." He began to scroll down through page after page of indecipherable sequence data. "If you wanted to get an idea for how big that is in *computer* terms, here you go."

The red panda's finger tapped the keyboard again and again and again, each keystroke shifting the visible page from down further and further. Arkady whistled under his breath at the sight of it; even though he couldn't discern what all of it meant, he at least understood why it had taken this team years and years to piece all of this together. "Compared to the full length of the genome," Lederle said, "this is almost nothing, too." Finally, after what had to have been several dozen 'pages' of the data, the sequence finally came to a stop.

"And this is actually it?" Il-Hyeong asked. "That right there was the Pyxis Sequence itself?"

"Well, the blueprints for it, at any rate," Lederle replied, opening up a new program and making his way through a new set of data tables.

"Are you sure that it works?" Arkady asked. He wanted to reach into the computer itself and touch that sequence of data points as if it could give physical assurance that the thing he'd sought for so long was actually real.

Resting back in his chair, Lederle adjusted his glasses. "Well, clearly, we haven't tried anything out on Pandora herself, yet," he said. "But what you just saw is the sequence that codes for the neurotransmitters needed to make her central nervous system function."

"If we're going to be extracting you, then we can't leave any hard copies of the data behind," Il-Hyeong said. "After we're done here, can you get us into the main Fan-Yin site in Highslope?"

Lederle shook his head. "No need. I physically brought the drive here, myself," he explained. "I know none of the other scientists have been back into the labs since the attack, so nobody will have noticed it's gone yet."

Il-Hyeong smiled and set his paw on the red panda's shoulder. "You've done a very good thing," he said warmly. "God will reward you for your service."

"I hope so," Lederle sighed. "We all have our calling in life, though, don't we?"

"Don't we just," Il-Hyeong said. He pointed with his free paw over toward the analysis device on the other side of the room. "What's that machine over there doing, exactly?"

Arkady turned to look at the machine as well, just out of reflex. Because of that, he was half a second too slow to stop what he saw happening next.

After pointing, Il-Hyeong had dropped his other paw, the one that had been on Lederle's shoulder, and grabbed his gun, which had been resting across his lap. He was probably intending to aim higher, but with Arkady reaching to intercede, the fox only had time to bring the pistol up to around chest level before pulling the trigger, firing once into the red panda's back.

The gunshot rung in Arkady's ears, sparing him from having to hear the sound that Lederle made as he coughed up blood. His eyes were wide with shock, and he stared at Arkady with a silent, pleading expression as the front of his shirt started to blossom with a rapidly-growing patch of dark red.

As Lederle began to slump out of his chair, Il-Hyeong caught him, cradling him gently in his arms. "It's okay now, brother," the fox whispered to him before placing a soft kiss on his cheek. "Your work is finished. God is waiting for you."

Arkady's paw was already wrapped tightly around the grip of his own weapon, but by this point, the damage was done. He could only watch, dumbfounded, with no solace to offer the scientist, whose eyes just slowly slid shut as his muzzle dropped open, the rest of his body going still a moment later.

Il-Hyeong lowered the body to the floor, then wiped his paws on his own pants. Still clutching his gun in one paw, he remained hunched down on the floor to reach for the computer case.

Seeing Il-Hyeong fire on the Carmine Order soldiers back at Fan-Yin despite orders had been one thing. Watching him execute unarmed prisoners in the basement of an abandoned building had been even worse. But here, to see Il-Hyeong kill Ethan Lederle without any provocation or even any cause that Arkady could discern was just so—

"Why?" The word seemed to spill out of Arkady's mouth all on its own. He realized, then, that he was starting to cry. At once, he found his resolve and forced it to come to the surface. "God in Heaven, Il-Hyeong, what the *fuck* did you just do?" His fingers gripped harder at his gun, but he couldn't bring himself to try to aim it just yet.

"I just had to watch a good man die in my arms, that's what," the fox replied without even turning to look at Arkady, his attention still completely on the computer case under the desk. "I was *trying* to get a clean shot to the head so he at least wouldn't know and wouldn't have to suffer."

Now Arkady brought his gun up. "Don't you fucking touch that," he barked, warning the fox away from the computer. "Have you really been trying to sabotage this mission the whole time? Are you—"

"God, Arkady, don't pretend you're going to shoot me," the fox sneered, even as he complied by getting to his feet. "Besides, this is Mission Accomplished. We should be happy."

"Accomplished?" Arkady said. "*What* exactly did this accomplish?" He looked down at Lederle, lying dead and still in a slowly-growing pool of his own blood. "How does killing the one person who can make sense of this—the one person who's been willing to help us—accomplish anything?"

"He *did* help us, Arkady," the fox explained. "He got us the very thing that we came here for. And now that we have it, we can get on a flight out of this godforsaken country as soon as the sun comes up."

"Yes, he helped us. He helped us, and you just shot him right in the fucking back!" Arkady kept trying to ignore the corpse by his feet, and the easiest way to do that was to focus more of his rage on Il-Hyeong. "He hadn't even finished ana—"

Il-Hyeong groaned. "What, hadn't finished cross-referencing your blood sample?" he said. "Who cares? We've got the Pyxis Sequence, now. It's all right in *here*." The fox tapped the side of his head with a single claw.

While Arkady had been held in anticipation that Dr. Lederle would be providing them with the genetic data they'd tried so hard to get, the ferret hadn't even considered that he'd been looking right at that very same data. Il-Hyeong's having recorded the visual display of the sequence to his memory module had been quick and brilliant thinking on the fox's part, and Arkady might have been calling it a stroke of genius if it weren't for the senseless killing that had just followed.

"Yes, okay, we have the sequence," Arkady conceded. "And yeah, wow, that's wonderful." Once more he looked down at Lederle. "What are we supposed to say to the Directorate Board about this, though? Who's going to make sense of the data when we get back?"

"Dr. Mayflower will know what to do with it, I'm sure," Il-Hyeong said. "And on the off chance that she doesn't, we can go to Novoprypiatsk and have the folks at Ajna check it out."

"And what if none of them can make heads or tails of it?" Arkady kept his gun leveled at Il-Hyeong, his finger running back and forth over the trigger guard; the fox looked unconcerned. "What'll we do then? Did you even..." Again, the ferret stole a look at Lederle's body, and he sighed with anger and frustration that felt like it would only be assuaged by actually pulling the trigger. "He was going to give this to us. He had already agreed to come back to the Château with us, to keep helping us."

"Or maybe he was just going to be a liability," Il-Hyeong said. "Clearly, the 'secrecy' of his Fan-Yin project left something to be desired, and if nothing else, having him along with us would have been the same as painting huge targets on our backs."

"And that gives you the right to just *kill* him?"

"Oh, come on," the fox said. "He was willing to die for this. You and I both saw him take a knife to his own throat."

"That still doesn't give you license to kill him," Arkady cried. "He... He had a family that he was going to get back to, and he—"

"Yeah, well, he'll see them if they get into Heaven when they die, too," Il-Hyeong said. His eyes began to wander around the room, scanning the various pieces of equipment. "What's done is done. We've got the Sequence. Let's head back home."

Arkady lowered his weapon. He thought about Ethan Lederle's family, somewhere in Xin-Banzhu. He thought about Lederle standing in his kitchen, ready to slash his own throat before betraying the secrets of the Iolite League and Project Scheherazade—no, Project Semiramis, as he knew it.

"I'm just... I can't believe you don't *care*," the ferret said. His eyes were starting to well up again as he looked at his friend, trying to fathom how and why the fox had become this creature so intent on killing everyone who crossed their path. "I mean, you just... you just murdered someone, Il-Hyeong." He didn't try to keep the sadness out of his voice. "Is finishing this mission really worth the cost to your soul?"

For a few seconds, Il-Hyeong was quiet, and his expression didn't change. Then, he let out a dejected sigh that, for some reason, made Arkady's spine tingle. "Wow. You actually haven't figured it out, yet, have you?"

"Figured out what's happened to you?" Arkady asked. "No, I should say I haven't. Could you enlighten me? Because to be pretty fucking honest I could use the help right about now."

"It's not about what happened to me," Il-Hyeong said. "It's about what happened to *us*."

"Oh, this ought to be great," the ferret grumbled.

Il-Hyeong ignored the snideness. "You and I have been turned into the greatest weapons the Iolite League has, Arkady. It's kind of brilliant, when you think about it."

"We're not weapons, Il-Hyeong. Yes, killing is part of what we do—when it's necessary. We're still not outside of God's judgment."

The fox smiled, and the glint in his eye as he grinned that toothy grin almost made Arkady take a step back. "But that's what's so brilliant about what they did, Arkady!" he said with a triumphant motion of his paws. "God has already rendered His judgment unto us, but our bodies are still here to do the work of the League and Sahasrara."

"God's judgment doesn't stop just because we're sent on some secret mission," Arkady said. "No matter how important it might be to the League."

"Of course it doesn't," Il-Hyeong responded. "Or, well, wouldn't, at any rate, if it the League hadn't fixed that for us."

Arkady stared back at the fox. "I'm sorry," he said. "I didn't realize that God had spoken to our superiors and called in for a rewrite of the Iolite Doctrine."

"See, I think that's part of your problem," the fox said. "I think your wit and your sarcasm are your defense mechanisms, and they're helping to keep you in denial for longer than I was."

"Can you stop talking in goddamn riddles and tell me what you're trying to get at?" Arkady demanded. "Because I'm running out of excuses to not just shoot you anyway for what you've done."

Il-Hyeong shook his head in disappointment. "Fine. If you're really having that hard a time following along, I'll spell it out for you," he said. "Remember last week? Back at the Château, when Dr. Mayflower and her team put us on the operating table and killed us?"

Arkady flinched. "What, the augmentation procedure?" he asked. "Come on, it wasn't *that* bad."

"Well, no, I see that *now*," Il-Hyeong said. "Just like I see the brilliance of freeing our souls from their mortal coils while retaining these bodies to carry on."

"I don't think anesthesia's got quite that much kick to it."

"Very funny. There's that wit again." Il-Hyeong rested his hips back against the computer desk. "Don't you remember what it was that Mayflower said? She said we were clinically dead for over half a day."

Arkady couldn't believe what he was hearing. "What, so now you're letting semantics dictate your moral code?"

"It's going nothing to do with semantics. It's everything to do with the fact that we were dead and left there, and the wonders of Iolite League science brought back these two... the two *shells* that used to be Il-Hyeong Quinn and Arkady Ryswife."

Within his mind, Arkady recalled the bizarre behavior his friend had been exhibiting over the last few days: his apparent disregard for his own personal safety, his complete lack of concern over personal ethics and morality, and now his current insistence that God's judgment of their souls was already complete.

"Dear God, you actually believe what you're saying, don't you?" Arkady said.

"Do you not still try to pray anymore?" Il-Hyeong asked. "You haven't gotten that hollow feeling, like God's not really listening to you, because there isn't a soul still in this body for Him to listen to?"

"I think it's natural to feel abandoned right now, when neither of us know who to trust or where to get help or how to help our friends."

"You're not really even Arkady Ryswife anymore, though," Il-Hyeong insisted, still waving his paws and his gun around with exaggerated swings. "You're just an amazing bit of science, a reanimated automaton or golem who just remembers *being* Arkady Ryswife."

"Okay, you know what?" Arkady said, trying desperately to not roll his eyes. "This is officially the most ridiculous conversation I've ever had with anyone. So, you know what? You go get on a plane headed back for Kyunjiu and then Deepwater, and you get the Pyxis Sequence out of your head and back to Dr. Mayflower as soon as possible. I'll stay behind and try to get Ming-Jun way from Kuai."

Il-Hyeong looked as though he wasn't ready to move on to the next part of the conversation. "I can prove it," he said with an air of finality in his voice. "Watch."

It looked like the most casual movement a person could make as Il-Hyeong lifted his gun just high enough to get off a single shot that struck Arkady right in the gut. The ferret stumbled back two full steps, feeling like he'd just been punched, then looked down and watched as blood began to coat his fur and clothing.

"You feel that?" the fox asked.

Arkady looked back up at the fox. He was almost too stunned to even feel betrayed by what his friend—his former friend?—had just done. His mouth moved and twisted, but he could think of no words to put to those movements, nothing that could do this disgusting situation justice.

"Do you know how many times I got shot while escaping from Fan-Yin Bioinformatics?" Il-Hyeong said, sounding like he was a salesperson trying to make a pitch. "Just hours before I came and found you in the bus depot down the street from Ming's apartment, good as new? It's like it's nothing. Look."

Il-Hyeong then fired three more times in rapid succession, three more bullets piercing Arkady's abdomen. After that fourth shot, the ferret fell backwards, landing on his tail and lower back before collapsing on the floor. His breathing was slow and labored now, and his whole body was writhing and twisting in pain. Already, he could feel himself getting colder.

"You're mad," he coughed as he looked up at the fox who now loomed above him as if nothing were amiss. "I'm..." He'd meant to say, *"I'm dying,"* but was he? He brought both his paws to his stomach, then held them up in front of his eyes.

His vision was blurry, but it was starting to focus again. His fingers and palms were smeared in quite a bit of blood, but was that enough? Should he have been bleeding more from having been shot four times in the stomach at point-blank range?

Should he be feeling more pain? Should he even still be conscious, let alone still be alive?

The wounds in his abdomen started to tingle awkwardly. The chill in his torso was already beginning to subside.

"Lie there and think about that for a bit," Il-Hyeong said, turning and stepping out of Arkady's field of vision. "Catch up with me later, and we can go back home together, you and me." The ferret could hear the fox rummaging with some more of Lederle's equipment, disconnecting the small computer case that lay under the desk.

Arkady stared at the ceiling. He felt like he should be waiting to die, but even before he heard the door slam shut as Il-Hyeong left, he knew that his shell of a body was going to linger on.

15. The Seventh Chakra

On the other side of Dr. Lederle's office, which by now had also become the fifty-first floor suite in Shambhala, Arkady saw Kentian McEvoy slumped against the wall. Blood gushed in messy, silent spurts from the pair of holes in the wolf's chest. His arms lay limp at his sides, cordoning off part of the pool of blood that grew and grew and grew around him.

Despite the bleeding, Kentian was still visibly alive. His stare was blank, fixed on Arkady without any emotion behind it. It looked almost as though he were dead, but every so often, he'd blink, and sometimes his snout would try to twist up and form a word or two, but no sound would come out.

Arkady couldn't bear to watch, but he couldn't move, either, and he didn't dare close his eyes—not now. The ferret lay in a pool of his own blood, though he could feel that his was no longer growing, and certainly not at the alarming rate that Kentian's was. Why did the wolf have to bleed so much? If he didn't stop bleeding soon, he was going to—

Don't die, Kentian, Arkady thought, trying to will those words directly into Kentian's head. He didn't want to try actually speaking, because that might make Kentian feel bad, seeing that Arkady could still speak without blood gushing from his mouth even though Arkady had been shot twice as many times as Kentian had.

Wasn't that worth a chuckle? Hey, what was a measly two bullets to an agent of Sahasrara, right? Surely, Kentian could live through something like that.

All he had to do was not die. Was that so hard? *Just don't die, Kentian.*

Just don't die. Just be like Arkady. Just lie there, relaxing, relishing the fact that you can't feel pain while your body starts to come back together. Just sit there and wait, healing wounds that a person's body has no business healing because that's just what you *do* when you're a living instrument of God's will.

Four bullets to the gut. Arkady hadn't even blacked out. He'd just fallen over in a heap, feeling the blood flow, feeling the heat leave his body until all of that just... stopped. While Kentian lay slumped, bleeding, his breathing getting slower and slower, Arkady could feel his strength returning. Not quickly, but gradually and nevertheless unceasingly. He was getting better.

Not Kentian, though. Kentian's lifeless gaze was the same as Arkady remembered it, after the wolf had been shot twice by Cibola, the villainous raccoon Arkady had failed to kill; the same as Arkady remembered it even as Kentian had died with his back to the hallway he'd been counting on escaping down; the same as Arkady remembered it when Il-Hyeong had dragged his blood-trailing corpse into the elevator because the fox had been unwilling to just leave him there, had been unwilling to just let him die.

Il-Hyeong. Il-Hyeong hadn't been willing to give up on Kentian. Il-Hyeong was a good fox, a loyal comrade, one who put his own life on the line for the people he called his friends, for the better world that Sahasrara had sworn to forge in the name of the Iolite League.

Arkady had messed up, Kentian had died, and Il-Hyeong hadn't been able to do anything about it. Arkady would have been willing to die for what was his own mistake. How fair was it, then, that the same Il-Hyeong could fire bullet after bullet into Arkady's body, and yet the ferret was no closer to dying the death he probably deserved?

"Dr. Mayflower and her team put us on the operating table and killed us," Il-Hyeong had said. It was true that you couldn't kill something that was already dead, but what Il-Hyeong was suggesting—that was madness.

But what *had* Mayflower and the marvels of Iolite League science done to him—done to both of them? The choking, metallic scent of blood that filled Arkady's nostrils now reminded him of the scent that had clung to Il-Hyeong when he'd woken the ferret up in the bus station alcove after they'd both escaped Fan-Yin. Half the fox's body, or nearly half, had been covered in dried blood, and for obvious reasons Arkady had only assumed that the blood had come from the fox's victims (oh, God, how many had fallen victim to Sahasrara on this failure of a mission?).

But there was no reason to doubt Il-Hyeong's statement, as he'd emptied half a clip into Arkady's stomach, that he'd been shot repeatedly in his own attempts to get away. Endorphins and drugs could push a person past his limits, force away the pain and convince him to keep going, but they couldn't repair a collapsed lung, couldn't get a person back on his feet after having his gut perforated.

What *had* Mayflower and her team done to Arkady and Il-Hyeong while they'd been under the knife? What else went into the augmentation, aside from giving the agents lightning reflexes, enhanced perception, and the ability to press on past fatigue and lack of sleep that would incapacitate lesser beings?

Il-Hyeong was certainly right about one thing: the two of them definitely weren't the same Il-Hyeong Quinn and Arkady Ryswife they used to be.

But to have died there on the operating table? For their souls to have left their bodies? That was going too far. After all, Arkady had—

Arkady had awoken screaming in the middle of the procedure! The surgeons hadn't been able to explain it, but had dismissed it as a mere unforeseen curiosity all the same. But it had happened. Arkady had been conscious. He'd been *thinking* and *feeling* and definitely alive.

He had to tell Il-Hyeong that. He had to find Il-Hyeong and tell the fox that he had it all wrong, that there was no loss of their essence, that they could still be the people they'd been before... before *this* mess.

Arkady lolled his head back to the side and stared at the empty spot on the wall where he imagined Kentian lay dying. Taking a slow breath and wincing from the effort, the ferret began to gather the strength to lift himself off of the floor. He pushed himself into a sitting position, then grabbed hold of the edge of the nearest chair and pulled himself to his feet. His abdomen was sore and tender as he moved, but with just a little less effort than it took to drag himself out of bed when hungover back in school, Arkady was back on his feet.

Once standing, the ferret could again see the body of Ethan Lederle, lying where Il-Hyeong had set it. The fox had crossed the red panda's arms across his body and had closed his eyes, giving him at least some sense of repose, but that didn't change the fact that he was dead, nor the fact that it was Il-Hyeong who had killed him in the first place.

Arkady then looked back at the empty spot on the wall, imagining Kentian in those last few precious moments of his life.

"Whatever's in that case had better be worth this," the wolf had said.

The ferret closed his eyes and muttered a soft prayer. "Whatever comes of this, I'll make sure that it was," he said to himself, before checking his gun and walking toward the door.

An hour and a half had passed since Il-Hyeong had shot him. The sun would be up soon, but for now, Arkady was left with only the faint, eerie glow of the pre-dawn winter sky. It was probably quite cold outside, too, but the ferret could feel very little of that.

Walking down the stairs of the FY-SES building, Arkady could tell that he had indeed stopped bleeding. His abdomen still hurt while he moved, but only slightly, and a quick, disbelieving check with his fingertips proved that the holes in his gut had, in fact, sealed up fully. Whether the bullets were still inside him, he was unsure; he certainly wasn't going to backtrack and check the floor of Lederle's lab now in order to find out.

If they were still inside him, and they posed some sort of threat to his well-being, he wasn't even going to worry about it. His own well-being had slipped past the boundaries of what he cared about, by this point. Right now, he had only two concerns: get out of Ridgecresent with the Pyxis Sequence, and come home with his entire team.

His friends. Could either of them even be called that anymore? Ming-Jun might have been playing the other side this whole time (but did Arkady really believe that?). Il-Hyeong had just shot him four times and left him behind (but weren't his ultimate goals still in line with what the Iolite League wanted?).

When Arkady got outside and made it to the FY-SES parking lot, he noticed that Dr. Lederle's car was missing. Il-Hyeong had to have taken it. So much for Arkady's faint hope that the fox might have conveniently been waiting outside to have a little talk after the ferret came to his senses and saw the light after being fired on.

What did that leave Arkady with for resources? The ferret ran through a mental list.

He had the money in his pocket, as well as the false identity as Samuel Togen of Kyunjiu. He had his gun and a single clip of bullets. That was about it.

How about potential help? There was Boots; Arkady considered heading to the wolf's apartment in Highslope before realizing that the wolf was probably still undergoing medical treatment for his broken arm (another thing to thank Il-Hyeong for). Dr. Lederle, of course, was dead.

That brought things back to either Il-Hyeong or Ming-Jun. Il-Hyeong had the Pyxis Sequence, and evidently also the only rationale he needed to act in the unconscionable way he did. While Arkady wasn't going to let that stand, the fox did at least appear to consider the mission over and done with and was just going to wait for the ferret to catch up with him—presumably at the airport, either the one in Thousand Leaves, or perhaps the one in Song Kang, given that the fox made no secret of his ardent desire to get out of Ridgecrescent, land of heathens.

Ming-Jun, on the other hand, had answers. Maybe she didn't have all of them, but she had to have *some* of them. She knew about the Carmine Order, and even if her decision was to stay behind to be with them (were they really her people?), Arkady wasn't going to accept or believe that until she looked him in the eye and told him herself. Il-Hyeong had obviously already given up on her, and maybe time would prove him right on that account, but for the time being, Arkady saw what he believed was still his chance to get to the bottom of things, once and for all.

Arkady wouldn't have stood a chance of convincing Il-Hyeong to come along on this last point of business even before the fox had shot him. So be it. Let Il-Hyeong get impatient and stop waiting for him. Let Il-Hyeong run back to Deepwater as soon as possible. Let him deliver the Pyxis Sequence to Dr. Mayflower so that Pandora could finally wake up. Arkady was going to prove that Ming-Jun Devra was not a lost cause.

Unfortunately, beyond heading back into the clutches of Kuai and the Carmine Order empty-handed, Arkady didn't yet have much of a solid plan for his venture. Though his wounds had healed, his clothes were still soaked through with blood, which would make operating around town more than a little bit problematic. Dealing with that, the ferret decided, was at least something that would resemble a starting point.

His appointment with Kuai was still over twelve full hours away. Given how much had happened in the span of two days, even that half day seemed like a daunting eternity. Would the Carmine Order really continue to stay away? Was Il-Hyeong really going to leave on his own if Arkady didn't track him down? What *else* could possibly go wrong over the course of the next several hours that hadn't somehow gone wrong already?

Plan for what you can plan on, the ferret told himself as he started walking. He needed to come up with a clear strategy, and to do that, he needed to get into a better place, both physically and mentally; for now, he needed to begin with smaller steps, and that meant getting himself some new clothes.

As he walked toward the center of town, the sun began to rise, though with the Holygate skyline blocking the horizon, there wasn't much light by which to see clearly. That worked to Arkady's advantage, though, since it meant that what few poor souls who were up and about at this hour would be less likely to notice the bloody mess the ferret was. Smell would be another story, of course, but what few folks Arkady did see were all in automobiles, and nobody paid him any regard.

The trudging walk felt interminable. Arkady considered stealing a car, like Il-Hyeong had done twice, by this point, but he had already resolved to break into the first clothing store he came across and he didn't want to compound his wrongdoings any more than necessary. *We* are *still responsible for our actions, no matter what Il-Hyeong might think.*

Around an hour or so later, Arkady finally arrived at a commercial district that looked promising. It was still too early in the morning for even most coffee shops to be open, though, and retail stores wouldn't open until later still. With resignation, the ferret accepted that his break-in plan was going to have to move forward, and so he kept his eyes peeled for the first suitable shop he could find.

He came across a small department store, and decided to go with that. After a few seconds of trying to pick the electronic lock, it became apparent that that approach was going to take too long and likely attract attention of its own, and so he instead bit his lip and smashed the glass door with the butt of his pistol. At once, the entire glass panel fell apart, its structural integrity ruined. In the aftermath of shattering glass, Arkady then heard the store's security alarm going off, but he'd planned for that contingency, as well.

Undaunted, the ferret hopped in through the smashed door and went straight to work looking for the first set of clothes that would both fit him and make him look unobtrusive. He settled on a pair of long, heavy pants, a long-sleeved shirt, and a short trench coat to help guard against the Ridgecrescent winter. He used his old clothing to wipe clean whatever blood he could from his pelt, getting rid of at least the stuff that was still damp. Throwing his old, bloodied clothing into one of the store's shopping bags nabbed from the front counter, Arkady then left behind a stack of Ridgecrescent dees to cover the price of the clothing as well as his best guess at what repairing the door would cost before he hurried to sneak out the back.

There out back, there was no obvious sign of how close the police might be, but Arkady still wasted no time. He slipped down the back alley and went a few blocks before ditching his bag of old clothes in a dumpster behind some other shop. The cops might find it eventually, but they'd be looking for evidence of theft, not foul play, and even if they did come across it, by the time anything came of it, Samuel Togen would be long gone.

The ferret took a circuitous route back to another one of the main downtown streets. More early risers were out and about, now, most of them likely heading to various service jobs, and none of them seeming to pay much heed to their fellow man. Arkady, with his own out-of-place demeanor, used that cover to his advantage, slipping on past passersby as he looked for some early-morning breakfast shop or always-open diner to camp out in for a few hours until the rest of the city woke up.

Solace had come in the form of a truck stop near an off-ramp from the highway that ran through Holygate on its way from Highslope to Thousand Leaves. Paying for damages and stolen merchandise hadn't completely broken Arkady's wallet, so he went first to the pay showers in the bathroom and stripped down so that he could wash himself clean of the copious amount of caked-on blood that still clung to much of his fur.

This was the second time in as many days, Arkady reflected, that he'd been forced to shower in some run-down public facility. Also, disturbing though the thought was, cleaning his pelt of dried blood was much more pleasant than washing up after taking a dip in a river tainted with sewage runoff. He'd be quite happy if he never had to do either again.

Once he was clean and dry, he got back into his stolen clothes and got a booth at the truck stop's diner, nursing a thick, syrupy mug of black coffee and picking at the largest breakfast he could stomach. He couldn't be sure if his lack of appetite came from having been shot so recently in the gut, or whether it was another unanticipated side-effect of the augmentation.

Again, it all came back to the augmentation. What else hadn't Arkady and Il-Hyeong been told?

Sitting calmly in his booth, Arkady tried to relax, and willed himself to feel all that he could. His nostrils were filled with countless different scents, but each could be distinguished with only a modicum of effort. There was the pungent aroma of bad coffee; grease coming from the kitchen, all the way out back; the hint of beer on the breath of the badger sitting at the far end of the counter.

He shut his eyes and focused even harder. With concentration, he could tell how many people were in the room without using his eyes (eleven, including himself). Smelling even deeper, he could detect the scents of individuals who were no longer present, who must have been sitting in the diner overnight, their scents still detectable even over the much stronger odors of smoke and alcohol, of the musk of a half-dozen different species and the exhaust fumes from the miniature fleet of trucks idling outside.

246

When he smelled the trucks, Arkady perked his ears, and realized he could *hear* the trucks as well, even from inside. The ferret then held his breath, no longer attempting to pick apart smells, but instead focusing on different sounds. Once more, he found that careful concentration opened up his senses more than he imagined possible. He could hear individual dishes sizzling away on the grill in the back kitchen; he could hear the rattling of the heating ducts and the electric buzz coming from both of the coffee makers as well as the microwave; he could hear the tired and dejected sighs of the badger at the far end of the counter.

Arkady opened his eyes back up when he heard the approaching footsteps of his waitress, a short weasel who nevertheless took obvious care in making herself look something resembling pretty despite working in a place like this. She flashed Arkady a smile as she refilled his coffee, a clear attempt at trying to share or establish some mustelid species bond with the ferret, but Arkady just smiled back and mouthed the word "thanks" without actually speaking.

Alone once more, Arkady took a tiny sip from his mug, then set it down, gripped the handle, and focused his thoughts again. This time, he directed his attentions inward, thinking only of himself. He closed his eyes and tried to shut away the outside world, to perceive nothing that was not Arkady.

This was not easy. His awareness was so heightened that it was difficult to consciously ignore it, especially after having spent the last few days experiencing a constant sensory bombardment that had forced him to acclimate. Willfully fighting that adjustment was, as to be expected, tricky. He started with the smaller stuff: the smells that had been lingering for hours, the sounds coming in from outside the building. By shutting those out first, he was able to work his way up to stimuli that were more and more difficult to ignore.

Bit by bit, scent by scent, sound by sound, the diner seemed to disappear around Arkady as he forced it all away. Rather than putting up a mental wall, it was more like closing curtains and shutting doors—acknowledging that the outside world was there, but that he wasn't going to pay attention to it right now. Blocking out the chatter of the patrons was like shutting windows to muffle the outside din; blocking out the glare of the lighting through his closed eyelids was like flicking off a switch.

Now, Arkady was truly alone with himself.

The sensation was remarkable. He was filled with a hyperawareness of himself and his body. If time could be measured by counting his breaths or the individual beats of his heart, then time had slowed to a crawl. He could fix his focus in on any part of himself, not as far down as the cellular level, but still with far more acuity than anyone had ever achieved before.

His nervous system stood out most. He could feel the major nerves running through his body, down along his limbs and tail, and he could feel where the surgically-implanted nerve connections had been installed alongside existing biological tissue. This was what enabled his body to have the reflexes it needed in order to act based on the heightened senses he possessed. This was what (*This was what turned him into a killing machine.*) allowed him to aim, line up a precision shot, and pull the trigger in under a second. This was what (*this was what put him outside the bounds of anything God had ever intended*) made him a living marvel of Iolite League science. This was what Pandora would be.

He was an amalgamation of flesh and machine, the fusion of ferret and synthetic components that masqueraded as real. That fusion, however, was complete: there was no break between what was his by nature and what had been grafted onto and into him artificially. All that he felt was Arkady Ryswife, the single entity, a masterpiece of biology, chemistry, and physics and oh so very alive.

Then, with great surprise, he became aware of something else. Something that was not Arkady Ryswife—something inside of him that was apart from him. A parasite? No. With the way his body had been designed and crafted, any such parasite would have been instantly identified and eliminated. Some type of symbiont, then, perhaps.

Whatever it was, it was manifold, and yet it was one. He felt it acting deep in his belly, causing the faintest tingle in the region where his skin, muscles, and viscera had been shredded by bullets (the bullets were definitely not still inside of him, he could now tell).

He also felt this presence in the roof of his mouth, where he'd scalded his sensitive palate on hot diner coffee. The skin there was healing, both naturally, he could tell, and also thanks to the efforts of whatever this *something* was. It refused to be pinpointed, though, not as if it were intentionally avoiding Arkady, but as if it simply wouldn't 'appear' readily to his senses, try as he might.

An idea sprung to Arkady's mind. He opened his eyes, and at once, he lost his grip on that special sense of self. No matter, though. A casual check convinced the ferret that no one was looking directly at him, and so in that window, he took his fork in his right paw and jabbed the tines hard into the back of his left.

He bit his lip to stifle his grunt of pain, but much like when he'd been shot, it didn't hurt as much as it should have. He pulled the fork back and quickly wiped the blood from the tines with his napkin, which he then crumpled up and tossed onto his plate. With that done, he looked at his injured paw.

Well, his barely-injured paw, at any rate. Granted, a fork wound was hardly a grievous injury, but even the four evenly-spaced dots of blood were hard to make out through the fur. Calling upon the same concentration he'd fought for earlier, he focused on that tiny red pattern, really trying to *feel* it through the veil of adrenaline and self-defensive numbness.

That same presence of "something other" was there, working alongside his own body to fix that minor wound. Each of the four holes made by the individual tines was distinct, and each was being patched up quite quickly. Even though the ferret had already been through the process of getting shot multiple times and then getting up and walking away as if nothing major had occurred, it was no less amazing for him to really feel his body at work, repairing the set of tiny puncture wounds he'd given himself.

In less than a minute, the skin had closed up completely, the bleeding stopped and the residual pain gone. The ferret flexed his individual digits and made a fist; there was no soreness or tenderness worth noting.

An assessment of Arkady's situation and the tools he had at his disposal suddenly looked much less dire. He might just be one person against the entire Carmine Order, if this were truly a worst-case scenario, but even then, he wasn't a typical person.

With his breakfast and his self-experimentation done, Arkady stayed at the diner for just two more cups of coffee before deciding he'd be pushing it if he stayed any longer. He left enough of a tip to be generous without leaving so much as to make him stand out, and then left the truck stop in search of a small public library.

The directory at the truck stop phone booth had led him to one that was just a couple miles away on foot, but even by the time the ferret got there, it wasn't due to open for nearly another full hour. Luckily, a modern metropolis like Holygate wasn't without its plethora of cafés and coffee shops, so Arkady was at least able to find someplace within a couple blocks where he could legally loiter in the interim. Besides, after what he'd been through, he doubted that too much caffeine would pose his body any threat.

During the wait, Arkady continued trying to hone his senses, focusing on the outward instead of the inward. Though he had no real fear of either Carmine Order assassins or Holygate police coming to find him, it would be foolish to not at least be in the right mindset. After all, he'd been wrong more than once about this mission so far.

Once the library was open, Arkady headed back and found it to be exactly the sort of place he'd been hoping for: older, a bit musty, and small. A library like this was bound to have a better selection for local interests, most especially local history, and with the librarian's help, the ferret accumulated a stack of books that would more than last him the rest of the morning.

Older books did indeed herald the historical wonder of Dianjiang Gardens, though—as Kuai himself had claimed—there was nothing officially confirming that the trio of buildings had been there since pre-civ times. He was able to find context dating back to within the first millennium of recorded history, which made Dianjiang Gardens at least three thousand years old. *Not unlike Château Sainte-Mireille,* thought Arkady as he examined some photographs from a comparatively more recent age.

Despite Dianjiang Gardens itself being well-chronicled in Holygate's history, Arkady had less luck finding anything about the Carmine Order. For most of the site's history, it appeared to have been administered by an organization called the Caan Bay City Group, though the most recent official documentation citing that was still close to five hundred years old.

Arkady also looked for anything that might hint at the existence of people speaking anything other than Language as the world knew it, but as he'd gathered from Ming-Jun's secrecy about *Zhōngwén*, there was nothing to be found on that subject.

The only real feasible connection that the ferret was able to make was the theory (long-running since olden times) that Dianjiang Gardens had originally been built with some religious or other special social significance in mind. Over the centuries, it had served as a museum, a tourist attraction, a private residence, a museum again, and probably many other things before its current incarnation as a teahouse and restaurant, but if it did originally have a more hallowed or sacred purpose, that might go at least some way toward explaining the fanaticism displayed by members of the Carmine Order.

How was all of it related, though? What did any of it have to do with the Iolite League and the Pyxis Sequence? What was it about the three books from Tomosabaki that would drive Kuai and his men to such lengths in order to obtain them?

Arkady wished that he could do some reconnaissance on Dianjiang Gardens, but he couldn't risk being spotted, even by the more mundane staff. If the Carmine Order had any indication that he was in the area at this time of day, then they'd know he hadn't gone back for the books as promised, and he couldn't risk that. He had no idea what other local sites might have significance to the Order, either; it was likely that Kuai would choose such a place for their meeting that evening, and the ferret might have better luck scoping out one of those locations if he only knew where they might be.

Being lost in ignorance of the facts was nothing new, though, as far as this situation was concerned. The trick, then, lay in making the best use out of the next several hours before it came time to meet with Jiangzhao Kuai and trade the two things that neither of them actually had.

It didn't come as any real surprise that Il-Hyeong wasn't waiting around the train station when Arkady came by. The ferret wasn't sure whether he'd even expected that the fox would actually be there, but he felt compelled to check just the same.

He wished that there was some way he could check to see if Il-Hyeong had come through. The rail route to Thousand Leaves was an extremely busy one, though, and there was no way that anyone who worked the ticket counters or the platforms would remember one specific (deliberately nondescript) swift fox having come through—even if that wasn't also a breach of privacy on behalf of the railway authority.

Arkady checked the giant clock in the train station lobby. If Il-Hyeong had left for Thousand Leaves on the earliest train he could have possibly caught, and then went from there directly to the airport, then he'd be about to land in Kyunjiu around now. Then, if that were true, by the time Arkady was meeting with Kuai, Il-Hyeong would be halfway back to Deepwater, to home and safety.

That was all assuming that he'd left as quickly as possible, which Arkady didn't think was the case. He'd have at least waited some amount of time for the ferret to catch up, as he'd said he would, after all. But what would he have done after that? Deranged as the fox may have become, his loss of morals didn't accompany any obvious loss of intellect. He had to have known that Arkady wouldn't leave without trying to get Ming-Jun, even if the Pyxis Sequence had been secured and the mission was otherwise complete. But would he leave Ridgecrescent and abandon Arkady to his foolish personal crusade? Or would he try again to convince the ferret of what he honestly believed was their new true nature?

A shadow cast itself across the floor in front of Arkady. The ferret turned, expecting to see winter clouds moving in to blot out the sun. Instead, he found himself staring at the hulking form of ex-Sergeant Berzeviczy.

The wolf was wearing a long-sleeved jacket, but one forearm looked much bulkier than the other, even under the layers of fabric. Clearly, he was wearing some kind of cast or brace, though it was remarkable that he wasn't laid up with a splint or a sling.

His nostrils flared as Arkady turned, but beyond that, his face showed neither friendship nor malice. "So, this is how it's going to be, is it?" he growled as a whisper, right into the ferret's ear. "Let's get down to it, then." The wolf motioned with his head over toward the hallway that led to the travel lockers.

Before Arkady had responded one way or the other, the wolf was already heading over there. He didn't even look back to see if he was being followed or not. Perhaps he was leaving himself the easy way out, in the event that Arkady wanted nothing to do with him—removing himself from further potential harm, out here in public.

Whatever Boots might want with him, Arkady at least owed the wolf an explanation. Boots had stuck his neck out for both him and Il-Hyeong, had really pulled their tails out of the fire, and in return, he'd gotten two dead partners, a broken arm and a...

And now a dead contact, to boot. *Well, this is going to be lovely*, the ferret said to himself as he followed after Boots, trying to determine how much the wolf could possibly know, at this point.

Around the corner, Boots stood waiting. He looked like he wanted to be leaning back with his arms crossed, but for obvious reasons, that wasn't possible. Arkady sniffed, and could detect faint hints of gunmetal somewhere on the wolf's person.

"So, following me, huh?" Boots asked. He added a snort. "Guess I shouldn't be surprised."

"Following you?" Arkady was so shocked that he actually laughed. "Seriously?" he asked as he recomposed himself. "No, Sarge, trust me: you're the *last* of my worries right now."

"You honestly expect me to believe that you just so happen to be here at this very moment?"

"I could say the same thing about you," Arkady replied.

The wolf sniffed at the air, his upper lip wrinkling as he did so. With what passed for subtle for a seven-foot-tall wolf, he scanned the crowd in the station lobby. "Where's your fox friend?" he asked.

There was a second where Arkady feared that Il-Hyeong might step out of the shadows at the mere mention of him. "That's actually why I'm here," Arkady said. "I was hoping that he'd be here, but... well, now I guess he's already gone."

"You don't know where your own partner went, huh? So, not only do you expect me to believe that you're not following me, but you also..." Boots' dubious expression started to change into a look of wry amusement as his words trailed off. "Wow. You're actually serious, aren't you?"

Boots didn't strike Arkady as the sort of wolf who would delight in ridiculing him, but just to be on the safe side, the ferret spoke up quickly. "Then I'm going to guess you're not following me, either," he said. "Look, have you seen Il-Hyeong?"

"Oh, no," the wolf said, shaking his head. "I'm done 'helping' you. If you want to prove that you're not out to get me, then just leave me be, and we'll leave it at that."

Just before Boots started to move, Arkady reached up and placed his small paw against the wolf's huge chest. "Please," he said. "I need to find Il-Hyeong. If you've seen him at all, just—"

Boots smacked Arkady's arm away without effort, and the ferret let him do it. "I said leave me be," the wolf growled. "Your problems aren't my problems anymore."

The wolf looked like he was going to try once more to break past Arkady, but the ferret moved with him. "Lederle's dead," he said. He kept his voice quiet, so that only Boots would hear it.

At that, Boots' eyes widened, and his lips started to pull back into a snarl before he forced a look of feigned calm back onto his face. "Even less reason for me to stay, then," he said, and then, with sheer mass and momentum that Arkady's speed and reflexes couldn't hope to counter, he barreled on past the ferret.

Arkady was quick to keep step with the wolf. "I can understand your wanting to skip town," he said. "But listen. I could use your help."

"What?" Boots stopped in his tracks, looking dumbstruck back at the ferret. "What makes you think I'd want to help you now?"

"I know you didn't get paid for your last job," Arkady replied. "But I can pay for this job *and* for what you're owed if you—"

"That's not what I mean," Boots interrupted, shaking his head. "What makes you think I'd ever want to work for you people again?" He looked almost like he was about to laugh. "Two of my buddies got killed doing this job for your freaky little cult, and now you're telling me that the original contact is dead, and *you* don't even know where your own partner is. Yeah, doing more work for you people sounds like a *great* idea."

Arkady opened his mouth, and then closed it again without saying anything. Was there even anything he *could* say to that? "That's not..." he started, but the words didn't go anywhere.

"I've got a train to catch," Boots said. "Excuse me."

After letting the wolf get only a couple of paces, Arkady once more went after him. "Don't think of it as a job from the Iolite League; think of it as a job from me." A few passersby perked their ears at the words 'Iolite League,' but none stopped to pay more attention than that, and some hurried away even faster.

Boots whirled around and shot the ferret an accusing look as he stopped abruptly once more. "For you?" he asked, and this time, he did laugh. "That's even *more* of a joke."

"Is it, really?" Arkady asked. "You seemed to want enough from me before that you—"

"I don't want your anything from you!" Boots' face was twisted up with a rage that he seemed to be unable to fully express. "I don't want anything from you except for your fucking cult to leave me the hell alone." Again, the wolf started to leave.

Arkady let him get a few steps before he shouted after him again. "Why do you keep stopping for me, then? Why not just ignore me and keeping on walking straight on to your train to wherever?"

The wolf's growl was a tangible thing, masked only partially by the bustling crowd. "Don't try to psychoanalyze me, boy. I've still got one good arm left."

"Go ahead and throw a punch then," Arkady responded as he closed the gap between them. He saw the wolf draw a breath, and for a moment, he thought a punch really was about to come at him—and he was considering allowing it to connect, whether because it'd make Boots feel better or because he might actually deserve it. When no such punch came, the ferret said, "What is it, Boots? What is it about me that fascinates you?"

"After all your people have put me through, you think I owe you an explanation?"

"No, I don't," Arkady said. "But here you are, continuing to talk to me." He then lowered his voice and offered a paw to the wolf. "Seriously, I know there's got to be something."

Boots left Arkady's paw hanging there in the air. "And what if you're just full of yourself?"

"You took me at my word and let me go after you captured me fair and square," the ferret said. "You keep asking me about the Butterfly Islands War, and even after my partner broke your arm, here you are, still—"

One of Boots' huge paws came up in a fist, but instead of striking Arkady with it, he just held it in front of the ferret's face, quavering. The wolf growled again, then set his arm down. "You're a nutjob," he said. "You're a nutjob and a cultist and I'm fucking *done* with you." He shoved Arkady in the chest (with a much weaker push than he could have managed, the ferret noted) and then stormed off toward the train platforms.

Arkady didn't follow; he just shouted again. "Where are you going?" he asked.

"Away," Boots called back, stopping long enough to get his words out. "Away from this city and whatever fucked up crisis you've created in it." He turned and looked over his shoulder back at Arkady, out of the corner of his eye. "See you in the next life, Mr. Ryswife," he said. "Or wherever it is you Iolite freaks go when you die."

With that, Arkady let Boots go. He watched the wolf go up to the ticket counter before turning away and heading back out the front lobby, biting his lip, feeling miserable for the whole thing.

Because Boots was right: good people had died trying to help him and Il-Hyeong—people who, as it turned out, couldn't even die.

Again, Arkady thought of Il-Hyeong. Would the fox ever regain the objectivity to do the right thing again, after all this? Was he even capable of caring about that anymore?

After all, what incentive was there to do good for a pair of Iolite freaks who had nowhere to even look forward to going when they died?

16. Conviction

It was Jenfei who was waiting at the hostess stand at Kuai's restaurant. One look at her, and Arkady immediately knew that she had been sent to wait specifically for him. She lacked anything resembling the meek demeanor of the other hostesses and waitresses he'd seen, and there was a definite fire in her eyes the moment she set her gaze upon him, a mix of eagerness and determination not unlike that of a soldier on the cusp of a battle.

Even walking into Dianjiang Gardens again after last night was a harrowing experience for Arkady. This was it: the inner sanctum of the enemy, and it was entirely possible—even probable—that the mere act of his daring to return after his first meeting with Kuai was the trigger for them to spring a trap. They'd already demonstrated that they were capable of having people shadow him and getting snipers in position to stop him and his team; the whole past day that he'd been in Ridgecrescent, someone might have been keeping an eye on him, seeing whether or not he'd made good on his word to Kuai.

None of that could be helped, though. He had to go through with things as if he had the full intention of meeting with Kuai on his own terms. Only then did he have a shot at appeasing him—or, if that wasn't an option, removing him from the picture. Either way, Kuai was the only path to answers and to Ming-Jun.

Jenfei's face offered no further hints as to which fate Arkady was walking into. She looked pleased, to be sure, but without knowing the *why*, that didn't tell Arkady much. He *could* tell that she tried hard not to let her gaze linger for too long on the briefcase he'd brought with him, and he hoped that was a good sign.

"I have a reservation," the ferret said as he walked up to the stand. "It should be under Ryswife."

The cacomistle's tail slid out of sight behind her. "Of course, Mr. Ryswife," she said, her voice still adding a full decade to her apparent age. "I see your reservation right here. Might I inquire as to the whereabouts of the rest of your party?"

"We'll be one short today, I'm afraid," Arkady replied. "I do hope that won't be a problem," he then asked, holding up his briefcase in one paw and tapping it with the other.

Jenfei looked down at the ledger, clearly merely pretending to consult it. "No, I don't suppose it will," she said. "If you'll follow me, then."

Arkady did follow her, noting that one of the cats from yesterday came to take over her place at a mere snap of the cacomistle's fingers. They headed out back, toward the kitchen as before, but instead of passing on through to the staircase, they instead walked out the fire exit. Outside, the smell of the eponymous gardens was so strong and sudden that it at once overwhelmed even those aromas from the restaurant itself.

Parked in the tiny cul-de-sac behind the building was a sleek black automobile, Ridgecrescent make. To Arkady's surprise, Jenfei herself got into the driver's seat, then opened the back door via a switch on her own door's console. There was no verbal invitation to get in, nor was one needed. Once Arkady was seated, the cacomistle began to drive off.

Inside the car, the smells of both the restaurant and the garden were cut off, and now Arkady could detect the same gunmetal scent he'd picked up when speaking to Boots earlier. So, Jenfei was armed. That was neither surprising not terribly alarming; it would have been foolish for Kuai to send her on her task without taking simple safety precautions, and at no point could Arkady afford not to remain wary of a trap or double-cross.

The hum of the engine was barely audible as the car drove out from Dianjiang Gardens and merged seamlessly into the city traffic. Having walked these roads much over the past few days, Arkady knew them to be old, but the ride was smooth, an effect of the vehicle's design doing something remarkable to diminish the impact of bumps and divots. Ah, the wonders of Ridgecrescent technology! The ferret couldn't help but think about Boots, and the things he must have seen, being on the front lines for the JDR in the Butterfly Islands War.

Noting to himself that Jenfei hadn't spoken a single word since leaving her post at the hostess stand, Arkady asked, "Are we in for a long trip?"

"Not so long that you can't afford to be patient," Jenfei replied in the same crisp tone Arkady had ever heard her use. "Or silent."

As Jenfei drove up onto an on-ramp, the briefcase sitting on the seat next to Arkady slid along the leather and bumped into the door. Kuai might have known that Project Scheherazade had obtained a set of books, but surely he hadn't seen the actual case they'd been inside at Shambhala, so there was no worry that he'd recognize a fake. The real case, along with the books and the tape recorder, were safe and sound, deep beneath Château Sainte-Mireille, where they'd hopefully stay for a long time.

If Kuai ever opened the case and examined the books within up close, he'd see immediately that they were just three old books from a library in Holygate, but Arkady wasn't planning on letting the raccoon get that far with his inspection. At best, his decoy books would serve as a distraction during whatever negotiations they got caught up in— and might buy Arkady (and Ming-Jun?) a second or two of time if they needed to cut and run.

"Are you a big reader?" Arkady asked Jenfei. "I'm curious as to how big a library the Carmine—"

"I asked for silence," Jenfei said. Her voice carried a militant edge, but even now, she neither snapped nor lost patience. "You are here to speak with Mr. Kuai, not with me."

Arkady guessed that they were still inside Holygate proper when Jenfei got off the highway a scant few minutes later. The ferret wasn't keen on wasting more effort in trying to engage her in weighted small talk, let alone pump her for information. She had the air of a well-bred, well-trained lieutenant to her, and having seen both the fanaticism of the Carmine Order's members and their soldierly devotion, Arkady knew that he wasn't going to unlock her psyche over the course of a simple car ride.

The section of the city that Jenfei had brought Arkady to didn't look much different than the downtown area where Dianjiang Gardens was. There were fewer tall buildings, but since Holygate was still a Ridgecrescent metropolis, "fewer" was a relative term. The nightlife crowd was certainly thinner, and more of the people on the street right now were wearing business attire than not. The majority of them were species who could more comfortably handle a nocturnal cycle, such as raccoons and foxes.

Soon, though, that small nighttime business district was left behind as well, and the lights of the city seemed to burst more vibrantly into life as the car barreled down the next few blocks. Now the streets were lined with nightclubs, late-night eateries, coffee shops and bars, all packed into tall but narrow buildings, with multi-tiered signs running vertically up their lengths, all of them bright and flashy, vying for attention. Here, the sidewalks were teeming with individuals of all species, with young people and old, the atmosphere one of joy and revelry—one that would jar the people back in Deepwater, who thought of Ridgecrescent only as a nation of xenophobia, religious oppression, and militaristic sovereignty.

A neighborhood like this would be rife with distractions, especially for someone like Arkady, who wasn't familiar with it. "Does Mr. Kuai own a nightclub?" he asked. "His business doesn't seem—"

"All you need to worry about Mr. Kuai's business is what business he decides to conduct with you." This time, Jenfei *did* snap her words, though her eyes remained dutifully on the road. "I will not ask you again to cease your questions."

Arkady had at least ascertained that Jenfei wasn't some emotionless robot. The fact that the cacomistle could be riled up wasn't the best piece of information he could have gleaned, but it was better than nothing. Using the silence that Jenfei had ordered, he studied the surrounding area, looking for any places of note, any potential escape routes, any workable roadblocks.

The car did not stop in that neighborhood, however. Jenfei continued to drive through the main nightlife strip, and then the roadway opened up, running past a large esplanade. At the far end of the park was a large, open-air band shell of a building that Arkady recognized as the Holygate Metropolitan Opera House. The building itself was lit up, but there did not appear to be a performance taking place this evening.

Jenfei began to slow down, and Arkady was expecting her to turn off into the parking lot for the Opera House, but she continued on a ways further, stopping instead in front of another building on the opposite corner. She put the car in park, got out without a word, and then opened Arkady's door from the outside.

Arkady got out, as well, then looked up at the building that was their destination. "Central Ridgecrescent Cultural Museum," the sign proclaimed. It wasn't a very large building, especially for a museum, but it was still several stories tall. Business hours were over, and only utility lighting appeared to be on right now.

Jenfei reached into her red silk gown and pulled out a key card, which she inserted into a slot next to the front door. She pulled the door open, and rather than hold it open for Arkady, she went on inside, pausing only to make sure that the door didn't just slam in his face. Once inside, the cacomistle nodded to the security guard seated next to the unmanned front desk, a bored-looking rabbit who seemed to recognize her. Jenfei continued on to the elevator lobby and pressed the button.

The silence was beginning to get overbearing. Was Jenfei's whole "silent treatment" a sign of professionalism? Or was keeping her own mouth shut the only way she felt she could keep composure around the enemy? Perhaps she was trying too hard, and if Arkady could—

Arkady's pondering was cut off by the elevator doors opening up far sooner than he'd expected. Again, Jenfei stepped inside silently. Testing her, Arkady stood where he was. The cacomistle merely made a sharp gesture with her head, a wordless demand for him to come in and stand next to her. The ferret complied.

Jenfei pressed the button for the roof, then the elevator doors slid shut. The elevator itself then began to rise, the sounds of the conveyance mechanism inside the shaft telling it to be quite old. Above the doors, the lights marking each floor passed slowly. Jenfei's long tail uncurled and recurled itself several times before the doors finally chimed upon arrival at the roof.

To Arkady's surprise, the roof turned out to be a glass-encased conservatory, some type of solarium or greenhouse. It couldn't have covered the whole roof, however, the ferret realized, since he hadn't spotted it from down on the sidewalk. The scents of greenery and flowers were both strong and pleasant, but altogether different from the floral medley back at Dianjiang Gardens.

A bronze plaque was set into the low wall of the stone entryway: *Donated by the Caan Bay Historical Society, 3413.* The bolts that held the plaque itself in place were marked with a variation of the same symbol on the uniforms worn by the members of the Carmine Order, the same symbol on the scroll that hung in Kuai's inner sanctum. It was doubtful that many visitors would even take notice of that tiny bit of filigree on the plaque's bolts, and those few who did would not likely give it much thought.

Even without his enhanced senses, Arkady couldn't have missed that detail if he wanted to.

Retaining her perfect poise, Jenfei led Arkady into the conservatory. Without stopping to concentrate, it was difficult to pick up the smells of individuals through the veil of ambient floral aroma, and so Arkady couldn't tell if Kuai was really waiting further within or not. This seemed like a weird place to bring him if this was all some elaborate trap, though.

As Arkady thought that, Jenfei stopped. She reached into the folds of her gown, then turned around, bringing a small pistol in line with Arkady's chest. "Now, Mr. Ryswife," she said, with no hint of either smugness or satisfaction, "Mr. Kuai is a very busy man, so if you'd kindly hand me that briefcase, we can both be on our way."

It was all Arkady could do to not roll his eyes right then and there. Was this really how it was going to go? He'd thought the Carmine Order was at least smarter than *this*, even through his own limited experience with them. Perhaps, in his having accounted for the possibility that Kuai would lay a trap for him, he'd given the raccoon too much credit that it would be a *good* one.

"All right, now," Arkady said, holding up both paws, the briefcase hanging from his right, "let's not be hasty. No one has to get hurt here." Arkady wasn't afraid for his own sake—not after seeing what getting shot four times at point-blank range had done to him—and though he knew he could power his way out of his predicament without real risk to himself, killing Jenfei would accomplish nothing, save earning him further ire from Kuai.

"I do have to admit that I'm impressed," the cacomistle said. "I left you ample opportunity to get the jump on me, and yet you didn't take it. Your honesty and integrity in your dealings is to be commended. The Order will remember that, I assure you."

Arkady grinned. "I wish I could say the same," he replied. "It's a shame that Mr. Kuai doesn't share those same values that—"

Jenfei suddenly turned her head to her right at the same moment that Arkady himself heard a rustling from that direction. She tried to swing her pistol in position, too, but was far too late in turning to stop the dark shape that barreled right into her as branches of greenery burst forward. Upon impact, the gun went off, its report fading before being replaced by the sound of a glass panel on the far side of the conservatory crashing in towards the floor.

As a solid punch connected with Jenfei's muzzle, knocking her head sideways, the black blur finally coalesced enough for Arkady to make sense of what he was seeing. Locked in a grapple with Jenfei, wearing her Sahasrara-issued infiltrator suit, was Ming-Jun.

Despite the rabbit's clean blow, Jenfei didn't go down. She snarled, blood dripping from her lip as she fought back, trying to turn her arm and wrist inward to get a shot off at her assailant. The cacomistle managed to wrench her arm inward, the barrel of her pistol pointing at Ming-Jun's head for the briefest of moments. Another gunshot sounded, but by then, the rabbit had smacked Jenfei's arm aside again, and the shot went wide, tearing harmlessly through the greenery.

Arkady took two steps back and drew his own gun, letting the briefcase drop to the stone path. He knew that with his absurdly-deadly precision and sense of timing that he could line up a shot that would hit Jenfei and not Ming-Jun, but he didn't want to take it until Jenfei's own gun was no longer a threat.

Ming-Jun and Jenfei both moved with keen agility. They swapped positions repeatedly as they grappled with one another, both of them throwing jabs or kicks when they could, Jenfei still trying to make use of her pistol. Ming-Jun's footwork was by far more impressive. Arkady recognized some Sahasrara training in her movements, which were also mixed with some form or style that he couldn't identify. The rabbit also had the advantage in body strength, and the fight would probably have already been over were it not for Jenfei's gun.

A third gunshot went off, but again, Ming-Jun had already deflected Jenfei's arm far to the side. Seizing the opening, the rabbit delivered a hard chop with her paw to the cacomistle's wrist; when the first blow didn't cause her opponent to drop her weapon, she tried again, and this time succeeded, the gun clattering to the smooth stone below.

"Never were the greatest shot, were you, *Jiànfēi?*" Ming-Jun snarled with a victorious grin that somehow looked frighteningly at home on the rabbit's face.

Jenfei drew her arms back, curled her tail, and then spat something in *Zhōngwén* before launching herself at Ming-Jun again. Now, Arkady had a much better window for taking a shot, but still he hesitated.

Are you really afraid of hitting Ming-Jun? he asked himself. *Or are you waiting to see how this all plays out? To see if this isn't some act staged to make you trust her implicitly again?*

The two women fought with frenzied, savage elegance. Jenfei's long tail whirled as she hopped and spun, throwing a series of sharp kicks that Ming-Jun had an easy time combating with her own. Again, the rabbit's footwork prevailed here, and after a few attempts by Jenfei to land a blow, the cacomistle took a savage snap-kick right to the jaw.

The blow was hard enough that Jenfei staggered and stumbled back. She was quick to recompose herself, but by then, Ming-Jun had moved into a lunge that Arkady recognized as coming from her broadsword forms. More important than assessing skill or style, however, was that Arkady could now tell that this was no staged fight: Ming-Jun was quite earnestly fighting for her life, and Jenfei was trying just as hard to kill her.

Ming-Jun landed a flat-palmed strike right against Jenfei's ribs, and while her opponent was still reeling from the follow-up blow, the rabbit spun her around and kicked her hard in the back of the leg. Jenfei collapsed onto her knees, but caught herself on both paws before she fell over completely. While the cacomistle was downed, Ming-Jun flicked her right wrist, appeared to snatch air with her left, and then reached down and pulled back, hard. A razor-thin line of red appeared in the fur of Jenfei's neck, and her paws scrabbled at the front of her throat as Ming-Jun tightened the garrote around it.

Arkady watched as Ming-Jun gritted her teeth and clenched her jaw, the white and gray fur rippling over her facial features as they distorted. She was pulling even harder now, her wrists crossed for leverage, and Jenfei's rasping breaths started to take on an unsettling wet tone, her struggles getting weaker by the second.

"*Xiǎotù*, release her." From around the corner, along the stone path, Kuai strode into view, a pistol similar to Jenfei's in his paw.

For a moment, Ming-Jun's paws went slack. She looked back at the raccoon with disgust in her eyes, then she released her hold on her wire garrote completely, letting it zip back up into its concealed holder inside her right sleeve. Immediately, Jenfei collapsed onto all fours, panting heavily now that she could breathe again.

Kuai kept his eye trained on Ming-Jun. He followed the rabbit's gaze down to Jenfei's discarded handgun. The two of them made eye contact, and Kuai just shook his head, taking another step forward, kicking the weapon aside with his foot. It disappeared into the undergrowth of the tangle of plants off to the side of the path.

Meanwhile, Jenfei reached up and felt at her own throat, then looked down at her paw and the blood that had come off on it. Spitting more blood onto the stone pathway, she started to drag herself to her feet. Arkady kept his gun ready, keeping his eye on Jenfei, but surreptitiously putting the better part of his attention on Ming-Jun and Kuai.

Once Jenfei was on her feet, she brought the back of one paw to her muzzle and wiped it clean of red spittle. She glared at Ming-Jun, looking like she might foolishly try to leap back into action at any moment. Ming-Jun held her ground, keeping both the cacomistle and the raccoon within her line of sight.

"*Jiànfēi*," Kuai said to the cacomistle without sparing her even the briefest look. "Go back to the restaurant. I'll take care of things from here."

Jenfei wheezed and turned to face Kuai. "*Shīfu*," she sputtered. Even with her voice shot, Arkady could tell that she was pleading. "Please, let me—"

"Go back to the restaurant, *Jiànfēi*," Kuai repeated with even more authority. The raccoon idly fingered the trigger of his gun as he licked between his lips and teeth while staring at Ming-Jun. "Your place is there, now."

Feeling out her sore jaw, Jenfei coughed, then spat a loose tooth out into her paw. She said not a word, but clutched her fingers around the tooth before hurrying back toward the elevator. No vestige whatsoever of her poise or composure remained.

Once Jenfei had left and was out of possible earshot, Kuai spared Arkady a brief look before leveling his gun at Ming-Jun again. "I'm impressed, *Xiǎotù*," he said. "Had I known that you could best *Jiànfēi* so easily, you might have been my second, in her stead. In another lifetime.

"Which only makes your betrayal that much more of a disappointment," the raccoon continued, shaking his head. "I was honestly hoping that you wouldn't show up tonight, but I knew in my heart of hearts that you would."

Ming-Jun kept her chin high. "Yeah, well, next time, pick someplace a little more secure to discuss your plans."

Kuai actually lowered his gun, and Arkady considered shooting him right there, but he couldn't ignore the chance that the raccoon might still be willing to talk. Dead, Kuai was useless to him, and he struck Arkady as the sort of man who would look death proudly in the eye if forced to chose between his personal safety and betraying his convictions.

"Oh, *Xiǎotù*," the raccoon said with a chuckle. "If I hadn't discussed the plans someplace where you could overhear them, how would you know to interfere?"

The look on Ming-Jun's face finally changed to one of disbelief. "You set Jenfei up?" she asked. "But she's—"

"She's a fool for not realizing that an agent of Mr. Ryswife's caliber wouldn't give up precious artifacts with just one woman pointing a gun at him," Kuai interrupted. "Still, her willingness to blindly follow orders has let me see your true colors at last, *Xiǎotù*, and I—"

"Stop calling me that," Ming-Jun snapped. "It's demeaning."

"No less than you deserve, then," Kuai said. He brought his gun back up. "Now, do me a favor and pick up that briefcase for me."

Ming-Jun didn't move right away. Arkady could see that Kuai's finger was definitely on the trigger; he was willing to shoot someone, here, if they made a false move. "Hold on," the ferret said. "Nobody needs to get hurt, here. We've both got something the other wants, so let's not do anything foolish, all right?"

Kuai had his gun pointed at Arkady now. "Ming-Jun," he said, stressing the different name, "please bring me Mr. Ryswife's case." The raccoon's muzzle broke into a faint grin, and his eyes narrow behind his glasses. "Then, Mr. Ryswife, we can discuss the trade agreement we made."

"This wasn't part of our agreement." Arkady let his eyes fix on Kuai's gun, then his own. Ming-Jun had started to move toward the dropped briefcase, and Arkady kept careful track of her movements as she approached.

As Ming-Jun bent to pick up the case, Arkady took one paw off of his gun and held it up. "Wait," he said. "I'll get it."

Kuai fired a shot into the stone pathway between the two agents' feet. Ming-Jun's long ears flapped backwards at the loud sound, and chips of fragmented stone grazed harmlessly against Arkady's leg. "I will shoot her, Mr. Ryswife," the raccoon said. "Both of you, if I have to." He pointed his gun at Ming-Jun, then waved it toward the briefcase. "Now, *Xiǎotù*, bring me the case; Mr. Ryswife, stay right where you are."

What value was Kuai to Arkady, by this point? If what Ming-Jun had said back at Dianjiang Gardens was true, then the raccoon had nothing with which to truly barter, and besides, Il-Hyeong already had the Pyxis Sequence. Information, then. Answers. Were there things— secrets about the Carmine Order, perhaps—that Arkady couldn't just find out from Ming-Jun?

The books. That what this was all about, at least to Kuai. Ming-Jun honestly didn't seem to have known what they were, back when they'd obtained them in Tomosabaki. Of course, she'd kept *all* knowledge of the Carmine Order and the *Zhōngwén* language secret from Arkady and from everyone else, so she could have just as easily muted her reaction to their significance.

But she wasn't loyal to Kuai—and since getting hold of these books had cost Kentian his life, Ming-Jun wouldn't willingly give them over to Kuai if she were aware of some greater purpose. Assuming, of course, that she realized that the books Arkady had brought were not the actual books Kuai was looking for.

Arkady let her retrieve the case, and allowed her to bring it over to Kuai. The raccoon held out one paw to take it from her, his other keeping his gun trained on Arkady. Just as he was about to grasp the handle, though, he instead grabbed Ming-Jun by the wrist. The rabbit was caught off guard, and she cried out as Kuai pulled her against his front and shoved the barrel of his pistol right up against the side of her head.

"Now, Mr. Ryswife," the raccoon declared as Ming-Jun's struggles quickly ceased. "Let's play a little game of truth or dare."

"I'm not playing any games with you, Kuai." Even with Kuai using Ming-Jun as a shield, Arkady's aim was effectively perfect. He could get a clean shot right to the raccoon's head and—

No. Too risky. Kuai's finger was right on the trigger, and the chance was too great that, in the throes of death, he'd discharge the weapon while it was still pressed against Ming-Jun's skull.

"Just one round," Kuai insisted. "And I'll make it very simple. Tell me truthfully: are the books in that case the three you promised to bring me?"

"Of course," Arkady said through gritted teeth. "Like Jenfei herself said: at what point during any of this have I been anything but forthright with you?"

Kuai nodded and grinned. "Just so," he said. "And so I'll give you one more free chance at this: if I have your little rabbit friend here open the briefcase, are the books I've asked for going to fall out?" He snarled as he pushed his pistol harder against Ming-Jun's temple. "Tell me truthfully. If you tell me 'no,' then we move on to a new discussion. But if you tell me 'yes,' and it turns out that you're lying, then poor *Xiǎotù* is going to have her brains blown out right here, right in front of you." His finger traced the trigger. "So, which is it?"

If Ming-Jun opened up the case, then Kuai would have to look down to see whether or not he'd been victim to a bait-and-switch. Would the position of the gun barrel move when he did that, even for half a second? Probably not. What if Kuai instead—

"Arkady," Ming-Jun said. "*Yī qī yī huì.*"

Kuai turned at once to look at her, his jaw beginning to drop. Ming-Jun continued. "*Yī qī yī huì,*" she repeated. "You asked me what it meant, back at that restaurant."

Arkady remembered, of course: the words from the pre-civ song they'd first heard on the tape, back in the hotel room in Seizo—the words that had so affected Ming-Jun when she listened to them, that she'd been humming to herself back in Highslope.

"How dare you?" Kuai growled to Ming-Jun. His face was awash with something resembling—no, it wasn't even mere resemblance. He was aghast, appalled. "How *dare* you?" he repeated. He continued to speak, but the words were lost to Arkady as he and Ming-Jun locked gazes with each other.

The look was subtle, but direct and determined, as was the oh-so-slight nod of her chin. Arkady returned the nod, then tightened the grip on his gun.

While Kuai was slack-jawed, castigating Ming-Jun for this transgression, the rabbit was momentarily able to duck her head down before he could react. Arkady pointed his gun down and fired, catching Kuai right in the side. The raccoon cried out, and as his weight shifted, Ming-Jun wrested herself free of his weakened hold on her.

Kuai buckled, the bullet having cleanly penetrated his flank. His arm dropped, and whether due to a spasm of pain or simple panic while trying to set up another shot, he pulled the trigger of his own gun. Ming-Jun shrieked as that stray shot struck her in the back of the thigh, causing her to collapse onto one knee before she could get more than a full stride away.

Arkady fired again, three more times. The first two bullets struck Kuai in the arm, causing him to scream as he dropped his gun. The third bullet shattered his kneecap, and now it was his turn to crumple there on the stone pathway, the scent of blood hitting Arkady's nostrils even from where he stood.

Ming-Jun scampered away, limping and clutching her injured leg as Arkady stepped right up to Kuai, gun held fast in both paws. The raccoon was down on his good knee, his other leg draped limply beneath himself, Arkady's gun pointed right at his head.

"Tell me about the books, Kuai," the ferret demanded. "What are they? Why do you want them so badly?"

Kuai clutched his injured arm close to himself before he looked at Arkady. His glasses were slightly askew on his muzzle, making the hatred in his eyes look somewhat pathetic as a result. "They mean nothing to you," he said. "They only—"

Arkady kicked Kuai in the face, hard enough to smash his glasses, but not enough to kick him over. "That's not what I asked!" he snapped. "I asked you to tell me what they are."

Coughing and sputtering, Kuai again looked Arkady in the eye. It was clear that, in the face of the pain he was in, his resolve was going to waver—but he was trying to tap into that fanatic conviction that members of the Carmine Order had always demonstrated up to this point. "You really want to know that badly?"

"They seem pretty important to you. Look at what you've been going through in trying to get your paws on them."

"Arkady," Ming-Jun said, sounding hesitant, but adding no further explanation.

Kuai closed his eyes and sighed. "Look," he said. "They're just... books. Books and a song."

"What's special about them?" Arkady asked.

"What's special?" Kuai scoffed as he laughed. "They're part of our culture. Our history. They belong to us."

Arkady shook his head. "No," he said. "You and your people have been on some kind of... paramilitary crusade, trying to get these books from us. What's written in them? What makes them so valuable?"

"I've already told you!" Kuai cried. "The Carmine Order exists to protect our culture. We just wanted to get that part of our history back from you."

"Ming-Jun," Arkady said without taking his eyes off of the raccoon. "Do you want to help Mr. Kuai jog his memory?"

Grunting with effort as she sat down on the path, holding her own injured leg, Ming-Jun took a few breaths. "He's telling the truth," she said. "His concern is protecting our culture."

"But what have *books* got to do with that?" Arkady demanded. He wanted badly to kick Kuai again, just for good measure. "What kind of books are they? What do they contain?"

Kuai shook his head. "I haven't seen them myself," he said. "From what *Xiǎotù* has told me, though, my guess is that two of them are old novels, and the third is some kind of philosophical treatise."

"Novels?" Arkady turned the word over in his head. "Novels?" he repeated. "Are you fucking *kidding* me?" This time, he did kick Kuai again, knocking his broken glasses clear off his face. "You really expect me to believe that you'd mobilize trained, armed combatants to get hold of a few pieces of *fiction*?"

"History!" Kuai shouted. "Over four thousand years of trying to piece together a history that nobody else can remember!"

Arkady could feel his paws shaking. "Tell me you're lying," he said, voice quieter now. "Tell me you wouldn't really do this—*all* of this—just for some old, dusty books that you don't know what they are."

Behind Arkady, Ming-Jun was trying to get to her feet again, but the ferret ignored her. Kuai seemed to be doing the same. "They're not just dusty old books," the raccoon said. "They're who we used to be— who we still strive to be."

"And *what* are you?" Arkady's arms were trembling. With his acute senses, he could smell the reek of fear coming off of Kuai. This was not a man who was ready to be a martyr for some cause; this was a man who was afraid. "You're some... some small-time crime lord who wants to play historian, from what I can tell."

"It's more than that," Kuai insisted. "You should know; isn't piecing together history what you do, too? Aren't you and I the same?"

Arkady actually laughed. "The same?" he said. "What I do—what we do, Ming-Jun and our companions—is liberate artifacts like these from selfish, egotistical collectors like you. Because our mission is to *restore* the fragments of the world's past so that everyone can learn from it."

"And yet in all of your searching," Kuai said, "in all of your records and books, you've never come across any mention of us, of *our* people, of *Zhōngwén*. What's your explanation for that?"

"You tell me," Arkady said. "But I'll tell you what I think," he added. "I think it's because you and your... your little crew aren't as significant as you want to believe. I think that—"

Ming-Jun cut him off. "It's because the world tried to get rid of us."

Leaving his gun pointed at Kuai, Arkady turned and looked over his shoulder at Ming-Jun. "What?" he said.

"It's true," Ming-Jun replied. "It's why we live in secret, even now. Better to hide it from the world than to risk losing our culture forever."

That any of what Kuai and Ming-Jun were saying could be true made Arkady's head hurt. Kuai did bring up a good point: how *could* such a group of people exist without Project Scheherazade having any knowledge? Moreover, why would Ming-Jun—who had already shown her lack of loyalty to Kuai—defend his position?

"But why not just reveal yourselves?" Arkady asked. "What risk could come from simply living in the open?"

"Our culture would be erased," Kuai responded, his face twisting up in pain as he reached to feel the gunshot wound in his side. "It is only by keeping our secret for all these millennia that our ways and our language have survived at all."

"And how can you be so sure of that?" Arkady asked. "You've kept your culture alive this long; who's to say that you wouldn't be just as successful at that without the added pressure of remaining hidden?"

Kuai sneered at Arkady, as if he couldn't believe the ferret's stupidity. "The reason we took to hiding in the first place was so that we would not lose our ways due to integration with the rest of society," he said. "And now, thousands of years later, where are the ones who chose not to hide? Gone! That's where." The raccoon's eyes were having a hard time focusing without his glasses, but he sought Arkady's gaze all the same, flashing him a sarcastic smile. "If the world were to face us now—a group of people who can communicate amongst ourselves in indecipherable words, with the know-how and dedication to escape notice of the common man and governmental authorities—then I'm sure that no one would be at all ill at ease with that, no."

"But it doesn't have to be that way, *Kuài-shīfu*," Ming-Jun said. The apparent honorific made Kuai shake his head to himself. "It's like I tried to tell you the other night," the rabbit said as she stepped closer to him. "The people on my team within the League *are* after the same thing we are, and with people like Arkady—people we can trust—I think that we can really—"

"Who are you to lecture me about trust, *Xiǎotù*?" Kuai spat. "You, who would promise to bring me the books you tracked down. You, who would kill *Jiànfēi* in cold blood in order to save a man you called 'leader' for years while lying to him every day of your life about who and what you really were." With a wry chuckle, he hung his head between his arms. "I wonder if there's anyone left you haven't betrayed, *tùzi*."

Ming-Jun clenched her paws together. She opened and closed her mouth, and Arkady could feel that she was searching for words.

"And you're some paragon of virtue?" the ferret said in her stead. "Tell me again about these books. You said Ming-Jun promised to get them for you?"

"And she lied," Kuai responded. "I'm going to bet that you never even brought them to Ridgecrescent with you, did you?"

Arkady took his finger off the trigger of his gun. "Why should she have?" he said. "So you could just sweep in, kill us all, and collect your precious little trophies?"

"Historical artifacts," Kuai said. "I wouldn't expect you to understand."

"No," Arkady said. "No, I think I understand perfectly, really."

Three books and a tape recorder. No secret messages, no mystical codes or divine wisdom to be found. Just books. Novels. Novels, and a song.

Il-Hyeong had huddled in the hallway of Fan-Yin Bioinformatics, praying to God, praying fervently to not have to kill people—people whom he subsequently gunned down, with Arkady's help. People, led by Jenfei, sent by Kuai, to help recover a set of books.

The two feline prisoners that Il-Hyeong had captured after that failed raid—the raid where Boots' friend and comrade Jenkins had been killed. The two prisoners, one of whom had been executed simply to get the other to talk—the other who then died as ignominiously as his companion, who died in fear after having betrayed his cause, after having been sent on a mission to kill a pair of agents so that Kuai could recover a set of books.

Arkady settled his finger back on the trigger of his gun.

There was Carson, the mouse who had been Boots' and Jenkins' driver, also slain by the Carmine Order, a collateral casualty in that same crusade to get to Arkady and Il-Hyeong and recover those books for Kuai. In the confusion and panic brought on by not knowing who could be trusted, even Boots had been hurt, hurt by Il-Hyeong, despite having been trying to help from the very beginning.

Poor Dr. Lederle, as well. He'd perhaps been the greatest help of all, having finally led Arkady and Il-Hyeong to the very thing they'd been searching for—the thing that Kuai had lied about having, had lied about wanting to trade for his precious, precious books. Dr. Lederle had ended up dead as well, a victim of—no, Lederle's death was squarely on Il-Hyeong. Arkady had to accept that. *(But would Il-Hyeong have had any reason to kill him, were it not for Kuai's selfish machinations?)*

Even Jenfei, Kuai's own second, sold out by her master, used as mere bait to draw out Ming-Jun, exposing her disloyalty as well. Even then, Kuai wasn't satisfied with hurting other people. He'd even said it, had admitted it outright: that he was willing to kill Ming-Jun, *Xiǎotù*, if she interfered with him getting his books.

And Kentian. Kentian's last words.

"Whatever's in that case had better be worth this."

It wasn't.

Arkady closed his eyes. He called up the mental image of the statue in the courtyard of Château Sainte-Mireille, the one with wolf, rabbit, tiger, mouse, fox, and bat holding paws, united in harmony beneath the all-encompassing motto of the Iolite League: *FOR THE BETTER WORLD*.

The better world was something that Arkady Ryswife believed in. The better world would be made and forged through belief and dedication to peace and love and unity. It would be forged by people like him, like Ming-Jun and Il-Hyeong, to be shared by people like Dr. Lederle's wife and children, like Vasilis Berzeviczy and Arkady's daughter, Pandora.

But not by Jiangzhao Kuai. The better world still waited somewhere out there, and there was no place in it for him.

Arkady's finger squeezed the trigger.

The spent cartridge case clinked against the stone pathway a few times, faintly audible as the echo of the gunshot itself faded. By then,

Jiangzhao Kuai was already dead, his lifeless body slumping to the ground a few feet away, a single, neat hole punched right between his eyes.

17. The Integrity of Angels

Ming-Jun was quiet. She hadn't said a word, either before or after Arkady had pulled the trigger. Like Arkady, she just looked down at the raccoon's body and at the look of fear and desperation frozen on his face.

Arkady holstered his gun and turned away. He tried to reconcile his conscience with the fact that he was glad that Kuai was dead. Repentance could not be attained so long as he held on to that selfish emotion, in taking joy—even in part—in committing such a sin. Perhaps later, that feeling would fade, and penitence might be his, but not right now.

"What happens now?" he asked.

Ming-Jun was still to his back. He could hear her breathing, a slight trembling that could have been from anxiety, relief, or exhilaration. "Well," she began, swallowing that word before continuing, "with Kuai dead, Jenfei is next in line. She'd take over, and—"

"I don't care about the Order," Arkady said, turning around. "That's not what I meant." He searched Ming-Jun's face for any sign of what she was thinking. Her eyes were tinged with sadness, but not consumed by it. "What happens with us, I mean? You and me."

The rabbit let out a held breath, then shifted more heavily onto her good leg. "Arkady, God, I'm..." Her chest heaved. "Please, you have to believe me. I didn't... I never thought that anything like this would happen. I swear, if I'd known that any—"

The apology cut off with a soft squeak as Arkady closed his arms closed around Ming-Jun's midsection, hugging her close to his front, muzzle tucked in against the crook of her neck. God, her scent was so reassuring. She was here, she was real, and he'd saved her. He'd sworn that he'd come back for her, refused to leave her behind, and now she was here.

Arkady let go of her, then set his paws on her shoulders, careful not to put any real weight on her. "It's okay," he told her. "I believe you."

A smile slowly crept across Ming-Jun's white-and-gray face. "Thank you," she said. Her smile began to fade as she looked back over at Kuai. "I wish that this all could have gone differently."

"It's not your fault. It's his. And he's paid for it, now."

Ming-Jun bit her lip, then sighed. "Is that why you killed him?"

"It's done," Arkady said, stepping away to put the body out of sight again. "Judgment is God's to render, now, unto him and unto me, both the same."

From behind, Ming-Jun touched Arkady's shoulder. "I'm not saying he didn't deserve it," she said. "I'm just—"

"It's done," Arkady repeated. "Leave it." Ming-Jun's paw came away, and she nodded silently.

The rabbit took a few steps in the direction of the elevator and stumbled, wincing and gasping as she bent down to grab at her injured leg. "Damn it," she hissed.

"Sorry," Arkady said. "I was hoping he'd drop the gun sooner."

Ming-Jun looked down at the red hole in her thigh. "Well, it certainly could have been worse," she acknowledged. "And hey, better a bullet in the leg than one in the head."

He knew that Ming-Jun had been referring to the fate she herself had avoided, but Arkady couldn't help but think of Kuai again. *He brought it upon himself. There are more important things to worry about right now.*

Hopping briefly on one foot, Ming-Jun made her way to one side of the stone path and sat down to check her leg out more closely. Arkady knelt down next to her to help. The bullet was lodged in the fleshy part of the thigh, and it would need to come out, but Dr. Mayflower would see to it that there was no lasting damage.

It was a shame that Ming-Jun hadn't been a recipient of the augmentation procedure. Or was a simple gunshot wound an acceptable payoff for not ending up with a mindset like Il-Hyeong's?

"I didn't bring my field kit," Ming-Jun said as her fingers picked some small, bloody clumps of fur out of the way. "I don't suppose you have one stashed in that decoy briefcase, huh?"

Arkady chuckled. "Just old, musty library books," he said. "Sorry."

Looking up from her work, Ming-Jun smiled back at him. "Just like old times?" she asked.

"Something like it," Arkady replied. After all that had happened on this sorry excuse for a mission to Ridgecrescent, it was doubtful that things would ever be completely like old times again, but for now, this would do.

The ferret looked at Ming-Jun's face again, studying the shapes made by the boundary between white and gray. "So is *Xiǎotù* your real name?" he asked.

Ming-Jun looked up again and laughed once. "Ew, God, no," she said with a grin. "It's sort of a nickname. It just means 'little rabbit,' is all." She patted Arkady on the shoulder. "My real name really is Ming-Jun."

"Good," Arkady replied. "Because pronouncing those tones right is a real pain in the ass."

They shared a brief chuckle at that, stopping when Ming-Jun winced at her leg again. With the moment having passed, she took a quick look around, then asked, "Arkady, where *is* Il-Hyeong?"

"I want to say he's halfway to Deepwater by now," the ferret replied. "But I honestly don't know for sure."

Ming-Jun appeared alarmed. "How can you not know?" she asked. "And why would he be on his way home?"

Arkady sighed. "It's... It's a long story," he said. "Let's just say that the mission is done and we can *all* be going home, now."

"Done?" Ming-Jun asked. Her eyes then widened in beautiful disbelief as realization dawned. "Wait, you mean you found it? You actually *found* it?"

The ferret nodded. "We did," he replied. "It's safe, and we'll be able to make sense of it once we get it back to the Château."

"How come you don't sound happier about that?" Ming-Jun asked Arkady as he helped her back to her feet.

"If I had to hazard a guess, Ming, I'd say that it's because Arkady has finally put together the pieces of the puzzle and has realized the truth behind it all."

Out from the row of botanical camouflage stepped Il-Hyeong Quinn, brushing dirt and bits of flowers off of his chest with one paw. He almost looked bored, but Arkady still recognized the faint vulpine ferocity in his eyes, even if those predatory instincts weren't currently directed at anything or anyone in particular.

"Il-Hyeong," Arkady said, taking his arm carefully out from underneath Ming-Jun's shoulder. "When did you get here?"

"Oh, some time before you did, at any rate," the fox said. He continued to exude laziness and boredom. "Are you telling me that you couldn't smell me, even through all this?" he asked, gesturing with his paw in a slow, casual circle.

Now that Il-Hyeong had mentioned it, Arkady realized that he *couldn't* smell him—not just because of the overwhelming floral scents of the conservatory, but because there didn't seem to be anything to smell. Being able to see the fox so close while still not being able to smell him was disconcerting; it was like he wasn't fully there, like he might as well have been a ghost.

If I pull my gun now, Arkady thought, *I can probably get a shot off before he has a chance to react.* At once, the ferret was horrified that violence had been his first reaction. No, whatever Il-Hyeong's intentions were, he'd had more than ample opportunity to strike from hiding. His morals were skewed, his methods reprehensible, but thus far, he had kept to the ideals of the Iolite League. He wasn't the enemy—not yet.

"Ming-Jun, take a step back," Arkady said at the same time as he took a step forward.

The rabbit didn't comply right away. "Arkady, what's wrong?" she asked.

"Yes, Arkady," Il-Hyeong said, "what's wrong? My assessment of the situation, perchance?"

"There's no 'situation,'" Arkady said. "We have the Pyxis Sequence. We have Ming-Jun back. We can all go home now."

Il-Hyeong clucked his tongue and shook his head. "Can we?" he asked. His gaze was on Ming-Jun, and now the rabbit did follow Arkady's advice to step away. "After everything you just heard and saw, you're still so quick to trust her?"

"Don't be ridiculous," Arkady said. "She just risked her neck to save mine."

"While also saving her own, I should point out," the fox added.

Arkady's fingers itched. He again considered reaching for his gun. "What are you even doing here?" the ferret demanded instead. "How did you even know to *come* here?"

"I followed Kuai," Il-Hyeong said. "I figured that I'd save you the time and effort of trying to deal with someone who was only planning to double-cross you anyway." The very front of his muzzle started to crack into a single-fanged grin. "But then I got up here, and I smelled that Ming was hiding out here as well, and I realized that a far better opportunity had dropped into my paws."

"Opportunity for what?" God, if only Ming-Jun could run, he'd order her to make a break for the elevators and just hope that he and Il-Hyeong were evenly matched enough that he could buy her the time she'd need to get away.

A look of disappointment crossed the swift fox's face. "An opportunity to see Ming's true colors, of course," he said, sighing. "Clearly, Kuai had no idea that she was here, but she hadn't been lying in wait for him, either, so something else was afoot."

"If you saw what just happened, you should be satisfied," Arkady said. "Let's not turn this into something it doesn't have to be."

"If I'm satisfied with anything," Il-Hyeong said, "it's with my having had the presence of mind to not take anything about this situation at face value. Not even Ming."

"Il-Hyeong," Ming-Jun called out, "I'm sorry I kept things from—"

The fox cut her off. "Spare me the theatrics," he said. "The only thing I care about is whether you're loyal to us or loyal to them."

If Il-Hyeong was beyond reason—if he was *incapable* of seeing reason, then this would all be for naught, and he'd decide whatever the hell his addled mind wanted. "Let's not jump to conclusions," Arkady warned, taking careful note of where Il-Hyeong's paws were, making sure neither was too close to his gun. "The Directorate Board will examine the situation after we get back, and if they think that Ming-Jun is—"

"Wow, Arkady," Il-Hyeong said with a laugh. "She got you good, didn't she? One of our closest allies, a member of our own inner circle, stabs us in the back, and you want to just smile, adhere to protocol, and do things by the book *now*, of all times?" His arm snapped up, and he pointed an accusing claw at Ming-Jun. "She's admitted to both deceit and to complicity with a group of people who tried repeatedly to kill us and to stop our mission!"

"It's not like that!" Ming-Jun cried. "The night before the raid on Fan-Yin, I—"

"I have to admit, you've been quite clever," the fox said, as if she hadn't even spoken. "The timing of your attack on the cacomistle woman certainly makes it look like your true allegiance is with us, but while that might be enough for Arkady to cast all doubt out of his mind, he's still refusing to see the greater picture, here, just like he has from the beginning."

"Agent Quinn, I am only going to give you this order once," Arkady said, resting his paw on his gun for effect. "Drop this. This is neither the time nor the place to argue about this. Agent Devra will accompany us back to the Château, and then we will follow due process."

Looking at Arkady's readied paw, Il-Hyeong barked out another laugh. "Oh, Arkady, *please*," he said. "Did you learn nothing from last night?" The fox used his muzzle to indicate the ferret's abdomen. Grinning, he then straightened up and turned his attention back to Ming-Jun. "No, I think we'll settle the matter of 'Agent Devra's' loyalty right here and now."

Arkady could smell the fear coming off of Ming-Jun now, in a way he hadn't even smelled when she'd been held at gunpoint by Kuai. That her own comrade could scare her so much was enough for the ferret to make up his mind: the time for hesitation had long passed, and he needed to take action.

Time slowed without conscious effort on Arkady's part as he whipped his gun into his paw and took aim. Bullets might not kill Il-Hyeong easily, but Arkady didn't want or even need that—he just needed to *stop* the fox, to take him out of commission and, if necessary, subdue him and take him back to Château Sainte-Mireille by force. That much, at least, he was prepared to do.

He had a perfect shot lined up right with Il-Hyeong's left knee. As the ferret's finger squeezed the trigger, though, the fox pivoted on his other leg and dodged out of the way, simultaneously bringing his own weapon to bear. Arkady saw the flash from the other gun's muzzle, then felt a searing pain that momentarily overloaded his body's advanced pain threshold.

Arkady's Zarna discharged once more into the flowers before clattering to the stone below, its sleek form slathered in red. The ferret's right paw was now a mangled, bloody stump, retaining only its broken forefinger and thumb; the digits that had been wrapped around the pistol's grip were gone, and in their place were only bits of splintered, shattered bone extruding from the red flesh.

"Come on, Arkady," Il-Hyeong said, his DKR-7 still at the ready. "I've just seen two people get shot in the leg back to back. Give me some credit."

In the aftermath of that gunshot, Ming-Jun nearly fell backwards. Her jaw had dropped, and she looked like she was searching for something to grab hold of for balance. Arkady tried to shift his attention from his missing fingers to Ming-Jun, willing whatever pain resistance he possessed to kick in.

"Have you lost your mind?" the rabbit shrieked. "What in God's name are you doing?"

Il-Hyeong swung his pistol over and aimed it at Ming-Jun. "As I just said, I think it's about time we settled the matter of your questionable allegiance." There was an odd lack of superiority in his voice, all of a sudden. His eyes were still cold, though, and he looked no less ready to make good on his threats. "And if Arkady's smart, he'll stay right the hell where he is; otherwise, he's getting another bullet someplace far more vital."

"Just let her explain herself," Arkady pleaded. Blood was still dripping from his paw, showing no signs of slowing. Even the augmentation's effects had limits, then.

"That's precisely what I intend to do," the fox replied. "Let's start simple." He brought his gun into alignment with the rabbit's already-injured leg. "Are you or have you ever been a member of this so-called Carmine Order?"

Ming-Jun sighed anxiously. "Yes," she said, "but—"

Before she could get another word out, Il-Hyeong fired again, striking her in the thigh and bringing her down onto one knee. "A simple 'yes' or 'no' will suffice, thank you," the fox proclaimed. "Now, a more difficult question, but a more important one: to whom do you owe your allegiance now?"

Her muzzle snarled up in both pain and rage, Ming-Jun looked about to spit out another invective of defiance. Arkady hoped desperately that she wouldn't, for her own good, and to his relief, he saw her head sag a bit, followed by a more dejected reply of, "To the Iolite League and to God, as always."

"Good," Il-Hyeong said. This time, he did not shoot, but Arkady could only wonder how long the fox was planning on prolonging this— and what he intended to do once he got all the answers he was hoping for, whether they were the ones he wanted to hear or not.

When neither Il-Hyeong nor Ming-Jun said anything for several seconds, Arkady took the opportunity to speak up. "There," he said. "Are you satisfied yet? Can we stop this pointless exercise already?" Was there even hope of getting Il-Hyeong to come back to the Château quietly if he did?

"I believe that Ming speaks the truth," Il-Hyeong stated plainly. "As for satisfaction? No, I'm afraid that her current loyalties are not the only issue we face." Holding his ground, the fox raised his pistol higher, watching Ming-Jun's face as he did so, waiting until she looked up again before he continued. "On the night before the Fan-Yin mission, you disappeared," he said. "The next night, the Carmine Order was waiting for us. How did they know we were going to be there?"

Ming-Jun's throat warbled as she swallowed a few times. "I told Kuai that we needed him to stay away. That—"

Another gunshot rang out, along with another cry from Ming-Jun as her right shoulder erupted in a burst of red. Her arm sagged limply, and blood ran down both the front and back. "You leaked Project Scheherazade's secrets!" Il-Hyeong snapped. "That you leaked them at all, let alone to members of an armed organization with its own hidden agenda, is betrayal and treachery that borders on blasphemy."

Arkady could see that Ming-Jun's wound was a nasty one—possibly crippling if it weren't treated with expert surgery as soon as possible. His genuine fear and panic for the rabbit's well-being was so bad, now, that his senses refused to focus, refused to comply with his wishes to just slow the moment down already, to buy him time to think, to come up with some kind of brilliant plan to get them all through this alive. If his body wouldn't comply, that still wasn't reason enough to let Ming-Jun suffer at the hands of a former friend.

Il-Hyeong might have expert aim, and maybe there was no way for Arkady to take him down without trading away his own life in the process. But standing there, watching, while she bled alongside him, would make him complicit, and just as guilty as Il-Hyeong. He might only have one shot to do something, so he'd need to make it count.

"I didn't tell him what we were after," Ming-Jun coughed. She cradled her right arm with her left, the blood running off at the tip formed by her bent elbow. "All he wanted was the books, I'm sure of it."

"And how did he know about the books, Ming?" Il-Hyeong demanded. No longer was sneering, vindictive and self-satisfied; now he was simply brimming with fury. "You told him about those, too, didn't you?"

"I was the one who told Dr. Lederle that gunmen and snipers had been sent to pin you down when you'd taken prisoners!" Ming-Jun shouted. Now, her eyes seemed to burn with a righteous rage all her own. "Kuai wanted you dead and I tried to save you!"

Il-Hyeong fired another shot into Ming-Jun's other leg, but this time, the rabbit only showed the barest hints of pain. "Do you think that makes up for everything else you did?" the fox shouted. He was brimming with anger.

Perhaps, now, Arkady thought—now, while Il-Hyeong was fixated on getting his justice. This might be his best chance to buy Ming-Jun some time. She might not be able to run, but if her endorphin levels were high enough that she could struggle past the pain, then maybe, if Arkady dove forward and tackled Il-Hyeong around the ankles, the rabbit might have a shot at getting to safety. Arkady probably wouldn't be able to escape the fox's wrath, afterwards, but so long as Ming-Jun got away, then—

A bullet whizzed by Arkady's skull, clipping his left ear, shaving off a small portion of it. Il-Hyeong had turned and fired so fast (or perhaps

Arkady had been so focused on the potential outcomes of his plan) that the ferret hadn't registered the movement until it was too late. "Arkady, so help me God, if you so much as move another inch, this next bullet is going right in your eye," the swift fox barked. "I don't want to kill you after everything else we've lived through."

"Il-Hyeong, please," Ming-Jun begged. "I don't know what happened to you, but please." She wasn't crying; there were no tears that Arkady could see. "Maybe you don't trust me or maybe you can't trust me, and I'm sorry, all right? I'm really, truly sorry." She turned and looked over at the ferret. "But what's Arkady done wrong?"

"I'd be more concerned with myself right now if I were you, Ming," Il-Hyeong said. "His fate and mine are already sealed; yours is still up in the air." The fox hesitated before taking his gun off of Arkady and pointing it back at Ming-Jun, but rather than aiming at her leg or shoulder, this time, the gun was pointed toward her head.

Ming-Jun looked right back at Il-Hyeong, her head held high. "Arkady," she said, eyes remaining firmly on the fox, "it's crucial that you remember what I'm about to say to you."

"I'll ask again." Il-Hyeong was at least speaking more calmly and quietly now. His free paw clenched into a fist, then quickly relaxed. "Do you think your noble actions absolve you of your betrayal?"

Arkady had seen Il-Hyeong execute too many people, now, for him to believe that the fox would spare Ming-Jun's life on anything but a whim. Was there even a right answer and a wrong answer to the question? It seemed that Ming-Jun was prepared for that eventuality, too, but what use did pride serve her now in not at least *trying* to placate him?

Still facing her would-be killer, Ming-Jun began to speak. *"Zài zhuāngyuán lǐ miàn—"*

Oh, God in Heaven, what did she think she was doing?

"—wǒ fángjiān de shūguì shàng yǒu gè zhōng—"

Il-Hyeong's aim started to waver, and his eyes went wide. "Arkady!" he snapped. "God, Arkady, what is she *doing*?" For the first time since the raid on Fan-Yin, Arkady felt fear coming from Il-Hyeong

It was then that Arkady realized just what Ming-Jun *was* doing. Quickly, with a twitch of his left paw, the ferret began to record the sound of her words into his memory module.

The rabbit continued to babble forth a stream of musical tones, that beautiful nonsense that only this secretive, select few could understand. That she wanted or needed Arkady to know this carried so much weight and expectation, and the ramifications of her speaking her language openly at all were nothing short of terrifying. He wanted to beg her to stop, to just shut her mouth and tell Il-Hyeong whatever he wanted to hear, but deep down, he knew that, if he were in her place, he'd have trusted her like this, too.

"*Tell* me!" Il-Hyeong demanded, pointing and gesticulating wildly with his pistol. "Tell me that you repent! Tell me that you're sorry for what you did, Ming! I need to know! I need to hear it!"

But Ming-Jun continued on in *Zhōngwén* as if she were in a trance, or perhaps as if she didn't even care that the fox had spoken. Il-Hyeong grabbed the grip of his gun with his other paw, in order to still the jitters and shaking he'd developed. "God in Heaven, is she speaking in *tongues*?" he cried out. "What manner of... of devilry *is* this?" As Ming-Jun continued to speak, the fox took a full step backwards and nearly lost his balance.

Arkady saw his chance, then. Il-Hyeong was rattled; his attention was divided and his aim was shaky. It was now or never.

With his left arm outstretched, Arkady dove for his pistol, lying on the floor, caked in blood. He braced himself for the impact as he tucked into a roll and went to spring up onto one knee as he came out of it.

Arkady brought up his gun to fire.

But Il-Hyeong had been faster than he'd anticipated; the fox was already aiming at the spot where Arkady had come out of his dive.

"Arkady, look out!"

Ming-Jun dove out in front of Arkady's field of vision.

Two gunshots rang out.

Time sped back up as Ming-Jun collapsed into Arkady's arms. He caught her full weight against his chest, and she lay draped across his forearms. The impact was sudden and strong, and Ming-Jun was limp, which made holding her that much more difficult. Arkady nearly lost his grip on his pistol, but as soon as he felt it beginning to slip, he was able to spare just enough attention to tighten his fingers.

Both bullets had struck Ming-Jun in the chest, and the smooth black material of her bodysuit allowed the blood to run over its surface with disturbing quickness. The rabbit coughed once, and more blood splatted out of her mouth and stained the white fur of her lower jaw.

Oh, God, no, this couldn't be happening. "No," Arkady whimpered, cradling Ming-Jun closer. "No," he repeated louder. "Oh, God, I..."

"Arkady," Ming-Jun said, another fresh trickle of blood leaking from the corner of her mouth as she struggled to speak. "Are you... all right?"

No, no, no, she couldn't have! What would have ever possessed her to—*no*, this wasn't right! "I'm fine," he told her. *Fine.* As if that word could possibly hold any meaning now.

The sound of Il-Hyeong's gun falling to the stone pathway made Arkady look up. The swift fox was standing as still as a statue, his eyes wide and his mouth agape. "Oh, God, Ming!" he called out before starting to race toward her and Arkady.

Before Il-Hyeong got more than two steps, though, Arkady brought up his gun and fired a warning shot that grazed the fox on his right side, just below the ribs. With that single shot, the damaged pistol fell apart, the grip cracking and splitting down the middle as the slide flew clear off the back. Despite this, the ferret still clutched the broken half of the gun tight as he shrieked, "Don't you fucking move! Don't you come one step closer!"

Ming-Jun lazily lolled her head in an attempt to look over at Il-Hyeong, but she was too weak already, and she just ended up slumping back into position, looking up at Arkady with eyes that had trouble focusing. "Did you... get what I said?" she said.

"Yes, yes, I got it," Arkady said. He could feel tears on his cheeks, though he hadn't noticed when he'd begun to cry. "Try to... try to just hold still, now," he urged her. There was little force in his words; he'd seen enough people die from gunshot wounds, and so had she.

"Good," the rabbit replied. She closed her mouth and looked up at the glass ceiling, aimlessly. "Thank you," she added, *"wǒ de péng yǒu."*

Her eyes began to roll up into the back of her head, then. The only thing that Arkady's senses wanted to pick up, suddenly, was the smell of blood—Ming Jun's, Kuai's, Arkady's own, Il-Hyeong's, even Jenfei's, all vying for attention.

"Ming!" Il-Hyeong shouted. He stumbled briefly, then began to approach again. In desperation, Arkady threw the remnants of his gun, but the makeshift projectile impacted harmlessly off of the fox's leg as he dashed forward.

"Get away from her," Arkady snarled. He held the rabbit closer, more possessively, even though he could feel that the life had already ebbed out of her.

Il-Hyeong began to shake his head violently in disbelief. "No, no," he wailed. "This wasn't supposed to happen this way. This wasn't what I came here for."

"Then why did you fucking *shoot* her?" Arkady's voice rose in pitch and cracked as his tears started to come harder.

"No," Il-Hyeong repeated. With the paw that had held his gun, he began to grope and scrabble at his face and muzzle, tugging at his whiskers, his ear. "This... this isn't my fault. I came here to save her!"

As gently as he could manage while still moving quickly, Arkady set Ming-Jun's body down on the ground, then dove over her and tackled Il-Hyeong to the stone walkway. The fox brought up an arm to ward off the impact, but he wasn't able to stop the ferret from dragging him down all the same. "You liar! You goddamn fucking liar!" Arkady growled as he and Il-Hyeong grappled there on the ground.

With just one paw and a bloody stump, though, Arkady was unable to keep Il-Hyeong pinned; the fox pushed the ferret off of his chest, then kicked him in the stomach, sending him rolling. They both sprang back up into a crouched position, facing each other.

Il-Hyeong's DKR-7 was lying right by where Arkady had come up, and the ferret immediately grabbed it. The fox had started crawling over toward Ming-Jun, but he stopped as Arkady got to his feet, pointed the gun, and primed it.

Resting on one knee, Il-Hyeong slowly turned his head up to look at Arkady. The left side of the fox's face was speckled and smeared with blood from Arkady's mangled fingers, and his ears were folded back in a submissive posture. He flicked his eyes briefly over at where Ming-Jun lay, and then turned his gaze back to Arkady.

"Go ahead," the fox said. "Do it." His voice was devoid of any emotion, any real strength or passion at all.

"I should," Arkady replied. The harshness of his voice was cut by a wet sob that came out along with the words. He took a tiny step closer. "I really, really should." His arm wavered, and he bit his lower lip, hard, as he steadied his aim.

Incredible resistance and recuperative abilities aside, a bullet to the skull would probably still do the trick of putting the fox out of his misery.

Il-Hyeong was crying, too, Arkady then realized. It was a silent cry, one marked only by the faint glimmer of tears along the lower rims of his eyes. When Arkady narrowed his senses, he could tell that the fox was actually shivering, and trying his hardest to stop himself from doing so.

Arkady could smell Il-Hyeong now, too. Unlike when the fox had first emerged from hiding, his familiar scent was in the air, plain as day. Had he somehow been disguising himself before? Perhaps through some unprecedented level of body control akin to what Arkady had discovered earlier?

"Do it," Il-Hyeong demanded again, his voice louder this time. "It doesn't matter what happens to me. This is just a shell, remember?"

"Do you really believe that?" Arkady asked. "Do you really, honestly believe that?"

The fox lowered his head even further. "If it's true, then think about it. We're all together now. All four of us."

That Il-Hyeong could be so blasé about that in the face of having just killed his own friend and comrade made Arkady's trigger finger start to twitch. If Kuai deserved to die, then surely Il-Hyeong deserved the same, did he not? He'd shown nothing but a casual disregard for everything he'd ever believed in, violating the sanctity of the life of others as well as his own soul in some mad desire for... for what? Arkady didn't even know what the fox was after, anymore.

"Why?" the ferret asked after swallowing back another heavy sob. "Why did you kill her?"

"She jumped in front of you. It was an accident."

"After you'd already shot her multiple times?" Arkady snapped. "After you demanded she repent at gunpoint?" His aim started to falter as he spoke, but he quickly steadied it again. "After all this talk and nonsense about reuniting our souls in Heaven, you honestly expect me to believe that you hadn't been intending to kill her from the moment you came here?"

"Not if it wasn't necessary!" Il-Hyeong cried.

Arkady pointed his gun down and fired into the ground, right next to one of Il-Hyeong's paws. "Necessary?" God, why hadn't he just put that bullet in the fox's head? "Necessary? What in the name of God and everything we're supposed to hold dear would ever make that 'necessary?' What has your deluded mind thinking that *any* of this has been 'necessary?'"

"Because someone has to *act*," Il-Hyeong insisted. "And that someone obviously isn't going to be you."

"Why not?" Arkady asked. "Because I haven't lost my grip on reality like you have?"

"No," Il-Hyeong said. "Because you're afraid."

Afraid? "Afraid of what?"

"Ever since Kentian died," the fox said, once more looking Arkady right in the eye, "you've been afraid to make the tough decisions—shit, you've been afraid to make *any* decisions."

"You shut your goddamn mouth. You have *no* right to say that to me after everything you've done."

"But I've at least *done* it, haven't I?" Il-Hyeong said. "You've been so afraid of letting people get hurt, forgetting that hurting people is *what we do*. And now that Dr. Mayflower and the rest have absolved us of any wrongdoing that comes with that, you still insist on—"

Arkady took another step closer; his gun was less than a foot away from Il-Hyeong's head now. "You're still hung up on that. You've latched onto that for some reason and *God* knows why you have, but you're putting yourself beyond self-reproach so that you can justify doing whatever the hell you want and you haven't even left yourself open to the possibility that you're *wrong*."

"Pull the trigger, then," Il-Hyeong said. The blood had begun to dry and darken in the pale fur of his face. "If I'm wrong, then God will judge my soul as He will."

"You think I won't?" Arkady focused on the fox's scent, trying to smell even the tiniest hint of fear coming from him. He found none. "Ming-Jun is *dead*. She's dead because of you. She's dead because she wanted to protect me. From something she thought I needed protection against."

Il-Hyeong began to speak, but Arkady immediately cut him off. "She died to save me from *you*. Tell me who the real traitor is, here, Il-Hyeong."

"I told you," Il-Hyeong said. "I didn't do it on purpose. If Ming had had her priorities straight from the beginning, she never would have been in this situation."

The rage inside of Arkady swelled so hard that the outside of his vision began to blur. All he could see was Il-Hyeong, this wretch of a fox, broken and yet remorseless. Il-Hyeong Quinn, who had at one time been Arkady's most trusted friend and comrade, who had put his own life on the line in service to the Iolite League and to Project Scheherazade, who had been so devout and dedicated that he refused even to abandon a teammate who was already dead, now had the nerve—the gall to say that it was Ming-Jun's own fault that he'd tortured and killed her.

Maybe the fox was right about one thing. Maybe Il-Hyeong Quinn really was dead, and the creature that knelt before Arkady now was just some shell that was a barely-recognizable echo of the person he'd once been.

18. Aftermath

Six years ago, Arkady had come to Holygate on the trail of an agent for the Octavians. Unfortunately for that agent, he'd been a fennec, which made him easier to spot in a crowd. Coming to Ridgecrescent had been a good move on his part, too, since that put him beyond official legal reach of the Iolite League.

What the fennec hadn't known, of course, was that Arkady and Sahasrara were outside the official legal scope of the Iolite League, too.

This had all been before Kentian had joined the team. Il-Hyeong and Ming-Jun had, on Arkady's orders, remained back aboard the Afortunadan luxury liner that the three of them had infiltrated as part of their original mission. This had left Arkady alone on Ridgecrescent soil: more exposed and more vulnerable, but also more able to work quickly and covertly.

Arkady hadn't learned the fennec's name before he'd been forced to kill him. Despite having been cornered and offered the chance for a peaceful surrender, the Octavian agent had instead chosen one final act of defiance. Arkady had shot him dead before he'd even gotten his gun out of its holster.

That had taken place around this neighborhood here, in an alley off of Heliotrope Way. At the time, Arkady hadn't paid any attention to the street signs, having been more focused on the chase, and so he hadn't recognized the name when Ming-Jun had given it to him the other night at Dianjiang Gardens. Now that he'd come, though, he remembered this place clearly.

Things never did go well in Ridgecrescent, did they? *Always so much death. So much senseless killing.*

"Il-Hyeong." At the sound of the ferret's voice, the fox lifted his head back up.

Arkady looked into Il-Hyeong's eyes. After a few seconds, the fox merely nodded his head silently.

Ten years the fox and the ferret had served alongside each other. A full decade of striving, together, to build the better world.

No actual sound came out of Arkady's mouth when he mouthed the word "goodbye" to Il-Hyeong. He made sure that his gun was lined up right, so that it would be clean and quick.

Then, Arkady bit his lip and closed his eyes, unable to bring himself to look his friend in the eye as he finally pulled the trigger.

A mere two years after the end of the Butterfly Islands War, Arkady's killing of that Octavian agent had caused a minor international incident. Officially, however, the Octavians didn't exist, and so Ridgecrescent had little recourse it could take with the case. The fallout from it all ultimately culminated in Arkady being extradited back to Deepwater.

The Iolite League, of course, hadn't taken any punitive measures against him, and the Directorate Board had, in private, commended him for going above and beyond the call of duty to track down and neutralize the enemy.

What would they think of him when he got back from Ridgecrescent this time? *"You come back from Tomosabaki having lost a member of your team, and then, on your very next mission, you lose the rest of them?"* Would his career in Sahasrara even survive something like this?

Not that it mattered much. The Pyxis Sequence was gone, and Arkady was coming home with nothing to show for his spectacular failure. At this point, it might even be too much to hope that they'd let him see Pandora one final time—Pandora, who now might never wake up and see the world Arkady had wanted to create for her.

"If this all goes wrong, there's an antique shop on Heliotrope Way." That's what Ming-Jun had said.

Well, things had all certainly gone wrong. Whatever she'd meant, it wasn't as if Arkady could make anything worse by going to check it out.

After pulling the trigger, the slide slid back harmlessly. There was no gunshot. There was no bullet. There was no gory hole in Il-Hyeong's skull.

Arkady dropped the DKR-7 to the ground and kicked it into the greenery in frustration.

"What now?" Il-Hyeong asked. "Do you strangle me to death with your bare paws?"

"Somehow I doubt that would kill you," Arkady said. "Though it might give me a sense of satisfaction."

Silence hung in the air between them. It was an awkward moment.

❁

"Times Gone By." That was the name of the antique shop. *Quaint*, Arkady thought as he put his paw on the handle and pushed his way inside.

The midmorning sun shone through the storefront windows, providing the only illumination inside. Motes of dust swirled through the air as the ferret took a step inside and looked around. The musty smell of old belongings that had passed through the paws of so many different owners over decades and centuries created quite the stale, unpleasant potpourri for an artificially-enhanced nose.

Most of the items on display were unremarkable. Project Scheherazade had amassed a trove of real artifacts, and by comparison, the wares of this antique shop—while admittedly cute or pretty—were mere knickknacks. There were quite a number of faded statuettes, and things like picture frames, candlesticks and other ornaments crafted from precious metals that were no longer practical to work with nowadays. Hand-drawn price tags hung from most of the items, the majority citing three- and four-digit prices in Ridgecrescent dees.

Now that Arkady had taken several steps further inside, he could smell, from further back inside the shop, the scent of a male shrew that he assumed had to be the owner. Angling his ears and focusing his hearing, the ferret could then hear the quiet rummaging coming from the back room.

Arkady lazily fingered a small tapestry that hung between two carved wooden posts that he recognized as being of Aléu make, from the Butterfly Islands. The woven scene depicted a group of crudely-drawn felines engaged in some type of dance or ritual. For something like this to end up in Ridgecrescent made it quite the find indeed. A quick glance at the price tag reaffirmed that.

There was a scurrying of short footsteps, and then a nice, eager, "Can I help you?" as the shrew emerged from the back. He was a short fellow, pushing fifty and wearing large glasses.

Could he help Arkady? Why had Ming-Jun even wanted him to come here in the first place? "I'm just looking for now, thanks."

"Well, let me know if you have any questions. I'd be glad to tell you all about anything we have here."

"What now, then?" Il-Hyeong asked. "I know you're not going to just let me go."

"You should be brought before the Directorate Board," Arkady pointed out. "But I don't believe for a second that you'd come quietly."

The fox let out a truncated, one-note laugh. "And give myself over to be executed?" he said. "No, Arkady, I wouldn't dare take that privilege away from you, my friend."

"The thought of trying to strangle you is starting to sound pretty appealing again."

"At least you'd be enjoying something," Il-Hyeong said. "And at least you'd be doing it yourself."

Arkady tightened his good paw into a fist, digging his claws into his palm out of frustration. "Why are you treating this all like it's just some kind of game?" he asked. "Is that really all this is to you?"

A thin, toothy smirk formed on the fox's snout. "We've all been pawns in this, Arkady," he said. "To Sahasrara, to Ajna—to Kuai and his Order. If that's not a game, then what is?"

In a sick and very twisted sense, Il-Hyeong's delusional belief that he had no soul started to make some small modicum of sense: if you were trapped in a game you couldn't win fairly, why not find a way to change—or break—the rules?

"You do realize that you're still insane, right?" Arkady said bluntly.

"If that's how you want to see it, then that just proves that you're still in denial."

The shrew shopkeeper finally noticed Arkady's bandaged stump, biting back an initial gasp of shock at the sight. The ferret had planned on getting himself to a hospital, but by the time he'd recuperated from the encounter on the rooftop, a fleshy, protective layer had somehow grown over the wrecked nubs where his fingers had once been attached. Presumably, Dr. Mayflower would be able to tell him more, once he got back. In the meantime, he at least had partial use of his thumb and forefinger, the broken bones having knit considerably overnight.

If the shopkeeper was disturbed by what he'd seen, he immediately turned right back to politeness. "By all means, if you need help looking at anything, I'd be more than happy to assist."

"I'll be fine, thanks." Arkady didn't want to be curt, but he was running out of ideas as to why he was even supposed to be here, and he wasn't even sure how much longer it would be wise to stall for time.

Why an antique shop? Why *this* antique shop? Did it have to do with the shopkeeper himself? Or was it, as Il-Hyeong probably would have said, another elaborate ruse on Ming-Jun's part to throw Arkady off of her traitorous scent?

That's when Arkady saw it.

In one of the back corners, on the wall over by the till, hung the sword that Ming-Jun had brought with her to Highslope—the one that had gone missing after the apartment had been abandoned. Arkady strode up to it, peering at it closely. Part of him wanted to be sure that it was, in fact, the same sword, while he knew at the same time that there was no way it could be anything else.

The shrew clapped his paws together. "Ah, the Kyunjiu broadsword," he said proudly. "You have a very good eye."

Arkady turned his head and looked back at him. "Don't you mean Quanyao broadsword?" he asked.

At once, the shrew's eyes narrowed. He reached up, readjusted his glasses, and licked his teeth once. "A very good eye indeed," he replied, much more quietly.

"You're weak. You're weak, and I'm not even sure how."

"Why?" Arkady asked. "Because I'm not inclined to kill everyone who might be an inconvenience, up to and including my friends?"

Il-Hyeong's upper lip pulled back. "Because you're supposed to be a weapon," he said. "You and I, weapons who work in tandem."

"Weapons," Arkady said flatly. "Weapons for what?" Why was he even bothering to listen to what the fox had to say anymore?

"Instruments of divine retribution," Il-Hyeong said. "Weapons for God Himself, to carry out His will in ways that His other subjects cannot."

With a sudden surge of anger, Arkady lifted his foot up and delivered a sharp kick to the kneeling fox's chest. He felt ribs crack as the fox let out a yap of pain. "And who gave you that idea?" the ferret demanded. "What makes you think that God needs weapons?"

Rasping for breath, Il-Hyeong looked up as he put one paw tenderly to his chest. "And just what is Sahasrara called, again?" he sneered. "'The sword of the Iolite League.' Of course God needs weapons. God needs all sorts of instruments of His will down here to carry out His divine plan. That's why the Iolite League exists!"

"Yes," Arkady said. "To create the better world, not... not some place where people can just do whatever they feel like and claim it's an extension of what God wanted!"

The fox winced as he laughed. "Of course not," he agreed. "Not everyone. Just people like you and me. And Pandora."

"You leave her out of this."

"But she's so key to the plan," Il-Hyeong said. "I thought that's why you were so upset about all this in the first place."

"I assure you that it is authentic," the shrew said, standing next to Arkady as the two of them looked at the sword. The shopkeeper seemed to be showing it attention that was nothing short of admiration. "Did you have any questions?"

"One or two," Arkady said. The trick was picking the right questions to ask. He needed to tip his hand just enough to discover what Ming-Jun had wanted him to discover. After all, she'd planned for this contingency in the event of her not making it out alive; whatever it was had to be of critical importance, at least to her.

He needed something that made his intentions unmistakable, yet which was also as innocuous as possible. Mentioning Ming-Jun was probably *too* direct. Making any open connection to involvement with the Carmine Order was likewise a bad idea, Arkady guessed. Ming-Jun wouldn't have sent him here without reason, though. After all, this was her backup plan—her final direction to Arkady in the event that the worst came to pass, which it certainly had.

There was really only one thing of true significance that Ming-Jun had left in Arkady's care. She'd entrusted him with one crucial thing that still played a role, even in the aftermath of last night's fateful confrontation.

"Could you tell me what '*yī qī yī huì*' means?" Arkady asked.

The shrew's face showed surprise that Arkady guessed was feigned. "Perhaps we should talk more in back, sir," the storekeeper said as he padded toward the front door, locking it and turning the sign from 'Open' to 'Closed.' "Come, sir," he added as he walked past Arkady again on his way into the back room.

Arkady half-expected the back office to be decorated with the same exotic stylings of Kuai's inner sanctum at Dianjiang Gardens, but in reality, it looked like any other office one would find in a small, hole-in-the-wall shop, complete with the out-of-date computer and notices tacked to the wall that looked like they'd been there for years. It was organized, though, and judging from the large stacks of paperwork, Arkady could tell that this fellow had ample documentation for the unique items he sold.

"Sit," the shrew said, pointing to the rickety, metal-and-plastic chair in the corner as he sat himself in his own much nicer office chair. "Get comfortable. I would offer you coffee, but I'm afraid it's been sitting there for several hours." He pointed with his muzzle to the coffee maker nestled against the wall. Arkady's sense of smell told him that, even before the coffee had cooled and partially congealed, it hadn't been of the greatest quality.

"I appreciate your taking the time to answer my questions," Arkady said. "I'm sure your time is very valuable."

The shrew smiled. "I can make time for this," he said. "So, '*yī qī yī huì*' you say? That is... an interesting thing to ask."

"I'm an interested party," Arkady said.

"Clearly," the shrew replied. "This is a difficult phrase to properly render in typical Language. The simplest way to put it would be 'once in a lifetime,' though this doesn't give the deeper meaning justice."

"She's not a weapon," Arkady snapped. His claws felt like they might actually draw blood from his palm. "That's not what this had been about."

"Hasn't it?" Il-Hyeong asked. "If she was originally designed as a project for Ajna, how could she be anything else?"

Arkady shook his head. "No," he said. "She's based on my genetic code. Her part in Project Scheherazade has always been under Dr. Mayflower's direction, for Sahasrara."

"You heard Dr. Lederle," the fox said. "This all started with his Project Semiramis."

"Then the direction of the project changed," the ferret insisted. "Obviously. Why else would it had been moved from Ajna to Sahasrara?"

"If you're not going to do me the favor of putting me out of my misery," Il-Hyeong said, "could you at least put more effort into connecting the dots yourself instead of making me draw all the lines for you?"

Arkady dove onto Il-Hyeong, tackling him to the floor. The fox put up no defense, fully allowing the ferret to get him onto his back. He ended up with Arkady astride his abdomen, the ferret's good left paw right at his throat, claws over the pulse point.

"If you're trying to goad me," Arkady growled, flexing his fingers, "it's working. So unless you really do have a death wish, I'd suggest you talk real quick and try real hard to make me understand why I should bother to leave you alive."

"You probably shouldn't bother," the fox said, closing his eyes. "But I'll humor you."

"It's a very old saying—ancient, even," the shrew explained. "It has its roots in old religion and philosophy, and to fully understand the phrase itself requires knowledge of other such things." He adjusted his glasses and regarded Arkady carefully. "More important than multiple layers of meaning, though, is how you know these words in the first place, yes?"

Arkady rubbed his right wrist with his left paw. His bandaged stump was starting to itch under its coverings. "I learned them from a friend," he said. "Though I suspect that she had a deeper meaning of her own in mind."

The shrew let out a jolly chuckle that surprised Arkady. "Perhaps she did. Or perhaps you're overthinking things a bit too much."

"I'm not sure I follow."

Chuckling again, the shrew leaned back in his chair and brought one leg up across his other knee. "This isn't magic and mysticism," he said. "You recognized a Quanyao broadsword, and you have words in another language that you don't understand. You're here because you need to know something, and I've already brought you out back here so that we can talk privately about it."

Arkady bit his lip. That'd teach him to get caught up in the moment. "You're not bound by some sacred code to keep this knowledge of yours secret?" he asked.

"Oh, no," the shrew said. "I most assuredly am. Though I'm not sure 'sacred' is the word I'd use." Setting both feet down on the floor, he leaned forward again. "Still, I've... let's just say I've been given reason to trust you, and leave it at that, yes?"

"Fine by me," Arkady replied. "You'll help me out, then?"

"What do you need to know?"

The ferret sighed. He knew what information he needed, but asking for it wasn't going to be a happy experience in the slightest. "I've got a message," he explained. "You might want to get something to write with."

Reaching into the pile of clutter atop the desk, the shrew procured a pen without much rummaging at all. "Let's hear it," he said, sliding a sheet of paper over in front of himself.

Arkady closed his eyes and accessed the memory module. He could retrieve the full content of Ming-Jun's final message, but that was going to require reliving those last few terrible moments up in the conservatory. It wasn't as if he had much of a choice, though.

"*Zài zhuāngyuán lǐ miàn,*" he began, mimicking Ming-Jun's tones as he watched the events play out before his minds eye all over again, "*wǒ fángjiān de shūguì shàng yǒu gè zhōng...*"

"Even if you don't want her to be used as a weapon," Il-Hyeong said, "even you have to admire the brilliance of what the Iolite League has accomplished."

Arkady didn't move his claws an inch. If Il-Hyeong made one false move, if he said the wrong thing, the ferret wasn't going to hesitate to rip his throat out. Being shot in the abdomen was one thing; having the carotid and the jugular both severed was probably another thing entirely.

"Yes, it is brilliant," the ferret said. "We have someone who will be able to act as a supercomputer with inspiration and imagination, in order to take the stories we tell her and make sense of them, to recapture what our world lost millennia ago."

"What we have," Il-Hyeong countered, "is a prototype unit. Beginning with her, the League will be able to construct a complete elite force of nigh-invulnerable loyal followers that have perfect reflexes, enhanced senses, who are capable of being programmed with all sorts of data, and who don't have souls to sully in their cause to bring about the greater good."

Arkady's fingers tightened around Il-Hyeong's throat. "That's not what she was made for."

"Then why apply all that biotechnology to people like you and me, Arkady? We're just the beginning. We were the field test. And we succeeded."

"You're the biggest failure in League history," Arkady snarled. "You were a brilliant and devoted soldier of peace and justice. Losing you from our ranks is worse than ten Butterfly Islands Wars."

"If you think I'm that capable," Il-Hyeong said, "then think of what Pandora will be able to do. Think of the perfection *she'll represent." A smile formed on his straining muzzle.*

Blood dripped from Arkady's bitten lip, and saliva froth fell from his tongue as he stammered out his words. "She'll be better than you could ever be. She can at least be programmed with the ability to tell right from wrong." To tell logic from insanity.

"If you're really upset by the notion of your 'daughter' being turned into a weapon like us, then by all means, go ahead and kill me," Il-Hyeong said. A narrow smile appeared on his muzzle. "Kill me, and

the Pyxis Sequence is gone forever, and you'll never have to worry about anyone misusing that soulless little girl in her tube."

If that was Il-Hyeong's attempt to snidely appeal to Arkady's sense of morality, then the fox had just made a fatal mistake. Arkady would not be mocked. He would not give in to a threat on Pandora's life and existence.

The ferret started to squeeze around Il-Hyeong's throat, and his claws, blunt through they were, started to pierce through the tender flesh beneath that layer of bristly, dusty-colored fur.

Even the skies above the Deepwater Archipelago looked like something out of some long-forgotten past life when Arkady had finally landed in Stewart. The towering skyscrapers of Ridgecrescent were nowhere to be seen. As far as the eye could see, there was nothing but ocean, idyllic landscape, and—barely visible on that tiny island to the west—the silhouette of Château Sainte-Mireille.

The sun hadn't even set when Arkady had ventured back down beneath the Château. The doors with the thousand-petaled lotus parted for him as easily as they ever had, but his reception had not been a warm one, despite the trials he had been through in trying to scrape his way back home alive. Dr. Mayflower had been pointedly silent as the ferret strode past the Hephaestus Chamber without stopping as he made his way to see the Directorate Board.

And now the ferret stood rather than sat in front of the Board, in full dress uniform. The eyes of badger, weasel, and gray fox drilled him with silent yet intense scrutiny. The scene looked less like a debriefing and more like a sentencing—though an actual sentencing, if it were necessary, would not come until later. For now, all Arkady could do was listen, and speak when spoken to.

"Your report so far does not speak well for you, Agent Ryswife," the badger said. "You have returned from Ridgecrescent not only having failed to obtain the Pyxis Sequence, but also having lost your entire team."

"I realize that, sir," Arkady said.

"And this having come right off the heels of your losing Agent McEvoy on your previous mission to Tomosabaki."

"I realize that as well, sir."

The three members of the Board exchanged glances. Given what Iolite League science had done to Arkady himself, the ferret almost wouldn't have been surprised if the doctors somehow *had* given the

Directorate Board the ability to communicate with each other via telepathic powers.

The weasel spoke up next. "Were your identity or the identities of your teammates discovered at any point, either before or after death?"

"Not to my knowledge, sir," Arkady lied. "We took precautions to maintain the false identities we had provided with for the mission."

The gray fox cut in. "An entire team of Sahasrara agents," he said with exasperation. "Top-level Sahasrara agents, all lost in the line of duty under your command." His shadowy form leaned ever-so-slightly forward. "Tell us, Agent Ryswife, why the Board should not just immediately cast you out based on your own admitted incompetence?"

Arkady kept his head up and his shoulders level. "I can think of no good reason, sir," he replied. "The facts remain as I have stated them."

There was a quick warning look from the badger to the fox, and then the badger turned to Arkady again. "The Board's final decision having yet to be made," he said, "we would ask that you clarify some of the points in your report."

"Of course, sir."

"You mentioned that Agent Devra was killed during the skirmish with this Kuai and his followers," the badger continued. "What was she doing out in the field with you at that point?"

Arkady felt his anger beginning to resurface, but he forced it back down. "She was backup, sir," he said. "Since Jiangzhao Kuai had demonstrated an intimate knowledge of the Pyxis Sequence at that point, I thought it best to have all active agents on hand to deal with any potential trouble."

"Despite the fact that Agent Devra had not undergone the same augmentation that Agent Quinn and yourself had?" the weasel asked.

"She had always been capable and competent in combat situations before, sir. I saw no reason to doubt her abilities in this instance."

The gray fox repeatedly tapped an alternating pair of his claws on the table. "And yet you appear to have underestimated the abilities of your opponents all the same," he said. "Or you overestimated those of Agent Devra."

"With all due respect, sir, I don't believe either of those to be the case."

"Your opinions aside, Agent Ryswife, these people still managed to kill her," the fox said. He was keeping the sneer out of his voice, now, probably because of the careful looks from the other two Board members.

Arkady kept his head straight. "That's incorrect, sir."

"I bet your pardon, Agent Ryswife?"

"Agent Devra was killed by Agent Quinn, sir."

If the Directorate Board was ever moved to sudden outbursts, then this counted as one. All three men stiffened where they sat, and this time they actively murmured instead of merely glancing at one another with significant looks on their faces. Arkady could have eavesdropped without any problem, but nothing they could have to say concerned him enough for him to bother.

"Killed by Agent Quinn, you say?" the weasel asked.

"That's correct, sir," Arkady replied. "Though I have no reason to suspect that shooting was anything but accidental, sir."

"And why wasn't this reported before?" the gray fox demanded. His claws gripped the far edge of the table as he leaned further over it.

"I noted truthfully in my report that Agent Devra had been killed in the skirmish between Sahasrara agents and Ridgecrest gang members. I felt that the specifics were of a nature sensitive enough such as to warrant only disclosing them in person, sir."

Even without advanced hearing, Arkady would have heard the fox's angry growl at his response. "And are there any other key 'specifics' you'd care to mention regarding the death of Agent Quinn, as well?"

"Agent Quinn isn't dead, sir."

"What?" the gray fox gasped. "It says in your report—"

Arkady had no qualms about interrupting. "It says in my report that Agent Quinn was lost in the skirmish," he said. "I never reported him deceased."

Rings of blood started to appear in the fur of Il-Hyeong's throat, circling Arkady's claws as they dug their way in.

This would be it, Arkady told himself. This would be his way of stopping the unconscionable monster Il-Hyeong had become. Reason had not worked. Pleading had not worked. Threats had not worked. What other recourse was there but this?

Il-Hyeong still did not resist. His breath seized in his throat as Arkady gripped, but he seemed willing to allow it to happen. If this was all doing Il-Hyeong a favor, more was the better to assuage any guilt Arkady might have otherwise.

But then, as he was grinding his teeth while preparing to tighten his grip even further, Arkady saw something that he hadn't seen before, not even when he'd been holding his gun to Il-Hyeong's head.

For the briefest of moments, in between struggled attempts to draw breath, Il-Hyeong's eyes showed a flash of sorrow—true sorrow, the likes of which Arkady hadn't seen since Kentian had died.

Sorrow. Perhaps it was sorrow that things had turned out the way they did. Maybe it was sorrow over the wrongs he knew full well he'd willingly committed. Or maybe it was sorrow that life had brought him to this point, to be killed by someone who had been his best friend.

Arkady relaxed his grip, then took his paw away entirely. The bleeding from Il-Hyeong's throat stopped almost immediately thereafter; the ferret's claws hadn't cut that deep, and the fox's augmented physiology would see to the rest in short order.

When Arkady staggered to his feet, Il-Hyeong remained on the stony pathway, looking up at the ferret in disbelief. Perhaps, then, he hadn't fully made his peace with God after all.

"Come on," Arkady said, motioning with his good paw. "Get up."

Il-Hyeong got first to his knees, then stopped. "What're you doing?" he asked.

"Just get up."

The fox hesitated, but then rose to his feet on his own. He rubbed at his neck and throat and took a few breaths, as if checking to make sure that everything was working properly. "Okay," he then said, looking down at himself. "Now I'm up. Now tell me what you're doing."

"I'm only going to offer you this once," Arkady said. "Come back to Château Sainte-Mireille with me. Appear before the Directorate Board."

Il-Hyeong rolled his eyes and shook his head. "Or what?" he said. "Or you'll try to kill me a third time?"

Arkady heard something in the fox's voice that he couldn't quite define. "You knew your gun was out of bullets, didn't you?" The ferret sighed and shook his head. "Just wanted to see whether I'd really do it, did you?"

"You did," Il-Hyeong said. "It's not my fault you didn't account for my clip not being full when I got here."

"I'm not going to kill you."

"Fine. I'm not going back to Château Sainte-Mireille."

"As you wish," Arkady said. He dipped his head in a shallow, barely-polite bow. "Farewell, Il-Hyeong." With that, he turned to leave.

Il-Hyeong took a step after him, then stopped short before calling out. "Wait!" Arkady turned back to look at him. "What are you doing?"

"I'm leaving," Arkady said. "I'm going to figure out a way to clean up this mess—" He tried to avoid looking at Ming-Jun's body. "—and then I'm going to go home."

"What, and just leave me here?"

"Well, it would probably be better for you if you weren't specifically 'here' when the authorities show up," Arkady said.

"And just what do you expect me to do?"

Arkady flashed the fox the hint of a humorless grin. "You're a secret agent. You'll figure something out."

Il-Hyeong snarled. "That's not what I meant," he said. "I mean... you're just going to let me go?"

"Since you're not coming back with me, yes," Arkady said. "But I'm going to tell the Iolite League what you did and what happened to you."

"So, no forgiveness after all, then?" The fox scuffed his toes on one of the stones underfoot. "Just too afraid to do the deed yourself, are you?"

The ferret shook his head. "You can probably outrun the Iolite League; I don't doubt that for a second," he said. "But you can never get away from what you've done here." He took another step closer to the fox. "And you're going to prove yourself wrong for me."

Il-Hyeong kept still. "What's that supposed to mean?"

"That you're not just some soulless machine who does God's dirty work," Arkady said. "The Il-Hyeong Quinn I've known is a good person, one who is honestly devoted to the ideals of a better society, of a better world to live in. So, yes, I'm letting you go, and I'm going to let you live out your own penance."

"And what?" the fox asked. "And just wait for me to redeem myself by turning over a new leaf?"

"Maybe it'll be something like that. Maybe you'll come around. Maybe you'll just go away and fade into obscurity, going into pious seclusion."

"And maybe I'll prove you wrong," Il-Hyeong said.

Arkady smiled again, and he once more saw that brief glimmer of Il-Hyeong's old self in the fox's eyes. "Maybe you will," the ferret agreed. "But if you do, then I will come back and find you, and I will kill you myself." With that, he turned away from the fox and started to walk toward the elevators. "And that, my old friend, is a promise."

"Agent Ryswife, this is unacceptable," the weasel said.

"As I said," Arkady replied, "I believe that Agent Devra's death was entirely accidental, and I believe that Agent Quinn's actions were the result of some kind of psychological disturbance resulting from an unexpected side-effect of the augmentation procedure he underwent before the mission, sir."

The weasel shook his head. "You are not qualified to diagnose your fellow agent's mental state," he said. "Moreover, any such issues and related steps of action would be for Dr. Mayflower to determine."

Arkady kept his head up. "Be that as it may, sir, at the time, we were in the field, and had no contact with any Sahasrara authorities," he said. "As the team leader, I took it upon myself to make a situational decision."

"And you overstepped your authority on that point, Agent Ryswife," the gray fox said. "Il-Hyeong Quinn has shown disloyalty to both Sahasrara and the League itself, and you have allowed him to remain at large, with vital knowledge of internal secrets, to say nothing of the fact that he has been outfitted with top-secret, military-grade biotechnology and is demonstrably dangerous."

"If I did exceed my authority, sir, then it is of course up to the Directorate Board to reprimand me as appropriate."

The gray fox seethed, clenching both his paws into fists. Then he sank back into his chair, clearly putting effort into keeping his cool. As he tried to relax, the badger spoke up in his stead. "The Board will decide any such punishment at a later time, Agent Ryswife," he said. "In the meantime, the simple fact of the matter is that our operation has been heavily compromised, and you are, at least in part, directly responsible for that."

"Perhaps not intentionally," the weasel hastened to add. "Which will also be taken under consideration."

"I am certain that the Board's wisdom will prevail," Arkady said, and only then did he finally bow his head in deference.

The gray fox leaned forward again. "You are dismissed, Agent Ryswife," he said. "The Board will take your report and testimony under advisement and render a decision in due time. Until such time, you are not to leave Château Sainte-Mireille."

"Understood, sir," Arkady said. "Sirs," he then added, bowing to the other Board members before turning to leave the chamber and return upstairs.

It was the third time in as many days that Arkady had been to see Dr. Mayflower for his current run of treatment sessions. Each lasted a full ninety minutes, which wouldn't have been so bad if Dr. Mayflower herself had stuck around to talk, but for the first two days, the kangaroo had found some too-convenient excuse to make herself scarce.

The real reason for her evasiveness was clear: she had a better idea than Arkady did about the fate of Project Scheherazade, and spending a prolonged period of time in the presence of someone she herself had helped make into a master of subtle senses would make it difficult for her to keep up a wall of feigned ignorance. Arkady didn't blame or even resent her for that. After all, from her position, how was she supposed to know how fragile or easily-upset Arkady might be after everything else had transpired?

On the plus side, after just two days, the fingers on Arkady's right paw had already almost completely regrown, now missing only the tips and claws. Today would likely be the last day of the main treatment, with a follow-up period of physical therapy to reestablish the strength and coordination of those repaired digits.

"Nanomachines," Dr. Mayflower had explained on the first day. "Your body is full of them, now. They're what's responsible for the accelerated healing you said you noticed." As she switched on the healing tube that had repaired so many of Arkady's broken bones in the past, she further explained, "With proper stimulation, the healing process can achieve truly remarkable things."

Arkady hadn't asked why he, Il-Hyeong and Kentian had never been informed of this infusion of nanomachines. He surmised that they were what allowed the body to survive and recover from the extensive augmentation surgery in the first place, which meant that the entire adaptation process had probably gone on longer than any of them had been aware. Chalk that up to another instance of the higher-ups not being on the level with their underlings.

Today, though, on the third day, Dr. Mayflower hadn't invented some reason to slip out during the treatment run. She wasn't particularly chatty, but she at least stuck around. Arkady waited a good five minutes before breaking the silence.

"It's okay," he said, causing her to immediately look up from the charts she was going over. "They told me this morning."

Mayflower took off her glasses and wiped them with her sleeve as she sighed. "I was wondering," she admitted. Setting her glasses back atop her snout, she came closer to Arkady. "How are you taking it?"

"They're at least letting me stay at the Château if I want to," the ferret said. "Though I'm not sure how long I'll stick around."

The kangaroo was visibly nervous around Arkady, and though she met his gaze, it felt more like she was only doing it because she was too afraid not to. "They told me that they were going to offer you a choice," she said. "Did they?"

"They did," Arkady replied. Inasmuch as one could call it a 'choice.' "I'm out on my own terms, though. That's how I think of it."

The Directorate Board had summoned him back that morning to render their decision. They'd informed him that Project Scheherazade was to be put on hold indefinitely, which had come as no real surprise. Next, they informed him that he could return to active duty within Sahasrara as soon as Dr. Mayflower had cleared him, so long as he was willing to undertake the next mission they planned to assign him.

The mission specifics were to track down and eliminate former-Agent Il-Hyeong Quinn. Arkady had refused.

"If you do leave," Mayflower said as she made some adjustments to the healing tube's inputs, "it'll be strange not having you around."

"Well, it wouldn't be forever," Arkady said. The Board had said that he was 'to be suspended from active duty until further notice,' which carried with it the undercurrent that said notice wouldn't be coming anytime soon, if ever. "There are still people here that I'd miss."

Finalizing her adjustments, Mayflower looked silently at Arkady for a few seconds, gnawing her lower lip with her blunt upper teeth. "We're not going to give up on Pandora, Arkady," she said. "It might take years to catch up on all the research we lost, but we've come too far to just throw away everything we've done."

Arkady leaned back into a more comfortable position. "Speaking of which, I actually had a question about that."

The kangaroo set a paw on the ferret's shoulder. "Of course," she said, her fingers squeezing reassuringly.

"Is Ajna going to be informed of Ming-Jun's death?"

The fingers on Arkady's shoulder immediately loosened and came away. "Ajna?" Mayflower said, making an admirable attempt at feigning honest confusion. "What does Ajna have to do with—"

"What does Ajna have to do with Ming-Jun and her involvement with Project Semiramis?" Arkady asked. "I'm going to have to assume a pretty close relationship there, seeing as she knew enough to get in touch with Dr. Lederle in her attempts to keep him safe."

The kangaroo took a full step backwards. "Arkady," she said nervously. "Please, it's not what you—"

"Oh, I'm not asking you to explain yourself, doctor," the ferret insisted. "I just wanted to say that it would have been nice to know, from the beginning, that we had a contact on the inside the whole time. It might have saved us a lot of trouble and probably some needless bloodshed, as well."

"Look," Mayflower said. "That's not my fault. The Directorate Board—"

"—had its reasons, I'm sure," Arkady finished. "And honestly, I don't care about that. Whatever might have gone down in the transition from Project Semiramis to Scheherazade no longer concerns me, after all." He leaned closer to Mayflower, then, as much as the immobilizing tube would allow. "What I do want to say is this:

"Ming-Jun is dead because she took a bullet for me. Two bullets, even. And I'm going to guess that she wouldn't have done something so foolishly noble if you'd told us ahead of time that Il-Hyeong and I were bulletproof."

The kangaroo opened and closed her snout. Her tongue clicked around inside her mouth with a quiet, spittle-laden sound.

"I just thought you should know that," Arkady said in closing.

Mayflower picked up a chart from her lab bench and hastily flipped to a random page. "I... The healing treatment should be set to go as-is, Arkady," she said. She shot a glance to the clock on the wall. "Give it another hour or so. If I'm not back, the equipment will turn off automatically."

She then did herself the favor of seeing her own way out, leaving Arkady to himself. The ferret watched the door close behind her, and then he just closed his eyes, leaned his head back, and waited.

It brought a smile to Arkady's face when the ferret thought about the irony that the Iolite League had given him the very means by which to go behind their backs so effectively. Already, the old halls of the Château carried sound well, which in Arkady's case meant that he could tell that someone was coming long before they stepped into view. Also, he could smell how recently certain individuals had passed through, giving him a better idea on when they would—or wouldn't—be likely to return.

His regrown fingers were at last whole again. They weren't very strong, but they gave him enough manual dexterity to work his lock pick (another thing the Iolite League itself had given him). It took him a matter of mere seconds to jimmy the lock open, and he pushed his way in past the door before closing it as silently as he could manage.

Once inside, he drew a relieved breath, and his nose was filled with Ming-Jun's scent. For a moment, the ferret allowed himself to bask in nonspecific, bittersweet memory, and then he cleared his head. Ming-Jun's scent was by far the strongest in here; as Arkady had hoped, no one had been in yet to see to her things.

He was sure that no one had seen him come inside. Hell, he was as sure as he could be that no one had even seen him leave his own room. *"The League will be watching you always, Mr. Ryswife,"* the gray fox on the Directorate Board had warned. Arkady believed the threat, too, but so long as he was here within the Château's own walls, he doubted they would be too concerned.

Now that he was inside, though, Arkady wanted to move quickly, in the event that, out of sheer, dumb luck, someone would choose now to swing by and finally take stock of Agent Devra's personal effects. Closing his eyes, the ferret then accessed his memory module and called up the translation he'd gotten from the shrew at the antique shop.

"Back at the Château, in my bedchamber," Ming-Jun had begun as she stared at Il-Hyeong's gun. Well, here Arkady was.

"On the top shelf of my bookcase, there's a pendulum clock." Arkady found both the bookcase and the clock in question. He'd seen it before, and thought as much of it then as anyone else might now: that it was a pretty if otherwise unremarkable piece of craftsmanship.

The ferret leaned up and plucked the clock from the shelf. It weighed a few pounds, and as its balance was ruined, the pendulum started to lose proper sway. *"Open up the panel in the back."*

Arkady did so. *"Inside, there are two books."* He reached inside and pulled out the first one. *"The red one is yours to keep."*

It was a small, thick volume, its edges quite frayed and yellowed. The cover was a faded red, on which was printed the title: *A Beginner's Guide to Contemporary Zhōngwén (New Revised Mandarin)*.

Arkady flipped through the pages, seeing a detailed mixture of writing as he knew it alongside the complex symbols of this other language. Before he could lose himself amidst those pages, he stuffed the book into his back pocket and looked back inside the clock.

"The other book has a name and an address written on the inside cover." There, tucked against the innards of the clock, was a slimmer volume, its pages far less brittle and aged. Opening to a random page, Arkady saw that the contents were handwritten, in Zhōngwén, penned with crisp, tidy strokes.

"I need you to get it to him, and he'll know—Arkady, look out!"

The ferret winced as his brain called up the mental flash of the visual memory that came with Ming-Jun's final words. The image went away as soon as it had come, though, and after shaking his head clear, he found the name and address Ming-Jun had mentioned.

Sliding the small, handwritten book into his pocket alongside the first, Arkady closed the clock and set it back into place atop the bookshelf. He'd see that Ming-Jun's last wishes were carried out, no matter where that road might take him.

"You don't have to worry," the shrew said as he handed the translation over to Arkady. "I promise that no one else will hear of this."

"I appreciate that," Arkady replied. He had his doubts as to whether that was true, but it wasn't like he had much of a choice. Il-Hyeong would ensure that the goodly shopkeeper never said another word to another living soul, of course, but Arkady was willing to take his chances.

The shrew started to lead Arkady out, but as he passed by the register, he stopped. "Here," he said as he reached up and took the Quanyao broadsword down off of the wall. "Let me pack this up for you, too."

Arkady stopped, stunned. "Oh, no, no," he said. "I... I couldn't, really. That must be worth a fortune."

"Not everyone has eyes quite as keen as yours," the shrew chuckled as he carefully got the blade boxed up. "Besides, this is more yours than it is mine, anyhow. I'm sure the young lady would want you to have it."

The ferret swallowed a lump in his throat. "At least let me pay you for it," he said.

Without looking up as he got the bundle ready, the shrew said, "I won't hear it. Besides, I wasn't expecting to ever sell this, anyway."

Arkady held his breath and nodded. "Very well," he said. "Thank you."

Just a few minutes later, the Quanyao broadsword was safely boxed up. "Here you are," the shrew said as he handed it over. "It's been a pleasure helping you today, sir ferret."

"Again, thank you," Arkady said, bowing as he accepted the sword. Not knowing what else to say without sounding awkward, he merely took his package and started to leave.

As he got to the door, he stopped and looked back at the shopkeeper. "One more question, actually," he asked. "What does 'wǒ de péng yǒu' mean?"

The shrew dusted off the spot on the wall where the sword had hung. "That means 'my friend.'"

19. Jurisdiction

News agencies all over the world had already decided on a name for it: the Sajeong Massacre. For days, now, the Consulate Guard had been engaged in open warfare in the city streets, attempting to quell an armed insurrection. There was no clear end to the fighting in sight, despite the fact that the government's forces were—as the news outlets were so quick and eager to point out—overpowering the resistance movement by a clear and overwhelming degree.

Proconsul Nwabudike crossed his arms together behind his back as he watched the violence taking place in the streets, not from the window of his state office, but via the large monitor screen that took up one whole wall of the board room. The fat raccoon hummed in thought as one news reel switched over to another, bearing a sensationalist headline in bold, blocky, red text: *BLOOD IN THE STREETS OF JUNG SIM WEON*.

"You see, Mr. Hamilton, what I have to put up with," the Proconsul said without turning around. "One can hardly curry favor with the rest of the world when the media biases the world so."

"That is always the trick, isn't it, Proconsul?" Arkady said. "But then, I take it that's why you've asked me here."

Nwabudike turned around and adjusted the badge of office that hung from his breast. He'd come to today's meeting wearing a stripped-down version of full regalia, as if he didn't want to seem "too" official while still obviously dressing to impress. He filled out his uniform generously, Arkady noted—a fact that file photos of the Proconsul were so often framed to avoid showing.

"I think we're both in the same business, you and I," the Proconsul said as he strode alongside the boardroom table, opposite Arkady, gingerly stroking the edge with one paw as he traveled its length. "Or, rather, we're in position to balance each other's end of the equation, as I believe they say."

Arkady didn't know who the 'they' in this situation referred to, nor had he heard anyone use that turn of phrase before. Still, it behooved him to humor the raccoon. "They do indeed," he said. "And how might I be able to balance things out on your end, then, Proconsul?"

(*"Blood in the streets of Jung Sim Weon!"* proclaimed the headlines. Even now, at this very moment, the people of Sajeong were dying.)

Nwabudike chuckled softly, and even that small laugh made his belly jiggle. "How indeed," he said. He stepped to the back of the room and opened up the cabinet that was set into the wall. "Naturally, Mr. Hamilton, it comes down to weapons, in this case." He produced a fancy-labeled bottle of whiskey from inside the cabinet, and poured some into two crystal glasses before locking the bottle back up.

"Well, then certainly, you've come to the right place," Arkady said with a smile as Nwabudike passed him one of the glasses. "The Duhamel Corporation prides itself on being the finest weapons manufacturer in the world." The ferret raised his glass to the Proconsul, and they both took a sip at the same time.

Whiskey had never been entirely to Arkady's liking, but ever since the augmentation, he'd been able to better appreciate the more subtle tastes when it came to the expensive stuff, and the Proconsul of Jung Sim Weon certainly liked the expensive stuff, it seemed.

Making a satisfied face as he swallowed, Nwabudike set his glass down, then took a seat, swiveling slowly. "And that's what I need," he said to Arkady. "The finest weapons available."

(The *finest* weapons. *"You and I, weapons who work in tandem."* That was what Il-Hyeong had said. And perhaps it was true that that's exactly what the Iolite League had turned them into.)

"Begging your pardon, Proconsul," Arkady said, "but it would seem to me—" He indicated the monitor with his paw, still holding his glass. "—that superior weaponry isn't something that you lack."

The raccoon's jolly face slowly melted away, and the look on his muzzle was soon replaced by a more sinister and self-satisfied smirk. "No, Mr. Hamilton, of course not," he said. "But these poor fellows mounting their doomed insurrection—ah, now there's a group of people who needs some increased firepower, wouldn't you say?"

Arkady withheld his own smile. "I'm a businessman, Proconsul, not a tactician," he replied. "But, on the surface, I'd have to say that you have a point." He'd done a lot of work to ingratiate himself into Nwabudike's favor, by this point, and it looked like the truth was about to make itself known.

"The quality of your company's weapons is not in question," Nwabudike said. "What I am concerned with, at this point, is..." He took another sip of whiskey as he looked up at the ceiling while searching for words. "...secrecy. I can only assume that in an industry with such, ah, questionable ethics, secrets are something of a concern to you, after all."

"Naturally," Arkady said. "After all, that's why they sent me."

Swirling the remnants of his whiskey around in his crystal glass, the raccoon abruptly set it back down on the table and looked Arkady straight in the eye. "I'll be blunt, Mr. Hamilton," he said. "Could your people arm these insurgents without anyone finding out?"

Now, Arkady allowed himself a smile. "I'm certain that we could," he said. "But if you're worried about our corporation making a secret attempt to aid these would-be usurpers, Proconsul, you needn't worry about that. Even if Kyunjiu is your neighbor, we—"

"No, no, Mr. Hamilton," the Proconsul said. "I fear no such thing. I want these insurrectionists to be armed."

The ferret set his own whiskey glass aside. "Again, I'm no tactician, but that seems a strange tactical choice on your part, Proconsul."

("I am but a humble messenger. Surely you can see that I alone pose no threat to you.")

"I'm sure it does," Nwabudike said, grunting with exertion as he rose to his feet, his chubby frame wobbling before he managed to steady himself on his thick, stubby legs. "But rest assured, Mr. Hamilton, that I am quite serious."

The raccoon strode over to the monitor again, once more crossing his arms behind his back. "Look at the news," he said. "The streets of my beloved capital of Sajeong are overrun with an undesirable element, and the world vilifies me and my government for taking steps to defend itself from this... this poor excuse for a rebellion. And why?"

He spun around with surprising grace to face Arkady again. "Why? Because this resistance takes up arms against the government without having either the coordination or the equipment to even put up a decent fight! And the media swarms in, and gets the world to blame *me* for the fact that these political ingrates are getting slaughtered for defying me!" He huffed and panted after his brief outburst, already worked up and out of breath. He stomped back up the boardroom table and drank down the rest of his whiskey with one gulping swallow before plodding over to the cabinet for a larger refill.

Arkady sat quietly, giving the Proconsul a chance to calm down after his moment of indignation and outrage. It was remarkable that the raccoon seemed to actually believe what he was saying, and just as remarkable that he'd trust an outsider like 'Manfred Hamilton' with these details.

Of course, to seal the deal, the Duhamel Corporation would need to know what it was getting into. Well, as far as Proconsul Nwabudike knew. The real idea was that the Duhamel Corporation would never hear of this proposal at all.

"I believe I see where you're coming from now, Proconsul," Arkady said as Nwabudike hurried his way through his second whiskey. "Arming the insurrectionists should be no problem, nor will it be a problem to do so clandestinely." He polished off his own drink, then declined a refill with a polite wave of his paw.

(*"The different species of this world are not as different as they may appear on the outside."* Book of Alexandretta, Chapter One, Verse One. One of the chief tenets of the Iolite Doctrine. Was it therefore really a bad thing to treat one selfish, corrupt leader just like any other?)

"My government will pay top dollar for such," the raccoon said as he took a seat again. "I need your people to understand that."

Arkady nodded. "An understanding that should be easy to reach," he said. "Though the real question now lies with just how much you're looking to buy, along with where you need it, when you need it, and how you need it to be delivered."

"At this rate," the Proconsul explained, "the resistance will soon be crushed. They need to be outfitted before that can happen." He took a breath and looked back over at the monitor briefly before shaking his head in disgust at what he saw. "They've got this leader, some fellow named Ryswife; he'll be desperate. I'll make sure that word gets to him of seized munition that are ripe for the plucking, and even if he suspects a trap, by that point, his little rebellion will *have* to go for it."

The ferret tapped his claws on the boardroom table thoughtfully. "So you ensure that the insurrection is well-armed," he said. "Better armed even than your own Consulate Guard?"

Nwabudike nodded. "Yes. I need my own men to be outgunned."

"So that when you send your troops in for the final strike, it is *they* who get slaughtered."

The raccoon's muzzle split into another disturbing grin. "Precisely," he said. "Then, this little uprising loses its sympathy, and the government of Jung Sim Weon can justify purchasing even more weapons from you, Mr. Hamilton."

"You quell the rebellion, and strengthen your military to boot."

"And we come out with the moral high ground," the Proconsul declared. "Everybody wins."

(*"...and with his men routed, he looked toward the sky and the moon, and he conceded that it was cleverness that had won the day..."*)

Arkady tapped his cuff link. "Did you catch all that, Boots?"

Nwabudike's eyes widened. *"Every word, sir,"* came Boots' reply directly in Arkady's ear. *"Crystal clear. Thing of beauty, really."*

The ferret got to his feet and drew the miniature, silenced pistol from the back of his pants. The Proconsul, too heavy to easily stand up from his chair, fell back down where he sat, and held his paws up in surrender. "Please," he gasped dryly.

"All apologies, Proconsul," he said. "Looks like the insurrection won't be so desperate after all."

The fear on the raccoon's face slowly shifted over into realization and then into rage as Hamilton's true identity dawned on him.

"For the better world, Proconsul," Arkady said as he pulled the trigger, firing a single bullet between Nwabudike's eyes. The pistol's silenced barrel splintered apart with that one shot, the synthetic polymer having served its purpose in getting past security. As the fragments clinked against the floor, the Proconsul's head lolled back in his chair, blood trickling down through the darker fur of the mask that ringed his eyes.

Arkady bent down to pick up his attaché case from off the floor, then depressed his cuff link again. "Get started on prepping that recording, Boots. Edit out all references to the Duhamel Corporation and then get it out to the stations. I want it to hit broadcast in exactly one hour."

"Will do, boss," Boots replied. *"See you when you get back."* With that, the line went dead.

Quickly adjusting his tie, Arkady stepped back out of the conference room and into the hallway. Whether the jamming device stowed in his briefcase had successfully blinded the security cameras or not would soon be known, one way or the other. He'd either be walking right out the front door or making a mad dash for the nearest fire escape.

Either way, Arkady Ryswife would be ready. After all, this was who and what he was now—what his service to the Iolite League had trained him to be.

What the Iolite League hadn't done, sadly, was provide any aid to the people of Sajeong while the government's own soldiers gunned them down. Once the conflict was over, they would be sure to take the forefront in international relief efforts, and that was commendable, in some small way. While the conflict raged, however, a group dedicated to peace and harmony could do little more than condemn the violence while remaining impartial.

This had left Arkady to—as Nwabudike had said—take charge of the resistance. If the Iolite League had taken issue with his having done so

("The League will be watching you always, Mr. Ryswife."), he was visible enough of a figure that they would have found him and stopped him. That the League had made no such attempts to remove him was enough for Arkady to conclude that he had their tacit approval—especially since he hadn't seen any sign of Sahasrara, Ajna, or the League's other five secret operations groups working on bringing an end to the crisis.

Over half a year had passed without Arkady seeing much sign of the Iolite League at all. He didn't doubt the Directorate Board in their promise that his leaving their jurisdiction would carry with it a lifetime of being under the watchful eye of any number of their agents—until such time came that he decided to return to the fold, or he became enough of a liability that they were forced to remove him from the picture entirely.

Thus far, however, it seemed like the Iolite League was willing to see the bigger picture, the same bigger picture that Arkady saw: that there was more at stake right now than what had happened with Project Scheherazade. The rest of the world still went on, day by day, and there were more important problems to solve, more crises that needed attending, and more people that needed saving.

It had been on those points that Arkady had been able to convince Boots to work with him. Oh, Boots still claimed to just be in it for the money (and since Arkady was no longer officially associated with the Iolite League, he had no grounds for refusal on that point), but even over the past few months, when he still continued to protest that it was nothing personal, Arkady could tell that the wolf still saw something in him that he would yet admit to.

He saw it back when we first met, Arkady often reflected. Whatever it was had some connection to the Butterfly Islands War, but Boots wasn't talking. Not yet.

There would be time, though—Arkady was sure of that. He and the wolf made a pretty good team, and he was confident that they'd remain one for some time to come. In a bizarre way, it was almost natural for them to turn to each other: neither of them had anywhere else to go, both of them the sole remaining members of their respective teams *(both of us misled by our leaders, and paying the price for it)*, and by now, they were even getting along.

Building security did not seem to be alerted to the assassination that had just taken place. Arkady still needed to hurry, but doing so obviously would draw more attention that he couldn't afford. He still had some time left to pretend that nothing untoward had happened, and if he was lucky, he'd get more than he needed.

In the elevator lobby, Arkady pushed the call button and then held his briefcase casually in both paws. He gazed out the window, looking at the streets of the city below. From this high up, he could see the sections where the citizenry—and where some of the people he'd been leading—had been fighting. Most of those areas were still marked by columns of dull smoke, even now.

The tangible world was imperfect, but peace and understanding were something to strive for all the same—something that could be achieved in this lifetime, while the soul was still bound in flesh, so that paradise could be attained here before moving on. That was a lofty goal, though, one that required people to work together in order to make it a reality.

And then there were some people who were an obstacle and a hindrance to that goal. Some people's eyes could never be opened to the greater truth of things, so deep was their selfishness, their own personal evil. If Il-Hyeong had understood anything, come that last mission to Ridgecrescent, it had been that people like Proconsul Nwabudike were not worth the effort to turn to the cause—not while others suffered because of them. If only the fox had been able to better see when the effort *was* worth it, and when people could still be saved.

People like Il-Hyeong himself. Arkady didn't know what Il-Hyeong had been doing since Ridgecrescent. All he knew was that, two months after that mission, the fox had crossed paths with Boots during a job the wolf had undertaken in southern Kyunjiu. As for what had transpired there, Boots wasn't coming clean. *"He saved my life,"* was all the wolf had said. *"Let's leave it at that."*

Il-Hyeong had been alive four months ago. He was still alive, that much Arkady still believed, just as he still believed that the fox was not the lost cause that even the Iolite Doctrine itself might deem him to be.

After all, Il-Hyeong had been a believer in the same things that Arkady was. Given time, he might open his eyes again, see that he had been wrong about himself and the things that he had done.

If he didn't, then Arkady wouldn't hesitate to do what Il-Hyeong himself would have wanted: he would take action, without hesitation, and he would end the fox if it meant putting a stop to the suffering of others.

But Il-Hyeong had been Arkady's friend, once. Faith would have him believe in that friendship. The last resort was just that: the last resort. In the meantime, Arkady would just have to believe that, someday, Il-Hyeong would come back, would repent and would return to the fold.

They could be on the same side once more, in the name of the things they believed in. And then Pandora could wake up, and—

No. No, that wasn't why. Arkady hadn't spared Il-Hyeong just for that. He *hadn't*. He'd been over this with himself time and time again since Ridgecrescent. That wasn't the reason. How many times had he come to that conclusion, now? There was still something left in Il-Hyeong that could be salvaged. He'd see to that. Somehow. Someday.

The chime for the elevator sounded. The car was empty. Arkady took one last glance down at the city below before stepping inside. He pressed the button for the lobby, then watched as the doors slid closed. No sign of commotion was yet to stir down the hallway that led to the Proconsul's meeting room.

The elevator began its smooth descent, but Arkady breathed no sigh of relief. He still had to get out of the building, and then find someplace to lay low before rejoining with Boots and the other members of the resistance.

Someday. Someday, Il-Hyeong would open his eyes again. Someday, Pandora would awaken. For today, Arkady had done his good deed.

The corrupt leader of Jung Sim Weon was dead. Soon, the insurrection—and the rest of the world—would hear of his plan to turn on his citizenry and on his own protectors, and his death would be justified. Jung Sim Weon would rebuild. And it would have help.

And tomorrow, down in the boroughs of Sajeong, the people would wake up, they would hear the good news, and they would get to breathe a sigh of relief as they basked in their own small slice of the better world.

Epilogue

Boots was used to people staring at him whenever he was out in public. It took effort for the average person *not* to pay attention to the huge wolf. This was nothing new, and he'd mostly inured himself to it, besides. Only every so often did those stares get to him.

The fact that he was in Afortunada made it worse. Here, on the streets of Corazón, the wolf had his own prejudices to fight. The average person might not be able to help staring at him, and he had difficulties not staring back.

The Butterfly Islands War had changed a lot of people. The better part of a decade had gone by since then, but Boots knew he wasn't the only person who hadn't gotten over it. Hell, a big part of him didn't *want* to get over it. Wasn't that his right?

In the meantime, he'd just have to accept the muted anger he felt inside of him as he walked through Afortunada's streets. Whenever someone around his age turned and looked at him, he would look back and wonder, *"Did you serve? Did your friends help to kill mine?"*

It was for that very reason that Boots seldom came to Afortunada for work. He trusted himself and he trusted his gut, but he knew he couldn't trust his own objectivity if the merc he was working alongside was someone who'd fought against the JDR back in the war. Call him stupid for wanting to think that way, but he was at least smart enough to avoid putting himself in that situation.

Boots had come to Afortunada this time as a personal favor, though. There were few people who could convince him to come here without putting up a fight. Arkady Ryswife was one of those people. The ferret hadn't stressed the personal importance of the matter, but even without knowing anything hinged on that, Boots would have agreed to the task.

So, here he was, lumbering down the busy main road at midday, carrying a small trunk in one big paw. Inside were a sword, an old, beat-up tape recorder, and a set of three books that Arkady had let him see briefly. The ferret had made some cryptic claim about milking a favor out of some doctor acquaintance of his, but Boots hadn't pressed for more.

Arkady had always been the secretive type. He pretty much had to be, nowadays. Boots had gleaned enough about the Iolite League to know that Arkady was a living liability just by virtue of what he knew. Boots had also pieced together enough to determine that the ferret's ruse about the Octavians, back when they'd first met, did in fact refer to an actual group.

Everyone had their own little way in which they wanted to try to change the world, it seemed. In that regard, perhaps Boots himself was no different. There were any number of people or organizations to work for, or work with. So why work alongside Arkady Ryswife?

The ferret looked like he should have been a mere child during the Butterfly Islands War, and yet clearly he hadn't been. As much as he looked like a young man on the surface, one good look at his eyes told an old soldier like Boots that he was gazing into the eyes of someone who had seen a lifetime of things both great and terrible.

No child from Deepwater who had seen the Pillar of Light would be struck by the true gravity of what they were seeing. Not in the way that someone like Boots or the Aléu or the soldiers on either side of the war had been struck by it. No young fellow in his early twenties could have experienced the breadth of pain and joy and loss that Boots had— not without still showing the mental scars, the kind that a person didn't learn how to fully hide until years and years later.

Then there was Tokiko Akitoshi. Boots didn't know much about her; Arkady had said only, "I was her friend," back when the wolf had asked the one time they'd gone to the grave in Holygate together. Arkady Ryswife didn't otherwise strike him as a sentimental man. Boots was content to leave him his privacy, and got the same in return.

Were they friends? Inasmuch as either of them had friends, Boots had to concede that they were. Otherwise, he wouldn't be in Afortunada making a special delivery. That, and he probably wouldn't trust the ferret with his life the way that he did.

The wolf came upon the low-rise apartment complex indicated by his map and made his way between the rows of buildings. Afortunada had neither the same standard of living nor the level of technology that Ridgecrescent did. Boots tried not to feel superior when it came to that. Hell, by most countries' standards, this was a pretty nice neighborhood. It was clean, well-lit, and there were no scampering children underfoot to run screaming at the sight of a seven-foot-tall wolf who plodded along with a dire purpose.

Why had Arkady picked him for this? It sounded like it was just a simple drop-off. Wasn't that something Arkady could do himself? Or, if it weren't, wasn't it at least something he could trust with somebody who looked a little less conspicuous?

"Arkady likes you. I'm not sure why, but he does." That's what Il-Hyeong Quinn had said that day, in their encounter in Kyunjiu.

There would be time to relive that later, the wolf told himself. For now, he just needed to stay on his toes, in case this mission carried hidden risks. It would be unlike Arkady to knowingly send him into a situation unprepared, but that didn't give mean he could let his guard down.

Maybe only crazy people trusted Arkady Ryswife. That might explain Boots after all. He chuckled to himself at that. And maybe Arkady Ryswife only trusted crazy people in return.

The wolf came to Building 2-3 and walked up to the door to Apartment 88, outside on the first floor. He sighed, hoping he wouldn't need to reach for his gun, and knocked on the door with a heavy fist.

Seconds later, the door swung open, and a short, white-and-gray rabbit gripped the frame as he looked up at the wolf. He appeared to be in his late twenties, in much the same way that Arkady didn't.

"Zhengyi Devra?" Boots asked.

The rabbit's ears twitched. "N-No," he said, shaking his head. "Sorry. I'm afraid you've got the wrong address."

He tried to shut the door in Boots' face, but the wolf grabbed hold of the top of it and easily kept it still. "Look," he told the rabbit. "I'm just here to drop off a package with you. A friend of mine has spent months trying to track you down across three continents, and I'd appreciate it if you just took this stuff already so I can go home."

"I don't want anything," the rabbit protested. "Tell your friend he has the wrong rabbit." He struggled in vain to shut the door again.

"Hey, I'm okay just leaving this here on your doorstep, if I have to." (Arkady had specifically told Boots *not* to do that.) "Let me just set this trunk down here, and let me give you this." He did set down the trunk, and then he reached into his coat, next to where his gun was hidden behind the padding, and pulled out the small booklet of gibberish the ferret had given him to deliver.

The timid rabbit took the booklet in his paws. "What's this supposed to be?" he asked, as if he was afraid of it.

"Just take it, okay?" the wolf said. "I need to get going."

The rabbit looked down at the small book and hesitated before opening the cover. His pupils went wide as he gazed down at the first page. After that, his paws started to shake, his eyes welled up, and then he shut them as he tucked his chin against his chest and started to cry.

About the Author

Kevin Frane grew up near Boston, studied Biology and Astronomy out in Western Massachusetts, then moved to Japan in a failed attempt to seek his fortune before winding up in the San Francisco Bay Area, where he has since gone native. In this new land of too many coffee shops, he has been writing for many years while also working as a video game producer. His short stories have appeared in anthologies such as *New Fables* and *ROAR*. His first novel, *Thousand Leaves*, was also published by Sofawolf Press in 2008.

About the Artist

Kamui happily reprises the role of cover artist after providing art for *Thousand Leaves*. Okay, Mr. Frane—time to get cracking on the next sequel.

His art blends anthropomorphic and atmospheric, digital and traditional, and has recently appeared on books including *Heathen City*, *New Fables*, *Heat*, and his tutorial collection, *Work In Process*.

About Sofawolf Press

Sofawolf Press was founded in 1999 by Jeff Eddy and Tim Susman with the goal of bringing professional-quality publication to the best in furry fiction.

Please browse our catalog at *http://www.sofawolf.com*.